More...

"Lyrical and he gets the sardonic, macho patter between men down cold. The finale is heartfelt and unexpected, and a final confrontation stuns with its violent and confessional precision."

—*Providence Journal Bulletin*

THE NIGHT VISITOR

"The author is indeed a treasure.... A hybrid of Tony Hillerman and Carl Hiaasen, but with an overall sensibility that is uniquely Doss."

—*Denver Post*

"The dialogue crackles, and the Southern Colorado atmosphere astonishes, especially at night."

—*Publishers Weekly*

"Fans won't be disappointed.... Doss pulls together an archeological dig, abandoned children, and a good, old-fashioned murder to pull off his latest success."

—*Chicago Tribune*

THE SHAMAN'S GAME

"Suspenseful and satisfying.... Doss has reproduced the land of the Southern Colorado Utes with vivid affection."

—*Dallas Morning News*

"Doss could be accused of poaching in Tony Hillerman territory ... but Doss mixes mysticism and murder with his own unmistakable touch."

—*Orlando Sentinel*

"Deft storytelling ... compelling ... ingenious ... intense ... a richness of prose and plot that lifts it out of the expected ranks of mystery fiction."

—*Arizona Daily Star*

GRANDMOTHER SPIDER

"Propelled by fast-paced action and intriguing characters ... like something out of Stephen King ... with snippets from Dave Barry."

—*Chicago Tribune*

Also by James D. Doss

Shadow MAN

JAMES D. DOSS

ST. MARTIN'S PAPERBACKS

SHADOW MAN

Copyright © 2005 by James D. Doss.
Excerpt from *Stone Butterfly* © 2006 by James D. Doss.

Cover photo © Scott Warren/Aurora.

Library of Congress Catalog Card Number: 2005046513

ISBN: 0-312-93664-8
EAN: 9780312-93664-8

Printed in the United States of America

St. Martin's Press hardcover edition / October 2005
St. Martin's Paperbacks edition / August 2006

St. Martin's Paperbacks are published by St. Martin's Press, 175 Fifth Avenue, New York, NY 10010.

10 9 8 7 6 5 4 3 2 1

For
Thomas A. Lopez
White Rock, New Mexico,

and

Bill McCabe
Alma, New Mexico

ACKNOWLEDGMENTS

I wish to offer my thanks to
Bret Doss
and
Dr. Joseph D. Matthews
Los Alamos, New Mexico

PROLOGUE

Though knowing this is merely a dream—an afternoon nap's delusion—you marvel at the intricately crafted illusion. Behold the panoramic canvas of earth and sky, with each line so finely drawn, every feature so infinitely detailed. Is the immensely gifted artist some hidden portion of yourself, or is the maestro someone else—someone altogether Other? Turning away from this cosmic question, you take another direction—along an alluring footpath that meanders between towering canyon walls. Feeling the soft crunch of sand and pebbles under your bare feet, you stroll alongside a shallow stream, in the cool shade of trembling willows—until a spray of sunlight warms your face. Now you proceed more carefully, avoiding pointy clusters of yucca spears—only to encounter a surly congregation of curiously sculpted, lichen-encrusted boulders. Are these artful stones pretending to be petrified souls—or might it be the other way around? As you ponder this conundrum, delectable scents of sage and wild roses waft past your nose. You reach out to pick a pink blossom, are startled by the rattling croak of a raven on yonder ponderosa. At your glance, Lady Darkwing takes to flight, soars over the mesa. She goes to console a spirit who sighs and moans over a few moldering bones.

Though the atmosphere is charged with an eerie anticipation of catastrophe, never has experience been so physically authentic, so concretely real. The single exception is Time, who slips past, stealing precious minutes and heartbeats and memories—the old thief moves far more swiftly here. Look to the heavens—see the flower-clouds wilt, only to blossom again, billow like ghostly schooner's sails, then fade into diaphanous bridal veils.

Down here, black shadows slip across the sands like spilled ink—soon they will wet your feet! You move on—a little faster now.

Nearing the mouth of the chasm, you hear someone approaching from behind. It is the old hag who conceals dreadful secrets in the wraps of her dusky garments. Attempting to flee the rustling skirts of night, you take long, heavy-footed strides. In a growing panic, you sense another presence, but in your twilight flight you pass within a few paces—only dimly aware they are there.

The still sentries can hardly be distinguished from the drought-stunted trees.

Indeed, they seem to be rooted here.

The warrior's spine is lodgepole pine, his lean limbs are corded like the bloodberry vine. But a spindly perception would be a misconception—this one does not bend in the wind.

Auntie is a hard, knotty old stump, twisted and bent from crown to trunk. She is known by her flinty, caustic bark—but it is her bite that leaves the toothy mark.

She has seen you! Hurry, hurry, hurry—

Wake up.

If you can.

1

COLORADO, SOUTHERN UTE RESERVATION

Without a thought of mentioning the passing apparition to her nephew, the Ute shaman watched the dreamer's phantom dissolve into a shadowy mist, evaporate into nothingness. It was unusual to encounter one of *them* out and about at this time of day, but during those wee hours just beyond midnight, one might see dozens of these tethered-to-the-body phantasms flitting about like nervous yucca moths. Daisy Perika believed that dreams prepared mortals for that time when the cord between body and soul shall be severed—and some must begin to serve their sentences as lonely, wandering ghosts. The aged Catholic fervently hoped (with God's help) to bypass this dismal interval, and proceed directly to that mansion her blessed Savior had prepared for her in Upper World.

Charlie Moon could not have imagined the thoughts percolating through the old woman's singular mind. Nor would he have wished for such a privilege.

The tribal policeman and his aged aunt stood on a curled-up ridge called the Cougar's Tail. A little more than a stone's throw away, the mouth of *Cañón del Espíritu* gaped as if it might swallow the entire valley whole, including Daisy's little trailer home. Neither Moon nor his closest living relative was concerned about such an improbable outcome. These sensible folk were peaceably watching the scarlet smear of sunset.

Moon pushed his black Stetson back a notch to a jaunty position, looped an arm around the old woman's shoulders. "You should move into town."

Daisy snorted. "Why should I do a thing like that?"

"I worry about you." The tall man looked down at the top of her head. "In Ignacio, you'd have neighbors to look in on you."

"Neighbors—hah! I'd sooner have a family of skunks nesting under my floor." Her lips crinkled into an enigmatic smile. *And it's not like I'm all by myself.* The shaman gazed into *Cañón del Espíritu,* far past where her eyes could see, way up there where the dwarf made his home in the abandoned badger hole, even into those dark crooks and crannies where a multitude of spirits mumbled and muttered while they waited for Middle World to end and Judgment to begin. From time to time, one of them would come to talk to her. It might be the Little Man wanting something sweet to eat, or a gaunt old haunt starving for some conversation. Daisy's dark eyes sparkled in the fading light. *I have all the company I need.*

The honeyed sun vanished behind Three Sisters Mesa. Before slipping into an unseen sea to bathe away the heat of day, she would pull a dark, star-sprinkled curtain down behind her.

The quiet in this remote place was more than the absence of sound. It was a peaceful river, flowing slowly out of the canyon. For a few heartbeats, it seemed as if Moon and Daisy were the only human beings in the world.

They were not, of course.

The planet was bustling and crackling with billions of busy people. All over the globe, on a multitude of stages, small and large dramas were being played out.

For example: About four hundred miles south of the Southern Ute reservation, something very big and bad and noisy was about to happen—an event that would, in time, unsettle the lives of Charlie Moon and his aunt Daisy.

NEW MEXICO
A few yards above Luna County
A few minutes below midnight

The warning kept hammering in the pilot's skull—*This is just plain nuts.*

William "Pappy" Hitchcock squinted at a tar-black sky that he imagined to be the root cellar of heaven. Or maybe not. It could be the penthouse of that other place. Whatever it was or wasn't, he had the most peculiar sensation—that curious spirits of earlier aviators were watching him, wishing him good fortune, a happy landing. He grinned, tipped his baseball cap at the ghostly audience. *Hey, Lucky Lindy ... Halloo, Antoine-Marie-Roger de Saint-Exupery ... Howdy there, Gus Grissom! Take a gander at Mrs. Hitchcock's favorite son. Ain't this a big, hairy horse-laugh? Me with this rickety old crate strapped to my butt, bumping along barely above the treetops, can't see the ground half the time, can't see the stars at all. And don't forget this humungous summer thunderstorm, lightning flashing, thunder booming—winds shifting and twisting all over the place! It's like everything and everybody is out to shoot me down—why, I wouldn't be the least bit surprised at antiaircraft fire!*

A heavy barrage of hail rat-tatted on the windshield, dimpled the aircraft's thin skin.

A caustic grin. *Well thank you for that.*

He estimated the odds of a fatal crash as somewhere in the neighborhood of even money. That was a bad neighborhood. And on top of that, the internal vicinity was distinctly unfriendly—every one of his surly passengers was airsick, wanted by Interpol, and packing. As if all this were not enough to make the trip sufficiently interesting, he was about to spring a highly unpleasant surprise on these outlaws. One might reasonably conclude that the captain of the 1940s-vintage aircraft was worried, or at least mildly concerned about the situation. If One did, One would be mistaken.

At least for the moment, Mr. Hitchcock was in fine fettle and form—particularly for a man of his years. He was also that rarest of all mortals—a genuinely happy person. This was because he had made a firm decision to put all of his troubles behind him. Most of them already were. Literally. A couple of hundred miles behind him was the Wings of War Military Aircraft Museum, from whose hangar—just hours ago—he had stolen the antique U.S. Army Air Force DC-3. As has already been alluded to, some of his troubles were more closely behind him. Back there in the cargo bay, the half-dozen heavily armed cartel soldiers watched over a big pile of laundry bags that were stuffed tight as ticks with twenty-dollar bills.

Hitchcock gave little thought to his disgruntled passengers; his professional duties required all of his concentration. His instructions had been straightforward:

1. Stay under the FAA radar.
2. Land on the makeshift strip exactly six miles south of the Mexican border, where the cartel's Humvee and laundry truck and troops would be waiting.

Carrying out Instruction Number One was *enormous* fun—snaking through serpentine canyons, surfing across rippling seas of silver grass, skimming over the crests of rugged mesas. Hitchcock figured he was flying about as low as he could get without clipping off treetops and colliding with high-jumping jackrabbits.

Executing Instruction Number Two might have been mere routine—a yawn. Except for the fact that he intended to add a dash of spice to the stew. Hitchcock planned to land the DC-3 at a makeshift strip just six miles *north* of the Mexican border, where *his* Humvee and *his* laundry truck and *his* troops would be waiting. Yes sirree—Pablo Feliciano and

"Doc" Blinkoe would be there and they'd be loaded for bear. Oh, this switch-and-run was just *too* sweet. What a fine way to cap off a long career!

Alas, as it would come to pass—the worst of Mr. Hitchcock's troubles were still out there in front of him. And coming up fast.

ON THE GROUND

Partly because he was the man with inside connections to the cartel, mostly because he had come up with the hijacking plan, but also because it would have taken both of his partners to outwit a bright twelve-year-old—Pablo Feliciano was the brains of the three-man outfit. The pump-action shotgun propped on his shoulder, the Colombian was busy doing what he did best. He paced back and forth, worried about what might go wrong. He could imagine all sorts of catastrophes. The DC-3 would crash or the sacks would be stuffed with newspaper instead of cash or the DEA would spot the airplane from a dirigible-mounted radar or the makeshift landing-strip lights would fail or they'd all end up in jail—something would surely go wrong. Maybe everything.

Dr. Manfred Wilhelm Blinkoe didn't have a worry in his head. What, exactly, he did have between his ears was something of a mystery. On account of the fact that he was sometimes heard having a conversation with someone who *wasn't there,* the orthodontist was considered by his two partners-in-crime to be mildly eccentric seven days a week—and on occasion, a borderline lunatic. He had, in fact, been diagnosed by various professionals as schizophrenic, manic-depressive, bipolar, possibly even the possessor of a multiple-personality disorder. These modest shortcomings had not disqualified him from participating in the current project, which no completely sane person would have considered for a millisecond. Blissfully unaware that he harbored even the slightest flaw, Blinkoe considered himself a genius with a flair for the romantic. And having inherited a considerable fortune from his mother, he was not doing this for the cash. Like virtue, adventure was its own reward.

At the moment, the wealthy eccentric-lunatic-genius-romantic was perched in the sooty-black Humvee, immediately behind a tripod-mounted M2 .50-caliber Browning machine gun. The deadly apparatus was fitted with a superb night-vision scope. Having checked and aligned the metal-link ammunition belt, he adjusted the focus on the Starlite optics, watched a lime-tinted coyote lope along a rocky outcropping 160 yards away. *What an easy shot that would be.* To resist the absurd temptation, Blinkoe elevated the air-cooled barrel, squinted at a clearing in the cloudy sky. Countless points of green light winked and blinked at him. *Nothing but stars and silence. It must be a lot like this on the dark side of the moon.*

The stillness was cut by a sharp *click-clack* as Feliciano pumped a 12-gauge buckshot load into the chamber of his favorite shotgun. This mechanical statement was followed by the soft sound of his voice. "If Pappy took off on time, the DC-3 should be about ten minutes away."

This produced a grunt from Blinkoe.

In the starlight, Feliciano could barely make out the clumps of creosote bush, smoke tree, and snakeweed, but their piquant scents wafted past his nose. He didn't care for the smells. Feliciano had never liked the desert or anything that came with it. Imagining the sands to be crawling with sidewinders, scorpions, and tarantulas, he mused about which he loathed the most. Decided on the hairy spiders. There was something eerie in the deliberate, arrogant way they *walked.* He looked at the Humvee, blinked at the crazy Anglo's thick profile. "If these hombres figure out Pappy Hitchcock's landed 'em on the wrong side of that Mexican border, there's going to be serious hell to pay."

"You said it." *About ten times you said it, just in the last hour.* "But don't fret, my melodramatic friend." Blinkoe took a grip on the Browning, made a wide turn on the tripod. "I can chop down big trees with this bad machine, and I'll make bloody hamburger out of those—"

"Shhhh!" The Colombian turncoat was holding a finger to his lips.

Off to the north, there was an uneven thrumming of engines, the whir of propellers whacking off dark slices of midnight.

Feliciano pointed his shotgun in the general direction of the approaching aircraft, went through the drill for the gringo's benefit. "Soon as he's over Apache Butte, I'll switch on the runway lights. After that old crate rolls to a stop, I'll give the dot-dash signal with my flashlight. There'll be five, maybe six of my countrymen on board, and I'm the contact they'll expect to see. After most of 'em have their boots on the ground, I'll hit the dirt and take the first shot. That's your signal to spray 'em with the machine gun. Pappy'll take out any that're still on the plane. But don't you stop firing till the last of those banditos are dead." The soldier of misfortune checked his sidearm. *And just to make sure, I'll see that every one of 'em gets a shot to the head.*

Blinkoe felt a sharp pain in his lower back, a sudden surge of fear. *Take it easy. It's not what you think it is—probably just a muscle spasm.* Buoyed by these self-reassuring assertions, he squinted through the scope. "Pablo, this is going to be *too* easy—a real turkey shoot."

Maybe he's right. Worrier though he was, Feliciano's favorite superstition had to do with how merely *saying* something could make it happen. He took a deep breath, nodded in the darkness. "Everything'll work out just fine."

It would be gratifying to report that the bold trio's optimism was justified by the subsequent course of events—one prefers to see the habitual losers win one now and then. And things did get off to a fairly good start.

As the DC-3 approached, the jury-rigged landing lights switched on without a hitch.

The venerable World War II aircraft touched down, bumped along the desert hardpan to a lurching halt.

The prearranged flashlight signal was given, accepted as genuine.

The Colombians evacuated the airplane with no more than normal caution.

After shouting an enthusiastic greeting to his betrayed comrades, Feliciano hit the ground, Blinkoe laid into them with Mr. Browning's supremely efficient killing machine. Two of the cartel soldiers managed to return fire, but the .50-caliber scythe cut them all down like noxious weeds.

The noisy part was over in less time than it takes to tell about it.

But the barbarous business was far from finished.

It was, in fact, just getting started.

Having been smited hip and thigh with lumps of lead, Mr. Hitchcock would be denied what he wanted most of all. Before the flood of dawn had washed away the last smudge of night, the pilot's blood-soaked body would be rolled into a remote arroyo, left there to rot.

Only weeks later—having slit a farmer's throat for stealing his girlfriend's spotted billy goat—Señor Feliciano would end up in a Mexican jail. But not for long.

Having taken himself a remarkably pretty young wife, Dr. Blinkoe would live in constant fear for his life.

2

As the accumulation of many winters pressed heavily upon her, Daisy Perika had become set in her ways. The Ute elder was a contented recluse; the mere thought of being far away from her little home at the mouth of *Cañón del Espíritu* made her shudder. On those occasions when she took a meal in town, Daisy preferred Angel's Cafe in Ignacio or Texas-Bob's Barbecue in Durango. But here she was—almost a hundred miles to the north, in Granite Creek—seated at a fancy, linen-covered table in the Stockman's Hotel Restaurant. The shrunken woman was flanked by two sizable men—Southern Ute Tribal Investigator Charlie Moon and Granite Creek Chief of Police Scott Parris. It would have been perfect, except for the fact that FBI Special Agent Lila Mae McTeague was seated directly across from Daisy, who had noticed how the pretty white woman was eyeing her nephew. Worst of all, Charlie was eyeing her right back. Daisy's face was set like granite. *I'll just pretend that she's not here.*

The table's delectable centerpiece was a three-layer strawberry jam cake, its inch-thick pink icing dotted with dozens of red candles. While they watched, Daisy opened her birthday presents.

Charlie's gift was a satellite telephone. It was astonishingly small and came with a nylon cord so she could hang it around her neck like a pendant.

Daisy Perika muttered her thanks for the gadget, which she thought resembled a fancy dog collar. When her nephew demonstrated how the thing worked, she grumbled that she could barely make out the tiny labels by the brightly colored buttons, much less read the script on the narrow little gray strip that served as a monitor.

Charlie assured his aunt that he had programmed in all the numbers she would need for an emergency. At the press of this button she would get 911, that one would ring his ranch landline, another one his cell phone. Wearing his now-pay-attention-because-I-am-dead-serious expression, he made it known that he expected her to wear the high-tech communications device all the time. Even when she was taking a bath. Especially when she was out walking in the wild canyon country around her home.

She solemnly vowed that she would and immediately dismissed the promise from her mind.

Scott's gift was an ebony cane; the head was a hand-carved soapstone owl. This would be nice for going to church, she told him. Daisy had a special affection for the white man, who was her nephew's best friend. She reached over to pat the *matukach* on the arm.

The FBI woman had brought her a lovely parcel—wrapped in embroidered white cotton, tied with a ribbon of Japanese silk. Daisy discovered a lovely Spanish shawl inside, gave it a once-over. *It's probably a Chinese knockoff.* While everyone watched, the shameless old woman found the label, squinted hard at it. Barcelona. *Well. I guess she's trying to impress me.* Which just went to show how calculating and sneaky these men-hunting white women could be.

A Portuguese waiter with the willowy frame of a bullfighter appeared, touched each candle on the cake with a butane wand. Completion of this operation took quite some time.

"Oh, my—look at that." The flames danced in Daisy's eyes. "There's way too many to blow out."

Lila Mae smiled. "Then let them burn."

Daisy pretended not to hear.

The FBI agent felt the slight. It was her face that burned.

By nature oblivious to petty thoughts or malicious intentions, Moon looped a long arm around his shriveled aunt. "Time to make a wish."

The ancient woman closed her eyes, shook her gray head. "Oh, God—I wish I was eighty again."

This produced a roar of laughter from the men, a brittle smile from Lila Mae.

Charlie Moon sliced the cake, passed ample portions around.

Daisy dug right in.

Lila Mae barely touched the rich dessert.

Sensitive about the tightness developing lately under his belt, Scott Parris left half of his helping behind, but pecked wistfully at the remains with his fork.

Moon, slim as a whip snake, completed his wedged section and helped himself to a second serving of the sugary confection.

The second hand on the wall clock went *clickety-click*.

Old times were recalled, mostly true stories were told.

During a momentary lull, the waiter brought a silver decanter of steaming coffee. The caffeine-rich beverage triggered further remembrances, even more audacious anecdotes.

In an attempt to break through Daisy's defenses, Lila Mae offered up an account of her sixth birthday party and a tiny white kitten with a "little pink bow" around its neck. Her father, she recalled, had presented the gift in a root-beer mug. Birthdays were a special time. She flashed her sweetest smile at the Ute elder.

The wicked old woman yawned in her face.

Even Charlie Moon noticed this. He shot his aunt a warning look.

This mild rebuke merely annoyed the birthday girl. *Why did Charlie have to invite that pushy woman anyway? I wish he'd brought along one of my friends instead—like Father Raes Delfino. Why didn't he do something nice like that?* These thoughts produced a deeply satisfying pang of self-righteous pity.

As if he had heard her secret wish, Charlie Moon passed his aunt a small package. "I almost forgot. Father Raes asked me to give you this."

Daisy turned the gift over in her hands. The parcel was wrapped in plain brown paper, tied with a stout length of twine. "Why didn't he bring it himself?"

"He left the Columbine a couple of days ago," Moon said. "He's going to spend a month in Italy."

Daisy sniffed. "I didn't know there was any shortage of priests over there." She borrowed Moon's steak knife to cut the string, unpeeled the wrapping. "It's a little book," she said. And indeed it was. The gold-leaf title on the scuffed leather cover was *The Little Flowers of St. Francis—Illustrated.* The pages were worn from many turnings. She squinted at the yellowed flyleaf where someone had written in blue ink, now faded: "To our Dear Son Raes Delfino on the occasion of his sixteenth birthday."

This must have been very, very precious to him. Tears filled the Ute woman's dark eyes. She thumbed through the book, stopped at a woodcut print—*St. Francis Praying on Mount Alverna.* Daisy was drawn in by the simple sketch. *I wonder if that's what the man who talked to birds really looked like.* As the shaman blinked in disbelief, the black-and-white drawing seemed to take on extra dimensions. Branches on bluish black spruce trees shivered in a chill breeze, a puff of cloud drifted across a sapphire sky, the grass under the saint's knees was green and wet with pearly dew. The man from Assisi turned his head toward the woman who held the book in her hands.

Daisy's mouth gaped. *What on earth . . . ?* In the blink of an eye, the saint's countenance had changed. This face was someone she knew. "Father Raes," she muttered, and heard Moon's voice come from somewhere far away.

"He said to tell you he'd be here in spirit."

The tiny version of the Catholic priest gave the old backslider a heart-piercing look.

Panicked, Daisy tried to shut the book. The covers were like welded sheets of iron; they would not move. Her hands trembled; she whispered: "What do you want?"

The others at the table were staring at the peculiar old woman. The general consensus was that she must be reading an interesting passage.

She watched the elfin apparition shake his head, heard his voice say: "Daisy, Daisy. Every morning, every night, I pray to God for your soul. The angels in heaven weep for you." With this pronouncement, the phantom priest collapsed into nothingness, the scene on the yellowed page reverted to the simple woodcut of the kneeling saint.

The small volume slipped from her hands.

Daisy understood that God expected her to do something. She knew exactly what it was. The penitent sinner resisted for a painful moment before she looked across the table at the FBI lady. "Uh—I guess I forgot to thank you for the scarf." She strained hard to get the words past her lips. "It's very nice." *There—that should make God happy.*

It made Lila Mae McTeague happy. She beamed at the unpredictable Ute woman. "I'm so glad you like it."

"I sure do." Daisy pulled the exquisite covering over her head. "I'll wear it to the next funeral I go to." She breathed a melancholy sigh. "And that probably won't be too far off. Most of my friends are almost as old as me and they're dropping dead like flies at the first hard frost." Another possibility suggested itself to her. *Or maybe some of them will be coming to say good-bye to me.*

◆ ◆ ◆

Barely three miles away, at another expensive eatery, two other diners were working out their entwined destinies.

The Stockholm Room at Phillipe's Streamside Restaurant was filled with soft amber light, joyful strains of *Brahms' Academic Festival Overture*—and a congregation of happy patrons.

Just beyond the green-tinted windowpanes, a small patch of night was gaily illuminated by a string of Chinese lanterns. Because the evening was chilly, the man and the woman had the Streamside Patio to themselves. A combination of effects conspired to make this a uniquely romantic spot—the lusty roar of Granite Creek's rolling waters, a low mumbling of thunder over the cloud-shrouded mountains, the hooked horns of a crescent moon, the winking flicker of a sugar-sprinkle of stars.

The lady in a black dress and pearls picked at the roasted remains of a freshly slaughtered chicken, tastefully nestled in a deathbed of wild rice and damson plums.

The well-dressed man with the forked beard relished his pork roast, caramelized onions, and buttered new potatoes flecked with a pox of chopped chives. It is true that Manfred Wilhelm Blinkoe gave the lady an occasional appraising glance; equally true that Amanda Anderson seemed barely aware of his presence.

Their tables were separated by a dozen paces.

It was just as well.

Manfred had a very attractive young wife at home and serious business on his mind.

The lady diner was down on men in general, having just left one behind.

Somewhere on the far side of the stream, a tawny wood rat scuttled among the dry leaves.

On a craggy cottonwood branch, a saw-whet owl spread her white-spotted wings, launched herself aloft. This *Aegolius acadicus* had her yellow eye set on the sliver of silver moon, harbored in her breast the happy ambition of landing there.

Like the robin-size owl, the woman was entertaining optimistic thoughts. For example, that she had reached the pinnacle of a successful career, had more than sufficient funds in the bank to purchase a spacious condo in Aspen, a fine house in Santa Fe. Better than that, she finally had more than sufficient evidence to divorce her lying, lecherous leech of a husband. To top it all off, she was still a fine-looking woman, well on the sweet side of fifty, and in perfect health. As she raised a long-stemmed wineglass to toast her excellent prospects, Amanda had enormous confidence in the future.

There was something else she had.

Seven seconds to live.

The short-timer felt the man's gaze tingle on the side of her face, turned to return the brazen stare. If she had not moved, the soft-nosed bullet would have struck her in the left temple, barely two centimeters above the ear. As it was, the crimson entry wound appeared on her forehead, just under the line of her hair—as if a magnanimous genie had placed a precious ruby there.

There was no pain.

There was . . . nothing.

Scott Parris was halfway home from Daisy Perika's birthday party when a sudden shower rattled on the windshield. There was a blurred flash of lightning in the east. He counted the seconds until a rumble of thunder tumbled off the mountains. *That was about a mile and a half away.* He smiled in the darkness. *A fine dinner with good friends and now a rainy night—just the thing for a good sleep.* This pleasant thought was interrupted by an unpleasant vibration in his shirt pocket. Only a half-dozen souls had his private number. The chief of police pulled over to the curb, frowned at the digits on the display. *That's Doc Simpson's cell phone.* He punched in the number, waited.

The medical examiner's voice crackled in his ear. "Scott—where are you?"

"On my way home—how about you?"

"I'm at Phillipe's. Enjoying my sweet little niece's wedding reception."

Simpson sounds like he's had a couple of drinks. "Good for you—give the lovely couple my best wishes for a long and happy life."

"I've already done that." A pause. "Scott—would you do me a big favor?

"Maybe." Parris grinned in the darkness. "If it don't have anything to do with lending you money."

"I'd appreciate it if you'd come over to Phillipe's. Right now."

"Tell me what for."

"I'll tell you when you get here."

Silly old goat. "Why can't you tell me what this is all—"

"Park on the south side, next to the kitchen entrance. But don't come inside—walk around back, to the patio. I'll be waiting for you." The telephone connection went dead.

The chief of police did a tight U-turn on the newly wet street, popped a couple of antacid tablets between his teeth, swore he'd retire before this time next year. *If I win the lottery.*

3

SCENE OF THE CRIME

The long strings of multicolored lanterns cast a bizarre tint of unreality onto the restaurant patio, where a large red-and-white table umbrella sheltered the remains from the rain. Scott Parris could not shake the absurd, nagging conviction that this ugly display had been staged for his benefit. It would turn out to be a setup for one of the medical examiner's tasteless jokes. Any second now, the woman in the black dress and pearls would sit up, smile at him, wipe the tomato paste off her face. Doc Simpson and Phillipe and the bearded guy he didn't recognize would start laughing their heads off. "April Fool," they'd say. "We sure had you going there!" But the first of day April was gone with the melted snows that swelled the roaring stream.

He took a few steps away from the small gathering, dialed dispatch on his cell phone. After appropriate orders had been barked out, the Granite Creek chief of police approached the umbrella, knelt on one knee. This had been a handsome, upper-class woman. The pearls would be the real thing. Another real thing was the small hole in her forehead. The lead bullet had expanded, so the exit wound would be at least an inch wide. He knew this because a yard away was a half-dollar-size fragment of skull, shiny with a smear of brain tissue, a long hank of dark hair attached to a flap of scalp. He braced a hand on his knee, got to his feet with a grunt. "Give me the short version."

Dr. Simpson shrugged under his rented tux. "The brief account is the only one I know. I'm inside, enjoying the reception. Phillipe comes over, gives me a nudge and a look. I follow him down the hall, through the kitchen, out the side door by the Dumpster. He tells me something horrible has happened, brings me around here." He pointed his chin at the body. "I find this lady. Just like you see her. She's dead, of course." Simpson continued in a professional monotone, as if he were talking to his microcassette recorder. "The lesion on the forehead has the appearance a small-caliber entry wound. Probably a hollow point, from the damage evident at the exit." Anticipating the question forming on the policeman's lips, the medical examiner jerked his head to indicate the second diner. "There was only one other person on the patio. A Mr. Dinko. He's a dentist."

"Orthodontist." The man stepped forward. "And the name is *Blinkoe*. Manfred Wilhelm Blinkoe."

The experienced policeman calibrated the witness in a single glance. About five-eleven, 180 pounds, a good fifty-five years old. Probably closer to sixty. Nearsighted, judging by the thick spectacles. The man's outstanding physical feature was a forked beard. "What happened here, Mr. Blinkoe?"

"*Doctor* Blinkoe, if you please."

Parris tried again. "What happened here, Dr. Blinkoe?"

The man swelled with a deep breath. "Because the wedding reception had booked the main dining room, the lady and myself were dining on the patio. She was seated there." He pointed at the table nearest the corpse's feet. "I was just over there, at the table by that garish blue flower pot." Oblivious to the light rain, he looked up at the dark sky, as if he saw something there.

"Did you know the victim?"

Blinkoe glanced at the corpse, shook his head.

Parris crossed his fingers, hoped for a yes. "You happen to get a look at the shooter?"

"Sadly, I did not."

It had been too much to hope for, but the policeman felt a surge of heartburn.

As if hoping to please the public servant, Blinkoe added quickly, "But I did hear the gunshot."

Well that's something. And something is better than nothing. "Just a single shot?"

"Yes. It was merely a little *pop*." The witness pointed toward the river. "And it came from directly behind me. From across the stream, I should think."

Parris stared at the tangle of brush on the opposite bank. It made sense. A hundred assassins could hide in that small, dense forest. Fifty yards beyond the thicket was a little-used county road where the shooter could have parked his car.

Blinkoe continued. "As chance would have it, I happened to be looking directly at the lady when I heard the shot—and saw the bullet wound appear in her head. For a moment, she merely stared"—he goggled his eyes to imitate the victim's blank expression—"then she toppled out of the chair. *Kerplop*." He made what was evidently intended to be a kerplopping gesture with his hand. "I was quite startled, of course—one never expects to see such a terrible thing. I immediately took cover behind the big flowerpot by my table. When I was convinced there would be no second shot, I approached the body and placed my finger on the lady's neck, just under the jaw. There was not the least hint of a carotid pulse. Having determined that the victim was dead, I entered the restaurant and summoned Phillipe."

The owner of the business nodded. "As soon as I was informed about the incident, I came to see for myself." He stared in amazement at the corpse. "There she was—exactly as Dr. Blinkoe had reported. By remarkable good fortune, the county medical examiner was inside, a guest at his niece's wedding reception." He made a slight bow to Dr. Simpson. "Naturally, I requested that he come outside at once and examine the body." He added hastily: "If there had been any sign of life, I would have summoned an ambulance. But sadly, there was no need. I conferred with Dr. Simpson, and we thought it advisable to be discreet." He glanced at the series of large windows that framed the ongoing celebration inside, added unnecessarily: "The wedding party has not been informed about this tragedy." He looked hopefully at the chief of police. "After all, what good would it do to disturb my happy guests with such terrible news?"

Straining to hold his temper, Parris addressed his remark to the surviving diner. "Do you recall what time it was when you witnessed the shooting?"

Manfred Blinkoe shrugged. "I did not look at my watch. But I would estimate that the poor woman was shot—oh, about twenty-five minutes before your arrival."

Twenty-five minutes! Parris ground his teeth. "Someone should have dialed 911 immediately."

Phillipe recoiled as if he had been struck by a snake. "But the woman was dead—what good would that have done?"

The professional lawman did not expect much from citizens whose experience was limited to running high-priced restaurants or fixing smiles that still had some personality. But the county medical examiner should have known better. "If one of you had called the emergency number right away, told us somebody had been shot on the patio, the department would have had uniforms all over the area within three minutes flat. We would've stood a fair chance of nailing the shooter. By now, the guy has had time to drive halfway to Durango. Or Leadville. Or Gunnison."

The M.E. withered under this attack.

Feeling mildly sorry for the old man, Parris turned his cold stare on Phillipe. "Here's the deal." He pointed a sausage of a finger at the man's chest. "You go inside and tell your guests that nobody leaves the joint."

Deeply wounded by the deliberately crude characterization of his four-star establishment, Phillipe gave the gastronomic Neanderthal a look of utmost disdain and pity.

Parris barely restrained himself from grabbing the businessman by the collar and shaking his teeth loose. "Do it right now. Or I will."

The restaurateur retreated with an inaudible mutter that suggested Parris's parents had never enjoyed the benefits of matrimony.

Dr. Simpson sidled up to his friend. "I'm sorry, Scott. I should've made the emergency call." He tried to grin. "Guess I may've had two or three martinis too many. And even when I'm sober, my old brain don't function like it did twenty years ago."

Parris patted the M.E.'s stooped shoulder. "Sorry if I snapped at you guys. A murder in my jurisdiction kinda puts my teeth on edge."

Feeling at least partially absolved of his sin of omission, Simpson turned his attention to the corpse. After shaking his head at what had been a lovely woman, he covered the body with a vinyl tablecloth. Only the lady's feet protruded, and her left arm.

The chief of police was staring at the fingers on the dead woman's hand. There was no wedding band. But there was a pale white circle on the tanned skin where one might have recently been.

The orthodontist cleared his throat. "Excuse me."

One of the woman's red high heels had slipped off when she fell from her chair. Parris was mesmerized by the exposed foot. "Yeah?"

"I am, needless to say, not an expert in murders and such." Annoyed that the policeman did not look at him, the witness unconsciously clenched his fists. "But if you will indulge me, I believe there is a distinct possibility that you may not have considered."

"Consider yourself indulged." Just under her big toe, there was a dime-size hole in the silk stocking. *I wonder if she knew about that.*

Blinkoe raised his voice. "I believe the bullet was intended for me."

As he turned his head to glare at the witness, Parris almost jerked his neck out of joint. "Why do you believe that?"

"Well, for one thing—the shot came from behind me."

"Yeah. I remember you said that. Is that the only reason?"

There was a hesitation. "I have a very strong feeling that I am the person who was supposed to die tonight."

He has a feeling. *Great.* "Look, I understand you've been through a traumatic experience, but—"

"I doubt that you understand *anything* about what I've been through." The man's eyes seemed to bulge from their sockets; the startling effect was magnified by the thick spectacle lenses. "Have you ever been shot at?"

The former Chicago cop felt the bad memories come flooding back. "Yes, I have." *More than once.*

Blinkoe blinked. "Oh—well yes, I suppose you would have been. In the line of duty and all that." He flicked a tiny piece of wet lint off his cuff. "That is one thing. But let me tell you, sir—it is not the same when you are dining at your favorite restaurant."

Scott Parris's blue eyes twinkled. "Yeah. I can see how that's enough to put a man off his feed. But the point is, you weren't hit." He glanced again at the corpse's bare foot. "It was this lady that got shot dead."

Blinkoe shook his head. "Nevertheless, I am virtually certain that the unfortunate woman was not the murderer's intended target."

"Dr. Blinkoe, take it from me. Any guy who can place a slug dead center in his target's forehead—even from just on the other side of the stream—is an expert marksman. If he'd had the bead on you, you'd be stone cold dead." He pointed at the corpse. "And I'd be talking to this lady about what happened when *you* got popped."

The witness assumed a stubborn expression. "I think I may have moved just as he fired the shot."

"Then the slug must've passed pretty close to you."

"Well, yes—I suppose it would have."

"Did you get nicked?"

"Well, no. Of course not."

"Did you hear a chunk of lead go zipping by?"

"I did not." Blinkoe bristled at this hardheaded cop. "But I tell you—that bullet was meant for me!"

Parris glanced at his wristwatch, wondered when the first GCPD unit would arrive. "Dr. Blinkoe, can you think of anyone who hates you enough to shoot you?" *Aside from me.*

Blinkoe struggled to return the lawman's bold stare. "Every man has his enemies—I suppose I have my share."

"Okay. So give me a name—and a motive."

The supposed victim finally averted his gaze. "I am not prepared to speculate on such matters."

Why does my only witness to a homicide have to be a nutcase? The policeman managed to retain a thin veneer of civility. "Then what do you want from me?"

Blinkoe canted his head, stared intently at the starless sky—as if the answer might be concealed in that dark space beneath the heavens. "I don't know. Protection, I suppose."

Parris closed his eyes, gently massaged the lids with his fingertips. "Witnessing a killing at close range is a nasty experience. Makes a man stop and consider his mortality." *Makes some of 'em downright goofy.* "But I expect you'll feel a lot better after a good night's sleep."

"Thank you for this halfhearted attempt to cheer me up. But what if you are wrong?" Blinkoe glared at a Chinese lantern as if he could not fathom what on earth the vulgar contraption was. "What if the murderer strangles me in my sleep? Runs me through with a rapier? Poisons my morning tea?"

Parris's patience had fallen below the quarter-tank mark. "Then you'll be dead."

The citizen scowled at the public servant. "I *beg* your pardon?"

Regretting his unprofessional retort, the weary chief of police made a final attempt to get through to this stubborn man. "Dr. Blinkoe, if you won't tell me anything specific about who might've taken a shot at you—or why someone might want you dead—there's nothing much I can do." *But what am I gonna do with this guy?* Like most "eureka" moments, this one seemed to come from nowhere. Parris proceeded with a wary caution. "Maybe you'd feel more comfortable having someone else look into it." He managed to look quite sympathetic. "Someone not connected with the police department."

Blinkoe's expression was an unhappy mix of bald-faced astonishment and acute pain. "You don't mean like a—a gumshoe?"

Parris maintained an earnest expression. "Nowadays, we call 'em private investigative consultants. PICs for short."

"PICs—really?" Blinkoe pulled at the left cusp of his beard. "I suppose it is not a totally absurd notion." He gave the cop a hopeful look. "Could you recommend a private investigative whatever—a PIC—who is both highly capable and very discreet?"

"Well, let me think about it." Granite Creek's top cop tilted his head back, pretended to consider a bushel of gumshoe-fruit hanging on a massive willow tree. Eventually, he nodded as if he had shaken the right one loose. "Yeah. I believe I know just the guy."

Anticipating such an outcome, Blinkoe had produced a small leather-bound notebook and a gold-plated fountain pen. "Please give me his name."

Cocked and loaded, Scott Parris gave him both barrels. A name. A telephone number.

The orthodontist jotted the information onto a blank page. "Taking on the services of a PIC seems a rather drastic course of action." He stowed the notebook and pen in his shirt pocket. "I will have to give it some thought."

Parris stared at the dead woman's big toe. The obscene little hole in her stocking was beginning to annoy him. *Please, please, let some of my uniforms show up.*

Blue and red lights flashing, the first black-and-white pulled into Phillipe's parking lot, screeched to a rocking halt. It was, as might be expected, the dependable Captain

Leggett. Parris was on his way to meet his second in command when he heard a sound.

"Hsssst."

He turned. "Who's there?"

A head appeared just above a mulberry bush. "Just Old Willie, the groundskeeper."

The chief of police smiled at the scarecrow-man who emerged.

"Old Willie" was worthy of his nickname. Tattered gray overalls hung on the aged man's skinny frame. He was hunched forward, walked with a cane. He removed a long-stemmed pipe from a mouth that bristled with untrimmed whiskers, stuck it into the pocket of the OshKosh B'Gosh bib, offered a skeletal hand to the lawman.

Parris shook the bony paw, stole a sideways glance at the squad car, where Leggett was closing the door. "So you work for Phillipe?"

"For almost three months, now." Willie chuckled. "But I wouldn't exactly call it work. I mostly potter around. Mow the grass once a week, keep the weeds from taking over the place." He tapped the cane against Parris's boot toe. "I knew you'd be getting around to asking me sooner or later, so I thought I should let you know right now—I heard that shot."

Parris forgot about Leggett. "Where were you?"

He pointed the knobby cane. "Sitting up yonder in my rocking chair, right in front of the storage building where we keep all the gardening equipment and fertilizer."

Parris squinted in the darkness, could barely make out a peak-roofed, slab-walled shed that was almost hidden in a cluster of willows.

Anticipating the next question, the old man said: "That Phillipe is an okay fella; he lets me bunk in there. After I'm through with my chores, I kinda settle in for the night. Sometimes I listen to my battery radio, other times I go for a walk down by the creek. But this evening, the radio was fulla static and it looked like rain, so I came outside to watch the thunderstorm build up over the mountains. When the shot was fired—I was smoking my pipe." Having reminded himself of this small pleasure, he retrieved the device from his pocket and restarted it with a kitchen match.

The chief of police put his hand behind his back, crossed his fingers. "Did you see the shooter?"

A slow shake of the gray head. "Didn't see a soul. Not when I heard the shot, and not later. What I mean is, I didn't see no one running away." He leaned heavily on the cane. "Which is kinda interesting, when you think about it. From where I was I could see the whole parking lot and most of the patio, where that poor woman got killed." He made a sweeping gesture with the pipe. "And you can see that both places are lit up almost bright as day."

Parris nodded. *Which means the shooter left by some other way. Across the river and through the woods* . . . Another GCPD unit was pulling up, and Leggett had spotted the chief of police. Parris's right-hand man was headed toward his boss. "I have to go have a word with one of my men. But stay put; I'll have someone take your statement."

The groundskeeper smiled. "Always glad to help the Law." He shook his cane at the cop. "But there is one thing."

"What's that?"

"I don't want my name to show up in the newspaper—this is just between me and the police."

"Not looking for publicity, eh?"

"I'm not looking to be the next person who gets shot at."

"Well, I wouldn't worry about it—you didn't actually get a look at the shooter, so—"

"You know that, and I know that." The groundskeeper took a long, thoughtful puff on his pipe. "But what if the bad guy don't know that?" He pointed the smoking instrument at the chief of police. "The killer might think I'm one of those witnesses that know a lot more than the newspaper is lettin' on." He clamped the stem hard between his teeth. "Chew on that for a while."

4

WHAT HARRIET SAW
LOOKING IN HER WINDOW

When Manfred Blinkoe stepped into the bookstore, it had been almost three days since the unfortunate incident at Phillipe's. Having selected a used volume (*Classic Bowie Knives*) and rendered up a crisp new twenty-dollar bill for his purchase, the orthodontist stood at the counter while the owner of Harriet's Rare Books completed the transaction. As she fumbled with the coins, the customer consulted his obscenely expensive wristwatch, which kept perfect time. *Eleven fifty-nine and thirty-two seconds.* He raised his gaze to the mirror on the wall behind her, liked what he saw. In an effort to make the reflection perfect, the vain fellow proceeded to straighten his red bow tie. He had barely managed to complete the small task when—staring at the silvered glass with an expression of astonished horror—he muttered: "Oh, no—he has returned. And so soon." Precisely, in fact, at high noon.

The book slipped from his hands, hit the counter with a heavy *thunk*.

This seismic event derailed the woman's rickety little train of thought. "Don't make so much racket while I'm making change!" When her customer did not respond, she gave him a dirty look. And saw it. Out there on the sidewalk. Looking straight at her.

Harriet dropped nickels and dimes all over the floor.

5

WHAT DAISY FOUND UNDER THE FLOOR

With the chill of last night's rain hanging heavy in the morning air, Daisy Perika pulled the woolen shawl more tightly around her shoulders. The tribal elder leaned on her oak staff, scowled at the pair of legs protruding from underneath her trailer home. *If it ain't one awful thing it's something worse. Yesterday, the television went on the blink. Week ago Sunday, the well pump popped a gasket. Last month, a spotted skunk crawled up under my house and died. And now this.* The more recent stink was, if possible, even more disturbing. She heaved a sigh, lifted a prayer to heaven. *God have mercy on a poor old woman.*

A raven sitting on a juniper snag spread its wings. And laughed at her.

Using the Ute tongue, Daisy mumbled a vulgar response to the foul bird. It squawked a raucous reply, departed in a huff and whuff of feathers. The shaman was watching the impudent creature wing its way toward Snake Canyon when she heard the low rumble of an automobile engine, the protesting squeak of springs on the rutted road. She got a tight grip on her walking stick. *If that's somebody bringing me more trouble, I will whack 'em right between the eyeballs!*

Manfred Wilhelm Blinkoe saw a spot of sunlight flashing off something metallic. He elbowed the attorney he had pressed into service as his chauffeur and pointed. "Right over there, Spencer—that must be the place."

"I should hope so," the ill-tempered driver snapped. "Aside from a single chipmunk, we have not encountered a sign of life for these last ten hellish miles." Spencer Trottman turned off the bumpy dirt road onto the hint of a lane that wound its crooked way through a thirsty grove of piñon and juniper.

"Don't park too close to the Indian woman's home—it is considered impolite." Blinkoe used the pedantic tone of one who has a superior knowledge of such matters.

"As you say." *I would have preferred to park thirty miles away.* The driver braked the white Mercedes SUV to a stop, shut off the ignition, turned to give his client a stony look. "Manfred, as your legal counsel and investment adviser, I am compelled to say it again—this is a fool's errand."

Blinkoe laughed. "Hah—that is why I brought you along!" Noting the hurt look hanging on Spencer Trottman's long face, he added quickly: "To keep a close watch over me, I mean. I expect you to deter me from doing some foolish thing that I might deeply regret for two or three seconds."

Daisy Perika pretended to be unaware of the arrival of the massive automobile and oblivious to the pair of white men in suits who emerged—as the attorney might have put it—*therefrom*. But therefrom the corner of her dark eye, she watched them approach in mincing steps, as if getting a little spot of dirt on their polished shoes would be a catastrophe. When they were within a dozen paces of her trailer, she turned abruptly—raised a hand to signal that they should come no closer.

The visitors stopped in their tracks.

Pegging at the ground with her walking stick, Daisy went to meet them. She paused a few steps away, blinked. Something was very odd. The taller, clean-shaven man was easy enough to see, crisp and clear as could be. But the bearded fellow was out of focus, sort of jittery at the edges. In the shaman's fertile imagination, there were two images of the man, one laid over the other—but slightly out of alignment. She blinked and the fuzzy twins merged into one. She heaved a little sigh. *Must've been something in my eye.*

The funny-looking fellow with the forked beard tipped his spiffy black homberg in a theatrical gesture. "Ah, excuse me, madam—would you be Ms. Daisy Perika?" He stared at her through thick spectacles.

She eyed the strangers with open suspicion. "I would if it'd be doing me any good."

Blinkoe was somewhat taken aback by this response. "How do you do, I am—"

"How do I *do*?" She pointed at the legs sticking out from under her trailer. "How would you be doing if first thing in the morning, you come outside for a breath of fresh air—and found a *dead body* under your house?"

The visitors stiffened, seemed about to bolt. It was the attorney who spoke. "Dead? Are you quite certain?"

"Well," Daisy admitted, "I haven't actually *touched* it to see if it's still warm. But this one sure looks stone-cold to me."

Rebounding from this unexpected revelation, Blinkoe displayed a morbid fascination. "But how did this unfortunate person expire?" He rubbed his hands together in happy expectation. "Might it have been an act of mindless violence?"

Daisy aimed a sullen glare at the man. "Well I didn't do 'im in if that's what you're thinking."

"Oh, I assure you, I did not mean to suggest—"

"Excuse me." Spencer Trottman cleared his throat. "But I

feel compelled to make an observation. It strikes me as distinctly noteworthy that the corpse is not *entirely* under your trailer. What I mean to say is that it is only *partially* under your home." His tone suggested that perhaps they had caught the old woman in the very act of concealing the body.

Daisy nodded. "Yeah, I guess you town people would think it's kinda strange. But when they're dying, people are a lot like skunks or dogs—they get this urge to crawl into some dark place, like caves or hollow logs. Or under a person's floor." She squinted up at the clouds and continued. "Last night was awfully cold and rainy. After I drifted off to sleep, it's possible the poor fella come by looking for help. Maybe he pounded on my door, but I was sleeping like a stone and he wasn't able to rouse me up. So he tried to scoot up under the trailer to get out of the weather—but before he got all the way, he gave up the ghost."

His gaze fixed on the dead man's boots, Blinkoe stubbornly returned to his question. "But what was the cause of death?"

Daisy turned her considerable imagination to the various possibilities. "Some awful disease, maybe. There's always black plague amongst the prairie dogs, and those gray jumping mice carry the falling-down fever and there ain't no cure for that. Then there's the six-eyed bloodsucking ticks and the hairy-faced flesh-eating wolf spiders." Her grim expression made it clear that they did not want to hear the grisly details of how the ticks and spiders went about their gruesome business. "Now I'm not saying it couldn't have been a gunshot wound or a knife in the back. Around here, bad things happen every other day." She leaned on the walking stick. "But that's not for me to figure out. I guess I'd better call the tribal police, tell them there's a dead man up under my trailer."

Trottman directed a whisper into his client's ear. "A loony old woman and a dead body. I *told* you we should not have come out here."

Blinkoe was unfazed. "Oh posh, Spencer—all this worry over a mere corpse. Why, I would not have missed it for all the world."

The Ute woman eyed the newcomers. "What brings you two out here—you make a wrong turn somewhere?"

In all the excitement, they had almost forgotten.

"Hmm. Let me see." Blinkoe pulled at the left fork of his meticulously clipped beard. "Oh yes. We have come in search of a Mr. Charles Moon. His foreman at the Columbine Ranch—a Mr. Bushman—informed us that Mr. Moon might be on his way here to pay a visit to his aunt, which is presumably yourself. Oh, by the way"—he nodded to indicate the stiff-lipped man—"this is my legal counsel, Mr. Spencer Trottman. I am Dr. Manfred Wilhelm Blinkoe."

The shaman, famous for her herbal cures, raised an eyebrow. "What kind of doctor?"

"I am an orthodontist." He had taken note of her teeth, which could use a bit of work, and added hastily: "Though I am no longer in active practice."

"It's just as well," the old woman said with a nod toward the presumed corpse. "I don't think you could do this one any good. I'd say his chompers is the least of his problems."

Trottman's spine jerked as if he had received an electrical shock. He pointed a trembling finger at the body under Daisy's trailer. "One of the legs just moved."

The old woman pinned him with her gimlet-eye stare. "You sure about that?"

He seemed suddenly to doubt himself. "Well, I suppose it wasn't all that much—merely a twitch."

"Possibly the onset of rigor mortis," the orthodontist suggested. *That would help establish the time of death.*

"Yeah, could be the body's starting to stiffen up." Daisy turned to see whether the leg might twitch again. "Or it could be it's somebody that's playing possum. This wilderness is full of crazies." The old woman set her jaw in the manner of one who is not about to put up with any nonsense from a would-be corpse. "Well I'll sure find out." She marched back to the trailer, yelled: "Hey! Are you a live one or a dead one?" Without waiting for a response, she kicked at a boot.

A big voice boomed out from beneath the trailer. "What?"

Daisy turned to grin at her visitors. "Just like I thought—

he was faking. And I'll bet you a dollar the yahoo's up to no good. He was probably stealing the root crops and canned goods I store under there, then played dead when I came outside." She made another kick at the boot. "You come outta there, you thievin' rascal."

The man under the trailer gave the wrench a final twist. *I'll stop a quarter turn before I strip the threads.*

As the visitors approached the woman's home, the orthodontist noted a rain-spotted Expedition parked in a clump of junipers. A pretty blue-and-white flower had been painted on the door. Blinkoe pointed at the automobile bearing the Columbine logo. "Excuse me, Ms. Perika. But the fellow under your home—might he possibly be Mr. Moon?"

Daisy pretended to be startled at the suggestion. "Well, now—why didn't I think of that." The old woman raised a hand to her mouth, snickered.

"Hah." Blinkoe elbowed his legal counsel. "The aged auntie has pulled our legs!"

Spencer Trottman was as far from being amused as is east from west. He glared at the Ute woman. "What is Mr. Moon doing underneath your home?"

"God only knows," she said with a shake of her head. "From time to time, my nephew does some strange things."

Having pulled himself out into the daylight, Charlie Moon jammed a pair of wrenches into his hip pocket, squinted up at the visitors. The uptight fellow looked like either a lawyer or a mortician. The man with the double-pointed beard was another matter altogether. *Where have I seen that face?*

Manfred W. Blinkoe introduced himself and Spencer Trottman to the tribal investigator.

Charlie Moon had heard the Mercedes engine a full nine minutes before the sounds had been detected by his aunt's old eardrums, but he had been too busy to take an interest in either their arrival or their conversation with his mischievous relative. "Sorry I couldn't come out to meet you. My aunt smelled something sour last night, thought another skunk had crawled up under her floor. It turned out to be the odorant they put in the propane. I was busy fixing a leak in her gas line."

Outraged by the Indian woman's contemptible shenanigans and her nephew's amiable explanations, the attorney was in a mood to take scalps and burn tipis. "Gas apparatus can be quite dangerous." He looked down his long nose at the sitting Indian. "I assume you are well qualified to make the necessary repairs." It was apparent that Spencer Trottman assumed no such thing. Indeed, he appeared to be eager to sue if he could find a client.

"I'm just your run-of-the mill handyman." The Ute grinned at his aunt. "She hires me because I work for nothing." He got up off the ground.

The attorney and the orthodontist watched the lanky figure unfold like a carpenter's segmented ruler—up to a height of seven feet above the top of his boot heels.

Moon brushed some dust off the seat of his jeans. "Anything I can do for you fellas?"

"Quite possibly." Blinkoe gave his attorney a look that brooked no argument. "Spencer, why don't you have a pleasant visit with this charming little lady while Mr. Moon and I go for a walk-and-talk."

"First, I got to get my hat." Charlie Moon headed for the Columbine flagship.

Blinkoe followed.

As he watched them go, blood vessels throbbed in Trottman's neck.

Daisy smiled at the irate attorney as if he were her closest friend.

"C'mon inside. I'll brew us up a fresh pot of coffee." *This should be fun.*

6

AN UNLIKELY CLIENT

The tribal investigator and the white man walked along the rutted road toward the mouth of *Cañón del Espíritu*. The long-legged Ute slowed his pace to allow his companion to keep up. "Well, Dr. Blinkoe, what's on your mind?"

"Business. I understand that you are a private investigator."

"I hold a license, but the cattle business keeps me pretty busy. Now and then I do an odd job for the tribal chairman, but that's about it."

"You are too modest."

Moon grinned. "You think so?"

"I have heard about the excellent work you did for Senator Davidson."

The Ute's antenna pricked up. "Where'd you hear about that?"

"Word gets around."

Moon hoped that not too much word had gotten around

about that fiasco. If the whole truth ever came out, he could end up doing a long vacation in a federal resort.

"And there's that investigation you did for Jane Cassidy—the woman praises you to the skies." The sedentary man was getting slightly short of breath. "On top of that, you come highly recommended by the Granite Creek chief of police."

The Ute stopped to look down at the odd man. "You know Scott?"

"I met him just last week." Blinkoe avoided the dark man's penetrating stare. "I suppose you've heard about the deplorable incident at Phillipe's."

Moon had heard. "You're the guy who was on the patio— with the woman who got shot."

"I was not precisely *with* her. I was dining alone that evening, as was the unfortunate lady." He shot the Indian a quick glance. "Did Chief Parris tell you about me?"

"He didn't have to. I saw your picture in the local rag."

"Oh, of course. The newspaper." Blinkoe's lips tightened. "I detest any sort of personal publicity."

"From what I recall, you're the only witness to the shooting."

"Which is not much help, I'm afraid. The shot was fired from someplace behind me. On the far side of the stream I should think."

"So you didn't see the shooter?"

Blinkoe shook his head. "It was quite dark except on the patio, which was illuminated by some absurdly tawdry Chinese lanterns." He swatted at a black wasp that buzzed past his nose.

"So why do you want to talk to me?"

The worried man bit his lip. "I think you may be able to help me." He clamped his mouth shut, tried to think of precisely how to approach the matter.

Moon decided to give the potential client all the time he needed.

They approached a narrow ribbon of a stream that trickled out of the mouth of Spirit Canyon.

◆ ◆ ◆

The hunter's Savage 110FP Tactical Rifle was chambered for
.300 Winchester Magnum—one of the best long-range car-
tridges available. He found a suitable spot behind a juniper,
seated himself cross-legged, rested the rifle barrel in a notch
between the trunk and a limb. Like all effective plans, this
one was simple. Put a round through the primary target, then
drop the Indian cop. A homemade silencer was screwed onto
the end of the barrel, so the shot wouldn't be heard by the old
woman in the trailer or the lawyer who was her guest. He had
no interest in these bystanders. Blinkoe was who he'd come
to kill. Once he had gotten the job done, he would walk back
to the truck, hide the rifle in the concealed compartment
welded under the pickup bed, drive away like an innocent
tourist. It would probably be at least an hour before the sur-
vivors began to wonder why Blinkoe and the Indian hadn't
returned, another thirty minutes before they went looking for
them. *And by the time they find the bodies and put a call in to
the police, I'll be miles and miles away.*

He closed his left eye, squinted his right at the high-tech,
antishake 9X telescope. *Okay . . . there they are. But a little
fuzzy.* He thumbed the focus knob, noted the distance on the
in-scope range finder digital readout. *A hundred and thirty-two
yards. Not exactly a slam-dunk, but I can do it.* The marksman
placed the crosshairs on Manfred Blinkoe's spine, snugged his
finger up to the trigger. And had an unsettling thought. *If I take
Blinkoe out first, the skinny Indian might take a dive into the
bushes and slip away. I have to kill them both. It'd make more
sense to drop the athletic-looking spear chucker with the first
shot, then pop Blinkoe.* With an almost imperceptible movement of the heavy rifle, he laid the crosshairs on the Indian's
chest. The Ute was nodding, evidently responding to something Blinkoe was saying. *Okay, Tonto. You've got about three
seconds left to live.* His finger began to tighten on the trigger.
Nobody on earth or in heaven can save you now. . . .

A sudden gust rattled the juniper branches.

"Damn—damn!" he muttered. Even a mild breeze would

make this a marginal shot, and now the wind was tossing dust in his face. He thought it over. *I can't afford to miss. There's only one way out of this place, and it's a long drive back to the paved highway. If the survivor dials 911 and reports a sniper, the local cops could throw up a roadblock before I could get back to the pavement.*

He waited for the annoying wind to subside.

It did not.

It seemed to have come to stay.

It was time to call it a day. This descendant of Cain was not overly troubled. There would be another time. Another opportunity. The essential thing was to stay in the game. He slung the nylon rifle strap over his shoulder, departed as silently as he had come.

Blinkoe picked up a small stick, pitched it into the crystalline water. He took a childlike pleasure in the small splash his minuscule missile made. The orthodontist blinked at the stream, watched the twig float away, vanish under an overhang of willow branches. He wished all his troubles would slip away with it. "That evening at Phillipe's, the person who fired the shot—missed."

The tribal investigator thought about this. "Unless I completely misunderstood what I read in the newspaper, the bullet hit the woman in the head. She dropped dead on the spot."

"Allow me to clarify. The assassin missed his *intended* target."

Moon thought he knew, but felt compelled to ask. "Which was?"

"Myself, of course."

The Ute watched a bald eagle circle above the canyon. *Why don't I ever get one of those slinky, good-looking lady clients like those hard-drinking detectives in pulp fiction. The rich blonde that wants you to find her missing sister who ran off to Hollywood with a trombone player. All I ever get is a thankless assignment from the tribal chairman or some botheration from one of these peculiar persons that—*

Manfred Wilhelm Blinkoe wrung his hands in exasperation. "Aren't you going to ask me how I know this?"

If it'll make you feel better. "How do you know you were
the shooter's target?"

"I sense you are humoring me." A pout pursed his lips. "I
don't believe that I shall tell you."

"Okay."

Blinkoe stamped his foot. "You are a most exasperating
man!"

"I didn't mean to rile you." The Ute patted Blinkoe's
rounded shoulder. "Tell me what's on your mind."

The orthodontist seated himself on a rotten cottonwood
log. "You must promise not to laugh."

"I'll do my level best."

It was some time before the man spoke, but when he did it
was with an intensity that surpassed his previous tantrum.
"Moments before the shooting occurred, I felt a strange, tin-
gling sensation. I looked up, toward the table where the
woman was seated. There, very near her, was . . ." He put his
face in his hands. "Oh—I don't know if I can make myself
tell you."

Moon sat down beside him. "If it'd help, I could tie you to
an anthill. Drive red-hot splinters under your toenails."

The *matukach* glared at the merry Ute. "Mr. Moon, I am
not devoid of a sense of humor. I laugh at the Sunday comics,
particularly FoxTrot and Agnes. And if I happen to see an elderly lady trip over her cane and tumble down the porch
steps, I positively go into hysterics. But this is a *very* serious
matter."

"You're right."

Blinkoe's expression was doubtful. "You promise not to
make sport of me?"

"Sure. Now tell me who you saw near the woman who got
shot."

"For the sake of conversation, we may refer to what I saw
as . . ." He gulped. "As It."

Moon arched a dark eyebrow. "*It?*"

Blinkoe avoided the Ute's gaze. "That's what I said."

"Uh, I don't know just how to say this—but what exactly is It?" Moon had no trouble looking puzzled. "Are we talking animal, mineral, or vegetable?"

The white man's face blushed pink. "Neither."

"I'm not sure I really want to know—but what does that leave?"

"It is nonmaterial."

Aha. "You mean like a ghost?"

"More like . . . a *presence.*"

The tribal investigator stared at his potential client. *Or maybe a hallucination.*

Blinkoe waited for a response. "Well?"

"Hmmm," the Ute said.

"What does that mean?"

"Means I'm thinking."

"Thinking what?"

You don't want to know. "You ever seen this 'It' before?"

"Oh, certainly—during the course of my highly eventful life, whenever I have been in mortal danger I have often become aware of my . . . uh . . . *companion.* This has occurred seven times during the past ten years, five of which preceded the violent incident at Phillipe's."

Moon did some elementary arithmetic. "Five plus one equals six." He said this with considerable assurance that he would not be contradicted.

Blinkoe cleared his throat. "The seventh sighting was *after* the shooting."

The tribal investigator looked over the canyon. The white-headed eagle was no longer there. "When and where?"

"Yesterday, in Granite Creek. More precisely, at noon—at Harriet's Rare Books."

"Anybody try to do you in?"

Blinkoe shook his head. "But I am certain that it was a warning. Whoever intended to murder me at the restaurant may have been lurking nearby, waiting for a second opportunity. I have no doubt the scoundrel will make another attempt."

"You tell Scott Parris about this . . . uh . . . this It business?"

"I did not." Blinkoe hesitated. "Forgive me for saying this about your colleague, but he is a bone-headed bumpkin."

Moon tried to look at least mildly offended, but could not pull it off.

"Which is to say—he is not the sort of person who would listen to any story that was more unusual than Jack and Jill Went up the Hill to Fetch a Pail of Liquid Refreshment. But I did inform him that I was the assassin's intended victim."

"And he didn't buy that?"

"No. In fact, he came very near guffawing in my face."

"But Scott sent you to see me." *Thanks a lot, pal.*

"He did." The peculiar man scowled. "I'm sure he merely wanted to be rid of me."

"Look," the Ute said gently, "I don't think I can help you. Nonmaterial stuff—that's not quite in my line of expertise." *Maybe he should talk to Aunt Daisy.*

"I am not an utter fool," Blinkoe snapped. "I do not expect you to go looking for . . . for my nonmaterial *companion.* What I want you to do is find out who's trying to murder me. And put a stop to it."

"Well, it does sound interesting." Moon flipped a pebble into the stream. "Problem is, I've got a big ranch to look after. And what little time I have left over, the tribal chairman keeps me busy with this and that."

"Then you're saying you won't help me?"

"Sure wish I could, but—"

"I cannot accept that answer." Blinkoe jutted his chin in the manner of one who has been driven to a difficult decision. "I'm sorry. But you leave me no choice in the matter."

Intrigued to find out what the man had in mind, Moon waited. He did not have to wait long.

Manfred Wilhelm Blinkoe put a hand inside his jacket.

Having met more than his fair share of crazies, the tribal investigator tensed. *If he pulls a gun—*

Blinkoe produced a pack of Bicycle Playing Cards, which he offered to the Ute. "I understand that you are a gambling man."

Moon inspected the box. The cellophane seal was unbroken. "Where'd you hear that?"

The white man allowed himself a small smirk. "I have my ways of finding out things."

"What've you got in mind?"

Blinkoe rubbed his palms together. "Name your poison."

"Straight poker will be the death of me."

"Done."

"What're the stakes?"

"My hard cash against your hard work."

"You'll have to be a bit more quantitative." Moon watched the orthodontist extract a wallet from his hip pocket. A *fat* wallet.

Blinkoe removed a thick sheaf of hundred-dollar bills, began to peel them off one by one. He offered the stack for the Ute's inspection.

Moon counted the crisp new hundreds. "There's a thousand bucks here."

"We'll play one hand. You win, you take the greenbacks. I win, you provide me with three days of your investigative services at no cost."

This sounded too easy. The Ute gave him a narrow-eyed look. "I shuffle, you cut, I deal."

"That will be quite satisfactory."

Moon ripped off the cellophane, opened the small carton. He checked the deck, offered it for Blinkoe's inspection.

The orthodontist expertly spread the cards into a fan, passed them back to the Ute.

Moon shuffled.

Blinkoe cut the deck.

Using the sandy earth for a table, Moon dealt five cards each. He watched the odd man check his hand. "How many do you want?"

"Oh," Blinkoe said with a shrug, "I suppose I'll stick with what I've got."

Moon knew a bluff when he saw one. He looked at a pair of fives. "Dealer takes three." He dealt himself a deuce, a nine of spades—another five! "I'll raise you three more days of services."

"I'll see that with another thousand dollars."

Moon laid his hand down. "Three of a kind."

"Well," Blinkoe said, "that is pretty good." He smirked. "But not good enough." He showed the Ute his hand. All hearts. Ten. Jack. Queen. King. Ace.

Moon stared like a man who has stumbled over a tombstone and found his name engraved on it. And today's date.

Blinkoe beamed at the Indian. "Well, well—looks like this is my lucky day."

The Ute spoke slowly, his words cutting like an ax. "Dr. Blinkoe—the odds against being dealt a royal flush are not even one in half a million."

"Is that a fact?"

"To be exact, it's one in six hundred and forty-nine thousand, seven hundred and forty."

"Then I am extraordinarily lucky."

"You're extraordinarily reckless. You should've gone for something barely believable—like a straight."

Blinkoe's voice went thin. "What, exactly, are you saying?"

"I'm saying you're an outright, bald-faced cheat."

"Sir, that is highly offensive." The player made a valiant attempt to appear outraged. "After all, you dealt the cards. How could I have possibly—"

"The old-fashioned way. You marked the deck, put it back in the box, used a heated butter knife to reseal the cellophane."

"Really, now—"

"And you had that flush stuffed up your sleeve along with all the other aces and faces you might've needed—depending on what I was holding."

"That is absolutely absurd."

"Then prove me wrong—take off your jacket, roll up your shirtsleeves."

"And if I refuse?"

The hostile Indian picked up the deck. "I'll check to see if the ace of hearts is still in this deck. Along with the rest of your flush."

The card cheat blanched. "Mr. Moon, I am compelled to make a critical statement—you are taking a friendly little card game far too seriously."

"Dr. Blinkoe, there is nothing more serious than poker."

"Oh, all right." He threw his hands up with an air of exasperation. "I admit it—I did play a bit of a prank on you. But it was all in good fun."

The Ute continued to stare holes in him.

"I have confessed—what else do you want?"

Charlie Moon told him what he wanted.

Blinkoe said a painful farewell to twenty hundred-dollar bills.

Moon counted the money twice. "If any of this turns out to be counterfeit—"

"Oh, posh. I would never consider such a monstrous deceit."

The Ute held a bill up to the sunlight. "Looks like the genuine article."

"Well of course it's genuine." *He is really a very picky fellow.* "I hope you will be willing to forgive and forget—"

He glared at the white man. "I can't think of anything makes me madder than a card cheat. Compared to you, a horse thief could teach Sunday school."

Blinkoe blinked. "You are really angry with me?"

"If you was on fire, I wouldn't spit on you."

"You should not be so judgmental." The shameless man looked away. "It is not my fault that I had cards in my sleeve."

This was more fun than he'd had in weeks. "How do you figure that?"

"I suffer from a serious medical condition." There was a well-executed hesitation. "If I reveal my humiliating secret, will you promise to keep it to yourself?"

"Sure." *This should be good.* "Cross my fingers."

The habitual liar took a deep breath, exhaled the contrived confession. "I cannot control myself. It is true that I am a compulsive cheater—but this fault is entirely due to a defective gene."

"Well, that throws a whole new light on things." Moon choked back a grin. "Is there any treatment?"

"Psychiatric counseling has been of no use at all." Blinkoe exhaled a martyr's sigh. "But last month, I met with a group of biomedical scientists in Palo Alto who are hopeful that advances in stem cell research will eventually provide a cure."

"You mean like implanting cells from an honest person into you?"

"It's a bit more complicated than that, but you are more or less on the right track. Needless to say, I have invested heavily in their research."

Moon was absolutely in awe of the man. "I guess I was a little hard on you."

"Does that mean you will agree to help me?"

"Haven't made up my mind yet. But if I do, it'll be for five hundred bucks a day. First ten days in advance."

"Ouch! That is rather steep."

"If you'd like to bargain, we could discuss paid holidays. A medical-dental plan. And a bonus if I have to work on Chief Ouray's birthday."

"Oh, very well. I accept your terms." Blinkoe glanced toward the trailer, where his impatient lawyer was waiting with the old Indian woman. "I suppose you'll want all sorts of personal information."

"*If* I decide to do some work for you, I would need to know something about your business activities."

"Other than a few investments, I am retired from the world of business."

"That must give you plenty of time to spend with your family."

"I am, sadly—an orphan. But I do have a devoted wife." Blinkoe rubbed a gold band on his finger. It was set with a heart-shaped stone. "This six-carat ruby was a gift from my loving spouse on our first wedding anniversary." He blinked moist eyes. "Pansy saved up every penny from her allowance." For a moment, he was so moved by this magnificent lie that he could not speak. He cleared his throat, glanced at the Swiss-made timepiece strapped to his wrist. "I suppose we should return to your aunt's quaint domicile. Spencer is a very impatient fellow; he's probably in a tiff by now."

"Whether or not I decide to take you on as a client, there's one thing I'm bound to do for you." The tribal investigator stared hard at the fascinating man. "I'm going to give you some advice."

M. W. Blinkoe looked mildly alarmed at the prospect. "What sort of advice?"

"The sort that might save your life. Here it is: Don't ever, *ever* cheat at cards again."

The response was immediate and scented with insincerity. "Oh, very well."

"You promise?"

"I give you my solemn word."

Moon grinned.

Blinkoe looked to be deeply hurt. "I don't like that look in your eye—do you think I would lie to you?"

"Well, you had your mouth open—and I could hear words coming out."

"I have informed you about my medical condition, Mr. Moon. You should make an attempt to be more tolerant. And understanding."

"Next time you have some aces and royalty up your sleeve, you're liable to run into somebody who's not nearly as tolerant and understanding as me." *Somebody who'll slit your throat and pocket your poke.*

7

DINING WITH DAISY

Having managed to lure the lawyer into her home, Daisy Perika pointed at a chair by the kitchen table. "Sit down."

Though Spencer Trottman was not in the habit of taking orders, he was far too civilized to invite a confrontation with this old savage. So he sat. And looked around. "Well, well." *Rather a tiny place.* "Have you lived out here very long?"

"All my life," she muttered as she puttered around the propane stove. "And don't ask how long that's been. I just had a birthday and I don't like to think about it." Daisy raised the top of the range, used a kitchen match to touch a flame to each of the pilot lights. There was a satisfying *pop*, then another. *Looks like Charlie got that gas line fixed.* She turned to her visitor, gave him a jerk of her head. "Come over here."

The lawyer got up from his chair. "What for?"

"I want you to get down on your knees in front of this stove, stick your head in the oven."

He paled. "I *beg* your pardon?"

She gave him a box of matches. "You got a young back and long arms; see if you can light the pilot. It's in the broiler, way near the back. I'm too old and stiff to try it—if I get down there, I might get all stove up." *Stove up—that's a good one.* "And if I did, I might not be able to stand up straight for a month."

The white-collar worker frowned at the grease-spotted linoleum in front of the stove, considered his razor-creased trousers.

Daisy pitched a newspaper onto the floor. "You can use that."

Trottman knelt on the obituaries, flicked a wooden match to life, stuck his arm into the broiler, closed his eyes in the hope that the subsequent explosion would not blind him for life—and by some good fortune managed to ignite the pilot flame. It was the first useful manual labor the attorney had performed in ages. It felt good. He got to his feet, brushed nothing in particular off his knees.

Daisy pointed at the floor. "Pick up the newspaper."

Now accustomed to being the Ute woman's house servant, he performed this task without protest.

She snatched the *Ute Drum* from his hands, stuffed it in a plastic wastebasket. "I don't get many visitors out here, so I'm not set up for entertaining people." She pointed at the ancient television set. "I'd turn on a baseball game for you, but that worthless box of tubes and wires is on the blink. The picture's all slanted, so when I want to watch *Oprah*, I have to tilt my head like this." She demonstrated. "And it makes my neck hurt."

His stiff face almost smiled. "Don't give it a second thought. I rarely watch TV."

"Then I'll make a fresh batch of coffee and heat up some Indian stew."

It would be impolite to refuse her hospitality. "Well—I suppose just a little coffee."

A few minutes later, Daisy Perika plopped a mug of black liquid in front of her guest. "You want any milk or sugar with that?"

Spencer Trottman shook his head. There was a rainbow sheen floating on the tarlike liquid. *It has a film of grease on it. She has not properly cleaned the cup.*

The old woman slammed a bowl down by his hand.

"Ah—excuse me, madam—"

"I'm no madam," she snapped. "And there ain't no young floozies in this house."

"Well of course not, but what I mean to say is that I really didn't want any—"

This feeble protest was interrupted. "It's an old Apache recipe. You'll like it."

"Dr. Blinkoe and I had breakfast only a short while ago. I really have no appetite for . . ." *for whatever this is.*

She stirred the stew, raised the spoon to his lips. "Open your mouth, so I don't spill it on your pretty blue tie."

Seeing no viable alternative but to obey, he opened his mouth.

Daisy shoveled the food inside.

He chewed. Swallowed.

"Now, isn't that good?"

His eyes were wide with surprise. "It is *delicious.*"

"Then finish it up." She seated herself across the table, started in on her bowl.

Spencer Trottman considered himself a chef of sorts. Halfway through his helping, he had to ask. "May I inquire about the recipe?"

"You start with some onions cooked in butter. Then you add some sweet corn and sliced summer squash."

He nodded. "And there's a pinch of paprika."

"I used a cup and a half."

Her guest looked as if he doubted this.

"I made the original batch outside, over a piñon fire—in my big copper pot. Took all day and half the night to cook it up."

"Oh."

"It was way too much for my freezer, so I canned it up in gallon jars."

He chewed at a piece of stringy meat. It did not taste like beef. "You must have used an entire lamb."

Daisy shook her head. "That ain't lamb."

The finicky man grimaced at his bowl. "Goat?"

The old woman snorted. "Lots better than that."

"Of course. I should have known. Pork."

"You're getting warm."

"Please—you really must tell me."

She leaned over the table, lowered her voice to a whisper that he could barely hear. "I guess you bein' a lawyer, you know how to keep a secret."

"Certainly." He crossed his heart. "I promise never to reveal the ingredients of your recipe."

"If you want to brew up a mess of Old Apache stew, first you got to catch yourself an old Apache."

Trottman was startled by this tasteless remark.

"Of course," Daisy continued in a thoughtful manner, "I prefer *Young* Apache stew myself, because the meat is lots more tender. But way out here off the beaten path, a person has to be satisfied with whatever happens by." She shot him a look. "You ever hear of Albert Stone Foot?"

He shook his head.

"Well, he was an old Apache who happened by one day." Daisy stopped chewing, put a finger in her mouth. "What's that?" The Ute elder removed the offending morsel, examined it, made a horrible face. "Ugh—I *hate* it when I get a 'Pache toenail in my mouth!"

The Mercedes SUV was a mile from Daisy Perika's trailer when Spencer Trottman finally spoke to his passenger. "So what did you think of Mr. Moon?"

"Honest to a fault," Blinkoe said. "A bit too ethical for my tastes. But considerably more intelligent than I had expected. I have no doubt he will live up to his reputation as a highly competent investigator." He grimaced as the automobile chugged over a pothole. "On the whole, I like him. And by the by, he will be looking into this threat on my life. You shall provide him with every cooperation."

"Of course."

Blinkoe turned his face toward the driver. "Did you enjoy your visit with Mr. Moon's aunt?"

The lawyer snorted. "The woman is a lunatic."

"Hah—did she play another trick on you?"

"She is a very coarse, crude person. It would not be going too far to describe her as a malicious old witch."

The orthodontist clapped his hands. "Oh please—tell me what she did!"

Trottman set his jaw. "I absolutely refuse to discuss it."

"Oh, very well then." *Spoilsport.* He turned away to stare at Chimney Rock.

Trottman was well aware that while Manfred Blinkoe had difficulty recalling his Social Security number or zip code, he seemed to have almost total recall of what he read in a half-dozen newspapers or watched on the television news. *Not that I believe one word that came out of the old woman's mouth. But it won't hurt to ask.* "Manfred, do you recall any news reports about an Indian by the name of Albert Stone Foot?"

"Certainly," the news junkie replied. "Mr. Stone Foot was reported missing last autumn on the Southern Ute reservation. There was quite an extensive search by tribal police and volunteers."

Trottman grasped for a straw. "Then he was a Ute."

Blinkoe shook his head. "Mr. Stone Foot was married to a Ute woman, but he was a member of the Jicarilla Apache tribe. He is presumed dead, but the body was never recovered."

The lawyer felt the bile rising in his throat. He braked the automobile to a sudden stop, opened the door, leaned out, gagged. But not one morsel of the Old Apache did he manage to regurgitate.

Charlie Moon finished his bowl of stew. "That was good enough to eat."

Daisy Perika got the pot, ladled him out another helping. "You'd naturally think so; you brought me the pig all the way from the Columbine."

"I can't take any credit for the pig. That was a gift from Dolly Bushman." For some reason, the Columbine foreman's wife was quite fond of his aunt. The full-time rancher, part-time tribal investigator, occasional handyman reached for a Saltine Cracker and remembered there was one last chore to do before he headed home. "Didn't you tell me your TV was acting up?"

"It needs some tweaking. But there's no big hurry." The crafty old woman smiled. *I have lots of ways of entertaining myself.*

8

THE PLEASURES OF A RANCHER'S LIFE

Having enjoyed a breakfast of fried eggs and broiled beef-steak, the owner of the Columbine took his third cup of heav-ily sugared coffee onto the west porch of the headquarters building. Before the start of the day's work, it was Charlie Moon's practice to take a few minutes to enjoy this remote patch of paradise. The sun was just showing a blushing face over the Buckhorn range, the mist-shrouded river laughed its uproarious way along a road cobbled with glistening black stones. A fresh breeze carried the honeyed scent of purple clover. The Ute raised his cup to salute the morning, and its Maker. The descendant of Adam forgot about his steaming coffee, drank deeply of unadulterated joy. For this eternal in-stant, his life was filled with perfect peace. Time hung still, as if the ponderous rotation of a trillion-trillion galaxies had ceased.

Dogs are not romantics. The hound made his creaky way

up the steps. Sidewinder regarded the human being he had adopted with a yellowed eye and cavernous yawn.

The man was away in some distant land.

To assert his presence, the dog bumped against the rancher's knee.

Moon looked down at the beast. "Howdy-do."

The animal responded with something that was either a rude belch or a canine expletive.

The Indian cowboy seated himself on a sturdy redwood bench.

The big dog plopped down at his feet, expelling a satisfied *whuff* from his lungs.

Quiet tiptoed back, settled down with man and beast.

Charlie Moon knew that he was blessed to have the loan of this wide river valley. Sunlight sparkled over the sweet waters, shimmered in the aspen leaves. There was so much beauty dancing about that it threatened to overwhelm him. He closed his eyes.

Peace is a precious and ephemeral commodity.

His coffee was cold when he heard the hoarse voice.

"Hey—boss!"

Moon watched his foreman approach in a stiff-legged walk. This determined gait suggested some urgent business. Trouble was what the cantankerous old man usually brought to the headquarters. Unless he had a serving of disaster or calamity to spare. "Morning, Pete."

The dog got up, raised its nose to sniff at the wonderfully odorous man.

Pete Bushman stopped at the bottom porch step, tugged at his scruffy beard. "We got us some problems."

Imagine that. Moon prepared himself to receive the daily ration of bad news.

The foreman dished it out. "I just got a call from Slope-Eye Piper, who got bailed outta the Granite Creek jail yesterday afternoon. Seems Slope'd spent the night carousin' around in town, and this morning when he was drivin' back to the Columbine, he passes the lane to that spread we bought over t'other side a the Buckhorns, he notices the gate is busted up some, so Slope makes the turn and drives down the lane to have a look-see and—"

"Pete, give me the short version."

Bushman took a deep breath. "Well—from the sign, Slope says it looks like some rustlers broke through the Big Hat main gate sometime last night, drove right up to the headquarters with a big truck, made off with maybe twenty head of our best Herefords." Bushman turned to squint at the eastern horizon. "I imagine they're in Wyomin' or Kansas by now."

The Ute got up from the bench, frowned at his foreman. "What about the men we've got stationed at the Big Hat—are they okay?" There was not a man on his payroll who would not fight it out toe-to-toe with cattle thieves. The fact that the cattle were missing suggested that the three cowboys must be hurt bad. Or worse.

Bushman's bushy face wilted under the boss's searing gaze. "Uh—none a our boys wasn't exactly there at the time." To clarify this confusing assertion, he pointed toward a distant place across the river. "I'd brought 'em back to this side a the Buckhorns, moved 'em over onto the north section, on the bank of the Little Brandywine. They was mending some a that old bob-war fence that's been there since Moses was tendin' sheep."

Moon was enormously relieved to know that none of his men was injured or dead. But leaving the Big Hat unguarded was inexcusable and Bushman knew it. The boss waited for an explanation. It was not long in coming.

"Thing is," the foreman half-whined, "we been kinda shorthanded since three of our top hands got jailed in Granite Creek for wrecking the Silver Belle Saloon and Portuguese Tom got sick with the bloody flux and little Butch went over to Denver City to get that tattoo took off his scalp and got a nasty infection that turned his eyes pink and yeller." The foreman kicked his dusty boot at a kidney-shaped pebble, missed it. "I figgered if 'n the gate to the Big Hat was locked up tight, well, it didn't seem likely that nobody would cut the chain and go in there to steal nothin'—I mean, they'd likely have thought we'd be bound to have somebody on the place lookin' after our stock—" Realizing he had stumbled into a grievous tactical blunder, Bushman stopped in midsentence, stared at the ground. Wished he could sink into it.

The slender Ute nodded his head slowly, like a buzzard pecking flesh off the foreman's bones. "But it was *me* that was fooled—I was the one that thought we had some men over there." He looked toward the Buckhorns, blinked into the face of a blazing yellow sun. "But maybe the thieves had a grain of sense, and figured that if the gate was locked there must not be anybody on the Big Hat. Columbine cowboys don't have a reputation of being so scared of rustlers that they lock themselves in at night."

The foreman got the message. "Uh—right. Tell you what, I'll put off mendin' them fences out past Pine Knob. I'll tell Slope-Eye to stay at the Big Hat and I'll send a half-dozen more boys over there with carbines and orders to make it hotter'n a west-Texas cookstove in August for any rustler who so much as—"

"I'll take care of the Big Hat." Moon's tone was flat, hard. "You look after the Columbine." To avoid saying something he would regret till his dying day, he turned away, disappeared into the headquarters.

The owner of the Columbine had not raised his voice or said an unkind word, but in all the years he had worked for Charlie Moon, Pete Bushman had never seen the Ute so flat-out angry. It was understandable that the boss was riled—nothing makes a stockman madder than getting his beeves rustled. It was the foreman's habit to argue about every decision Moon made, but this time Bushman shrugged at the empty space where the tall man had been standing. *I s'pose it could've been worse.*

Sidewinder descended the porch steps, paused long enough to growl at the bearded man.

The foreman hardly noticed.

The hound raised a hind leg, emptied his bladder in Bushman's boot.

Pete Bushman noticed. He also danced, shrieked a curse that would have made an inebriated longshoreman blush.

His duty duly done, the hound sauntered away toward the horse barn, where he would curl up and nap in the straw.

Charlie Moon stood in the cool darkness of the massive parlor, feeling extremely hot under the collar. Big fists clenched, he stared at a heap of piñon embers smoldering in the fireplace. *I shouldn't have been so hard on Bushman. He's as good a foreman as any from Montana to New Mexico, and everybody who walks on God's earth makes mistakes. But twenty head of purebred beef stolen—that'll amount to a good chunk of our profit for the whole year!* The rancher removed an old horseshoe that had hung on a brass hook below the mantelpiece for nine decades. It was the Columbine's "lucky shoe." He took hold of the thing with both hands, straightened it out. It was not *perfectly* straight, but in this world perfection is a hard commodity to come by. Feeling marginally better, Moon bent it into a U again. Not a perfect U, but it would have to do. He hung the good-luck piece back on the hook, glared at it. *See you do a better job from now on.*

There was a banging on the door. It was not Bushman's knock.

Moon ignored it.

The second rapping was louder.

Charlie's old F-150 pickup and his Expedition are parked side by side. So he must be around here somewhere. The logician was County Agent Forrest Wakefield. He knocked on the seasoned oak a third time.

The door was jerked open. The Ute rancher's rangy frame filled the space.

"Hi, Charlie." *He looks like he could chew up a railroad spike and spit out carpet tacks.* Wakefield took off his brand-new cowboy hat, held it over his heart like a shield. "How you doin' today?"

"Peachy." Moon gestured him inside with a nod. "What's up, Forrest?"

"Oh, somma this and somma that." The county agent came inside, blinked in the low light. "That coffee I smell?"

Moon led him across the parlor, down the hall, into the spacious kitchen. "I can't remember—you like it black?"

"Cream and sugar, if you please."

"Oh—right." Moon prepared the beverage, put the mug and mixings in front of his guest.

Wakefield added a dab of cream, two spoons of brown sugar, took a sip. "Mmmm. That just hits the spot."

"You want some breakfast?"

The county agent looked around the kitchen. "You got anything already made?"

"A leftover beefsteak. Some biscuits I can warm up for you. And there's gallons of jam and jelly."

"Ahh—that'll do just fine."

After he had finished his second breakfast of the day, the county agent burped. "Charlie, you sure got it made in the shade. I wish I had me a place like this. Quiet. Peaceful. No neighbors for miles and miles." He leaned back, tilting the wooden chair on its hind legs, watched the rancher wash the dishes. Well acquainted with the Indian's quiet moods, Wakefield happily carried on with his monologue. "You know, Charlie—when I got out of high school, I didn't want to go to veterinary school up at Fort Collins."

The dishwasher put a platter and mug in the drying rack. "You didn't, huh?"

The visitor shook his head. "Did it 'cause my daddy was a vet. And I didn't really want to be a county agent, neither. But that's what Uncle Simon did for a living over in Grand Junction, so I sorta drifted into this line of work. It was kind of a family tradition."

Moon seated himself across the table from his guest. "What'd you really want to be?" The Ute bet himself ten to one the answer would be "cowboy."

Wakefield scratched at his sunburned neck. "An actor."

"That a fact?"

"You bet." The county agent sighed. "But Pop wouldn't hear of it."

"I guess he was worried you'd leave the wide-open spaces behind—head straight for Hollywood."

"Give me half a chance, I still would." Wakefield squinted at a rectangular frame he constructed between his thumbs and fingers. "Big silver screen." The county agent's eyes glazed over. "Always saw myself as a tough Bogart kinda guy. G-man, maybe. Or gangster." He raised his hand, aimed an imaginary pistol at a defenseless bread box.

The rancher stared thoughtfully at the slender, blue-eyed white man. "Yeah. I can just see you. Blond doll hanging on one arm, Tommy-gun cradled in the other. Nasty old cigarette dangling from your lip."

The would-be actor perceived this romantic image, nodded his whole-hearted approval. "You got it." He gave Moon a hopeful look. "I do a great Cagney impression. One of my favorite lines was in *Blood on the Sun*—it's a great old 1946 flick. The Cag was Bob Sharkey."

"*Blood on the Sun* was 1945," Moon said. "Cagney played Nick Condon."

Wakefield was goggle-eyed. "You sure of that?"

"Bob Sharkey was his role in *13 Rue Madeleine*. That was in 1947."

"Oh. Right." *I never know when Charlie's kidding me.* "Anyway, you wanta hear my Cagney?" In preparation, the county agent cleared his throat.

"I'd rather have red-hot coals stuffed under my eyelids."

"You're kidding me."

"No I'm not."

"Oh."

"What brings you out to the Columbine?"

Wakefield remembered, made a face. "The sort of thing that makes me hate to be a county agent."

Moon mirrored the grimace. "I don't like the sound of this." *Maybe I should've listened to his Cagney.*

"Well, here's the thing Charlie—there's a medical test I got to run on a random sample of your herd." *I'll try to put the best face on it, but it'll be like primping up a warthog.* "Won't cost you a thin dime though; Department of Agriculture's paying for the whole business."

The rancher was greatly relieved to hear this. He beamed at the county agent. "I am greatly relieved to hear this."

"Forrest Wakefield," the owner of this name said, rolling the syllables over his tongue. "That's a great actor's name—don't you think?"

"It's not as good as Spencer Tracy. But I like it a little better than Engelbert Humperdinck."

"Actually, Mr. Humperdinck wasn't an actor, he was a—"

"I know what he was. What's the medical test for?"

Wakefield blushed. *I might as well just say it straight out and get it over with.* "Uh—it's for a prion-caused ailment technically known as Creutzfeldt-Jakob disease. The layman's term is mad cow dis—"

"I know what Creutzfeldt-Jakob disease is." Moon clasped his hands together as if he were about to offer up a prayer. "What's happened, Forrest—a case been found in Colorado?"

"Oh, my goodness no." The government employee shook his head hard enough to make his neck bones crack. "Most certainly not. To the best of my knowledge. My *direct* knowledge. Of course, I am not apprised of every single incident that—"

"Then why do you want to check out my stock?"

"The story is—uh—I mean I am informed by my superiors that the USDA needs some big ranches in the Rocky Mountain states to evaluate a brand-new, in-the-field blood test for C-J prions." He tried to make it sound like good news: "And whadda you know—the Columbine got selected!"

"A dubious distinction." Moon got up from his chair, leaned to stare at the public servant. "Give it to me straight—what's the downside?"

"Oh, none at all." Wakefield looked at his right hand, examined the manicure he'd paid ten dollars for in Denver. "Of course, with any of these new procedures there can always be some *minor* problems that pop up."

"Define *minor.*"

"Well—take for instance . . . false positives."

"Like where the test says one of my steers has mad cow disease even though it's perfectly healthy?"

"Right." He smiled at the rancher, like a teacher pleased with a bright pupil. "That's a false positive all right."

"What happens then?"

"Oh, the Stage-C rules kick in. We quarantine your operation till we can test every animal with the older methodology. Which is considerably slower, but known to be reliable."

The rancher pointed at the wall. "Forrest, I got over two thousand head out there grazing on forty-one sections."

"I'll only need to test a random sample of about ten percent." The county agent did a quick mental calculation. "After you get 'em penned, testing a coupla hundred will only take us about three or four days. Maybe five or six. Once we actually get started, that is. And I'd have to call in some help." He pulled at an earlobe. "You know how hard it is to get qualified veterinary technicians these days?"

"No. And I don't much care."

"Look, it's not all that likely that there'll be any false-positive results from the new test." He frowned at the rancher. "Last five years or so, you bought any stock out of Canada?"

Charlie Moon jammed the black John B. Stetson down to his ears, stomped out of the kitchen.

"Hey," Wakefield called out, "where you going?"

"Away from here," Moon rumbled.

9

WHAT HAPPENED ON COPPER STREET

The two of men walking along the sidewalk were big in different ways. Charlie Moon was slender, more than a head taller than his companion. The Ute's best friend was mostly broad shoulders and gorilla chest. But the size of a man is not measured in inches and feet. It is quantified by what is inside. Inside, these were sizable men.

The chief of police tipped his fawn-gray hat, returned an elderly lady's smile. He spoke to the Ute. "Something has just occurred to me."

"And you feel bound and determined to share it."

Parris suppressed a slight shudder. "It's sorta one of those Jungian things—like when the shrink is chatting with his lady patient, who just happens to mention this rare Egyptian beetle that's never been seen ten miles from the Nile, and bam! There the bug is in downtown Vienna, crawling along on the doc's windowsill."

He's been reading again. "Let me guess—you joined the book-of-the year club?"

"Nah, nothin' like that." Parris blushed like a twelve-year-old. "I been dating this cute psychologist. And she's really, really smart."

Charlie Moon had a witty retort right on the tip of his tongue, but gave his friend the gift of silence.

"Oh, yeah—now I remember. That beetle, that's what's called a Jungian *coincidence*."

"Synchronicity."

Parris squinted at his friend. "What?"

"Mr. Synchronicity is a first cousin to Miss Coincidence, but he comes with an extra syllable—which makes him considerably more high-tone." Inordinately pleased with himself, Moon kept right on going. "Your everyday run-of-the-mill coincidence—why, they're so common that folks give 'em away as party favors. But your USDA-Prime synchronicity—that product goes for ten to twelve dollars a pound."

"I wish you wouldn't do that." Parris strained to recollect his thoughts. "Where was I when you threw me off?"

"Sharing a coincidence?"

"Oh, right. It's kinda creepy. Here we are—two coppers—walking the beat on Copper Street." He paused in midstride, pointed at the sidewalk. "Charlie, I don't *believe* it. Look at that—two brand-new pennies right there, faceup! Now what do you think of that—is that one of them grade-A synchro-coincidences or what?"

"Well, if you want my two cents, I think you need to get out more. But not with psychologists. Date yourself a flirty waitress or a rich widow woman who has a big house on Greenback Street. Besides, you are the only copper on this team." The Ute raised his nose in the air. "Me—I am a highly respected tribal investigator."

"I stand corrected." Parris shot his buddy a narrow-eyed Sherlock look. "Being a highly trained detective, I have detected something remarkable in your remark. D'you want to know what?"

"Absolutely not."

"Good—then I am bound to tell you. Normally, you say something like [he mimicked the Ute's deep voice]: 'I, Charlie Moon, am a full-time rancher and part-time tribal investigator.' " Parris allowed his throat to relax to its normal state. "The fact that just now you did not mention the beefy portion of your chosen vocation leads me to believe that something is sour back at the Columbine." An irksome smirk. "Am I right?"

Moon had already reported the rustling incident to the state police. Plus the Cattleman's Association and the Brand Association. Potential buyers in ten states had been notified and provided with branding information and nose prints. There was nothing the local chief of police could do about it. *Except rag me about not being able to keep my beeves from getting stole.* "I would rather not talk about ranching today."

Parris's blue eyes twinkled merrily. "What is it—ol' hairy-face Bushman giving you trouble again?"

The Indian grunted in a dismissive manner.

"If it's not your foreman, it's got to be your cows. I bet they've come down with incurable bovine constipation that'll wipe you out and ruin your minor reputation."

"There's no such sickness as bovine con—"

"Then what is it—hoof-and-mouth disease?"

"No!" The rancher looked around to see who might have overheard this reckless remark. "And don't even *say* that out loud."

"Have you turned superstitious on me?" Parris snickered. "You think just *saying* something bad can make it happen?"

"Of course I don't." The thoroughly rational man glared at his friend. "But those superstitious things happen all the time, whether a fella believes in 'em or not." Moon took a deep breath. "So let's talk about something else. Something cheerful."

"The deteriorating situation in Saudi Arabia? The riots in Pakistan? Baseball?"

"Any of those'll do just fine."

"There's a rumor going around that there's a hundred-year curse on the Cubs."

"That's nice." Moon spotted a sign that made his mouth water. "How about a little pick-me-up snack?"

They entered Ye Olde Ice Cream Parlor, which was not yet a month olde. The Ute called for a triple dip of Strawberry Delight in a king-size sugar cone. Mindful of the slight bulge at his waistline, Scott Parris purchased a small cup of Soy Frostie.

As they walked past a JCPenney, the Ute licked at the ice cream. It was good. Very much good. He began to feel better. Very much better.

Parris used a pink plastic spoon to pick at the healthy protein concoction. *This is twice as good as a hornet flying up your nose.* "What's really on your so-called mind, old chum?"

"Coupla days ago, while I was down at Aunt Daisy's place—"

"What were you doing there?"

"Fixing a propane leak under the floor. While I was doing this, a Dr. Blinkoe tracked me down."

"Propane leak, huh? Those can be dangerous."

"Forget about the propane. Let's talk about Dr. Manfred Wilhelm Blinkoe."

Granite Creek's top cop frowned. "Manfred Wilhelm Blinkoe? Hmmm." He took a mincing bite of processed soybean dessert. "There must be ten thousand Blinkoes in the local phone book, but does *Manfred Wilhelm* ring a bell for me?"

"It ought to bust your eardrums wide open. Dr. Blinkoe is the citizen who believes somebody is out to do him serious bodily harm. Somebody else gets shot, Blinkoe figures the bullet was actually meant for him. He is what some people who are less charitable than me would consider paranoid. And you put this joker on my trail."

"Oh, sure—*that* Blinkoe—the forked-beard orthodontist who was dining on the patio at Phillipe's last week when the poor woman got shot." Parris tossed the paper cup into a trash can that resembled a penguin with an open beak. He licked the spoon one last time, fed it also to the facsimile of the Antarctic fowl. "But it hurts me to hear the 'you put that joker on my trail' remark. I merely referred a potential client to my best buddy—in hopes that you might jump at the opportunity to make an honest dollar doing some useful work. Not to mention keeping your hand in the investigating business. I would not want you to get out of practice—lose your touch, so to speak. Such as it is. Or was."

Moon took the last bite of the sugar cone, wiped his fingers on a handkerchief. "What I'd like to know is—"

"Wait—don't ask. I can read you like a comic book. In the interest of efficiency, let me tell you what it is you want to know."

"Go right ahead."

The chief of police raised a massive, hairy hand, counted off his little finger. "Number one, you want to know if we have a probable motive for the shooting. Answer is affirmative. The lady was a former prosecuting attorney from Cook County, Illinois. She was responsible for putting at least nine dozen bad guys behind the walls." He counted off the next finger. "Number two, you are curious about whether we found a weapon. Another definite yes on that one. We are talking .22-caliber model M 6787 Hi-Standard target pistol. This fine piece of machinery was equipped with a first-class silencer—not something your average target shooter carries in his hip pocket. And he tossed it right after the shooting— Officer Alicia Martin fished it out of the stream. This shooter is a pro, and pros hit what they aim at. Your client was never in the least danger of getting popped."

"What makes you think Dr. Blinkoe's my client?"

Parris smirked. "When have you ever turned down a fee?"

"It wasn't quite like you think. Dr. Blinkoe suckered me into a hand of poker." Moon shook his head. "You won't believe this—this slicker draws a royal flush and doesn't even blush."

The older cop scowled. "I never did like orthodontists. When I was a kid in Indiana, there was this Dr. What's-his-name who kept sending me birthday cards. Christmas cards.

Valentine cards. Even these horrible Halloween cards with jack-o'-lanterns that had big jagged teeth. There never was nothing wrong with my choppers." He paused to smile at his reflection in a drugstore window. "But it kinda gave me a dental inferiority complex. I didn't smile till I was almost thirty years old."

"That is a terrifically sad story," Moon said. "But let's get back to the business at hand. You were telling me all I wanted to know about the shooting. So far, you only counted off two fingers."

"Oh, right." Parris turned down another digit. "Three, you want to know have we determined the original owner of the pistol—"

"Nope. That was more like number eighteen. Three is: Do you have any idea who pulled the trigger?"

The chief of police clenched the counting hand into a fist the size of a cantaloupe, jammed it into his jacket pocket.

Moon grinned at his best friend. "Well?"

"You shouldn't have interrupted me. Now I've lost my place. Which gets me confused about what I've already told you." He aimed a squinty-eyed glare at the Ute. "Anyway, you shouldn't be asking me so many questions. Technically, Mr. Tribal Investigator—in this burg you are a regular citizen. I shouldn't be telling you diddly-squat about what's what."

The amiable Ute shrugged. "Okay."

They approached a corner. The traffic light turned red.

Parris waved at the driver of a passing school bus. "So— are you going to do some poking around for Dr. Blinkoe?"

"You are the chief of police," Moon said.

"Well—thank you for this timely piece of information. But despite rumors that I am approaching the ragged edge of senility, I remain acutely aware of what my occupation is. I also know the name of the current president of the United States and can still tie my shoes without assistance."

"I am glad to hear it." Moon patted the older man on the back. "Now see if you can focus on this concept—I have a license from the great sovereign state of Colorado. This piece of paper permits me to perform confidential investigations. If a private investigator takes on a client, he does not make a habit of revealing information about that client's private business to a publicly funded constabulary. Including the chief of police."

Parris snorted. "Nobody likes a smart-mouthed P.I."

Moon laughed. "But everybody loves a middle-aged cop who can still tie his shoes."

"Danged right." Parris grinned at a slender, dark-eyed girl in a pink satin dress.

Hardly noticing the chief of police, the young lady smiled shyly at the tall Ute, who flashed a bright one right back at her.

Parris was stung by this. *Why do the oldies grin at me and the young ones ogle Charlie?* He sucked in his gut, rubbed at his scalp. *I got to go on a serious diet . . . maybe get a hair implant.*

"So," Moon said to his friend, "do you have a suspect?"

Parris shrugged under his new blazer. "We might." He glanced at the canny Ute. "So are you going to do some poking around for Dr. Blinkoe?"

"I might."

The chief of police was determined to get the upper hand. "You ought to ask your FBI sweetie pie about the shooting at Phillipe's."

At the mention of the pretty lady's name, Moon could not help but grin. "Do you refer to Special Agent Lila Mae McTeague?"

"How many feds are you holding hands with?"

Moon ignored this. "The Bureau jumping on the case because of the potential out-of-state connection?"

"Sure. And forget the 'potential'."

"Go ahead, get it out of your system."

"Agent McTeague, who normally works out of Durango, has set up a part-time office right here in Granite Creek. She did this just two days after the shooting at Phillipe's."

Moon stopped dead still. "She's working here in town. Are you serious?"

"Serious as a bad case of hoof-and-mouth."

The stockman grimaced at the sickly reference. "Where's her office?"

Parris gave him the address. The blue eyes twinkled. "I'll bet you even money the hit was connected with the murdered prosecutor's history in Illinois."

"How much money we talking about?"

Don't want to scare him off. "Ten bucks?"

I've already been cheated by one slicker this week. "You probably already know who the shooter is."

"Maybe I do. Maybe I don't. You lay down your ten-spot, you take your chances." He gave the Ute a sideways glance. *Charlie can't resist a wager.* "So—you on for the bet or not?"

"I'll cover your ten." Moon tried to put the picture together. A killing in a small Rocky Mountain town wouldn't get the attention it would in her hometown. Scott Parris didn't have the resources for more than a run-of-the-mill investigation. Six weeks later, it would be old news. A cold case. But shoot the Cook County prosecutor down in the Chicago Loop and there'd be a hundred cops assigned to the investigation—and they wouldn't let up until they had the killer by the neck. Not if it took sixty years. "You figure somebody with a grudge found out the prosecutor was headed for a Colorado vacation, sent a Chicago shooter out here to do the job while the lady was a long way from home?"

"Possibly." Parris hesitated. "But these modern times ain't like the old days, when the Family would put some Cicero thug on a flight from O'Hare to Denver, where he'd rent a car, drive down to Granite Creek, check in to a hotel, then look for an opportunity to blow the brains out of another tourist from the Windy City. These days, they outsource the task to someone who already knows the territory."

"You figure some guy from Denver brought the Hi-Standard pistol to our fair city?"

"Why Denver?"

Moon shrugged. "There can't be that many contract killings to do in Colorado. You'd expect a person in that line of work to set up shop in our largest city—where most of the action is."

"You might think so." Parris smiled at another pretty young lady, who stole a glance at the Ute. "But nowadays, there are freelancers in the business. They might live anywhere. Pueblo, Salida, Durango—or maybe in some little mountain cabin. These part-time operators typically only do a job every year or two, to supplement their legal income. Rest of the time, they're your friendly local barber or postman or . . ." Parris waved at a postman across the street. "Point is, we got to keep our thinking up with the times."

"Yeah," the Ute said. "I guess everything changes."

The traffic light changed.

On the far corner of the intersection, the angular figure of a stick man flashed on a glass panel; his segmented legs walked in jerky fashion. For those who did not get the graphic message, a sign below the little man said WALK NOW. Obedient to the electronic summons, the lawmen crossed a little avenue called Shady Lane. It was a dead-end street.

Parris's pager buzzed in his shirt pocket. He checked the number, glanced at his Indian friend. "I need to get back to the station."

Moon watched the chief of police stalk away, then strolled another three blocks on Copper Street. *It is nice, once in a while, having nothing in particular to do. Let the Columbine take care of itself. I am footloose and free as a pronghorn antelope on the wide-open plains, happy as a coyote with a mouthful of warm jackrabbit—*

At that moment, something quite odd occurred. It may have been a case of happy serendipity, cosmic synchronicity—or no more than a simple coincidence. But Charlie Moon noticed that he was standing directly in front of the place of business where Manfred Wilhelm Blinkoe claimed he had last seen It.

Harriet's Rare Books.

I should walk right on by, forget this Blinkoe guy. Let him solve his own problems. Sensible thing to do is head on back to the Columbine, tend to my cattle operation. The tribal investigator considered this latter course of action. *I need to make some telephone calls, find a caretaker to keep watch over the Big Hat so the rustlers don't come back and haul off the rest the stock east of the Buckhorns. And I need talk to my county agent about that new government test for mad cow disease—maybe there's some way to duck that bullet.*

None of this sounded like a great deal of fun.

Or, I could just drop into this nice little bookstore and ask the lady a simple question or two.

10

THE PERFECTLY ORDINARY BOOKSTORE

Charlie Moon pushed on the door; it responded with a harsh, brassy squeak. *Hinges could use some oil.* The inner sanctum was illuminated by the few rays of sunlight that penetrated the front window. There were books everywhere—lining dozens of unpainted pine shelves, stacked on the floor, piled in pyramids on tables. There was not a sound, or any sign of life, human or otherwise. *I thought all of these places had cats.* He considered announcing his presence, but the fragile silence seemed to be the glue that held the place together. One muffled "hello" might bring the whole establishment crashing down. *The lady who runs this outfit may be in the back. Or maybe she stepped out for a few minutes, headed down the street for a bite to eat. I'll just mosey around for a while, have a look at the books.*

Charlie Moon moseyed over to a shelf marked WESTERN,

began to scan the authors' names. One shelf was filled with Zane Grey, another with Louis L'Amour. On a top shelf, nudged up against a few old paperbacks by Lee Floren, Al Cody, and Michael Hammonds, were several works by Will James that piqued the rancher-cowboy's interest. *Lone Cowboy* was there, but Moon already had a fine copy of that one. He inspected volumes of *Big-Enough, Sand, Sun-Up, Cow-Country,* and *The Drifting Cowboy.* Then he spotted *Smoky the Cowhorse*—which turned out to be a first edition. *I've got to have this one.* He felt something hard and cold press against his spine. Instinctively, he froze.

"Gotcha!" the raspy voice crackled.

It sounded like a woman. A very angry woman. Moon did not dare look over his shoulder. "Excuse me—can I ask you a question?"

"*May* I ask you a question."

"Sure—you go first."

"I was correcting your grammar, bonehead!"

"And I sure do appreciate it." He had another go at it. "May I ask you a question?"

"Sure. Say your last words."

"What's that sticking in my back?"

"The business end of a pistol."

"I figured that. What caliber?"

"Thirty-two Colt."

"Cocked?"

"Don't need to be. It's a double-action." A gurgling chuckle. "But if it'd make you feel better, I will cock the blamed thing."

"No, don't bother yourself." He felt beads of sweat on his forehead. "Is it loaded?"

"Damn right it is!"

"Then I hope you'll be real careful."

"*Very* careful." She nuzzled the muzzle up against his spine. "Now you put that highly valuable first edition Will James back up on the shelf."

Moon did as ordered. "I take it you don't want to sell this particular item?"

"Don't get sassy with me, you low-down, no-good book thief!"

"Look, ma'am—I didn't have the least intention of stealing any of your—"

"Oh, shut your mouth." The pressure on his backbone eased. "And turn around. But do it slow and easy."

He turned. Slow and easy. Stared down at the elfin figure of a slender woman with a narrow, pinched face. The hair was a yellowish gray. In the blue dress and white apron, her appearance suggested an Alice in Wonderland well past the bloom of her youth. Moon estimated that if she managed to grow four inches, she would be pushing five feet.

The heavy chip on the woman's shoulder caused her to lean toward suspicion. "One short-person joke and you're dead meat."

"It never crossed my mind."

"Now look me straight in the eye and tell me you are not the yahoo who's been sneaking in here for months, stealing my best stuff while I'm on the potty."

"Okay." There was no way the seven-foot Ute could look her straight in the eye. He watched the old revolver tremble along with her hand. "I ain't the yahoo who's been sneaking in here for months, stealing your best stuff while you're on the—uh—potty."

"Why should I believe you?"

"Because I'm illiterate?"

The gun barrel dropped to point at his left knee. "You can't read?"

"Not a word."

Her mouth gaped, something almost like pity softening the hard little face. *He must be one of those basketball players that got through grade school without having to crack a book.* "Is that the honest-to-God truth?"

"Nope. It's a flat-out falsehood." He dared to smile. "Just wanted to see if I could get you to relax a bit—so maybe you wouldn't shoot me by accident."

"If I shoot you, it won't be no accident." Her gray eyes lost the flinty look. "You sure you ain't a book thief?"

"I can't swear to it—but I wasn't last time I checked."

"Well, I guess you could be tellin' the truth." She studied his face. "You don't look smart enough to steal free samples at the supermarket."

"Thank you." Moon took a deep breath of the musty atmosphere.

She squinted at the overly tall man. "What're you doing in my store?"

"Uh—looking for a good book to read?"

She aimed the pistol at the top shelf. "You want to buy that Will James *Smoky the Cowhorse* first edition?"

"Please don't take this the wrong way, but the way I see it—a man shouldn't have to make a decision about a purchase whilst confronted by a lady who's packing."

"Times is hard, cowboy." She tapped the end of the Colt barrel on his belt buckle. "Amazon and them other dot-coms has taken away half of my business. So what about *Smoky the Cowhorse*?"

"What're you asking?"

There was the barest hesitation. "Ninety-nine dollars?"

"That's a little pricey for my budget." He saw her thumb go to the hammer. "But I'll take it."

"Ah, what the hell." *I kinda like him.* "You can have it for eighty-nine." She pointed again with the pistol. "Reach up there, get it off the shelf so I don't have to bring the stepladder." The woman stuffed the Colt revolver into an ample apron pocket. "But I don't take credit cards or checks. Cash on the barrelhead, that's my policy."

"I hope if you find out I don't have that much money in my wallet—you won't murder me."

She shrugged. "I'll take your IOU. And you can have the book for seventy-nine bucks."

"That's a deal." He removed *Smoky the Cowhorse* from its place between *Drifting Cowboy* and *Cowboys North and South*. Looked at the title page. "Well look at that, it's signed by ol' Will himself!"

"Not it's not, you big smart-aleck." She headed for the counter. "As you might've guessed, I'm Harriet."

"Actually, that would have been my second guess."

The proprietor of Harriet's Rare Books stopped, turned. "What was your first?"

"Elizabeth Taylor." His expression was deadly earnest. "When she was about sixteen."

The tiny woman blushed. "What's your name, you big shameless liar?"

"Charlie Moon."

"Moon. I've heard that name before." A frown creased her brow. "And come to think of it, I believe I've seen you in town once or twice. But you've never come into my store before."

"I never felt the need of any extreme excitement."

She gave him a suspicious look. "You that Arapaho who runs the Columbine Ranch?"

"I'm the Southern Ute who owns the Columbine. And," he added with pardonable pride, "the Big Hat. Which is right next door, just across the Buckhorn range."

It was coming back to her. "You're some kind of Indian cop, aren't you?"

"Yeah." *The kind that should've stayed home today.*

"You really come in here to look for a book?"

"Not entirely."

"I knew it! What're you up to—you after a crook?" Hard-boiled detective mysteries were her meat.

Might as well get right at it. "You know a man by the name of Blinkoe?"

"I wish I could say I didn't." Her tone was distinctly hopeful: "Is old Weird-Beard in trouble?"

He nodded. "Big trouble and then some."

"What's he done?"

"Promise you won't tell a soul?"

"I swear on Grandma O'Gilligan's grave."

"Then I guess I can trust you." Moon frowned at the memory of the imagined event. "Last night, Dr. Blinkoe came out to the Columbine to do an extraction. I hate to tell you this, but that quack broke off my foreman's wisdom tooth, left two of the roots down in the jawbone, took his two-dollar fee without so much as a 'Sorry, bub,' and left the ranch in a big hurry." He lowered his voice to a whisper. "Me'n the boys are huntin' him down. We lay hands on this Blinkoe bird, Pete Bushman will pull all of his teeth with rusty wire-pliers, then hang him personally. Probably from a cottonwood limb, though I prefer sycamore myself."

"Orthodontists don't pull teeth, *Bean Pole*. They straighten 'em."

"So you say. But this is my story, and I'm stickin' to it."

She smiled, went behind the counter. "Dr. Blinkoe comes in here two or three times a month—and generally takes something home. He'll buy anything on nineteenth-century dentistry, so I'm always on the lookout for those. He also likes books on western history. And weapons."

"Weapons?"

"He's interested in antique pistols. U.S. Cavalry swords. Collectible stuff like that."

A coal-black cat appeared from somewhere, leaped onto the counter between Moon and Harriet. After asserting its considerable presence, the feline creature made a point of ignoring both of them.

"That's Mississippi Snowball," she said with a small grimace. "I don't much like cats, but this one belonged to the previous owner. He won't eat mice and he won't go away."

Moon leaned on the counter, rubbed Mississippi Snowball's back. "Has Dr. Blinkoe been in lately?"

"Last Tuesday." She glanced at a clock on the wall. "It was a few minutes before noon—I remember because I was about to shut the place and go get some lunch. Hadn't had but two customers all morning, then here comes Goggle-Eye Doc with the funny beard."

"Did he find something he liked?"

"He was looking at a book about Bowie knives. And he ended up buying it." She stared at the cat's yellow eyes. "But not before he was startled by something."

Moon eyed the black cat. "I bet I know what spooked him."

The smirk was all over her face. "I bet you don't."

"Bet you this much." Moon put four shiny quarters on the table. All in a row.

Harriet removed a dollar bill from a cigar box, slapped it over the eight bits. "You're on, high roller. Now, what caused my customer to drop the book?"

"Why that's plain as the sparkle in your pretty eyes." He watched her blush again. "You snuck up behind him, jammed that Colt *pistola* into his back, accused him of theft, tried to bully him into buying the Bowie knife book for three times what it was worth."

"That's a tempting notion, but it's not what happened." She snapped up the dollar and change.

Moon waited for a return on his investment.

She put the greenback plus profit into her cigar box. "If I told you what actually happened, you wouldn't believe it."

"Don't matter a whit whether I believe it or not—long as it's a good story."

"You wouldn't mind losing your money to hear a flat-out lie?"

"Not me. I'm a cattle rancher—money means nothing to a stockman."

Harriet jerked her head to indicate something behind her. "You see that mirror on the wall?"

"I do." What he saw was his reflection. And the dusty window framing a live motion-picture of Copper Street.

"Well, Dr. Blinkoe was paging through the *Classic Bowie Knives* book when he sorta slowed down." She picked up a Cajun cookbook to demonstrate. "Slow as sorghum molasses oozing off a tablespoon, he looks up, right over my head." She turned to point at the frame of silvered glass. "Right at that mirror."

"What happened then?"

"Why, he turned pasty-white as an uncooked biscuit. No, make that an anemic marshmallow. Then he said, 'Oh, no— it's back!' Or something like that."

"He happen to mention what *It* was?"

"He didn't have to." The small woman looked past Moon, toward the street. "I saw him myself."

Moon arched an eyebrow. "The *It* was a *Him*?"

"Well of course it was!"

"And where did you see It—I mean *Him*? In the mirror?"

"No, you big telephone pole." She pointed at the front window. "He was standing right out there on the sidewalk—looking in through the glass."

The Ute was muttering to himself. "Then It . . . was just a man."

"But not just *any* man," Harriet snapped. "This old blister was Dr. Blinkoe's twin."

Moon felt a deep chill creep along his spine, right up the nape of his neck to the back of his hat. "You absolutely sure about that?"

"Sure as week-old roadkill stinks. The fella outside the window was the spirit and image of Dr. Blinkoe." She shuddered. "Just imagine—*two* of them Weird-Beards loose on the streets!"

11

THE ESTATE ON MOCCASIN LAKE

As soon as he was out of town, Charlie Moon slipped a Chet
Atkins CD into the slot. The disc spun up with Canned Heat.
A dozen miles north of Granite Creek, while Mr. Atkins was
plucking and picking "Centipede Boogie," the Expedition
began the gradual descent from an arid sandstone plateau
into a wide, shallow portion of the Moccasin River basin.
Overhead, the midday sun sizzled, a filmy sheet of cirrus
shimmered, a sinister formation of Messerschmitt Nazi
blackbirds dived at a hapless B-24 raven on its way back
from a cross-channel run. Below this nostalgic display, an in-
terlocking patchwork of dry and irrigated fields pretended to
be a giant brown-and-green quilt that some thoughtful
grandma had spread over the sleepy valley. The road made a
gradual arc to the left, aligned itself with the rocky stream.
Suggesting a chance encounter of land and water serpents,
road and river proceeded along their winding way west.

During the guitar picker's rendering of "Jitterbug Waltz," Moon slowed at a sign. The script on the redwood plank informed the motorist that he was about to pass Moccasin Lake Estates. He turned the Columbine flagship onto a narrow asphalt lane that was in better condition than the blacktop road he had taken from Granite Creek. Manfred Wilhelm Blinkoe had recited the directions over the telephone. Take the second right, which is Sundown Trail, then hang a hard left on Deadwood Lane. The orthodontist's residence was reportedly at the end of Deadwood. And so it was.

Moon pulled to a stop in the shade of a picture-book spruce, graciously allowed the late Mr. Atkins sufficient time to fade away under his "Rainbow" before he shut down the CD player. The Ute sat quietly in his big automobile, examined what could be seen of the Blinkoe property.

In the paved driveway that terminated at a detached garage, a glistening yellow Mercedes sedan was parked beside a freshly waxed gray Chevrolet pickup. A much older, rusty GMC pickup with Kansas plates was half hidden on the far side of the garage. A muddy black Suzuki motorcycle had been leaned against a utility pole.

A steep stairway provided outside access to an apartment over the garage. Someone was looking out between a slit in the red-and-white curtains. The pale face disappeared as soon as the Ute looked up. *That'll be the guy who rides the Suzuki. Maybe he looks after the place when the Blinkoes are away.*

Sheltered by a small forest of ponderosa, spruce, and transplanted aspens was the place Dr. Blinkoe called home. The massive house—Moon estimated twenty rooms—was constructed of brown and orange bricks. The porch roof was supported by a half-dozen fluted granite columns. Mullioned windows were lined up along the first and second floors. In the attic, a few smaller windows peeked duncelike from under gabled hats. Massive red sandstone chimneys shouldered up against each end of the structure.

A grassy lawn fell off gradually to the edge of the lake, where a redwood dock jutted into still waters. A magnificent pontoon houseboat was tied there, a twelve-foot bass boat floated beside it. As if the lake water might not be entirely suitable for his bathing, a kidney-shaped swimming pool had been placed in the shade of the trees. A few pine and spruce cones floated on the surface. Moon smiled. *Dr. Blinkoe knows how to live. And has the means to do it.*

Moon was opening the Expedition door when Manfred W. Blinkoe appeared on the porch. The man with the forked beard wore crisply ironed khaki slacks, a black turtleneck sweater, old-fashioned penny loafers.

Behind the spectacles, Blinkoe's bulbous eyes bulged with enthusiasm. "Hey, there—Charlie." He waved at his visitor. "Did you have any problem finding the place?"

Moon assured him that his directions had been more than adequate.

He hurried out to shake the Ute's hand, then glanced back at the house. "My wife doesn't know why you're here. I told her you were interested in buying my boat."

The man could not hiccup without telling a lie. "Which one?"

"What?"

"We'll have to keep our stories straight." Moon tried not to grin. "So am I interested in the big boat or the little one?"

"Uh—the houseboat, of course. I mean, why would you want the small one?"

"Actually, I wouldn't mind having a bass boat on my lake."

His lake? Balderdash. It's probably nothing more than a dug-pond. Knowing no other way to smile, he grinned crookedly at the Ute. "You have an honest-to-goodness lake on your ranch?"

Reading Blinkoe's mind, the proud owner of the Columbine nodded. "Sure do. Great big one, too. Chock-full of native trout." *And Lake Jesse wasn't made by damming up a fine creek and filling a sandstone canyon with water.* Nature had made Moon's alpine lake thirty thousand years ago, using a glacier for a plow.

The wealthy man jerked his chin toward the lake. "Let's amble on down to the houseboat, where we can confer in private."

It was a minute too late for that.

"Hey—Manny."

Moon looked toward the source of the shrill voice. A stunningly shapely young woman stood on the porch, hands on her hips. She wore a tight black dress with a deep V neckline. The silk garment did not quite reach her knees. Cornsilk-yellow hair framed the pretty face, flowed over her shoulders in a honeyed waterfall. He could not help staring.

As if he had not heard the summons, the allegedly deaf husband set his face toward the dock and began to amble thataway.

She called out again in the screechy voice. Louder this time. "Hey!" For punctuation, she stamped her foot.

Recognizing defeat, Blinkoe turned, padded toward the porch.

The Ute followed.

Mrs. Blinkoe looked over her husband's head at the tall, slender man.

Moon removed his black John B. Stetson. Smiled shyly at the cover girl.

Blondie cocked her head. "Who're you?"

"Uh . . ." The Ute tried to remember his name. Did. "Charlie."

"Charlie who?"

His response was faster this time. "Moon."

"You really interested in Manfred's dumb old boat?"

Moon glanced at the sleek bass boat. "Yes, ma'am. And I'll buy it if the price is right." *Like fifty bucks.*

"Ah, he'd never sell you that big tub." She glared at her husband. "Would you?"

Blinkoe shrugged. "I'm thinking about getting a larger one."

The young woman approached the Ute. "I'm Pansy Blinkoe."

Moon had no trouble putting on a stupid look. "Oh—I didn't know Dr. Blinkoe had a daughter."

The pretty face broke into a smile. "Oh, you are just *shameless.*" She took the visitor's arm. "And I like that."

Moon's face burned.

Pansy felt the heat. "Before you look at Manny's silly old barge, you want me to show you around the house?"

The Ute looked to his host for permission. *Do I?*

Blinkoe caught a wicked look from his wife, surrendered. "When you're through with the guided tour, I'll be down at the boat." No longer having the heart to amble, the man of the house shuffled slowly away toward the dock.

Pansy took her guest across the sixty-foot-long parlor, down the carpeted hall, into a huge corner bedroom. A pair of bay windows looked down onto the lakeshore. "Isn't this pretty?"

The man nodded dumbly.

"You know what room this is?"

He thought he did. "The master bedroom?"

The blue eyes burned at him. "Manny ain't my master, mister—and he don't sleep in here. This is *my* bedroom." She pointed a carmine fingernail at a canopied bed, provided an utterly unnecessary piece of information. "That is *my* bed."

It was high time to change the subject. Moon focused on a large color print in a frame over the mantelpiece. "Who's that?"

"My mommy and daddy, of course." She pouted. "Don't you see the family resemblance?"

He admitted that he had. Mommy and Daddy also had pretty blue eyes. But not nearly so pretty as Pansy's.

The young woman released Moon's arm, kicked off her red slippers, plopped down on the bed. Flat on her back. She smiled prettily at the dark stranger.

He barely managed not to stare at the woman.

She looked halfway through him. "You didn't come way out here to look at some stupid old boat. What're you really here for?"

"You want the unvarnished truth?"

"No man ever tells a woman the truth." She giggled. "But get as close as you can."

"I'm in the beef-ranching business."

"Hah," the pouty mouth said. "I don't believe a word of that."

Then I'm making some progress. "And I'm not all that interested in the boat."

"I knew it!"

"It's the motorcycle."

"What?"

"The one out by the garage."

"Oh, you don't want that."

"You're not willing to sell it?"

"It don't belong to me."

"Then maybe Dr. Blinkoe will make me a price."

"That ain't Manny's motorcycle. It's . . . it's Clayton's."

"Clayton?"

"Clayton Crowe. He's my brother. Before I was a Blinkoe, I was a Crowe. That ugly old GMC pickup belongs to Clayton too, but it don't run half the time."

"Then I'll have a talk with your brother about the motorcycle."

"Oh, no. Clayton is—he's sick today. Real sick. In bed with the flu or something."

"Sorry to hear it."

The blue eyes narrowed. "You really want to buy a dirty old motorcycle?"

"Not unless the price is right. Mostly, I'm just enjoying talking with you."

"No you're not." She tugged at her wedding band. "You're just teasing me."

"Well, there's nothing wrong with that. Truth is, I really do own a cattle ranch out west of Granite Creek. And I'm here to do some business with your husband."

"What—you gonna sell Manfred some cows?" *It would be just like my stupid husband to buy a bunch of stupid cows and put them out to graze in the stupid yard.* "Well?"

"Can't say."

She pushed herself up on an elbow. "Why not?"

"My business with Dr. Blinkoe is confidential."

Pansy fluttered the long eyelashes. "You won't even tell poor little me?"

"I especially won't tell poor little you. If you want to know, ask your husband."

"Oh, foo." She got off the bed, found her slippers. "I hate my husband."

"I don't believe that."

"Don't you?" She did not wait for a response. "Tell me something, Mr. Moon. Do you think I'm pretty?"

Moon found himself stumbling around for an answer.

"Just tell me this one thing. Do you think I have a nice smile?" She flashed it at him.

Dazzled, Moon muttered, "Well—'nice' don't get halfway there."

"Thank you. Now let me tell you something." She pointed in the general direction of the lakeshore. "When you go down to the dock to see my stupid old husband, you know what he'll tell you?"

Moon shook his head.

"He'll tell you that when he picked me up in Reno, I was waiting tables—when I wasn't turning tricks. That I wasn't nothing but a bucktoothed hillbilly slut."

"I don't believe he'd ever say a thing like that."

"You believe it, cowboy! And then he'll tell you that *he* made this pretty smile. That four of my top front teeth are fakes."

The Ute gentleman did not know what to say. But he said it anyway. "I don't care what anybody says, Mrs. Blinkoe— you've got a million-dollar smile."

Tears filled her eyes. She fell back onto the bed, stared at the ceiling. A hint of the screech returned to her voice. "I hate all men to death. They're all a bunch of rotten, no-good, stinking liars." She pointed at the nearest member of the despicable gender. "Including you."

He had backed his way to the door. "I am sorry you feel that way."

The blue eyes flashed at the exasperating man. "You

should be." Pretending to think he could not hear her, she murmured, "If you'd been nice to me, I might've been nice to you."

Moon put his hat on, pretended not to hear. Made himself disappear.

12

THE BOAT

Manfred Wilhelm Blinkoe took the tribal investigator on a tour of the houseboat, which had SWEET SOLITUDE painted on both of her aluminum pontoons. The lower deck boasted a glistening stainless-steel galley, two comfortable bedrooms separated by a full bath. Though marginally smaller, the upper deck was dominated by a well-appointed parlor. This walnut-paneled room featured a regulation-size pool table, a suite of comfortable leather couches and chairs. The control room was just aft of this space, and jutted a full yard above it. The upper deck was all windows; the flat roof bristled with antennas and lights. As a backdrop to the spoked captain's wheel, there were two panels filled with modern navigation and communication instruments. As the proud captain explained the function of each, Moon did his part by nodding and looking suitably impressed. When the show-and-tell was complete, the men returned to the lower deck.

Blinkoe leaned with both hands on the polished brass railing, gazed expectantly toward the house. Pansy was at the window, like he knew she would be. Watching. "Did she show you her bedroom?"

Moon ignored the question.

"She's a very good-looking woman, my Pansy."

"She is a special lady." He gave his client a warning look. "You're a lucky fellow."

"You won't believe this," Blinkoe's eyes narrowed, "but when I met Pansy, she was waiting tables in Reno. That's what she did in her *spare* time. And as for that pretty smile, why, she had teeth like a woodchuck—"

"Dr. Blinkoe, unless what you're about to tell me bears directly on the question of your personal safety, I don't want to hear it."

The orthodontist gave the Ute a wide-eyed look. "I was only going to tell you about the work I did on her dent—"

"Keep it to yourself."

Blinkoe's mouth was still open. About to say something.

The Ute shot him the do-and-you'll-die look that had once stopped a full-grown cougar in its tracks. "You understand me?"

"Okay. You don't want to hear it, fine." Blinkoe waited a few racing heartbeats. "So what did you and Pansy talk about?"

This was getting tiresome. "Ask her."

Anger was welling up in Blinkoe's throat. "Who are you working for—me or my wife?"

"Neither of you." Moon produced his wallet, removed the hundred-dollar bills. It was like saying good-bye to twenty of your best friends, but he pressed them into the noxious man's hand. "But I like her a lot better than you."

Blinkoe stared at the small fortune. "You drove all the way out here to return my money?"

"That wasn't my original intention." Moon looked toward the house, felt Pansy staring straight at him. "I'm here to give you some advice."

"More advice, eh?" A wry smile crinkled his mouth. "About my compulsive tendency to cheat at cards?"

"Tell you the truth, I don't care if you carry six-dozen aces around in your sleeves."

Blinkoe clenched the bills in his fist, plopped down in a canvas deck chair. "What, then?"

"First time I saw you, you told me that whoever shot that woman at the restaurant was aiming at you. At the time, I figured you were a little bit paranoid. After I talked things over with Scott Parris, I didn't have any reason to change my mind."

"Then why—"

"Let me have my say."

"Very well. Say away."

"After I talked to the chief of police I dropped into Harriet's Rare Books."

"For what purpose?"

"To find out what *It* was."

Blinkoe dismissed this with a snort. "Well, I could have told you that would be a waste of time—no one can see It but myself."

"Harriet saw It."

"Balderdash! The woman is a sixty-six-year-old fruitcake."

"You want to hear her description?"

"I can hardly wait." Blinkoe smiled. "In fact, I am all a-twitter with anticipation."

"She said the It was a Him."

The fork-bearded man raised his left eyebrow by a millimeter. "Indeed."

"You want to hear more, or have you stopped twittering?"

"Oh please go on! The suspense is barely noticeable—or practically palpable. I cannot remember which."

"She said It was a fella who looks enough like you to be your twin."

Blinkoe lost the smile, along with most of the blood in his face.

The Ute picked up the grin. "What do you say to that?"

"She could not have possibly seen . . ."

"Seen *what*?"

Blinkoe assumed a passable poker face. "I cannot say."

Knowing his man, the Ute spooned out a double dose of dead silence.

Blinkoe gazed at the lake. Finally, he sighed. "Oh, very well. 'It' is my doppelgänger. My spirit-twin."

"Run that by me again."

A searching look from the white man. "Don't you know what a doppelgänger is?"

"Sure I do—same thing as a spirit-twin." Moon leaned toward the orthodontist. "You say you saw this whatsit at Phillipe's right before the woman was shot, and again in the mirror at Harriet's bookstore. But if your ghostly twin showed up right here and now, sat down in your lap—I wouldn't see him?"

"No." The haunted man shook his head. "You certainly would not." *At most, you might see his shadow. . . .*

The Ute played out his hand. "But Harriet saw him. She said your look-alike was just outside the store, looking in the window. That's why you spotted him in the mirror behind the counter."

Blinkoe ejected his portly self from the deck chair. "But the silly woman could *not* have seen my doppelgänger—besides myself, no one has ever seen him!" He paced up and down the deck, pulling at the left fork of his beard. "This report is truly irksome."

"I'd say it's truly bothersome."

Blinkoe stopped to regard the Ute. "Bothersome?"

"There was no ghostly doppelgänger, Dr. Blinkoe. There's a small chance it was some guy passing by who just happened to look a lot like you." He made a careful inspection of the orthodontist. "But since it'd happened just a few days earlier at the restaurant, it's a lot more likely that some knothead glued a two-pointed beard on his chin, made a point of letting you get a gander at him."

"But why on earth would anyone—"

"Besides me and you, who else knows about your doppelgänger?"

Blinkoe hesitated. "Hardly anyone. My wife, of course. And over the years, I suppose I might have mentioned the phenomenon to one or two close friends."

"It makes an interesting story—and interesting stories have a way of making the rounds. Maybe some wise guy decided he'd have a little fun with you."

"Do you really believe that?"

"I won't believe anything till I've got all the facts lined up in a row." Moon glanced at the house. Pretty Pansy had vacated her post at the window. "I came out here because of the bothersome possibility."

"Which is?"

"The look-alike that's stalking you might not be pulling a prank. He might be a serious nutcase." The Ute watched a small flock of black ducks skim the surface of Moccasin Lake, land with a muttering flutter of wings. "He might even be seriously dangerous."

Blinkoe shook his head stubbornly. "You didn't see what I saw. The image in the mirror was *exactly* like me! As for Harriet seeing him, it is possible that she is a sensitive who has the remarkable ability to discern what not one person in a million is able to perceive."

"Those are pretty long odds," Moon said. "I'll lay you ten to one that what we're dealing with is no ghost. Your 'twin' is flesh and bone."

Blinkoe stared at the ducks without seeing them. "I appreciate your practical, down-to-earth approach, Mr. Moon. You might even be right." The troubled man jammed his hands into his jacket pockets, fumbled around as if his fingers were seeking loose change. "There are, according to accounts I have read, cases where unrelated persons may hear the doppelgänger's voice or see his image. There are even very rare instances where the doppelgänger reportedly takes on substance—replaces the original person." An uneasy pause. "Not that I can vouch for such tales."

"Even if you did, I wouldn't believe 'em."

Blinkoe cleared his throat. "In any case, I believe that I am in danger of losing my life."

"I won't dispute that."

"Then what shall I do?"

"Tell me who wants you dead."

The pale man shook his head. "I can't."

"Can't or won't?"

"Let me put it this way—I don't know his name. But he'll be a professional."

"Professionals work for money. People who pay hard cash for killings generally have a serious reason to want someone dead."

Blinkoe heaved a heavy sigh. "Before I settled down to a respectable life, I was involved in two or three rather reckless adventures."

"So was I." The tribal investigator watched a sleek duck take a dive. By the time the waterbird reappeared, he had counted to five. "But as far as I know, nobody's gunning for me."

Blinkoe opened and shut his mouth three times before he spoke. "I am suspected of taking part in a very rash act. Those who consider themselves to be the injured parties have evidently decided to even the score. I need protection from a ruthless, powerful organization that is international in scope, but I cannot turn to the federal authorities." He turned to stare at the Indian. "The feds—how shall I say it—have no partic-ular sympathy for me." He shifted his gaze back to the care-free waterfowl. "They would like to lock me up."

"Sounds like a knotty problem. Why'd you come to me about it?"

"Because you have a remarkable track record for getting results." He skipped a shiny half-dollar across the water, watched the ducks take flight. "Apparently, your reputation is overblown."

Moon grinned at the extravagant man. "I could've told you that."

Blinkoe fell back into the deck chair. "Let me summarize

the situation. While I was dining on Phillipe's patio, a hired assassin attempted to shoot me. For whatever reason, he missed. But he has not given up. He will be back. I am convinced of this because my doppelgänger only visits me when I am in mortal danger. What I need is professional help. Because I cannot turn to the conventional authorities, I came to you." He gave Moon a hangdog look. "Is there *anything* you can do to help me stay alive?"

"I'll talk to Scott Parris, give him a heads-up about your look-alike so the local PD can be on the lookout."

"Is that all?"

The tribal investigator gave it some thought. "You could drop out of sight until things get sorted out. Or hire yourself some professional bodyguards, keep 'em on duty twenty-four/seven. Or both."

"I see. Not particularly original ideas."

"That's because they're tried-and-true. Keep a low profile. Hire yourself some knuckle-draggers to stay between you and the shooter."

"Very well. I will consider your recommendations."

Moon took a step toward the gangplank, paused. "There is one other thing you should do."

"Tell me."

Moon told him.

As Blinkoe listened, he blanched. After Moon had made his solemn recommendation, the orthodontist shook his head. "You don't know what she's like—the unadulterated hell she's put me through."

Moon watched the man's face. "Will you do it?"

"If I can muster up the gumption." Blinkoe stared at the lake's lime-green surface, then stuffed the roll of hundred-dollar bills into the Ute's shirt pocket.

"What's that for?"

"A retainer. Against future contingencies."

"I'd better be going." *Before you change your mind.* On the way to his car, Charlie Moon looked out of the corner of his eye, saw the face in the apartment over the garage. According to the merry Ute's view of life, every day should have at least a small measure of fun. On an impulse, he mounted the outside stairway three steps at a time, pounded on the door.

It opened almost instantly, framing a tall, slender young man with bushy blond hair. He wore baggy U.S. Army surplus fatigues, scuffed combat boots. "What?"

You don't look sick to me. The tribal investigator flashed his badge. "You Clayton Crowe—Mrs. Blinkoe's brother?"

There was a spark of alarm in the young man's brown eyes. "Uh—why yes I am."

"This is a fine day—the kind of day that makes me feel really good." Moon frowned at the man in the doorway. "How're you feeling?"

"Just fine, thank you." He eyed the eccentric stranger from head to toe. "What exactly do you want?"

The Ute pointed down at the muddy motorcycle. "That fine Suzuki machine—is it for sale?"

The young man shook his head.

Moon showed no sign of being discouraged by this negative response. "Would you take a hundred bucks for it?"

The owner of the fine Suzuki machine set his jaw. "I most certainly would not!"

"Okay, then." Moon tipped his hat. "Guess I'll have to keep on looking."

13

THE LADY COMES CALLING

Charlie Moon was crouched behind his aunt's ancient television. Having removed the rear panel, he was probing around with a screwdriver. The was a crackling noise, followed quickly by an "Ouch!"

Daisy Perika scowled at her nephew. "What'd you do to my TV?"

"I didn't do nothing to the danged thing. It was the other way around—it *bit* me!"

"TVs don't have teeth—what'd you bite you with?"

He gave the flyback transformer a dirty look. "With about twenty thousand volts."

"It's your own fault. You should've turned it off."

Moon gave her a hopeful look. "How about I bring you out a new one?"

"I already told you, I don't want no new one—I like my

old one." She got up from her chair at the kitchen table, cupped a hand to her ear. "I think I hear a car coming."

"It's a full-size pickup," the young man said. "Got a shock absorber about to go." This much he could tell from the sounds made on the rutted lane. He smiled and added: "It'll probably be a Chevy."

Daisy watched the big Chevrolet pickup brake to a rocking stop behind her nephew's Expedition. "You think you're so smart. Tell me what color it is."

He studied the dusty innards of the TV set. "Sounds like a gray truck to me."

"You cheated," she shot back. "You was expecting somebody." A thoughtful pause. "Who's driving the truck?"

Moon scowled at a selenium rectifier. "It was going awfully slow. So I'd guess it was a woman."

"What kind of woman?"

"Don't know for sure."

"Make a guess."

"Okay. She's a good-looking young lady. Yellow hair. Big blue eyes. Nice smile." Very *nice smile.*

So he's met her before. But there are some things men don't notice. "What color's her purse?"

"Uh—black?"

"Red. And you think you're such a hotshot detective." Daisy opened the door, stepped out onto the rickety wooden porch. The young woman wore faded jeans and a white blouse that—in Daisy's view—was two sizes too small. The tribal elder sniffed her disapproval. "Who're you looking for?" *As if I didn't know.*

The woman glanced hopefully at the Columbine's Expedition. "I've been searching all over the county for Mr. Charles Moon."

"You've found him. Come on in."

Pansy Blinkoe squinted her big blue eyes at the mean-looking old Indian woman. "Uh—thank you kindly, ma'am. But I'll wait out here."

Daisy smiled. "Personal business, huh?"

The pretty young lady flashed a smile that raised the temperature several degrees. "Yes ma'am."

She is going to ma'am *me to death.* The grumpy old woman squinted at the offender. "You one of them Texans?"

"No ma'am. I'm originally from Tennessee."

Ma'am-ing must be spreading all over the country. Daisy turned away from her visitor. "Charlie, come on outside and talk to this sweet little *matukach* girl."

After they had walked a dozen paces from the trailer, where the strange old woman was watching through a little window, Mrs. Blinkoe was ready to speak. She had a hard time looking the Ute in the face. "I called your ranch, talked to Mrs. Bushman. She said you were probably at your aunt Daisy's place, fixing something or other. She gave me directions on how to get here, but I'm afraid I got lost over and over."

Moon stuck his hands into his hip pockets, smiled down at the doll-like figure. "This is a hard place to find."

"And you didn't answer your cell phone."

"I keep it turned off most of the time."

"Why?"

"I've noticed that when it's turned on, it's more likely to ring."

"Oh." She almost flashed the pearly smile, unconsciously put a hand over her mouth.

Let's get this over with. "What can I do for you?"

"Nothing. I just wanted to thank you."

"For what?"

"You don't really know?"

"If I did, would I ask?"

She searched his dark eyes, could see nothing there. "It's about my husband."

"Dr. Blinkoe all right?"

Her blond head made a jerky nod. "Oh yes, Manny's just fine. In fact—he's been *awfully* nice the last few days." She blushed a rosy pink. "He promised never to—" *This is very hard.* "You remember all that bad stuff I told you?"

"Mrs. Blinkoe, if I happen to hear anything unpleasant, I make a serious attempt to disremember it. Especially when it's none of my business."

She looked at her red shoes. "I mean about what Manfred might tell you about the bad things I did when I was in Reno."

Moon did not reply.

"Did he tell you any of those awful things about me?" *Please, please, say he didn't.*

"No ma'am. He certainly did not."

Pansy took a deep breath.

Moon thought she would hold it till her skin turned the same color as her eyes.

She let it out. "Well, it's all true."

"Look, it don't matter a smidgen to me what—"

"No, please. I've never told anyone about it. But I want to tell you."

He waited, braced himself for the pain.

Now she looked him right in the eye. "When Manny met me in that restaurant in Reno, my teeth was ugly. I couldn't help that. But to make ends meet—I did some things a nice girl shouldn't do. But only twice, that was all. And it's true I married Manny mostly for his money, and because he made me these new teeth." She smiled, exposing the merchandise. "The denture comes out. You want to see what I look like without it?"

He shook his head.

"Mr. Moon, I want you to tell me the truth about something."

I know I'll regret this, but . . . "Okay."

"Do you respect me?"

That's easy. "Yes I do."

"Do you like me?"

That wasn't hard either. "Yes ma'am. I certainly do like you."

She reached out to touch his sleeve. "Can I call you by your first name?"

He nodded.

"Then you can call me Pansy." She hesitated. "Charlie—if

it was a couple of years ago, and you met me before I went to Reno—before I married Manny—before he made me my pretty new teeth . . . before I—" She could not go on.

"Yes," he said. "Yes I would."

Tears filled her eyes.

He looked away. *I hate it when they do that.*

"Right after you left, Manny came inside. He sat down by me and held my hand, and—"

"Mrs. Blinkoe, this doesn't sound like it's any of my business—"

"Hush!"

He hushed.

"And he apologized for all the bad things he'd ever said or done." She sighed. "And you know what else he did?"

He shook his head.

Pansy fumbled around in her purse, produced a large platinum compact. On its face was a five-pointed star—fashioned of tiny diamonds and rubies. "I saw it in Denver last year, just *drooled* over it. I thought Manny'd get the hint, but my birthday came and went, then Christmas, and then our anniversary, so I figured it was a lost cause. Then, last night, he drops it in my lap. 'Pansy,' he says, 'this is for you.'" She stuffed it back into her purse. "Ever since you paid us a visit, Manny has been very sweet to me." She aimed the Big Blues at him. "And I think you had something to do with it."

This was extremely embarrassing. Moon looked off toward the yawning mouth of *Cañón del Espíritu,* tried to think of something to say.

"Of course, I don't expect you to admit it."

Good.

"Charlie, would you answer me one last question?"

He shook his head.

"But you don't even know what it is!"

"Sure I do. You still want to know what my business is with your husband."

"But you won't tell me?"

"Nope."

She sighed. "You know what?"

"What?"

"I respect you for keeping Manny's confidence."

Uh-huh. Like she-cougars respect jackrabbits. His dark face split into a wide grin. "Then you're not mad at me?"

"I am very, very mad at you." A slow smile parted her lips. "But since you're so nice to me—I'll get over it." *And then I'll be nice to you.*

After the chevrolet pickup pulled away, Daisy watched Charlie Moon mount the porch in a single step. "Who is that white woman?"

Moon was beginning to wonder about that himself. "Mrs. Pansy Blinkoe."

The Ute elder searched her memory, made the connection. "She related to that funny man with the two-pointed beard?"

"She's his wife."

"Well if you ask me, she's a good twenty years too young for the likes of a goggled-eyed old geezer like that." A suspicion grew in her mind. "Is Mr. Fork-Beard rich?"

"He's pretty well off."

"Hah—that explains it." She gave her nephew the gimlet-eye. "Is that married woman sweet on you?"

The tormented man closed his eyes, imagined a happier land. *I think maybe I'll move to Alaska. Build me a little log cabin on one of them offshore islands. One with no telephone. No mail service. No relatives.*

Daisy read much into his silence. "You know what—I kind of like that FBI woman you've been hanging around with. You know, Lola Fay McPig."

"That's Lila Mae McTeague."

It took all of the Ute woman's willpower, but she managed to get the words past her teeth: "Even if McPig ain't an Indian, she might still make you a halfway decent wife."

"I'm sure Miss McTeague would appreciate the ringing endorsement. If she happens to propose, I'll keep your approval in mind."

"Hah!" Hard as Daisy tried, that was all she could think of to say.

Charlie Moon pointed a Phillips screwdriver at the television. "I don't believe I can fix that thing."

"Well I never thought you could." She glared at her victim. "If you was a good nephew, you wouldn't let me limp along with that old piece of junk—you'd bring me a brand-new television out here." Her mouth twisted into a wicked smile. "One with a remote control and a great big screen."

14

HIS QUIET TIME

He was all decked out in a captain's hat, navy blue seaman's jacket, white linen slacks with thin red stripes down the sides, and white canvas deck shoes. If his face had not been so long, Manfred Wilhelm Blinkoe would have cut quite a jaunty figure. The owner of *Sweet Solitude* wore the hollow-eyed look of a wartime sailor about to depart for an unknown, unfriendly port. As if harboring some awful premonition, he gazed at his young wife with a terrible intensity. "Well, I suppose it's about time I got under way."

She nodded.

He reached out, gently caressed her golden tresses. "I'll miss you."

Wincing slightly at his touch, Pansy turned to look across Moccasin Lake, where a dense forest of willows concealed the northern shore. "I'll be all right." She chewed on her lower lip. "When'll you be back?"

"Oh, about a week." Blinkoe rubbed at the finger where the ring set with the heart-shaped ruby glistened in the late afternoon sunlight. "Maybe ten days." He stared at the woman until her beauty made him ache, then followed her gaze to the lake. "You know how it is with me. At least once a year, I have to have some quiet time."

"Yes," she said. "I understand." And so she did.

A pair of blue-black tree swallows swooped low, glided by like ghostly afterthoughts.

Pansy examined a painted fingernail. It had a tiny crack. "Will you call me while you're out on the lake?" Sometimes when he was away, he didn't call for days on end.

"Sure. When I'm in the mood, I'll check in." He gave her a searching look. "Will you be here in the evenings?"

She looked up quickly. "Where else would I be?"

"Oh, I don't know. Just thought you might go into town with your brother." He frowned at Clayton Crowe's apartment over the garage. Something moved at the window. *So my brother-in-law is up and about. The lazy, good-for-nothing bastard!* "You two could have a nice dinner at Corky's Barbecue. Or maybe take in a movie at the Lido."

"I don't know—Clayton don't like to go out much." She bit at the offending fingernail. "I may go to town by myself. If you call and I'm not here, just leave me a message on the machine." She shot him a brittle look. "I'll get back to you— when I'm in the mood."

"Look, honey-bun . . ." He started to reach for her with both hands.

Pansy had already turned, was walking way. Without glancing over her shoulder, she said, "Hope you don't get too lonesome out there."

M. W. Blinkoe stared as his shapely wife made her alluring way up the winding flagstone path. He watched the door close behind her, waited for her face to appear at a window. It did not.

He boarded the luxurious houseboat, climbed the metal stairway, started up the twin Mercury engines. After checking the gauges, he returned to the lower deck, untied the nylon rope hitched to the dock post, cast off for an uncertain destination.

The U.S. Army Corps of Engineers' dam was nineteen miles west of the Blinkoe residence. At sunset, the captain of *Sweet Solitude* was almost halfway there. He pulled closer to the northern shore, within a hundred yards of a jutting sandstone formation known as Whiskey Point. He shut down the engines, dropped anchor.

Blinkoe pottered around the immaculate galley until he had made himself a Polish-ham sandwich on pumpernickel rye, heated up a helping of Bear Creek Cheddar-Potato Soup. He placed the sandwich on a flowered china plate, ladled the soup into a matching bowl. After his supper, he checked his nine-thousand-dollar Bern Aristocrat wristwatch. Not quite nine P.M. He cleaned off the dinette table, turned on the CD player, listened to a splendid rendition of Schubert's *Death and the Maiden* while watching the moonlit ripples on the water. Finally, he broke out a new deck of cards, tested his wits at a lonely game of solitaire. Blinkoe toyed around with Joker Canfield, Mother's Klondike, Westcliff. Nothing worked; the cards stubbornly refused to cooperate. The disgruntled man made a stab at Devil's Despair. The game was aptly named. He pushed the recalcitrant deck aside, stared at the window, saw only a sad-faced reflection. *What is to become of me?*

Instantly, he felt a sharp pain in his lower back, near his left kidney. Blinkoe ground his teeth. "I *wish* you would not do that!" A pause. "I have a lot to think about—now please don't pester me." He listened intently, nodded at the amorphous shadow that had materialized. "Yes, of course I realize we're in this together. But you're certainly not helping the situation. Just this once, trust me." Gradually, the ache subsided. As it did, the Shadow Man faded into nothingness.

Once the heavy part of midnight had settled onto the lake, it was so quiet that Blinkoe could hear his heart thumping and pumping. *I'd give a thousand bucks to have somebody here to play me just one hand of poker.* He could think of only one thing to do. The cardsharp returned to solitaire, where he would sink to that most degrading of behaviors—cheating himself.

Long after his normal bedtime, Blinkoe was still wide awake. Still cheating. He did not hear the new sound on the lake—under the sigh and whisper of waters breaking on the shore, it was virtually undetectable.

Silent as an ebony swan, the sooty-tinted rubber boat skimmed across the water. The two men in the small craft were dressed in flat black nylon jumpsuits. They did not speak, carried no identification. But on his webbed belt, each wore a canvas-holstered 9-mm automatic pistol and a sheath knife with a four-inch ceramic blade. Along with other essential tools of their trade, a Czech-made submachine gun was packed in a waterproof case. The professionals boarded the *Sweet Solitude* without the least notice from the captain of the vessel. He was unaware of the visitors until one of them touched him on the neck.

Blinkoe yelped, flung his cards across the deck.

Less than an hour later, a pair of men paddled the rubber boat back toward Whiskey Point. Only seconds after they stepped ashore, a violent explosion lifted the houseboat off the surface of Moccasin Lake. A few thousand fragments—including bits and pieces of the unfortunate occupant of the luxury craft—were scattered over the waters. For several minutes, a greasy scum of diesel fuel and rubbish burned on the surface of the lake.

Quite soon, all was peaceful again. Serenely silent.

Until a famished cutthroat trout broke the surface, took a tasty chunk of flesh.

TWO DAYS LATER

Since she had occupied the small office in Granite Creek, one event in Lila Mae McTeague's life had been quite predictable. If she was not at her desk, she made the call on her

cell phone at 3:58 P.M. If she did not, the Man would call her
office telephone precisely two minutes later. Today she was
in the office. At 3:59 P.M., the FBI special agent took a small
key from her purse, opened the desk drawer where the cipher
telephone was concealed. At 3:59:30, the elegant lady removed a pearl earring from her right ear. She watched the
second hand rotate around the face of the Seth Thomas clock.
At two seconds before four o'clock, the telephone buzzed.
She picked up the receiver. "McTeague here."

The assistant special agent in charge of the Denver Field
Office requested that she deliver her daily briefing.

From previous experience with the assistant SAC,
McTeague understood that "briefing" implied *brief*. "I had a
late lunch with Chief of Police Scott Parris. He reports that
state and local police and Lake Patrol Authority have recovered a considerable amount of wreckage from Moccasin
Lake. Condition of the fragments suggests a powerful explosion, followed by a fire. Working hypothesis is that someone
placed a packet of HE on board prior to departure from the
Blinkoe dock. The detonator could have been fired by remote radio control, or by an attached timer. I think it more
likely that someone boarded the vessel while it was at anchor and—"

The Denver SAC interrupted with a pointed question.

"Yes sir. Even though no remains have been recovered,
Dr. Blinkoe is presumed dead. In the event human tissue
should be found, the state police will submit samples for
DNA analysis, but Dr. Blinkoe has no known living relatives." A pause. "Yes sir, that is correct—the presumed victim
was an orphan. The other possibility would be to examine his
medical history, determine whether there are any extant tissue samples to compare to—" She grimaced at the harsh
voice in her ear, nodded at the invisible supervisor. "Yes sir. I
realize that you know that. I merely intended to—" Another
nod. "Yes sir. Good-bye, sir." Special Agent McTeague returned the headset to the cradle, slammed her desk drawer
shut. *Crabby old goat!*

15

BEGINNER'S LUCK

The plump, middle-aged woman pried off the plastic lid—realized she had opened a serious can of worms. Dottie Neffick made a face at the writhing mass of night crawlers. *That is so icky!* She turned to the man beside her. "Pat, I just can't do this."

Patrick scowled at his wife, snatched up the coffee can, grabbed at her fishing line, deftly impaled a medium-size worm onto the barbed hook. "There," he grumbled. "Now see if you can cast it out by that big boulder." He added in a weary tone: "And try not to get it snagged on that log again."

Her face flushed with enthusiasm, Dottie made a surprisingly elegant overhead cast. Snagged it on the log. "Oh, dear." She giggled. "If I'd *tried* to do that, I bet I couldn't have—not in a month of Sundays."

Fresh out of snorts and scowls, Patrick stoically cut the

line with his pocket knife, attached another hook and sinker, baited the line with a second worm.

His wife smiled. "Thank you, dear."

This time, he made the cast. *That should be a good spot.* For a moment, the plastic bobber lay on its side, then jerked upright as the lead sinker settled out at four feet. He returned the brand-new rod and spinning reel to the woman. "Now sit still—and watch the cork."

She raised an eyebrow. "What cork?"

"The float. When I was a boy, we used bottle corks. So I still call 'em corks." *If that's okay with you.*

"Oh—d'you mean that little plastic ball-thingy?"

The experienced fisherman groaned. *I should've left her at home.*

Dottie was not perturbed by his silence. She watched the "cork." After a few seconds she tightened her grip on the rod. "Oh, Pat, look—it's moving! Should I pull it in?"

"That's just the current. Don't you do nothin' unless the cork goes under. Then you give it a good jerk. That's to set the hook." *These women, you can't learn 'em nothin' 'bout fishing, so I don't know why I even try.*

"This is *so* exciting." She shuddered with the delectable joy of the experience. "I don't know why I never did this before. From now on, every time you go fishing, I'm coming along."

"Wonderful," he muttered. A green fly buzzed by, followed by and by by a yellow butterfly. In the branches overhead, a jay began to fuss and cuss about something or other. *Yes sirree, this sure is the way to live.* A blissful minute passed. Then another. Patrick had almost forgotten that Dottie was with him. Then—

"Pat!" She reached over to jerk at his sleeve.

"What?"

"I think I have a bite."

He looked for the red-and-white float. It wasn't there. Suddenly her line went taut. *It's probably just a piece of driftwood.* "Might as well give it a yank."

Dottie gave it a yank. "Oh my goodness—it's a big one!"

He noted the sound of alarm in her voice, sensed an opportunity. "Probably a big water moccasin."

She paled. "Really—are there poisonous snakes in these waters?"

"Sure." He chuckled. "Why do you think they call it Moccasin Lake?"

"Oh, Pat—you're teasing me."

In a generous mood, he hoped Dottie had snagged herself a big channel catfish. She'd probably fall in with it. *Now that'd be something to tell the boys about.*

While Patrick watched, the ecstatic fisherwoman reeled in her catch. "Gracious—it feels like it weighs a ton!"

It ain't puttin' up any fight, but it does look like it could be a sure-enough lunker. "You want some help?"

"No, I do not." *You men think a woman can't do anything but wash your dirty clothes and cook three meals a day and change diapers.* "I can do this by myself, thank you."

He scratched a match across his Big Mike overall bib, touched a sulfurous flame to his pipe. *She'll never get 'im in. I bet she breaks the line. Then she'll take to hollerin' and squallin' to beat the band and she'll blame* me *for losing her great big fish. She'll say I should've helped her—even after she told me not to.* This day was turning out pretty good after all.

When her catch of the day was finally on the edge of the bank, Patrick and Dottie stared blankly. Comprehension finally kicked in, followed by horror.

The fisherman felt his breakfast gurgling up into his throat.

His wife flung her rod and reel away, stumbled backward. The woman's moan turned into a long, keening wail.

16

HER DAILY REPORT

In ten tick-tocks, it would be 3:58 P.M. the FBI special agent SET the 8X binoculars aside, removed the single-purpose cell telephone from her purse, punched the programmed button.

The assistant SAC picked up on the second ring. "Talk to me, McTeague."

"The official ID of the body part is scheduled for four o'-clock. I'm in the unmarked van, parked a block from the medical examiner's home. Chief of Police Parris and Tribal Investigator Moon arrived about twelve minutes ago. About five minutes after that, Mrs. Pansy Blinkoe and Mr. Spencer Trottman arrived in Mr. Trottman's vehicle—" She nodded. "Yes sir. Mr. Trottman is the family attorney. Mrs. Blinkoe is probably leaning on him for moral support as well as legal advice. I'm planning a fortuitous meeting with Chief Parris at about six P.M. Shall I call you back as soon as I determine the results of the ID?" She heard a clipped affirmative response, a click in her ear. McTeague dropped the cell phone back into her purse. *This is really dumb—I shouldn't be spying on my colleagues. I should be in there with Charlie Moon and Scott Parris, finding out firsthand what's going on. But this silly cloak-and-dagger business is the assistant SAC's pet idea, so there's no point in suggesting the direct approach.* She thought it over. *Things need to work out so the stuffed shirt* orders *me to terminate the surveillance.* McTeague thought she knew how to make this happen.

THE ORDEAL

Leading the way, the aged medical examiner switched on the lights over a narrow stairwell, descended into the cool, faintly chemical atmosphere of the mortuary. The occasional cadaver that came his way was stored in the basement of the pathologist's three-story Victorian home. Dependent almost entirely on grinding automobile crashes, drug overdoses among the student body at Rocky Mountain Polytechnic University, and the occasional fistfight gone too far at Paddy's Bar, business was not brisk. Despite the lack of material, Dr. Simpson loved his work.

Pansy Blinkoe followed Chief of Police Scott Parris down the stairs. She was trailed by family attorney Spencer Trottman. Charlie Moon was the last to descend into the cellar. Since his early childhood, the Ute had been taught to fear human remains—especially of those who had recently died by violence. On occasion, a dead body would fill the tribal investigator with an inexpressible sense of dread. At other times he was able to approach a corpse with all of the objectivity required by his profession. This was not one of those times. Moon had seen the man only days ago, when the spirit was still firmly connected to the flesh.

The medical examiner flicked another light switch, led the solemn procession into a boxlike room with a gray concrete floor, gray cinder-block walls, a gray acoustic-paneled ceiling. Recessed into one wall were six stainless-steel drawers.

After a quick, chilling glance, the woman looked away.

Dr. Simpson had conducted this difficult ritual many times, and understood the necessity of starting out slowly, easing them into the hard part. With a practiced casualness, he produced a small plastic bag. "Mrs. Blinkoe, does this look at all familiar?"

Pansy and the family attorney nodded in unison; it was the woman who spoke: "That's Manny's wristwatch." She frowned. "Where'd you find it?"

The M.E. stuffed the bag back into his pocket. "I removed it from the remains."

"Oh." Her face went chalky white.

Now for the hard part. Simpson turned a brass key in bin 2.

Pansy drew back, grabbed Moon's arm. "Do I have to do this?"

The Ute did not know what to say.

The attorney did. "No, Mrs. Blinkoe—you do not." Trottman glared at the M.E., as if expecting an argument.

"That's right," Dr. Simpson said. "It's entirely voluntary. We do prefer to have the remains positively identified by the next of kin, but if you would rather not perform this service, we can ask someone else." The pathologist's eyes twinkled as he regarded the feisty lawyer. "Perhaps Mr. Trottman would stand in for you."

The attorney bristled. "I certainly will." He gave the woman a tender look. "Mrs. Blinkoe?"

Pretty Pansy brushed away a wisp of golden hair. "No, I can do it." She braced herself. "Go ahead."

The medical examiner nodded, opened the insulated door, pulled out a stainless tray that was seven and a half feet long.

The woman, the lawyer—even the hardened pair of lawmen—caught their breath.

It was Pansy Blinkoe who spoke. "I don't understand— where is he? I mean . . ."

Dr. Simpson regarded the roll of cotton cloth, turned his gaze on Scott Parris. "Didn't you tell her?"

The chief of police reddened. "Uh—no. I guess I forgot. I

mean, I thought you had already . . ." He simply ran out of words.

The M.E. shook his head, turned to the woman. "Mrs. Blinkoe, I'm terribly sorry about this. What happened was, the person who—uh—discovered this specimen in Moccasin Lake did not recover the *entire* remains."

A look of cold horror was creeping over the woman's features. Pansy Blinkoe seemed to have aged a decade. "What do you mean?"

Simpson patted the cloth-wrapped parcel as if it were his favorite puppy. "What we have here is one of the limbs."

Her hand found her mouth. "Limbs?"

The M.E. nodded. "Left arm."

She stared at the unruffled pathologist. "But . . . why . . ."

Scott Parris turned his hat in his hands. "Ma'am, we have physical evidence indicating there was a terrific explosion on your husband's houseboat. Enough to do considerable damage to the—ah—remains."

"Oh, God." Her shoulders began to shake. She leaned heavily on Charlie Moon.

The Ute had felt her pain surging through him.

Trottman glared at Moon, patted the woman on the arm. "Mrs. Blinkoe—are you all right?"

Taking a deep breath, she nodded. "Let me see the . . . the . . ." She simply could not say it.

Simpson unwrapped the *thing*.

She stared at the torn shoulder muscles, the blackened biceps, the forearm, the upturned hand. "It doesn't look . . . real."

The M.E. nodded at what he considered a lovely specimen. "That's a normal reaction, Mrs. Blinkoe. A limb apart from a body strikes us as rather an odd thing to see. But it's real enough. What we need to determine is whether this belonged to someone you know." He turned his grandfatherly gaze on the young woman. "Can you identify this left arm?"

Her pretty head nodded. "That's his ring."

Simpson's round little baby face turned slightly pink. "For the record, Mrs. Blinkoe—*whose* ring?"

Pansy pointed at the horrid assembly of flesh and bone and skin. "Manny's—my husband's."

Trottman stared at the gruesome exhibit. "Yes. Manfred always wore his ruby ring."

The now-official widow closed her eyes, took a very deep breath. Exhaled. "Manny bought it years before we met. Inside the rim, he had the jeweler put all three of his initials. M.W.B." She added needlessly: "That was in case if he ever lost it, he could prove it was his."

"That's all we need to hear." Like a jolly butcher wrapping up a plump pork roast, the medical examiner rolled up the severed arm in the cotton cloth. "You fellows take the lady back upstairs. There's a fresh pot of coffee in the kitchen." As a thoughtless afterthought, the lonely old man added: "And there's a big Virginia ham in the fridge. Honey-cured. If you want to hang around for a while, we can make some sandwiches." It did not occur to the pathologist that his guests might not have an appetite.

17

THE NIGHT VISITOR

Feeling squeaky clean and considerably refreshed, Pansy Blinkoe reached for the gold-plated shower valve, turned off the skin-tingling spray of hot water. She stood very still, eyes closed, drip-dripping . . . whispering the words of a brand-new mantra.

Manny's gone.
Manny's not coming back.
Manny's dead!

Sucking in a gulp of the humid atmosphere, she continued.

I'm here.
I'm going places.
I'm alive!

She opened her eyes, focused on the shower wall, watched a plump bead of water slip down the surface of a cobalt-blue Mexican tile.

Outside the Blinkoe home, there was a *presence* in the darkness. It moved about the grounds with the easy familiarity of one who *belonged*.

Pansy Blinkoe stepped out of the shower, toweled herself almost-dry, slipped into a black Japanese silk bathrobe that was ornamented with impossibly crimson lotus blossoms, padded down the carpeted hallway, opened the door to her elegant bedroom, flicked on the overhead light. She seated herself at a pink marble vanity, began to brush lovely tresses that tumbled over her shoulders in a molten, golden waterfall. She gazed at the reflected woman, considered her options. *I'm still young. I could sell this big house, move to L.A. or Miami. Buy a smaller place, maybe on the beach. I could make some new friends.* Men *friends.* She smiled at the pretty face in the looking glass. It smiled back with the brilliantly white dentures Manfred had provided. *At least he did that for me.* She was about to give the hair another vigorous brush when her body went cold enough to freeze and shatter. Here is what was the matter:

In the mirror, just over her shoulder, she could see her bedroom window. A shadowy figure had materialized there. The familiar face was not smiling.

A MINOR IRRITATION

Tucked snugly into his bed, Spencer Trottman was immersed in the deepest of sleeps, enjoying the most pleasant of dreams. He walked along a grassy path, beside a crystalline stream. The bank was carpeted with iridescent green moss and tiny blue flowers. He was suddenly confronted by a small, freckle-faced boy. The child removed a toy telephone from his pocket. It rang once. Twice. The youngster stuck the thing to his ear, nodded, offered the instrument to the dreamer. "Here, mister—it's for you."

For the third time, the telephone on the bedside table rang. Almost awake now, Trottman rolled over, grabbed the instrument, almost dropped it, made an admirable recovery, put it on the pillow beside his head. "Wha—what?"

A woman's voice screeched in his ear. "Spencer—is that you?"

It's Pansy. He squinted at the alarm clock dial. Ten minutes past one. "What is it?"

Another shriek in his ear. "He's here!"

"Who's here—what are you talking about?"

Her voice dropped to a throaty whisper. "Manny's here—I *saw* him."

The attorney pushed himself up on an elbow. "That's not possible."

"I don't care whether it's possible or not," she said through clenched teeth. "I saw his face. Plain as day."

Trottman stared at the black window. "When did you see him?"

"Just a minute or so ago."

The man who had been so rudely awakened put his bare feet on the cold oak floor, felt a shudder in his legs. "You had a bad dream, that's all. After what you've been through lately, it's hardly surprising that—"

"It wasn't no dream—I'd just got out of the shower. I saw Manny while I was wide awake and brushing my hair."

She's either drunk or hallucinating. Or both. "Pansy, I have to ask you this. Have you been drinking?"

"No, you silly bastard—I have not been drinking." A pause. "Well, I did have a little glass of wine at dinner." *Maybe two. Or three.*

A glass of wine probably was your dinner. He swallowed a yawn. "You've had a rough day, identifying Manfred's remains and all. Hey, that was enough to give *me* the shivers."

"Look, I am telling you I *saw* him."

There is no point in arguing with her. "You might've seen

Manfred's ghost. From what I've heard, people who've lost a loved one occasionally have experiences like that."

"He was not a 'loved one' and you know it."

He blinked in the darkness. "What do you want from me?"

She made a half-sob. "Well, for starters you could show a little sympathy."

The attorney smiled. "I'm sorry, Pansy. I'm actually very fond of you." *More than you'll ever know.* "It's just that your call woke me up and I'm still sort of groggy—"

"Manny's come back to torment me."

He rubbed at his eyes. "Maybe you should take a sleeping pill."

"No, no, *no!*" Her transmitted voice rose and fell as she shook her head past the telephone. "I'm afraid—I need to talk to somebody about this."

"Why don't you talk to your brother?" Clayton Crowe lived over the Blinkoe garage. Surely he wouldn't mind holding his little sister's hand till she calmed down.

"I haven't seen Clayton for days—he's off on one of his trips, probably whoring around in Denver." She shouted in his ear: "Spencer, I will *not* sleep in this house tonight." *Maybe not ever again.*

Trottman got to his feet. "Then where will you sleep?"

There was a hesitation. "I thought you might have some idea."

Does that mean what it sounds like? Probably not. "Tell you what, Pansy—I'll get you a nice room over at the Stockman's Hotel."

"Don't bother. I'm coming to your place. Right now."

Why not? "Okay. Come on over. I'll put on a pot of coffee."

"Fine. We can sit up all night and talk." She took a deep breath. "Seeing Manny's face has really put the scare in me. There's some stuff we need to go over."

"What kind of things?"

"I'm thinking of moving away. To California. Or Florida." Now it was a little-girl's voice. "And there's something else I need to tell you. It's about Clayton."

Spencer Trottman heard a metallic click, stared at the

mute telephone. He sat down on the bed. Under the best of circumstances, Pansy was unpredictable. He doubted that she would actually show up. *Once she gets in her pickup, she'll probably just keep on driving.* He wondered whether he would ever see the pretty young woman again.

18

MISSING PERSON

Charlie Moon pulled the Columbine Expedition over to the curb, nudged it up behind a new Chevrolet squad car that was assigned to Granite Creek's chief of police.

Scott Parris had the engine running. He waved, making an impatient gesture for his buddy to get in.

The tribal investigator slid in beside his best friend, slammed the door.

The town cop jerked a thumb at the passenger-side shoulder belt. "Buckle up, cowboy—we are going to ride."

Moon fastened the restraint. "Good morning to you, too."

"What's the matter, Slim—haven't had your usual twenty-thousand-calorie breakfast?"

"Haven't even had a smell of coffee." Moon looked pained. "I left the minute I got the call from your graveyard-shift dispatcher." He glanced at the wily white man. "So what's this all about?"

Parris was already barreling down Copper Street. "Don't know for sure. We'll find out when we see the citizen who called the station at five A.M. He asked for me by name." He shot his friend a merry look. "He also asked for you."

"*Who* asked for me?"

Relishing his role in perpetuating the small mystery, Scott Parris spooned the information out in small bites. "Prominent local attorney." He toggled the siren switch to produce a single wail.

As they barreled through a red light, Moon braced himself. "Mr. Trottman?"

His foot heavy on the accelerator, GCPD's top cop hit the northern edge of town at seventy-six miles an hour. "That's the guy."

"Where are we headed?"

"To meet with said attorney."

Moon knew that Trottman's office and home were in Granite Creek. On the south side of town. He pointed this out.

"He's waiting for us at Moccasin Lake Estates." Parris looked toward an uncertain future. "More particularly, at the home of the late Manfred Wilhelm Blinkoe."

The first time Charlie Moon had met Manfred Blinkoe's attorney, the man had been immaculately clean, well groomed, outfitted in an expensive suit and spit-shined black oxfords. On this gray morning, the troubled man resembled an out-of-work pool shark with a hangover. The lawyer had bloodshot eyes, mussed hair, an insomniac's glassy stare. The effect was enhanced by his wrinkled slacks, dusty Roper boots, and loose-fitting windbreaker over a Broncos T-shirt.

After the chief of police and his passenger had extracted themselves from the confinement of the low-slung Chevrolet sedan, Trottman shook hands with each of the lawmen. "Thanks for coming." He gave the Ute an apologetic look. "Both of you." He turned to frown at the Blinkoe residence. "I've been here since before daylight. Something's not right."

Parris followed the man's gaze. "What's the bottom line?"

"Mrs. Blinkoe isn't here."

"So she's not at home." The chief of police raised an eyebrow. "Any particular reason why I should be concerned about that?"

"Perhaps." Trottman shrugged. "Perhaps not."

Parris struggled to keep the hammer from falling on his hair-trigger temper. "Would you care to clarify that?"

Trottman smiled sheepishly. "Sorry. Guess I'm not making much sense. I've been up most of the night."

"Okay. Start at the beginning."

Assaulted with a sudden fit of shivers, the attorney zipped the jacket to his chin. "Mrs. Blinkoe called me last night." He glanced at the rising sun. "Well, to be precise, she called me quite early this morning. About one A.M."

"Okay." Parris watched the man's face. "I may want a detailed statement later, but right now give me the two-bit version. What'd she call you about?"

Trottman looked at the damp grass. "Uh—she said she was scared."

The police chief's antenna went up. "Scared of what?"

"When she was in her bedroom, she saw somebody. In the mirror."

At the mention of a mirror, Charlie Moon felt an odd chill. Parris pressed on. "Who'd she see?"

"She *thought* she saw . . . her husband."

Parris cocked his head. "Let me make sure I get this straight—Mrs. Blinkoe claimed she saw her dead husband in her bedroom mirror?"

Another nod from the Blinkoe family attorney. "I told her it was due to all the stress, that she should try to get some sleep. But Mrs. Blinkoe was really upset. Her brother wasn't at home and she insisted that she wouldn't sleep there, not last night anyway. I offered to call the Stockman's Hotel, get her a room. But I don't think the poor woman was ready to sleep anywhere. She said she was coming into town—to my place." He hesitated. "To talk." He tried to smile. "You know how women are. Something upsets them, they have to talk about it."

Parris frowned at the lawyer. "I gather she didn't show."

"No." Trottman rubbed his tired eyes. "As you know, the drive takes barely thirty minutes. After almost an hour had passed, I thought maybe she'd changed her mind, taken a sleeping pill and gone to bed. But just to be on the safe side, I called her. Mrs. Blinkoe didn't answer the land line, so I tried her cell phone. Still no answer. I thought she'd probably just switched off the phones, so I went back to bed. But hard as I tried, I couldn't get a wink of sleep. So after lying there staring at the ceiling for hours, I drove up here." He pointed at an empty space beside Manfred Blinkoe's Mercedes sedan—a few spots of oil blemished the asphalt drive. "Her pickup was gone and there weren't any lights on in the house, but I banged on the front door. I wasn't surprised when there was no answer. So I came around the back of the house, to the garage, to see if I could raise her brother." He glanced up at the loft apartment. "You can see that his old GMC pickup is here, but his motorcycle is gone, so I guess he still hadn't returned from wherever he was. Mrs. Blinkoe told me he'd been gone for days. I said, 'To hell with all this foolishness, I'm going home. And I'm going to charge the Blinkoe Estate full rate for the hours I've spent out of my bed tonight.' "

Parris and Moon exchanged grins.

Trottman did not share their good humor. "But come have a look at this."

They followed the attorney past a bushy willow to the rear entrance.

He pointed. "Just as I was about to leave, I noticed that."

The lawmen stared. The glass in the rear door was broken. As if someone had rammed a good-size rock through it. Or maybe his fist.

Parris approached with due care of what might turn out to be evidence. There were only two dime-size fragments of glass on the back step. He looked through the shattered pane. The rest of the glass—about a dozen large shards—was inside, scattered across the kitchen floor. One chair was flat on its back. Parris turned to eye the attorney. "You been in the house?"

"Well, yes. I thought it advisable to determine whether

anyone was inside—perhaps in need of my assistance."
Trottman was blushing. "I don't have a key, of course—but
the door was not locked."

That made sense. The same guy who broke the glass
would have reached inside and thrown the bolt.

The lawyer rubbed a palm across his uncombed hair. "I
had a look around. There was a chair knocked over in the
kitchen, but no other—uh—signs of a struggle. I checked out
the whole house. There was no one at home. All the same, I
thought I should summon the police." He glanced at the tribal
investigator. "And, because he had been working for Manfred, I thought Mr. Moon should be notified."

Parris offered Trottman an amiable smile. "You wait out
here." Following standard operating procedure, Parris first
called out, inquiring whether anyone was at home. As expected, there was no response. He gave Charlie Moon the
let's-go look, used a handkerchief to turn the knob. The lawmen entered the Blinkoe residence. Aside from the hardwood
floor squeaking under their boots, there was no sound.

It took only a few minutes to verify the accuracy of
Spencer Trottman's report that no one was inside. And basement to attic, aside from the upended kitchen chair and broken glass, there appeared to be nothing amiss in the
three-story home. The lawmen made a second visit to the
lady's bedroom. They stared at the only mirror in Pansy
Blinkoe's pink-on-pink boudoir. "If she was sitting there,"
Parris pointed at the vanity, "she would have had her back directly to the corner window. So if she saw somebody in the
mirror, it was probably some Peeping Tom waiting for the
lady to undress."

Moon considered this a plausible explanation. "And if she
had her dead husband on her mind, any night-crawler's face
might've looked enough like Dr. Blinkoe's to make her heart
skip a few beats."

"Sure," Parris said. "So she calls the family attorney, un-
loads the story on him, tells him she's coming to his place.
She's plenty spooked, so in her hurry to get out of the house
she knocks over the kitchen chair, doesn't bother to pick it

up. Then, on her way to see the family attorney, she changes her mind, makes a snap decision to take a drive somewhere else. Like Salt Lake or Albuquerque or Casper. Anyplace where ghostly faces don't show up in your window at night."

Parris thought about this scenario. "But that don't account for the broken pane in the kitchen door."

Moon pitched in to help his friend. "Rattled as she was, Mrs. Blinkoe gets outside, realizes she doesn't have her pickup keys—and she's locked herself out of the house. She breaks in to get her purse."

The chief of police liked it. Far stranger things had happened. He mentioned two or three that had occurred during his days in Chicago. Like the Hindu snake-charmer who'd disappeared from a locked cell, and the hopped-up hillbilly taxi driver who drove his Checker cab into the Halstead Street Methodist Church and tried to purchase an airline ticket to Paducah.

Moon had his own examples. Like the wild-eyed Apache who got stopped at a roadblock, made a run for it, climbed a cottonwood tree, and howled like a wolf, and that time when a dead Ute woman showed up at the Sun Dance. Once you understood what was going on, these things made perfect sense. Well, except for the case of the corpse·who'd come to the Sun Dance. That one still didn't bear thinking about.

"There's one thing that's making me a mite uneasy," Parris said.

"I can't imagine what," the Ute responded.

Aha—Charlie's finally slipped up. "Then you haven't noticed?"

Moon had noticed. "Oh, you mean the gray Ford sedan parked up by the road?"

The chief of police ground his teeth. "Nobody likes a show-off."

"Don't you believe it." Moon patted him on the back. "*I* like you."

"Okay, smart guy. But I bet you didn't spot her yesterday."

"Sure I did."

"Hah!"

"What does that 'hah' mean?"

"It means, 'then tell me when'—and 'what was she driving?'"

"You won't take my word for it?"

"Double hah!"

"Okay, if you put it that way. Agent McTeague was parked up the street from Doc Simpson's place. Tan Chevy van. Government license plate UKL-228. There was a small crack in the left—"

"That'll do."

"—rear taillight."

Parris tried hard, finally thought of the word. "I am chagrined."

"I am visibly impressed with your vocabulary. But with whom are you chagrined, my erudite friend?"

"With *youm,* that's whom—for not telling me you'd spotted that FBI tail."

"Well, Mr. Chagrined, you sure didn't tell me you'd seen Mc—"

"And I'm ticked off with Special Agent McTeague. If the lady is so danged curious about the Blinkoe homicide, why skulk around like some kind of two-bit spy?"

"Because that's the way they do things at the FBI. And she's probably enjoying playing Jane Bond."

"What a waste of taxpayers' money—why don't she just walk right up and ask me what she wants to know?"

Charlie Moon had already given this quite a lot of thought. "Maybe she figures that what you know ain't worth finding out about."

"Thank you, Chucky. That did wonders for my self-esteem."

"Anytime, pardner."

Special Agent McTeague pulled away. *Sooner or later, one of them will spot me. Then Scott Parris will get all . . . what is the colloquial expression? Oh, right. He'll get all "bear-cat-growly"—and he'll call me up and demand to know what I'm up to, spying on him. I'll inform the assistant SAC that there's no use in continuing my surveillance. The A-SAC will criticize my tradecraft, then order me to inform the chief of police about the Bureau's interest in the Blinkoe case. I'll hint to Parris he should insist that Charlie Moon has to be brought into the FBI loop. He'll want to know why. And I'll say, "Why, because the late Dr. Blinkoe has undoubtedly confided in Charlie."* Being very pleased with herself, the clever lady smiled at the road ahead. *Men are so easy to manipulate.*

19

DEALING WITH PERSONNEL ISSUES

Early morning in the high country was never warm. Moon stood in front of the brick fireplace, held his palms out to the crackling pine logs. The parlor in the Big Hat headquarters was not as grand as the one in the massive log structure at the Columbine, but the fire cast a cheerful twinkle in the Ute rancher's dark eyes. He spoke to the pair of men standing behind him. "Even though you two aren't experienced stockmen, you can still make yourselves useful. We've had us some trouble lately with cattle thieves. My hope is that with a couple of armed toughs on the place, we won't lose any more stock."

The man who called himself Curly pulled at a cauliflower ear. "If somebody comes lookin' for trouble, what're the rules of the game?"

Moon continued to stare at the flames. "Call the

Columbine, then give 'em as much trouble as you can spare till I can get here with a truckload of armed cowboys." He turned to regard the men. Curly had a little brush of a mustache under his flattened nose, but not a hair on his shiny head—not even a trace of eyebrows. The older man, who was clean-shaven, stared myopically at the Ute from under the bill of a tattered Dodgers cap. "But there's nothing on the place that's worth getting yourselves killed for. So here's the drill: If things start to look dicey, do whatever's necessary to stay healthy."

Curly turned to his companion, who had a heavy revolver holstered on his hip. "Cap, d'you think you could you shoot a man if you had to?"

Cap nodded. "I've killed my share of men." He grinned. "Including a couple of Arabs."

Having served as a mercenary in a dozen troubled countries, Curly was pleased to hear this. "You was in one of them wars in Iraq?"

The baseball cap rotated twice to indicate a negative response. "*These* Arabs were in Newark."

Curly decided to let that dog lie.

Moon was about to add further instructions when the cell phone in his pocket buzzed. *I got to remember to turn that danged thing off.* He put the instrument under the brim of his hat. "Hello."

Scott Parris's voice crackled in his ear. "Hello yourself, Charlie. Where you at, ol' buddy?"

"Here at the Big Hat. Breaking in a couple of new hands."

"You mean cow-pie kickers?"

"I mean straight shooters."

"Gunslingers, eh?"

"You don't really want to know."

"I've known about your rustling problem ever since the day it happened."

"So why aren't you out there looking for my cattle?"

"Hey, I'll put Officers Knox and Slocum on it." The GCPD chief of police added a "Ha-ha."

"Don't do me no such favors," Moon grumped.

"Suit yourself." Parris switched to a more serious tone. "Look, Charlie—I got to see you. Right away."

"About what?"

"I'll bring somebody along to explain that to you."

"Who?"

"Your favorite federal agent."

Moon grinned. "Lila Mae?"

"Who else? I called her this morning, demanded to know why she'd been following me around. At first, she played it real cagey—said she was busy, would have to get back to me. Which means she had to call her boss and ask him, 'What do I tell the chief of police, Mr. Special Agent in Charge of the Entire Galaxy?'" Parris chuckled. "And she did. Get back to me, I mean. Said the Bureau would like to 'collaborate' with the GCPD on the Blinkoe homicide, and his wife's disappearance. After thinking about it some, I said she'd have to talk to the *both* of us. She said she couldn't make that decision, she'd have to check with her supervisor. She called me back again, just above five minutes ago, said she had the Bureau's permission to bring you into the loop."

The Ute glanced at the clock on the mantelpiece. "When should I expect you?"

"Oh, a couple a hours."

Moon said his good-bye, stowed the phone in his pocket. The new hires were staring holes in him. He smiled. "We're going to have some visitors."

Cap rested the heel of his hand on the revolver handle that jutted out at his side. "Who?"

The Ute shrugged. "The Granite Creek chief of police. And an FBI agent."

The men stared in numb disbelief.

Cap finally managed to squeak out a quartet of words. "Are you *kidding* us?"

Moon shook his head in a gesture of one put-upon by Life. "One of the things that makes running a ranch so difficult is hiring men who don't have something or other to hide from the law." He eyed Cap sternly, then Curly. "The chief of police is an old buddy of mine, and has a tendency to look the other way where my hired help is concerned. But, boys, let me tell you one thing I know from long years of experience with the tribal police—it don't *ever* pay to mess around with the FBI. Nothing gets past those folks. So if either of you two are wanted for counterfeiting or kidnapping or robbing banks, I'd just as soon you didn't tell me anything about it. That way, if Agent McTeague happens to match one of your homely kissers to a Wanted poster and puts the cuffs on you—hey, it's not like I knew anything about it." He turned to watch the flames lick resinous bark off the pine logs. "If there's any reason you fellas don't want to hang around, you can always hit the road before the fed shows up."

LILA MAE'S REVELATION

Scott Parris pulled his black-and-white to a rocking stop in the scanty shade of an elm that didn't know whether it was dead or alive. The low, rambling Big Hat headquarters was not as impressive as Moon's big log house on the Columbine, but it had a comfortable, lived-in sort of look.

Charlie Moon was standing on the porch. A pair of men flanked him.

McTeague unbuckled her shoulder restraint. "Those fellows with Charlie don't look like cowboys to me."

"They're not," Parris said. "He had some cattle stole off this place a while back. Those guys are sort of—guards."

The FBI agent took a closer look. The bald one was cradling a .30-30 carbine in the crook of his arm. The older one in the baseball cap toted a big pistol on his hip. "Guards? Those are a couple of thugs."

"Of course they are," Parris said with a grin. "And if those rustlers show up here again, I imagine they'll wish they'd gone somewhere else instead."

Charlie Moon stepped off the porch to shake hands with

Parris, tipped his black Stetson at McTeague. Moon noted the evil eye she was aiming at his new hands. He turned to make the introductions. "The shiny-headed fella is Curly."

I might have guessed. "How do you do?" she said.

Curly didn't tell her how he did—he merely leered at the good-looking woman.

The rancher continued. "The mean-looking *hombre* calls himself Cap. He claims to be a good hand with a six-gun, and not all that bad with the pots and pans. Boys," he said, "the lady is Special Agent McTeague. She works for the FBI, so watch your step." He nodded to indicate the man beside the fed. "This is Scott Parris, my old buddy. He's chief of police in Granite Creek. The reason you're looking after the Big Hat is that Scott is not interested in hunting down cattle thieves."

Parris grinned at the Big Hat hands. "Hi, fellas."

Cap touched his cap.

Curly was still grinning at the woman.

"Come inside," Moon said. "While Curly finds himself a rattlesnake and bites off its head, Cap will dish us out some lunch."

After the meal, Parris released a happy burp. Remembering the lady, he apologized.

"Forget it," McTeague said. "I have three older brothers." She smiled at her host. "Charlie, that was the best beef Stroganoff I've had west of the Mississippi. Your man Cap is a first-class chef."

Moon glanced at the man who was the object of this extravagant compliment. "I don't know. I thought it was lacking . . . a certain something."

Cap scowled at the owner of the spread, started jerking plates off the table.

As soon as the cook was out of earshot, McTeague whispered to Moon, "I believe you have hurt his feelings."

The Ute snorted. "Guys like Cap don't have *feelings.*"

Parris nodded. "Charlie's right. You start being nice to hardcases, it goes right to their heads. First thing you know, they start thinking they're actual human beings."

"Yeah," Moon said. "Then they'll be wanting regular wages."

The FBI agent stared at the Ute. "You mean you don't pay—"

"I bet all these guys get is thirty bucks a week and found." Parris scratched at his belly.

McTeague looked at Parris, then at Moon. "Found?"

"Room and board," Moon said. "Beans and bed." He shot a hurt look at Parris. "And for the record, I pay 'em *forty* dollars every Friday night."

She threw her napkin down. "But that's illegal!"

"Not if I don't get caught." Moon nodded at Cap, who sidled over to the table. "Mister, have you or that bald-as-a-doorknob chum of yours got any complaints about your treatment here on the Big Hat?"

The cook opened his mouth as if to make a beef, hesitated.

"If you do, you can tell this lady," Moon said. "She has got your best interests at heart."

There was a shrug, a rotation of the Dodgers cap.

Moon grinned at his favorite FBI agent. "See?"

McTeague shot the Ute a dark look, smiled at the exploited man. "The lunch was delicious."

This earned her a pleased grin before Cap returned to the sink.

Moon picked up his coffee mug, leaned back in his chair. "So what brings you two coppers to the hospitality of my humble table?"

"Ask her," Parris said. "She's only dropped me a hint or two."

McTeague raised a perfectly arched eyebrow, looked over Moon's shoulder at the chef.

"Hey, Cap," Moon yelled. "You can take a break."

The underpaid worker pitched a dishtowel aside, shuffled out the porch door.

Having rehearsed her small speech, McTeague delivered it flawlessly. "The Bureau has decided to take an interest in the Blinkoe homicide."

Moon looked from the FBI agent to the chief of police.

Parris shrugged. "Hey, it's no skin off my nose. If the FBI wants to help me, that's just dandy."

The tribal investigator blinked. "No knotty jurisdictional issues?"

"Not with me." Parris helped himself to a homemade oatmeal-and-raisin cookie. "Over the years," he said between satisfied chews, "a man learns to go with the flow. Live and let live. And so on and so forth."

Moon shook his head. "Don't take this the wrong way, pard—but I find this roll of baloney kinda hard to swallow."

"That's because I didn't mean a word of what I said. If this fed starts stepping on my toes, I'll run her out of town."

"I am greatly relieved to hear it," Moon said. "All of this fraternizing with the FBI could ruin your reputation for being a grumpy old lawman."

McTeague was about to bristle. "Can it, you two."

Moon attempted a contrite expression. "Yes ma'am."

Feeling not the least contritious, Parris managed a second burp.

"Here's the deal." The FBI agent spoke barely above a whisper. "At precisely fourteen hundred hours tomorrow, the Denver Field Office will issue a news release on the Blinkoe homicide."

Parris grinned. "Ain't this perfect? The FBI has just got interested in the case, and first thing they do is plan a news release—now why didn't I think of that?"

McTeague gave him The Look. "Shut up and listen."

He did.

"I have been granted permission to give you guys a heads-up." McTeague glanced at the door leading to the porch. Cap and Curly were in the yard, standing under a cottonwood tree. "For some time now, Dr. Blinkoe has been a person who was—shall we say—of interest to the Bureau."

The lawmen waited for the other boot to drop.

It did not.

Parris snorted. "Blinkoe is a 'person of interest' to the Bureau—that's it?"

"Don't ask me for details that I am not at liberty to provide. But I am instructed to tell you this: If either of you happens across any information that might have the slightest relevance to Dr. Blinkoe's untimely demise, you are to report to me immediately." McTeague stared at her coffee. "I wish I could tell you more."

Moon waved off the halfway apology. "It would probably be the kind of stuff that puts a man off his feed. Me, I wouldn't want to hear it."

"Well, speak for yourself, Charlie. Me, I wouldn't mind hearing just a tad more." Scott Parris thumped a knuckle on the table. "It just so happens that Moccasin Lake—where Dr. Blinkoe's boat was blasted to flinders and splinters—is in my jurisdiction."

McTeague stared at the chief of police. "So?"

Parris had no answer to this vague question.

Moon attempted to disarm her with a grin. "Is our official business done with?"

The fed said that it was.

The host beamed at his guests. "You two want some serious dessert?"

Though suffering from a belt that kept shrinking, Parris could not resist. "What've you got?"

"I'll let Cap show you." The rancher yelled for his sidearmed cook, who shortly appeared with his thuggish sidekick.

At the rancher's command, the man under the baseball cap served up two hot apple pies from the cookstove oven. He topped this display off with a gallon of hand-cranked banana ice cream.

At Moon's invitation, Cap and Curly joined them at the table.

Having recently slipped off his diet of raw carrots, raw apples, and oat bran, Parris put away a quarter of a pie with gusto. Pronounced it "better than Mom ever made."

Lila Mae McTeague enjoyed her share, heaped additional compliments on the chef. She also patted Scott Parris on the arm, made her apologies for being so opaque. Explained that she was "under orders."

The chief of police shrugged his broad shoulders. Said not to worry about it. "But while you're in my town, don't spit any tobacco juice on the sidewalk, good-looking—or I'll drop you in the jug and swallow the key."

Charlie Moon was a happy man. Ice cream and pie and apologies and forgiveness. It made for a perfect day.

20

TO GATHER HERBS

Daisy Perika trudged along the twisting, rocky path that snaked miles into *Cañón del Espíritu.* Well aware of the possible consequences if she stubbed her toe on a root and fell, the tribal elder kept her gaze fixed on the ground. *I could crack a hip bone, and not be able to get back up again.* She had forgotten about the pendant telephone suspended from her neck. *I could die out here and nobody would know till somebody happened by and found my bones with all the meat gnawed off by the foxes and coyotes. If I should give up the ghost before I get back home, I hope Charlie Moon remembers where to put what's left of my remains, and which dress I want to be buried in.* The image of her grinning skull, the chewed bones outfitted in the purple dress with the silver threads in the collar, sent a rattling shudder through Daisy's bent frame. This morbid portrait was counterbalanced by the happy realization of how her friends—especially Louise-

Marie LaForte—would be horrified. The old woman snickered at the image of gaped mouths, eyes like fried eggs. Now
that would be a funeral to remember.

After this most recent birthday, death was continually on
her mind. But as she hobbled along with her walking stick,
Daisy had time to consider other matters. Such as blessings.
The longtime resident of the little trailer home at the mouth
of Spirit Canyon appreciated how fine the sun felt on the dark
blue shawl draped over her shoulders, how wonderfully spicy
the sage-scented air smelled. She also thought about the
Catholic priest who had retired from the church at Ignacio.
When he wasn't traveling all over creation to places like Italy
and Mexico, Father Raes Delfino stayed in one of the cabins
at Charlie's Columbine Ranch. Daisy was grateful to her
nephew for providing this home for her favorite priest, but it
would not have occurred to the cantankerous woman to tell
him so.

The farther she got into the canyon, the higher the sandstone walls towered, the longer the shadows were. With each
step she took, Daisy recalled Father Raes's stern warnings
that she should have no communion with the *pitukupf*.
Though hardly any of the *matukach* believed in the existence
of the dwarf who had attached himself to the tribe a thousand
years or more ago, the Catholic priest did not doubt the existence of such creatures. He had told her tales of far stranger
things he had encountered while working among those naked
tribes in the South American jungles. Like frog-gods and
leopard-people and huge snakes that ate human babies. She
shook her head at such rubbish. South America must be full
of superstitious folk, and some of it had rubbed off on the
priest. The dwarf, of course, had nothing to do with superstition—even though only a few privileged Utes had encountered the *pitukupf*. And as far as she knew, Scott Parris was
the only white person who had ever laid eyes on the little
man, but Daisy wondered whether Father Raes might have
also seen him at least once. It was certainly possible—the
dwarf had appeared in church one Sunday morning, sitting
right beside her in the pew! Such disgraceful impudence—a

less-merciful God would have scorched the little heathen with a bolt of lightning.

Daisy paused, used a sleeve to wipe sweat off her forehead. *I wish it would cool off some. But who cares what I wish for?*

There was a sudden rumble of thunder over the Three Sisters.

A moment later, a fragrant breeze sighed along the canyon floor.

Ahh . . . that feels good. She looked up at the blue ribbon of heaven winding along above the canyon. *Thank you, God.* Thus restored, the aged supplicant resumed her steady pace.

Though far away in a foreign land, Father Raes seemed determined to occupy her thoughts. She had solemnly promised the priest that she would not seek out the dwarf, but that did not rule out chance encounters. After all, should she stay inside her home, hoping to keep herself away from the *pitukupf*? It was too silly to think about. And if she happened to take a walk in the canyon, would any reasonable priest expect her to avoid that abandoned badger hole where the *pitukupf* lived? Certainly not. She had as much right to be here as any other creature, including the troublesome little man. *It's not like I came up here today to see him.*

The thunder made a sound like two tons of freshly dug potatoes falling out of a wagon.

Daisy adjusted the strap of a hemp bag that was slung over her shoulder. By the time she returned home, it would be filled with a variety of roots and berries and herbs that the medicine woman used in her trade. The bag just happened to contain a few items the dwarf would appreciate. Like a small package of lemon drops, a can of Canadian Mountie powdered tobacco, a few strips of buffalo jerky. Plus an inexpensive pocketknife. *But that don't necessarily mean I brought this stuff for the little man. A knife can come in handy for trimming leaves off a bloodberry vine. And I might want to suck on a lemon drop or two, just to wet my whistle. A piece of jerky to chew on wouldn't hurt either.* Daisy chuckled. *I might even decide to take up dipping snuff.*

A blue-black raven soared down from the craggy edge of Three Sisters Mesa, landed directly in front of the old woman, cocked its head. Awked a throaty squawk.

Daisy paused to lean on her oak staff, raised an eyebrow at the creature. "And a good morning to you, *Taqo-ci.*" *What brings Mrs. Darkwing down here to visit with me?*

The bird ruffled her feathers, muttered a few garbled comments about this and that.

The Ute elder nodded. "I know just what you mean," she said, and continued her measured uphill tread.

The raven skip-hopped along beside her.

As they continued on their way, the odd pair exchanged tasty gossip about several ghostly friends they shared, and one or two of flesh and blood. The conversation continued until ordinary topics were exhausted. Daisy found a black splash of shade under a brushy juniper, seated herself in its coolness. As she rested, the Ute woman offered her feathered companion a piece of jerky.

The gift of food was gratefully received. *Taqo-ci* put a foot on the dried buffalo flesh, ripped off stringy shreds with her black beak, gulped down every salty morsel.

After the sun was two diameters higher, the raven mentioned the ghost of an Anasazi woman who wanted to confer with the shaman. It had to do with her remains, which had been buried ages ago in the narrow canyon on the other side of Three Sisters Mesa. Her brittle old bones had been exposed by a spring flood. Surely, the Ute woman could do something about this calamity.

Though wary of Snake Canyon, Daisy agreed to receive the troubled spirit. *I could send Charlie up there to cover those bones.* But she advised the raven that the Anasazi haunt better not show up while she was sleeping.

This condition was agreed to by the intermediary.

By now, Daisy had gotten her second wind. She gripped the walking stick with both hands, heaved herself to her feet.

The human being and the bird continued their journey in silence.

Daisy's musings returned to the priest who, the way she

saw it, had deserted his post. The man was not yet seventy summers old—far too young to retire. A happy thought occurred to her. *Since Father Raes ain't the reservation priest anymore, he don't have no authority over me. It's likely that any promise I made him don't hold.* She nodded to agree with this conclusion. *Sure. Since he's not working for the Church, maybe he isn't even a real priest anymore.* One flawed assumption conjured up another. *I bet the bishop took his white collar away. It would serve him right, leaving us like he did. And we don't have a regular priest at St. Ignatius yet, just that Father who drives down from Granite Creek once a week. Sooner or later, we'll probably have us a permanent pastor.* She sighed. *I probably won't like him, and I sure won't tell him about the* pitukupf. Daisy scowled at an unsettling thought. *I bet the new priest will go see Father Raes to ask about all the people in the church, and that little Jesuit will spill his guts about me. I can just hear him:* "Daisy Perika isn't a good Christian—no matter how many times I try to set her straight, I've got a hunch she sneaks off to talk to that infernal dwarf-spirit—trade him food and stuff for information." The imaginary conversation angered her. *Sure. Them priests stick together like a wad of cockleburs. And the new Father will start wagging his finger at me, saying,* "Now, Daisy, don't you have nothing to do with that dwarf. God's people don't keep company with such folk." The injustice of these imagined plots was enough to give her a surge of heartburn.

She turned to speak to her companion, but the black bird had departed without a word. This was not a great surprise; feathered creatures tend to be short on manners. A deer or raccoon or even a squirrel would not have left without some sort of good-bye.

Daisy Perika noticed that she was within a few yards of the spot where the *pitukupf* hung his tattered little hat. Tired from the long walk, she unslung the hemp bag from her shoulder, seated herself on the sandy soil, rested her back against a half-dead piñon trunk. Thus situated, she leaned the walking staff in the fork of a brittle branch and carried on the imaginary conversation, defending herself to an imaginary priest. *Look here, Father—if a tired old woman wants to sit herself down to rest—and it turns out she's within a few steps of the little man's home—is there anything wrong with that?* In her mind's eye, the cleric hesitated, then allowed as how that would probably be permissible. *As long as you don't make any effort to communicate with the creature.* Daisy put an innocent expression on her wrinkled face. *Why would I want to talk to the* pitukupf*? He's nothing more than a pint-size trickster. Always wanting some food or trinket before he'll tell me anything, and when he does open his mouth, he generally talks in riddles.* The backslider stole a glance at the crumbling old badger hole, which was partially concealed under a huckleberry bush. She dismissed the phantom priest, began to talk aloud to herself. "This is a good place to gather up some of the stuff I need." Indeed, right by her side was a fine little specimen of Corydalis. The herbalist took her time, patiently working the bluish gray plant up, root and all. By itself, it was not very effective, but in combination with valerian or skullcap and a couple of secret ingredients, this would be good for treating nervous twitching. A practitioner had to be very careful, of course. It was important to use exactly the right preparation, and you'd never give the medicine to a pregnant woman. She deposited the plant in the hemp bag, removed the plastic Ziploc filled with buffalo jerky, selected the best-looking strip, stuck it between her lips, and began to chew. *That tastes pretty good. And it's nice and peaceful here.* After she completed her small meal, Daisy closed her eyes.

Within a moment, she was drifting off. Toward that Other place.

21

RUDELY AWAKENED

It seemed that Daisy Perika had barely dozed off, when she felt someone kick the sole of her shoe.

The sleeper twitched, opened her eyes in a glassy stare. "What—who's there?"

It was, of course, the little man. Being barely knee-high, he looked the sitting woman straight in the eye.

Though delighted that the *pitukupf* had decided to show himself—sometimes the shaman went for months with neither sight nor sound of him—she scowled at the elfin creature. "What do you mean—kicking at me like that?"

He ignored this question, just as he had the first.

Daisy blinked, managed to focus on the rude little fellow. He did not look well. His skin had a sickly yellowish tint, his eyes squinted and watery. A dirty blanket was draped around his skinny frame, almost concealing the green shirt and buckskin breeches. His splayed feet were bare. Moreover, he shivered and quaked. Unexpectedly, he sneezed.

Oh my, I don't want to catch no dwarf virus. The woman pushed her back against the tree.

The pathetic *pitukupf* was eyeing the hemp sack.

Daisy had intended to bargain some information in exchange for the gifts, but now she felt an uncharacteristic surge of pity for the forlorn figure. *Poor little runt lives in a hole in the ground and don't have no family, or even a TV to watch.* She made a gesture with her hand. "Go ahead. Take what you want."

He did.

She watched the dwarf stuff packets of jerky and candy under his shirt. He opened the blade on the folding knife, cackled a little laugh as he rubbed the shiny steel blade on his blanket. Daisy began to regret her impetuous generosity. "Go ahead," she whined, "rob a poor old woman who don't have hardly any income but her Social Security. You probably don't care a whit about my troubles."

The *pitukupf* sneezed again, wiped his nose with the back of his hand.

Nasty little germ bucket, you could at least ask me why I came to see you.

To her amazement, he did ask—in an archaic Ute dialect the tribal elder strained to understand.

Daisy Perika got right down to business. In the current version of the tribal tongue, she told him about the pretty young *matukach* woman with yellow hair, how Charlie Moon had been working for her husband—a peculiar man with a forked beard—and how the man's boat had blown sky-high and now he was dead and on top of all that, Pansy Blinkoe had run away and nobody knew where she was. Could the little man tell her anything?

The *pitukupf* stared at the shaman as if she were a particularly hideous toad, finally took a step forward—pointed the blade of the gift-knife at her throat.

For the first time in the decades she had known him, Daisy felt more than a tingle of fear. *He is going to kill me!* She tried to mouth a protest, to throw her arms up for protection. She was unable to speak—her entire body was paralyzed.

The little man reached out with the tip of the stainless-steel blade, deftly pulled one of her eyelids down. Then the other.

The shaman was plunged into a darkness like none she had ever known.

Down, down, she went. Down and under.

I knew it. I am dying. But where am I going—into Lower World? Oh, God—I should've listened to Father Raes. . . .

Her spirit floated in a sea of nothingness, for ages it seemed. Then, somewhere just short of infinity, a tiny speck of greenish light.

She moved toward it.

Daisy was greatly relieved to be in Middle World, and in familiar surroundings. There in the distance was a landmark from her childhood—the V-shaped profile of Gunsight Mesa. Below, along a strip of highway, was a scattering of homes and barns—and a church with a rusty iron cross on the bell tower. *That looks like St. Cuthbert's at Garcia's Crossing— the little town where Daddy used to take us when he wanted to buy some sheep.* An instant later, the visionary found herself inside a musty-smelling room. The sandstone floor was dusty, the whitewashed walls were cobwebbed in the corners. The dismal space was illuminated by a narrow, slitlike horizontal opening near the ceiling.

Daisy gradually became aware of a murmuring. There were others there with her—three, she thought. Yes, now she could see a pale-faced young woman with yellow hair, and a middle-aged man and woman.

Yellow Hair was sitting, hands tightly clenched, speaking to the older woman. "Prudence, I feel so lucky to be here with you folks. I didn't have any idea what'd happen to me—or where I'd end up."

The grandmotherly woman responded in a lyrical His-

panic accent. "We're pleased to have your company." She reached out to pat her husband on the arm. "Sometimes, me and Alonzo get awfully lonesome."

The thin little man smiled, nodded his agreement.

Prudence sighed. "It seems like we've been here for ages, but time has a way of passing. I believe we'll be leaving fairly soon, for our new home. From what I've been told, some of our old friends will be close by—practically next door."

It was apparent that Daisy's presence had gone unnoticed by the occupants of the room. She did not recognize the older couple, but the young woman was well known to the uninvited guest. It was that young white girl who had come to the trailer to see Charlie Moon—the wife of that man with the funny two-pointed beard. Pansy Blinkoe. The shaman realized she had misjudged the dwarf. *The* pitukupf *has sent me right to the place where she's hiding.*

The unseen visitor watched every movement, listened to every word. When she had heard enough, Daisy turned toward the window. She gazed through this oblong portal to the outside world, saw the cross on the church steeple. *This house is next door to St. Cuthbert's Church. If I wanted to, I could find my way back here.*

Daisy Perika opened her eyes. The sun had slipped behind the largest of the Three Sisters. The hemp bag was there at her feet, but the *pitukupf* had evidently retreated to his lair. The aged woman's back and legs ached, her feet and hands felt like lumps of ice. She had no doubt that this was the remnant of the dwarf-induced paralysis. Shivering in twilight's gray chill, she reached for the oak staff, slowly pushed herself to her feet. As she looped the bag over her shoulder, her skin began to prickle with excitement. *I have to get back home before dark. And the first thing I'll do—even before I heat up something to eat—is make a telephone phone call to Charlie Moon.*

Perched on a dusty ledge on the sandstone cliff, the blue-black raven emitted a low, rattling chuckle.

• • •

By the time she opened the door to her warm, cozy home, food was uppermost in Daisy's mind. And after a satisfying supper of scrambled eggs and buttered bread, the weary woman was drawn to her bed. She switched off the lights, slipped her bones under the covers, pulled the quilt up to her chin. *Tomorrow will be soon enough to call Charlie.* She yawned. *Not that he'll pay the least attention to . . .* The thought was terminated with a snore.

22

A DEBT OF HONOR

At Spencer Trottman's invitation, Charlie Moon seated himself across the desk. The tribal investigator crossed his long legs, capped his knee with his hat. "Thanks for seeing me on such short notice."

"You are quite welcome." Trottman put on a thin smile. "I assume that your visit must have something to do with our mutual client, the late Dr. Manfred Blinkoe."

"You're right about that."

The attorney tried to read the gambling man's poker face. "Is there something you want to tell me?"

The Ute shook his head. "There's something I want to give you."

"Indeed?" Trottman could not imagine what.

Moon removed a manila envelope from his inside jacket pocket, tossed it on the glass-topped desk.

Trottman arched an eyebrow. "What's this?"

"Two thousand dollars."

The eyebrow went a notch higher. "Please explain."

"It was an advance from Dr. Blinkoe—for services I wasn't able to provide." Moon got up, put the Stetson on his head. "I figured it should go to his estate."

Having never had any dealings with an honest man, the attorney stared in disbelief.

HAVING SLEPT ON IT

Following a breakfast of green-chili stew and warmed-over biscuits, Daisy Perika eyed the pendant telephone and chewed over her thoughts of the preceding day. *Charlie's polite and pretends to listen to what I have to say, but he never pays any attention to my visions or anything the* pitukupf *tells me. He thinks I'm just a silly old woman who talks to a little man that ain't really there. So when I tell him where that* matukach *woman is hiding, I won't tell him how I know.*

Daisy slipped on her reading glasses, studied the miniature telephone. The colored buttons were so tiny. *This is not for a normal-size person. I should have given it to the* pitukupf, *let him wear it around his skinny little turkey neck. Maybe the dwarf would give Charlie Moon a call, ask how are you, you big jug head, and what is the price of beef these days?* The thought made her grin. But what had Charlie said? Oh yes, the red button is 911, the blue one is his cell phone, the yellow one is the ranch, the green one is to redial the last number you called, the pink one is . . . She could not remember what the pink button was for. Daisy pressed the blue button. It rang several times before she heard the recorded message.

> *The number you have dialed is not responding. If you wish to leave a message, please press one and wait for the tone.*

Phooey! I'll try his ranch. Daisy pressed the yellow button. A woman's voice answered. "Columbine."

Daisy snapped at the invisible person. "Where's my nephew?" As an afterthought, she added: "And who're you and what're you doing in Charlie's house?"

"Ah—is this Mrs. Perika?"

"Who else would it be, calling from a dinky little telephone that's hanging on a string around my neck? Now tell me—what's going on up there?"

"Well, ma'am, this is Dolly Bushman. Charlie ain't at home right now, and when he's going to be away from the headquarters for a long spell, he generally sets his phone to ring here at the foreman's house. Would you like to leave him a message?"

"No, I wouldn't." *Not with you.* "So where is he?"

"He's gone to see a lawyer about something. A Mr. Trottman, over at Granite Creek."

Oh that lawyer—he's the one who liked my Old Apache stew. Needing a favor, Daisy softened her tone. "Do you have Mr. Trottman's phone number?"

"I think so. Just a minute." Dolly was back in less time than that. She read the numbers to Charlie Moon's aunt. "Mrs. Perika, I believe that's for the lawyer's cell phone, but I could look up his office phone for you in the book and—" The kindly woman heard a click in her ear.

This one ain't programmed in, so I'll just do it the old-fashioned way. Taking considerable care not to make an error, Daisy Perika used a wooden toothpick to punch in the attorney's telephone number.

Several rings, then:

> *The number you have dialed is not responding. If you wish to leave a message, please press one and wait for the tone.*

The frustrated woman clenched her teeth. *So, Mr. Trottman ain't answering his stupid phone either. I'll just ring Charlie's cell phone again and leave a message for him.* She gave the button a poke. Waited through a dozen rings. Heard the now-familiar recorded voice.

The number you have dialed is not—

She deftly pressed 1, waited for the tone. "Charlie, I just tried to call you on that lawyer's phone, but he ain't picking up." She took a deep breath, puffed up like an angry horned toad. "I wanted to tell you that I know where you can find that white woman—I'm talking about Blinkoe's yella-headed wife. She's holed up in a place close to St. Cuthbert's Church, which is over at Garcia's Crossing, which is just south of Gunsight Mesa. And if you can't find her with those directions, I guess I'll just have to lead you by the hand and *show* you right where she is." A pause. "And don't you go asking me *how* I know—I have my ways." Imagining the look on Charlie's face when he got an earful of *this,* she smiled. "Call me right away." Daisy pressed the Off button. *Well, I've done my part.*

She waited all day for Charlie Moon to return her call— even forgot to have her lunch. By twilight, she was fuming. *He's probably out somewhere chasing them stupid white- faced cows. Or white-faced women. Or worse still . . . Maybe he heard my telephone message and decided it was just some more silly old woman's talk. Not even worth his taking the time to call me back.*

It was long past sundown when she gave up. The famished, weary woman did what must be done.

She had her meager supper, went to her little bed.

23

THE URGENT VISITATION

Having slipped quickly through that frenzied region where dreams and madness are concocted, Daisy Perika now drifted effortlessly in those dark currents whose silent voids are familiar to the aged and to infants. Her soul was at rest. Until . . .

Someone whispered in her ear.

Wake up, old woman.

Who are you?

Come with me.

Why?

Hurry!

The sleeper felt this *someone* take her by the hand.

Daisy was only dimly aware of getting out of bed, sleep-walking from her bedroom onto the kitchen's cold linoleum floor, opening the trailer door, stepping onto the rickety wooden porch, half-stumbling down the pine steps. She peered through slitted eyelids, shivered in the chilly night air. *This doesn't make any sense . . . I must be dreaming.*

The unseen *someone* tugged urgently at her hand.

Go toward the trees. Hurry.

The old woman opened her eyes. *I'm not asleep—I'm really outside! Well this is crazy—I could freeze to death.* She turned toward her trailer home.

She heard the voice again. There was no more urging— this was a command.

Do NOT go back.

In an effort to shrug off the spell, the annoyed woman spoke aloud. "It's cold out here—I'm going inside."

No. The grip on her hand tightened.

She tried to break free. "You mind your own business—"

Within the thin boundaries of an instant, there was a thunderous quartet of sensations.

A flash of bright, orange light.

A blast of skin-scorching heat.

A horrendous booming.

A gigantic, red-hot hand slapping her. Hard.

Now the old woman was truly unconscious. After a timeless moment, she floated back to the hard surface of physical reality. Daisy could not move. As a few fragmentary concepts coalesced, a singular coherent thought began to form.

I must be dead.

She blinked, waited for her eyes to focus. She stared at the flickering of yellow light reflecting off the bunched needles of a piñon.

If I'm not completely dead, then I must be pretty close to it.

Daisy managed to raise herself on one elbow, moaned at what she saw. A twisted steel skeleton of her trailer was all that remained. Flames leaped and pranced like demented dancers in a hellish ballroom.

Tears puddled up in her eyes. *My home is gone—and all my stuff.*

Weary of this life of sweat and toil, the old woman fell onto her back, stared at an inky sky. She spoke aloud to God.

"Well, that does it. I'm old as the mountains, I've outlived three husbands—the only family I've got left is Charlie Moon, and he don't come out here to see me except on Sundays." *Or when something's broke and needs fixing.* "And now I don't even have a roof over my head."

Daisy closed her eyes to the world. In a croaking voice, she began to sing. "Swing low, sweet chariot . . . comin' for to carry me home." She tried hard to recall the other words to the spiritual. And did. "I looked over Jordan, what did I see . . . a band of angels comin' for me." She swallowed the lump in her throat. "Comin' for to carry me ho-ome."

The tears flowed freely now.

She licked parched lips, sang more loudly—so God would be sure to hear. "Swing low, sweet chariot." She repeated this phrase a dozen times, while mulling over her thoughts.

If Father Raes Delfino gets back in time, he can say some words over me. Aside from Charlie Moon, I wonder how many people will show up at my funeral. Cousin Gorman for sure; he'll be stuffing his face with the free food. And Oscar Sweetwater will probably give a big speech—the tribal chairman don't ever miss a funeral or a chance to shake hands with some voters. And Louise-Marie LaForte will be there, poor old thing—I expect she'll cry buckets for me. I hope Charlie Moon remembers to have me buried in my purple dress. The one with the beads sewed onto the collar with the silver thread. Maybe I should leave a note. She scratched at the sandy ground with her fingernail. It was tedious work, but she kept at it. REMEMBER MY PURPLE DRESS YOU BIG JUG HEAD.

There, that should do it. Daisy continued to sing the song until her throat was dry and scratchy as sandpaper. Finally, she looked at an empty sky. Squinted.

Okay, God—I'm done singing. I am ready to go.

She waited.

And waited.

Dear God, you know how I don't like to complain, but laying out here on this hard ground hurts my back. And in case I forgot to mention it, I don't see no angels or chariot. The sense of being ignored by her Creator weighed heavily on the vain old woman. *Well, then—if you ain't gonna send no angels, maybe I just won't go!* As she considered the possibility of living for another year or two, the notion began to seem not only bearable but downright appealing.

Daisy sniffed, smelled the pungent odor of burned hair. *Oh no. I must be cooked to the bone.* She imagined a face hideously scarred by flames—little children screaming at the sight of her.

Someone spoke to her. "It's nothing to worry about. Just a few blisters." There was a pause before he added: "And your eyebrows and some of your hair got singed off."

It was a familiar voice. She turned to stare at the man squatting beside her, his face illuminated by the flames. "Nahum—is that you?"

He nodded.

For someone who had decided to live a little while longer, his presence was not good news. Nahum Yaciiti had been gone from Middle World for a dozen years—ever since that tornado killed him and most of his sheep. The earlier thought returned to haunt Daisy. *Maybe I'm already dead and just don't know it.* "Nahum—"

"You're not dead."

"You sure?"

The Ute shepherd nodded again.

Daisy reached up to her face, gingerly pinched her cheek. *Maybe he's right. I don't* feel *dead.* Grunting painfully with the effort, she pushed herself up on both elbows. "What happened?"

Firelight flickered in his eyes. "Looks like your place burned down."

She managed to sit up. "I can see that. What I want to know is how—"

"I'd say you're in kind of a fix."

Daisy understood what he meant. *I've got half my hair burnt off. No place to live. Not a bite to eat, no water to drink. It's miles to the nearest neighbor. Charlie Moon won't be here till Sunday, which is three days away.*

"You worried?" Nahum turned to smile at his cantankerous old friend.

"Why should I be?" The tribal elder scowled at the smoldering ruins of her home. "Everything's just dandy."

Angelica Pettibone had departed from the Durango airport only minutes earlier, climbing straight out from runway 20 to an altitude of eight thousand feet. The pilot banked the small aircraft into a gentle eastbound turn, continued her ascent into the crystal-clear night sky. Following her brief call to Flight Service, the filed Visual Flight Rules flight plan was active. Now she dialed the aircraft radio to 118.57 MHz, made the initial call-up to Denver Center, provided her aircraft's call sign.

The controller's response was immediate. "Niner-Mike-Echo, Denver Center. Say request and type aircraft."

She thumbed the microphone switch on the control yoke. "Denver Center, Niner-Mike-Echo is a Cessna 172, en route from Durango to Colorado Springs on VFR flight plan. Request flight-following."

"Niner-Mike-Echo, squawk one-seven-two-three and indent."

The pilot dialed the radar transponder from 1200 to the requested code. "Niner-Mike-Echo squawking one-seven-two-three and *indent*." She pressed the Indent button that would cause her radar blip to "bloom" on the controller's display.

"Niner-Mike-Echo, radar contact twenty-five miles east of Durango."

The pilot was about to respond when her eye caught a glint off to the northwest. She blinked, took another look. *My God—it's a fire.* "Ah, Denver Center, Niner-Mike-Echo has an apparent structure fire in sight on the ground. Estimate it's about five miles northeast of my position." She checked her sectional chart for terrain or other obstacles. Finding none, she banked the aircraft and headed directly for the glow. "Denver Center, Niner-Mike-Echo will overfly the fire to get GPS coordinates."

"Niner-Mike-Echo, no traffic in your area."

Angelica pressed the Flight Plan button on the GPS unit, watched the display switch from the moving map to a text page listing the various waypoints she had selected earlier.

Unseen and unheard by the Ute elder, the sweet chariot swung low over the flames that were licking up the last morsels of Daisy Perika's home.

The pilot dialed the selector knob until the Set Waypoint "soft-button" appeared. Taking due care to maintain her altitude in the mountainous terrain, she pressed the button just as the Cessna passed over the fire. "Denver Center, Niner-Mike-Echo has coordinates for the structure fire."

The controller responded. "Niner-Mike-Echo, Denver Center ready to copy."

FORTY-FOUR MINUTES LATER

Sirens screaming, emergency lights flashing, the first fire truck came rumbling along the dirt lane.

While a half-dozen helmeted firemen sprayed the smoldering residue of Daisy's home, an emergency medical technician tended to the former occupant.

After the enthusiastic EMT had poked and prodded and chatted her way through a preliminary examination—and pronounced her patient fit—she tapped a painted fingernail on the turquoise rectangle dangling from the Ute woman's neck. "That's a real pretty pendant. Where'd you get it?"

What is she talking about? Daisy looked down at the thing. *Well, my goodness.* It was the little telephone Charlie Moon had given her. For use in emergencies. She looked around for Nahum Yaciiti, eager to tell him about this joke on herself. But the shepherd had departed for other pastures.

24

THE SUMMONS

When the telephone jingles in the dead of night, it is always unsettling. Twelve times out of thirteen, it will be a wrong number—some beer-soaked guy calling from Poko's Lounge who wants to talk to his ol' buddy Leo. He refuses to believe this isn't Leo's number. You hang up, he calls you right back. "Hey, Leo ol' buddy—whassup, bro?" There's no way to strangle him without getting out of bed, driving all the way down to Poko's. Maddening. Then there's that thirteenth call. The one that matters.

Charlie Moon rolled over in bed, snatched up the receiver, listened to a terse report of a fire and a survivor. "I'm on my way." He pulled on his jeans and boots, grabbed a shirt and hat, clomped down the stairs and outside into the chilly stillness. The Expedition was moving before he slammed the door. As the big automobile rumbled over the Too Late bridge, roared past the foreman's house, Daisy Bushman woke up, blinked at the clock. "Where on earth is the boss off to at this time of night—and in such a big hurry?" Her husband responded to this query with a grunt and a snore.

A graveyard-shift state policeman stationed along the route reported to his dispatcher that the Columbine flagship was "flying low," but did not give chase. He had heard the radio chatter about the fire out at Daisy Perika's place. The tough cop said a prayer for the old woman. And her nephew.

Skidding to a halt behind a fire truck, Moon was not aware that he had trimmed nine minutes off his previous record from the Columbine to the mouth of *Cañón del Espíritu*. Ignoring the smoking ruins, he took long strides toward the old woman, who was barely enduring the protective presence of a hovering EMT.

When Daisy saw her nephew coming, she curtly dismissed the white woman and got to her feet.

Reaching out for Daisy's shoulders, Moon did a quick inspection. She had some hair singed off, a couple of blisters and a bruise on her cheek—and looked confused. "You all right?"

"I'm okay," she muttered, and pointed a trembling finger. "But look at that!"

He turned toward where her home had been for more than half a century. Little remained that was recognizable. Bucked up in the center, the charred trailer frame resembled the skeleton of a beached whale with a fractured spine. There were bowed rows of steel ribs where the walls had been, a few dangling roof supports, here and there scorched aluminum panels that had crumpled and melted in the intense heat. Litter of various sorts was scattered about. An album of photographs had come to rest on a juniper limb. Daisy's trusty 12-gauge double-barreled shotgun had also been ejected by the blast. Someone had propped it up against the fire truck.

The weary woman shook her gray head. "My home is burnt up, all my stuff is gone." She raised her hands to the heavens. "What am I gonna do?"

Moon had a ready answer for that. "First of all, I'm taking you into town for a good breakfast. Then you're going home with me."

Daisy allowed the young man to deposit her in his automobile.

Moon shut the door, heard a raspy, "Hey!" He turned to see the sooty face of a fireman.

"You her relative?"

Daisy's nephew nodded.

"I'm Dave McDonald, fire chief." The white man craned his neck to look past the tall Ute. "The old lady gonna be all right?"

"Yeah." For the first time since he had been awakened by the telephone call, the rancher managed a weak smile. "She's tough as a two-dollar steak." He frowned at the ruins. "Any idea what started the fire?"

The fire chief followed the Indian's gaze. "The BIA fire inspector'll come out and do a thorough investigation."

The tribal investigator detected a hint of an undercurrent beneath the man's words. "But you already have a notion of your own."

"Yeah," McDonald said. "But it's not official or anything."

"All the same, I'd like to hear what you think."

"I think it's the same old story." He motioned with a jerk of his head. "Come over here, I'll show you."

Moon followed.

McDonald stopped near the remains of the trailer. "See that, how the floor is all pushed up in the middle?"

"Yeah."

The fireman squatted. "See that pipe?"

Moon saw it.

He grinned at the Ute. "You know what that is?"

Moon knew perfectly well. "That's the propane line."

"What's left of it." The professional firefighter picked up a half-melted curtain rod, aimed it at something he found very interesting. "See that fitting?"

Moon nodded dumbly.

McDonald pitched his pointing stick aside. "That joint is

cracked. Probably because some half-wit repairman gave it one twist too many." He tilted his head, stared up at the tall young man. "You got any idea who might've been messing around with her propane line?"

The handyman tried to speak, felt his throat constrict.

The fire chief watched the Ute's face turn to stone. *He either don't know or won't say. Maybe he's covering up for some backyard mechanic. Well, it's not my job to find out. I'll leave the investigation to the BIA fire inspector.* With a grunt, McDonald pushed himself to his feet. "Gas would've leaked out till it displaced most of the air under the trailer." His expression was a bitter mix of sadness and frustration. "Too bad the old lady didn't smell it and call the gas company. They would've sent somebody out to fix it *right.*"

Moon was startled to hear his voice. "What do you think set the gas off?"

McDonald was pleased with the Indian's interest. "It's almost always an electrical spark." He pointed a gloved hand. "Look right over there."

Charlie Moon looked, saw nothing but piles of blackened rubble.

The fire chief explained. "That's the electrical relay that activates from a pressure switch to turn the well pump on. Once the gas-to-air mix was right, a little spark from those relay contacts would act like a detonator." He threw up his arms. "Blow the place sky-high." He turned to look toward the Expedition. "Since it went boom in the middle of the night, she must've been in bed. I wonder how on earth she managed to get out alive." This led to another thought. "I bet she got up in the middle of the night to use the toilet. When she flushed it, the water pressure dropped low enough to turn the well pump on." *Sure. That's bound to be what happened. I'll drop a hint to that red-hot fire inspector—show him he ain't the only one who can figure these things out.*

It seemed like a long drive from Daisy's place to Ignacio, where they would have breakfast. As he stared at the road, Charlie Moon's thoughts ran in the same weary circle.

Maybe the gas fitting I broke wasn't the cause of the fire. It's possible the blaze started in the kitchen stove, or the furnace, or under the water heater. Wherever it started, it would've finally touched off the propane line. Maybe I wasn't to blame. But even if I wasn't, I should've checked that fitting after I tightened it down. But I got distracted when she kicked me on the foot, and then I started talking to Blinkoe and his lawyer. Maybe the gas fitting wasn't actually leaking. . . .

There were miles and miles of silence behind them when Moon finally spoke to the little woman buckled down in the passenger seat. "Can you remember what happened last night?"

Daisy Perika sighed. From time to time, it was a heavy burden, having a nephew who had been an SUPD police officer for years and now was a big-shot tribal investigator. Charlie was always asking pointless questions. "A lot of stuff happened. I got my house burned down and my eyebrows singed off."

Moon slowed, stopped, allowed a crippled dog ample time to cross the road. "When did you realize the place was on fire?"

"I don't know for sure." She rubbed gingerly at the bruise on her face. "I guess it was sometime after the big boom knocked me across the yard, and I had time to come to my senses." Daisy watched the three-legged mongrel disappear into a weed-choked ditch. "And don't you make no smart remarks about my senses."

Moon was in no mood to crack a joke. "Something must've caused you to get out of bed." He recalled what the fire chief had said about the well-pump relay spark igniting the gas under the floor. "Maybe you had to go to the bathroom."

"I don't remember." She shot him a sharp look. "But if I did have to get up and empty my bladder, it's no business of yours."

"Where were you when the explosion—"

"Outside. Just a few steps from the porch."

She must have woken up when she smelled smoke or saw the flames. "What were you doing outside?"

Daisy looked out the window at the moving scenery, watched a straight-backed troop of pines march by. "Somebody woke me up, took me by the hand, led me outside."

Moon stepped on the brake, pulled off the road, parked in front of Goodall's Feed and Grain Store. "Who?"

She blinked, gave him a puzzled, innocent look. "Who what?"

He had played this game before. "Who woke you up, took you by the hand?"

Daisy looked at the back of her wrinkled hand. "Oh, it was Nahum Yaciiti."

He stared at her. "Nahum, huh?"

She felt a hunger pang. "I think I'll have three scrambled eggs for breakfast. And two biscuits."

Moon pulled back onto the blacktop, shook his head. Nahum Yaciiti was dead and gone. Had been for some years now. Dead, that is. But as far as Daisy was concerned—not gone.

At Angel's Cafe, Daisy Perika was grateful to realize that the story about the fire had not yet hit town. Otherwise all kinds of sad-eyed folks would have been patting and consoling her and saying things like you poor thing and ain't that just an awful shame. She ordered the Cowboy Special. Three eggs, two pork-sausage patties, a heap of home fries, biscuits and gravy.

Having taken care of the cranky old lady, the morning waitress turned her attention to the skinny Ute. *Charlie looks like he just buried his best friend.* Peggy readied the ballpoint pen. "What'll you have, honey?"

Charlie Moon didn't look up at the sweet-talker. "Coffee."

More times than she could remember, Peggy had brought this man breakfasts that would have satisfied a starved lumberjack. "Coffee—that's all?"

He nodded, stared blankly.

Charlie Moon's not hungry—well, now I've seen every-thing and I'm ready to die. The waitress hurried away.

Daisy studied her nephew's solemn face. "Charlie, you don't need to worry about me. I'm not one of those soft town-Indians that live on sugar cookies and soda pop." Her dark eyes flashed with determination. "I've got the *old* blood running through my veins. Our ancestors went through wars and starvations and plagues." She forced a half-smile. "Even fires." The hard-faced woman leaned over the table, clenched her nephew's arm. "When times was bad, the People suffered. Some of 'em died. That's just the way the world is. But those that was able would put one foot in front of the other—and keep right on going. And that's exactly what I intend to do."

Moon took her gnarled skeleton-hand in his. "I know you'll be all right." *I'll make sure of it.*

25

STARTING OVER

Daisy Perika's first day at the Columbine was a bustle of moving-in activity, and being the center of attention, the displaced woman hardly had a moment to herself. Pete Bushman felt compelled to follow the Ute elder around, "help" her put odd bits of furniture into her new bedroom, hang framed pictures on the wall, and offer all sorts of sage advice about how to adapt to the rigors of the ranching life. The foreman's wife loaned Daisy a portable television, fussed over her with hugs and kisses and comforting words until she felt suffocated by Dolly Bushman's well-meant sympathies.

Charlie Moon spent the day at the ruins of his aunt's home at the mouth of *Cañón del Espíritu.* He returned with a collection of items that had survived the fire. Shutting herself into the privacy of her downstairs bedroom, Daisy watched *Oprah* in the afternoon, whiled away the evening hours with faded family photographs, jars of canned fruit and vegetables, plastic bags of multicolored beads, the fine buckskin drum that had hung on her kitchen wall for decades, the shotgun she had once used to shoot at a UFO, and a Tennessee Forge cast-iron skillet. She examined each small treasure with considerable pleasure before storing it on a closet shelf, in a chest of drawers, or under the bed.

On the second day, her nephew took her into town to shop for clothing and other such necessities as she might require. Charlie paid the bills.

On the third day, Charlie left her alone with instructions to call on Dolly Bushman if she needed anything she could not find. This provided Daisy with an opportunity to explore the big log house that was her nephew's home and the hub of the Columbine Ranch. She would pause now and then to murmur and sigh about the part of her life that was forever lost.

On the afternoon of the fourth day, Daisy took an egg-and-bacon sandwich to the porch, seated herself on a cedar bench. The sun was rolling down the slope of an alpine peak, into the saddle of Dead Mule Notch. A breeze off the river was balmy and sweet with purple-aster perfume. She leaned back against the wall, took a bite of the tasty snack. *Egg sandwiches are good. Especially with a layer of crispy bacon. And a little touch of ketchup.* She was evidently not alone in this opinion—before she had taken a second bite, a startling event demolished her appetite.

What happened was this: While the succulent sandwich was clutched in her hand, eighty-six pounds of Something Big and Hairy came thumpity-thumping across the porch, arched its way over her lap, snatched her snack in a pair of toothy jaws, vanished in a flash of hind legs.

This caused the poor old soul to lose control of her bladder—and let out a horrific screech, as if she had discovered a centipede doing the jitterbug in her ear.

Charlie Moon burst through the door. "What's the matter!"

When she found her voice, Daisy managed to yell: "My sandwich—big [expletives deleted] ugly [expletives deleted]—took it right out of my [expletives deleted] hand—"

Her nephew committed two errors: (1) He laughed. (2) Too loudly.

Big jug head. Daisy got up from the bench, gave him a sharp kick in the shin.

The main force of this blow was absorbed by his thick horsehide boot.

Charlie eased the fighting-mad woman back onto the bench, seated himself beside her. "There's nothing to be scared of." He gave her a comforting hug. "The was just ol' Sidewinder."

"I'm not blind as a cave bat." She pointed toward where the animal had skedaddled. "That wasn't no rattlesnake!"

He agreed that no serpent had pinched her food. Sidewinder was, in point of fact, a canine creature. More specifically, a dog. A normally placid, God-fearing hound—who became an outright terrorist when food was around.

As far as Daisy was concerned, this had to be Charlie Moon's fault. She inquired whether the desperate beast was starving, and if so, why wasn't he fed?

Moon explained. "Sidewinder has his own kind of ethics—he hates to accept handouts. He prefers to steal what he eats."

Daisy offered the opinion that if that dog ever tried to take food from her mouth again, he would end up eating buckshot.

Her nephew made her another egg-and-bacon sandwich.

The lady had this meal at the kitchen table.

Following this incident, things calmed down a bit.

But the days were long and lonely.

Charlie Moon's absences from the Columbine became more frequent. He would leave with the sunrise, return home when the stars twinkled over the mountains.

Having little else to do, Daisy became curious about her nephew's cattle business. Suppertime questions about his various activities were met with shrugs and mumbles. There were "lots of things to look after." "Seems like if it ain't one thing it's another." "Went to see a man about some hardware." "Had another meeting with the county agent." And other such uninformative generalities. Realizing that a busy rancher had plenty of work to do, she gradually stopped asking questions. But little by little, the old woman began to feel less like a member of the household than a bothersome guest. *If Father Raes hadn't gone off to Italy, I'd have somebody to talk to. I bet he has breakfast every morning with the Pope. Or at least a cardinal.*

There was one minor consolation. Every evening, at precisely ten o'clock, the telephone in the ranch-house parlor would ring. (Nine fifty-nine P.M. was when Louise-Marie LaForte's daily dose of television enlightenment concluded; the dreadful evening news was "more than a poor sold soul like me can bear.") If Charlie Moon happened to be at home, he ignored this particular call. Daisy would take the instrument to a rocking chair, press it against her ear, listen to the French-Canadian woman's voice.

"Hello, hello," Louise-Marie would say. "Is anybody on the line?"

"No," Daisy would answer in a monotone. "This is a recorded voice. At the beep, please put two quarters in the slot. *Beep!*" Or some such silly thing.

"Daisy, is that you?"

"No," she'd say. "This is Doris Day." Or Orphan Annie. Or Kermit the Frog. Or some such foolishness.

"Ha-ha," would be the inevitable reply. "Daisy—you are such a card!"

And then the old friends would get down to chewing over the business of the past twenty-four hours.

On the tenth morning, Daisy stood at the parlor window, watched Charlie Moon pull away in his old Ford pickup. The boss was followed by Pete Bushman in a Jeep, little Butch in a huge fire-engine-red F-350, the Wyoming Kyd in a GMC flatbed truck that was loaded with tools and a crew of sleepy-eyed cowboys. *They're probably going off to mend a fence somewhere. Not that my nephew would bother to tell me.* Daisy set her jaw. *I have got to stop worrying about what Charlie is doing every day. I need to find something to do myself.* She rolled a few notions over in her mind, decided that for starters a nice long walk would be just the right medicine. The dust from the Columbine caravan had hardly settled when she got hold of her walking stick, headed for the back door. *That pushy Bushman woman may come looking for me.* This thought put some pepper into her stride.

Before she got her foot on the ground, Daisy had decided on a destination.

A few steps from the porch, Sidewinder materialized by her side.

Daisy scowled at the ugly dog. "Shoo," she said, swatting at him with the stick.

The hound sidestepped the intended blow and—just out of the reach of her staff—continued on his zigzagging, stopping-to-sniff dogtrot. Sidewinder even cast her an affectionate glance. The crotchety old animal seemed quite pleased to be with the crotchety old woman.

After a hundred paces or so, when her guard was down, the dog moved closer.

She was startled to feel something wet and warm take a droolish lap at her hand.

Daisy knew when she was licked. *Oh well. At least he'll be some company.*

It took the aged woman a considerable chunk of morning to make her way up a rock-strewn ridge's modest grade, pass through a hushed glade of evergreens, ferns, and mosses, finally emerge on the fringe of a grassy, flowered skirt. A mile away—or was it ten?—an alpine lake pretended to be a pool of molten glass. Raising a hand to shield her eyes from the sun, Daisy gazed at a sturdy log cabin that was nestled among a picturesque grove of aspen and spruce. This was the nice little place Charlie Moon had provided for Father Raes during his retirement. *And what does that fussy little priest do then? Stay here, so I can come pay him a visit when I take a notion? No, he goes off to some foreign land to hang around with people that don't even speak American.*

Daisy knew something that every member of her gender eventually came to understand—you simply cannot depend on a man. When you need them the most, they are gone fishing with an oafish drinking buddy, off to fight a war, or paying a call on the Pope.

But it was not only the priest's inexcusable absence or the unreliability of men in general. For days, something else had been gnawing at her—an injury she could not quite forget, and what was worse—she could not quite remember! Not until this very moment. Daisy stopped in her tracks. Of course.

During all her time on the Columbine, Charlie had not said one solitary word about the urgent telephone message she had left for him. *Maybe he don't care where that Blinkoe woman is hiding.* She raised her stick, took a hearty whack at a winged grasshopper, which fluttered away unharmed. *Or maybe he already knows where she is.* But another, more hurtful possibility was what galled her. *He doesn't think I know anything worth hearing about. Far as Charlie's concerned, I'm just a silly old woman who pays too much attention to dreams and visions.* And, of course, to the *pitukupf*. Her nephew did not even believe in the existence of the dwarf, much less that a tribal elder could learn important things by listening to what the little man had to say. Daisy wished she could think of some way to teach her smart-aleck nephew a lesson. A clump of gray clouds was settling over the mountains, threatening wind and rain, so she turned her face toward the ranch headquarters. Sensing her intention, the hound led the way. As she plodded along, the sly old plotter considered several possibilities, dismissed them all as either unworkable or unlikely to impress her nephew.

When a boisterous chorus of lightning legs tap-danced thunderously along the Buckhorn peaks, she had the inspiration. Oblivious to the dog waiting a few paces away and to the patter of rain on her back, Daisy paused on the ridge above the Columbine headquarters. A mischievous smile creased her wrinkled face. *Yes. That's exactly what I'll do.*

That evening, just before ten P.M., the Ute woman was standing by the current version of Mr. Bell's invention, waiting for it to make the usual noise. It did. She snatched it up, waited for the familiar voice.

"Hello, hello, is anyone on the line?"

Daisy imitated a girlish tone. "This is Mexican Jack's Pizza Parlor—may we take your order?"

"Daisy, is that you?"

"No." She snickered. "This is Mexican Jack."

"Ha-ha. Daisy—you are such a card!"

She took the telephone into her bedroom, seated herself on a comfortable chair. "Louise-Marie, do you still have that old black rattle-trap you call a car?"

There was a tense silence before the answer came. "Well, yes I do but—"

"Does it still run?"

"I suppose so, but I hardly ever drive it anymore. Not since I had my operation and—"

"Listen to me, Louise-Marie. There's something we have to do—something *really important*." She lowered her voice to a husky whisper. "I want you to show up at Charlie's ranch at nine o'clock tomorrow morning." Her nephew was always gone by that time of day. "And I don't want to hear none of your sissy excuses." That old white woman was such a scaredy-cat. If all the Europeans had been like her, Columbus would still be sitting on a dock somewhere in Spain, whittling little pine boats for Japanese tourists.

Louise-Marie responded in a whinish tone. "But, Daisy dear, it's been so long that I don't even remember how to find my way there and besides—"

"If you'll stop interrupting and let me slip a word in edgewise, I'll tell you exactly how to get from there to here." The happy conspirator proceeded to do this, and with gusto. Giving directions to the timid and confused—this was Daisy's long suit.

26

GETTING EVEN

As Daisy Perika had expected, Charlie Moon and his crew of cowboy-roughnecks left the Columbine at sunrise. She took a wool blanket and a mug of black coffee outside. Having seated herself on a comfortable birch rocking chair that faced the morning end of the porch, she pulled the blanket over her shoulders. As the warm sunlight slipped along the pastures, she sipped at the steaming black brew, hoped Louise-Marie would show up on time.

A bluebird winged her way by, found a perch on a spindly willow branch.

In the barn down by the river, an energetic mare kicked at her stall.

A westerly breeze playfully rolled a tumbleweed across the yard.

Daisy enjoyed all of these blessings.

Sidewinder popped his head up just long enough to peek over the floor of the porch.

The Ute woman pretended not to notice the furtive movement. She removed a biscuit-and-sausage-and-something-else sandwich from her apron pocket. Held it under her nose. "Mmmm. That sure smells good." She smacked her lips. "But I think I'll save it for later. Right now, I'll just sit here and enjoy my coffee." With a theatrical air of utter carelessness, she laid the tasty treat on a straight-backed chair beside her.

She counted off a minute. Then another. Then . . .

The head popped back up again. And just as quickly down.

When the occasion demanded it, Patience was a virtue the old woman could call to her service.

The present faded to past.

Sunlight moved along the redwood planks, stopped to warm her feet.

Underneath the porch, there was a barely perceptible grunting, also a curious bumping and thumping.

Her lips curled into a wry smile. *He's gonna slip up behind me.* The crafty old woman put her coffee mug on the floor, closed her eyes, began to rock. She imagined herself singing in the choir at St. Ignatius. *Amazing Grace—how sweet the sound. That saved a wretch li-iike me.*

There was no further indication of movement under the plank floor.

Daisy suddenly felt the hound's hard stare on the back of her neck. And with her eyes still shut, she saw something that made her skin tingle. What she saw was *herself.* From behind. It was like an old moving picture, in black-and-white. The vision was somewhat fuzzy at the edges, but she could clearly make out the back of the rocking chair, her old gray head, a square post supporting the porch roof. The shaman was fascinated by the singular vision. *It's like I'm seeing through that dog's eyes.*

Sidewinder watched. Waited.

Gradually the woman's vision faded.

Daisy began to sing out loud. "Through many dan-gers, toils and snares, I have already come . . ."

The beast, who took some pleasure in hymns, pricked his ears. After she had been there *ten thousand years* he decided it was high time to make his move. And move he did. Up onto the porch in a single bound went the hound, head and shoulders slung low, six long strides, mouth open wide, hind legs kicking off jackrabbit-style in a powerful leap—the straight-backed chair went a-crashing and a-tumbling.

Daisy threw up her hands in mock alarm, wailed: "Oh my red garters—what was *that*? Was it a big mountain lion—a terrible gray wolf?—a thunderbolt straight from the top of Black Mountain?"

The dog slid to a halt at the end of the porch, turned toward the object of the carefully planned assault. The biscuit-and-egg-and-something-else sandwich was clamped in his mouth. The canine's eyes laughed at the old woman.

"Why no," Daisy said with a hooting laugh, "it was only an ugly, stupid old food-stealing dog." She shot her victim a poisonous look. Precisely what *something-else* was—was known only to the cook.

Seasoning.

More specifically, three heaping tablespoons of extra-hot ground red cayenne pepper. One pinch was enough to season a big iron pot of pinto beans or keep the fleas out of your socks. One teaspoonful was enough to fell an ox. She waited for the symptoms. The dog would gag, she thought, then froth at the mouth. *Maybe fall down and go into spasms and convulsions. Maybe even die. That'd teach him a lesson he wouldn't forget.* Daisy was a hard woman.

Sidewinder wolfed the sandwich down. Trotted across the porch to where the human being was seated. Licked her hand.

The red pepper remnants burned the skin on her fingers.

But she had faith in her diabolical concoction. *He swallowed it before he got a good taste. But sooner or later, somewhere down inside his gullet, it'll hit him like a red-hot coal.* In a fit of hopeful whimsy, she imagined the thieving animal doing a couple of backflips before he dragged himself down to the river to gulp down ten or twenty gallons of water. *Any second now.*

The seconds ticked away.

The dog, locally famous for eating watermelon rinds, old rubber tires, even lumps of anthracite, stood there for quite some time, trading expectant stares with the disappointed woman.

Are you a real animal—or some kind of skin-walker with dog hide stretched over your bones? In the shaman's world, stranger things had happened. Finally, the human being blinked.

Having stared Daisy down, Sidewinder stretched himself out beside her rocking chair. He slipped off into a delightful dream where his newly arrived benefactor appeared with a heaping tray of the delicious sandwiches. Deep in sleep, the hound licked his lips.

27

ON THE ROAD AGAIN

Daisy heard a painful grinding and coughing. Disappointed to determine that it was not the dog, she turned in her chair. *That sounds almost like a car.*

It was. An almost-car.

The venerable Oldsmobile rattled the heavy boards on Too Late bridge. Pulling a billow of dust along behind, the black automobile made a wide U-turn, stopped beside Charlie Moon's Expedition.

Roused from his sleep, the hound blinked with moderate curiosity at the tiny white woman who emerged from the vehicle.

While her friend approached the porch, Daisy rocked.

Louise-Marie LaForte was walking with the aid of a cane. A white patch was taped over her left eye.

"You're late," Daisy said.

"I'm sorry, dear." Louise-Marie leaned against the porch,

looked up at the enthroned Indian woman. "It's been so long since I was here, that even with your directions I got all bumfuzzled and befuddled. I had to stop a dozen times and ask people where I was. One smart-aleck little boy told me I was in Little Rock, Arkansas." She cast a quick glance at the hound. "I've been so curious about what's on your mind that I hardly got a wink of sleep last night. Now tell me—where are we going?"

Daisy got up from her chair. "I'll tell you after we're on the road." She gave the white woman an appraising gaze. "You look like something that just crawled out of a coffin—you been sick?"

Louise-Marie nodded. "You know about my hip replacement last November. Well, in January my sugar diabetes started giving me fits. In March my liver turned my skin yellow, and right after that I had a bad attack of colonitis." Recalling problematic kidneys, gallbladder, and spleen, she continued with the defective-organ recital. "Then, just last week, I had a cataract removed." She pointed at her *good* eye, which had a distinctly milky appearance. "If I come along all right, the doctor will take this one out right after Thanksgiving."

Gripping her oak walking stick, Daisy eased herself down the porch steps. "With you crippled and three-quarters blind, I don't know if it's safe for me to ride with you."

The driver shrugged this off. "Oh, I do all right."

Sidewinder trotted along ahead of them.

Daisy pointed her stick at the rear bumper. "Isn't that a new license plate?"

Louise-Marie's head rocked in a slow nod. "Ever since the Ignacio town police started fussing at me about having a fifty-year-old plate on my car, I put a new one on every month."

The Ute woman gave the *matukach* motorist a look. "I thought they only had to be changed once a year."

"I wouldn't know about that. But my late husband collected plates from all forty-eight states—"

"I got news for you, Louise-Marie—there's fifty states in the union."

"Oh, that's right—I keep forgetting. Anyway, he had plates from Alaska and Hawaii too, and some foreign countries. Out in the garage, I've got dozens and dozens of 'em, so first day of every month, I take one plate off and put another one on." As she pointed at the current selection, there was an unmistakable sparkle of pride in her eye. "That one there is from Mexico."

Daisy shook her head. "The cops catch you tootling around with a Mexican plate, they'll take away your driver's license quick as a shot."

"Hah—I'd sure like to see 'em do that!"

"Oh, right," Daisy said. "You never did get a driver's license."

This conversation was interrupted by an urgent sound. It was a keening whine, which might have been either a failing gas turbine or a windmill calling for lubrication.

The women gave the hound the desired attention.

He ruffed up a little bark.

Louise-Marie leaned to pat him on the head. "Poor old poochy-poo—what does oo want?"

"Probably a red-hot tamale with a side of Tabasco sauce," Daisy said. *Or maybe a glass of ice water.* It was never too late to hope.

Sidewinder gave the Ute woman a peculiar look. Something odd glinted in his eyes. Something like intelligence, only better.

Almost mesmerized, Daisy was holding her breath. *He is talking to me. But not with words . . . with pictures.* The better to see them, she closed her eyes. What she saw more clearly now was the hound. But Sidewinder was not standing in front of her. The beast was in the Oldsmobile as it sped down the road, his homely head hanging out the window, tongue flapping in the breeze like a black flag!

Louise-Marie watched this silent intercourse with a delightful shiver of apprehension. *I do believe that Daisy is falling into one of her trances.* Two seconds later, unable to bear the suspense any longer, she tugged at the Ute elder's sleeve. "What is it?"

Startled, Daisy took a moment to compose herself, then smiled at the brute. "He wants to come along."

Disappointed at such a minor revelation, the owner of the vehicle shook her head. "I don't like to have animals in my automobile. He might decide to move his bowels or something and—"

"Sidewinder is car-trained." Daisy opened the rear door, pitched her walking stick onto the floor.

The animal climbed inside, sniffed at this and that, stretched his rangy frame across the backseat, yawned to show a mouth bristling with formidable teeth.

Accepting this latest defeat, Louise-Marie scooted herself behind the wheel. The small woman took some time to get situated on the stack of pillows that raised her just enough to see under the top rim of the steering wheel. She cast a Cyclops glance at her friend, who had gotten into the passenger seat. "Daisy, you should get yourself a car and learn to drive it."

This suggestion being too foolish to waste a word on, the Ute woman responded with a snort.

"Now just watch what I do," Louise-Marie said with a pedantic air. "First, I make sure this gear gizmo is in P. Then, I put my foot on the brake thingy." She pointed at her right foot. "You see where it is—right next to the gas thingy."

"I don't need to see no *thingies*," Daisy snapped. "You're doing the driving. Me, I'm just along for the ride." But she was watching her friend's every move.

"Then I turn the key—see those little needles jump up?" More pointing. "That's how much gas we've used, and that one's the oil something-or-other, and that's the T—which has something to do with the tires, and that's the Bat, which I have never figured out. And this big needle in the middle—it tells us how fast we're going."

"Is there anything that'll tell me how long I've got to sit here before you get this jalopy moving?"

Ignoring the snide remark, Louise-Marie started the engine. "Now, with my foot still on the brake thingy, I'll put the gear gizmo into D, which makes it go forward." *I don't know why they didn't call it F.* She pulled the lever. There was a slight lurch as the engine engaged the automatic transmission. She continued to give freely from her store of knowledge and experience. "The one thing I always do, is never put it into R, because that'll make it go backwards." *Which should be labeled B.* She set her chin. "Always Go Forward, that's my motto."

Daisy muttered a tart remark about where the widow LaForte could go. Her and all her kin. She had the good manners to use the Ute language.

The French-Canadian woman was oblivious to all but her demonstration of automotive locomotion. "Now watch what happens when I take my foot off the brake." The car began to move forward. Slowly. She gripped the steering wheel with both hands. "And you steer with this."

Daisy snorted. "Any fool knows that."

"One would assume so," the driver said. "I just wanted to make sure." She allowed herself the faintest hint of a smile.

Suspecting that she had just suffered an insult, Daisy scowled at her teacher.

Taking an interest in the goings-on in cockpit, Sidewinder hung his paws over the front seat.

Louise-Marie steered the car in a wide circle, looping around a cottonwood tree. "Now I'll put my foot on the gas. But oh, so gently."

The car accelerated. Oh, so gently.

Despite herself, Daisy was becoming interested in a procedure she had previously ignored. It did seem to be awfully simple. *And anything Louise can do, I could do twice as good.* A dreamy look slipped over her wrinkled face. *If I had my life to live over, I'd learn to drive a car. Maybe even a motorcycle.* She closed her eyes, the better to see a striking image of herself. Nineteen years old, slim and shapely, shiny black boots, tight yellow slacks, brown leather jacket sparkling with a hundred silver studs. Perched on a big red Harley, going ninety miles an hour down the Alamosa Straight. Big smile flashing like the midday sun, black hair flying in the wind. It was something grand to behold.

The elderly motorists motorized slowly down the lane.

Louise-Marie turned to beam encouragement at her reluctant pupil. "You see how easy it is? And it's never too late to learn."

As it happened, they were approaching Too Late Creek.

At the very instant the front tires rumbled onto the bridge, the hound licked Louise-Marie on her right ear.

The startled lady squealed. "Haaa-eee!"

The Olds responded to a vigorous twist of the steering wheel, sideswiped the sturdy pine railing.

Daisy grabbed for something to hold on to, prayed to God to save her from a plunge into the cold waters.

They passed over the bridge with nothing more than another dent on the fender.

On the other side, the driver chuckled. "That dog sure did surprise me." *Almost as much as in the fifth grade, when Elmer Hooper kissed me in the cloakroom. I wonder whatever happened to Elmer after he went off to barber school—*

Daisy slapped her hand on the dashboard. "Stop the car!"

Louise-Marie pushed the brake thingy to the floor. "What?"

"Get out."

"But why—"

The Ute woman was already scooting across the seat. "Because from here on out, I am doing the driving."

Earlier, when Louise-Marie LaForte had passed by the foreman's residence on her way to the Columbine headquarters, Dolly Bushman had been running the noisy vacuum cleaner. This being the case, the foreman's wife was unaware that Daisy had a visitor. The worn carpet was moderately clean now, and Dolly had other chores on her mind. For the last few minutes, she had been stalking a hyperactive fly. Now it was on the window screen. *Got you this time, you nasty little fiend . . . now hold still while I lower the boom.* She was about to swat the grown-up maggot into oblivion when she noticed something coming down the lane from the Too Late bridge. The black car was going so slowly that she was certain it was going to stop. *Who in the world could that be?* For the moment, she forgot about the pesky insect. Though the Oldsmobile was moving in an odd, jerking fashion—as if it might expire on the spot—it did not stop. Dolly watched as the vehicle lurched uncertainly by her house. *Well I declare, I must be seeing things . . . that looks like Charlie's aunt at the wheel. Oh, Lord—what is she up to now?* The practical woman made an instant decision. *Well, whatever's going on, I don't want to know anything about it.* She closed her eyes.

The fly executed a tight figure eight, came to sit on the swatter. Then on her nose.

28

SOUL MATES

Though the captain of the hijacked Oldsmobile was beginning to regret having yielded her ship to this mutinous old pirate, Louise-Marie LaForte remained outwardly placid. From time to time, she offered helpful words of encouragement. "For someone who's never drove a car before, you are doing fairly well." When the lurching of the vehicle began to make her feel nauseous, she offered thoughtful instructions. "It isn't actually necessary to pump the gas up and down to get the fuel to the motor. Just try and hold it steady."

By the time they were approaching the highway end of the miles-long ranch lane, Daisy's confidence was increasing. *I think I'm getting the hang of the thing.* The speedometer indicated that she was going slightly in excess of twenty miles per hour. The intersection with the paved road was coming up fast. She turned her head to look at the white woman's patched eye. "Now tell me again, how do you slow this thing down?"

Louise-Marie shrieked: "Look out!"

The driver turned her face back to the windshield, discovered that the sneaky machine had decided to head off in another direction. Directly in front of the hood was something like a tree. Only it wasn't. It was one of the massive redwood beams that supported the arch over the Columbine entrance. Instinctively, Daisy jerked the wheel. Her instincts were not well seasoned. She had jerked it the wrong way. As they plowed through a fence, two strands of barbed wire scraped over the hood, up the windshield, over the roof. The old car bumped along, dived into a shallow ditch, surfaced on the other side.

Her jaw set like stone, Daisy held on to the steering wheel. Closed her eyes.

Louise-Marie was screaming something about Judgment Day and Lord Have Mercy.

Having never enjoyed such sport, the hound was howling a joyful note.

When Daisy opened her eyes, she was astonished to see the blacktop highway stretching out in front of her. A sign on the shoulder informed passersby that Granite Creek was sixty-two miles away. *Well, that wasn't so bad. And it sounds like the motor's still going.* She pressed her foot on the accelerator. The car gave a wheezy cough, started moving.

The French-Canadian woman had collapsed on the seat. "Oh," she said. "Oh, oh. What happened?"

"Nothing happened," Daisy snapped. "I just took a short-cut." *What a prissy old sissy.*

Louise-Marie raised herself, opened the eye that was not patched. "Oh, look—my poor hood is all scratched!"

"Don't worry about it," Daisy piped back. "When we get to town, I'll buy you a brush and some paint. Red, maybe." Daisy imagined Louise-Marie painting the old black car red. Red like a woodpecker's head. Daisy sang the words out loud. "Red like a woodpecker's head—red like a woodpecker's head—la la la!"

Louise-Marie turned her head a full ninety degrees, fixed an uneasy stare on the driver. *It has finally happened—she has completely lost her mind.*

Daisy began to cackle. Life in this tired old world was what you made it. Go by the recipe they gave you, it could turn out to be pretty flat. But add enough salt and pepper . . . *This is going to be a fine day.*

Though Daisy was not aware of it, not so far down the road a kindred spirit waited.

If she had known about this other soul (whose name rhymed with "Rocks") she might have put the Oldsmobile in R and backed up all the way back to the Columbine. What she did know was that the road was smooth and long and straight. It called to her. *Roll on, Mamma.* Daisy rolled. Not too slow. Not too fast. But as the bald tires sang a siren's whining song on the blacktop, the Detroit City automobile put the miles behind it.

As they were approaching the outskirts of Granite Creek, Louise-Marie opened her mouth to speak. "Daisy, dear—I think you'd better pull over. I need a few minutes to do something."

The driver was in no mood to slow down, much less stop. "Whatever it is can wait till we get there."

"Get where?"

Daisy loved a mystery. "Where we're going."

"I can't wait that long."

"You got to pee?"

"No. My sugar's going up."

She is more trouble than a sack full of skunks. "How do you know that?"

"I just know." There were the usual signs. Louise-Marie had a slight headache; little green-and-yellow spots floated in front of her eye. She assumed a forceful tone. "Now you pull over and stop, so I can give myself a shot."

THE COPS

On the very best day of their lives, Officers Eddie "Rocks" Knox and E. C. "Piggy" Slocum were not among Granite Creek's finest. As they motored along in the GCPD black-and-white, they were not even close to the median.

Though fearless to a fault, Knox had no sense of balance. He was, in a word, reckless. In another word, dangerous.

Slocum was a sweet, guileless man who would go out of his way to help an elderly lady cross a busy street. Whether she wanted to go or not. He did not even slightly resemble the hard-eyed heroic type. It was as if he had absorbed all of the fear that would not stick to Knox.

Together, they did not compensate for each other's short-comings. Combined, they were a menace of misguided energies and misconceptions. Chief of Police Scott Parris was well aware of this pair of personnel problems. More than once, he had placed Knox with a sensible partner who (it was fervently hoped) would keep him out of trouble, and Slocum with an officer who had plenty of common sense. It never worked out. No one could work with either of them longer than a few days. And so the misfits were destined to ride in the same unit.

It was Piggy's day to drive, his partner's duty to procure necessary refreshment. Knox had visited the Mountain Man Bar and Grille to purchase half a dozen Lead Life Savers, which was what the manager of that establishment had dubbed the one-pound, deep-fried, sugar-encrusted dough-nuts. These tasty pastries were a favorite of cops, long-haul truckers, and backsliding dieters who were determined to commit caloricide. Having just returned from this errand, Knox was opening the passenger door of Unit 144 when he saw the classic automobile pass by. He slipped inside, dropped the bag of delectables on the floor, pointed. "Follow that car."

Piggy's little eyes were focused on the greasy doughnut bag. "Why?"

"Don't *why* me, Pig—just get after that old heap." Knox

fastened his shoulder strap. "But you can take it from me, those are bad guys."

The driver countered in a petulant whine. "First, can I have me a doughnut?"

Knox hated whiners. Especially chubby whiners. "The city's work comes before your belly."

Though he considered this a totally absurd thing to say, Piggy pulled 144 out onto the highway.

"Look," Knox muttered, "it's already slowing down. They've spotted our black-and-white. I told you these was bad guys."

The doughnut-deprived cop hoped not. He hated confrontations. Especially with motorists who were likely to be armed. Such folk were not afraid of you, might even be spoiling for a fight. "You want me to switch on the emergency lights?"

"Negative on that." Knox had a demented glint in his eye. "We don't want to spook 'em. Just stay back fifty yards or so."

Piggy's face twisted with concentration. "How much is that in car lengths?"

Why do I have to spend five days a week with a dimwit? "Half a football field."

"Oh, right." He slowed. "Hey, look, Eddie—I think it's going to stop."

Knox did his lopsided C. Eastwood grin. "Close in a little bit."

Piggy moved in on the Olds, squinted at the suspect vehicle. "Eddie, that looks like a Messican plate to me."

"Hah—what'd I tell you. It'll be some Juarez dope pushers."

The driver did not like the sound of this. "It might just be some tourists—"

"Tourists my ankle bone—you watch what happens when I call in the plate." Eddie Knox thumbed the microphone button, forwarded the alphanumeric information to dispatch.

Dispatch keyed the data into a Sun Microsystems terminal, clicked Retrieve with the optical mouse. The response flashed on the screen in four seconds flat. The FBI data bank—which contained every current license-plate number in the Western Hemisphere and most of Europe—had no such plate listed. Not in Mexico. Not in Lithuania.

Knox grinned at his partner. "What'd I tell you?"

"Golly, Eddie. I don't see how anybody could have a plate that wasn't on the computer."

"Well, it's clear enough to me—these slickers made that plate themselves. Which proves they are outlaws of one kind or another." He unholstered his service revolver, checked the cylinder, snapped it shut again. "This could be something big, Pig. Maybe they're not Mexicans at all. Could be a crew of rag-head terrorists that slipped over the border into El Paso. Or Chinese spies scoping out our air-force base. Or a Colombian drug kingpin and his armed-to-the-teeth driver." Knox preferred the latter. Drug dealers were what floated on sewage. Either way, the end of the thing was likely to be a bloody shootout. He echoed Daisy Perika's sentiment. *This is going to be a fine day.*

Piggy was gripping the wheel with white knuckles. "Listen, I think we should—"

"This is no time for *thinking*." There was a flinty edge to Eddie Knox's voice, a flat rattlesnake look on his face. "This is a time for action."

The driver gulped. "What should we tell dispatch?"

"Forget dispatch, Pig. We can handle this business all by ourselves." Knox switched off the communications console.

29

CLOSE ENCOUNTER OF THE WORST KIND

Daisy Perika pulled the Oldsmobile off the pavement, onto a graveled space in front of the Ford dealership. "Where is that brake thing you step on?"

Louise-Marie LaForte's head was pounding now. "It's right to the left of the gas thingy."

Daisy frowned at the floorboard. *Right to the left?* But she found it. Put her foot on it. The car came to a halt.

"Now put the gear gizmo in P, which is for Pause."

"Put what gizmo where for what?"

Louise-Marie was searching her purse for medical supplies. "The lever with the little white knob on it—push it up from D to P."

Daisy did this. *That wasn't hard. I should've learned to drive years ago.* She rested her hands on the steering wheel. *I could save up part of my Social Security. Why, in no time flat, I could buy my own car and—*

There was a sudden tapping on the window.

Startled, Daisy turned her head to look.

A big, ugly face looked back at her. A policeman's face. He made a rotating motion with his finger.

What does he want?

She heard his bullfrog voice through the glass. "Roll the window down."

This was an automobile without buttons to push. It actually had a roll-down window. Daisy found the handle, performed the operation flawlessly.

The cop gave them the eye, felt a pang of disappointment. *Just a couple of old biddies.* But there was something funny about that Mexican license plate. He grinned at the dark-skinned woman. *I wonder if she speaks any American.* "Good day, señora. Could I have a look at your driver's license?"

Hardly knowing what to say in a situation of this kind, the driver did not respond.

She probably don't talk nothing but Mexican. The better to bridge the language gap, he shouted in her ear: "I need to see your operator's license!"

Daisy jumped. "Don't you yell at me."

She sounds more like an Indian than a Mexican. Knox lowered his voice to its normal stone-shattering level. "Your driver's license, please."

Fast thinking under stress was the Ute elder's specialty. "I am a citizen of a sovereign Native American nation—I don't need to show you my license." One fabrication led to another. "Just last year, our ambassador to Washington, D.C., worked out a deal with the President of the United States; none of us Indians has to worry with things like driver's licenses or paying taxes or doing jury duty."

The old babe has brass, you gotta give her that. Knox's mouth split in a happy grin. "Soon as I have a spare minute, I'll check with the White House. But for right now, I'll have to ask you to shut off the engine and give me your ignition key. And then you'll have to get out of the vehicle, ma'am."

Daisy clenched the steering wheel. "No."

The tough cop was not used to hearing this obnoxious word. He repeated it. "No?"

Daisy's mind was racing for an excuse. "I don't have to take no orders from you—I have diplomatic immunity."

Knox laughed. *Wait till the boys back at the station hear about this.*

The member of the sovereign Indian nation did not like being made sport of. Daisy had swallowed that dose which is widely known as "just about enough."

Maybe I can talk some sense to the passenger. The better to see inside the car, the lawman lowered his head.

Because the police officer had approached on her blind side, Louise-Marie had not seen him coming. Though vaguely aware of the presence of the public servant, the diabetic had more urgent business to attend to. She was busy injecting her arm with insulin.

The grin slipped down to his chin, then fell right off Knox's face. *I don't believe this.* His tone was stern. "Shut off that engine *now*. And I want both of you old hens outta the car."

There was another bark—this one from the rear seat.

The policeman was momentarily distracted by the hound's toothy muzzle, which appeared over the driver's left shoulder. It was as if the old woman had magically sprouted a second head.

Knox's right hand instinctively went for his sidearm.

Daisy's right hand went for the gear-stick gizmo with the little white knob on the end. She pulled it down to D for Depart, stepped on the gas thingy.

There was a hail of gravel behind the Olds, an angry shriek from the cop.

Louise-Marie still had the needle in her arm. "Daisy—I'm not done yet. What are you doing?"

Having given the rearview mirror a glance and seen the *matukach* doing a one-legged dance, the Ute elder set her face toward the Shining Mountains. "I'm leaving my troubles behind."

◆ ◆ ◆

Piggy Slocum watched his partner hip-hop away from the suspect vehicle. *The bad guys have run over Knox's foot—and they are making a run for it!* He switched on the emergency lights, toggled the siren switch, pulled forward to get his injured partner.

Knox, still bopping around on his good foot, waved him on. "Don't let 'em get away, Pig! Go—go—go!"

Daisy Perika heard the siren wail. It was loud and getting louder. She could see the red and blue lights in the mirror. Under different circumstances, she might have pulled over and stopped. But the Ute elder was furious with the ugly *matukach* cop who had laughed in her face, and she assumed he was driving the police car.

Piggy swerved across the center line. His intention was to pull up beside the fleeing bad guys, let them know what a hopeless spot they were in. He prayed they were not armed.

Daisy saw the police car coming up fast on her left. Over the years, she had watched her share of chase-scenes on the television screen. If the cop tried to force her off the road, why two could play at that game! *Once he gets up beside me, I'll just give the steering wheel a quick yank, run him right into the ditch.*

It would not be necessary.

Officer Slocum was not capable of holding two thoughts in his mind at the same time. This being the case, while he was thinking about crossing to the other side of the road, he had not considered the hazard of oncoming traffic. Now, something very large and very yellow loomed just ahead of him. It was closing fast. His overriding thought was to live for another minute. Piggy swerved to avoid a collision, headed off the highway, through the Qwik-Stop parking lot, a brand-new chain-link fence, an apple orchard, another fence, into a pasture where his right front tire hit a jagged stone and popped. He skidded, went into a sickening turn, came almost to a halt. The car hesitated, as if it could not make up its mind. Gravity took charge, eased the vehicle onto the passenger side. Piggy came very close to being annoyed. *Well this is one helluva note.* Hanging in his safety harness, the horizontal cop switched on his communications console. "Dispatch, this is Slocum, in Unit 144. Can you hear me awright?"

"Dispatch reads you five-by-five, 144."

"I got a officer injured near the intersection of Moss Road and Eickleberry Lane."

"Identify injured officer."

"Oh, it's just ol' Eddie Knox. Some suspects in a black Oldsmobile ran him down. Same Olds whose Messican plate he called in."

"What is Officer Knox's condition?"

"Eddie's kinda hoppin' around and cussin' a blue streak. I think he got his foot runned over."

"Are you in pursuit of suspects?"

Piggy shook his head. "I was only able to pursue 'em for about—uh—two or three football fields till a big yaller school bus forced me off'n the highway."

"What is the condition of your unit?"

He hesitated. "Ol' 144 is . . . ah—kinda crapped out. What I mean is, I ain't able to go nowheres right now. Partly on account of I had a tire blow out."

"Roger that. Stand by."

Not much else I can do. Although I wouldn't exactly call it standing.

The situation seemed dark indeed until he realized that somehow, in all of the bumping around, something nice had happened. The sack of Lead Life Savers was within his reach. Piggy secured one of the two-thousand-calorie delicacies. Tasted it. Found it good. Mighty good.

Dispatch's scratchy voice interrupted his snack break.

"Unit 144, an ambulance has been dispatched to Moss Road and Eickleberry for Officer Knox. Report your current position."

Piggy choked down a mouthful. Looked thoughtfully at the cockeyed world beyond his windshield. "Well, I'm kinda halfway upside down." He took another bite, tried to tilt his head. *It'd be a lot easier to swaller if I was right-side up.*

30

ALL IN A DAY'S WORK

Chief of police Scott Parris pulled his black-and-white over to the curb, got out, stomped around the front of the low-slung Chevrolet.

Eddie Knox returned the boss's glare.

Piggy Slocum concentrated on a crushed Coke can in the gutter.

"Well," Parris said, "what happened here?"

Knox set his jaw. "We saw a suspicious vehicle, ran a make on the plate. It wasn't in the database, so I approached and asked the driver for her driver's license. Crazy old Indian woman said she didn't need no kinda license because she come from a 'sovereign nation' and—"

Parris raised his hand to silence the man. "Save the details for your written report. What I want to know is what's all this stuff about you being run down by the vehicle?"

"When I asked for the ignition key, she run over my

foot—and it hurts like seven kinds of hell." The limping man stuck out a tire-scuffed boot for the boss's inspection.

The chief squinted at the display. "Eddie, correct me if I am wrong. But unless I have forgotten which leg you had amputated about twelve years ago, that is your *prosthetic* foot. And I don't see how something that's made of pine or birch could hurt."

"Well, you're wrong on both counts. For one thing—" the amputee tapped his finger on the artificial limb, "this ain't wood. It's a high-tech fiberglass-and-carbon composite." He eased a little more weight on the inert member, winced. "And second, there is such a thing as phantom pain."

Parris scowled at the eccentric man. "Are you telling me that when the motorist ran over your high-tech fiberglass-and-carbon-composite foot—that it *hurt?*"

Knox looked like a very angry bulldog who wanted to bite something. Anything. "Well of course it hurt—that's what phantom-limb pain is *for*. I can feel the ache in all five of my toes!"

Parris could feel a sharp pain in another portion of his anatomy. He tried without success to stare Knox down, then turned his attention to the other half of the team. "Slocum, I understand you came within a gnat's whisker of going head-on with a school bus."

Piggy shook his head. "Oh, no sir. I missed that bus by a good first down."

The chief of police frowned so hard it hurt his face. "First *what?*"

Knox saw his opportunity and took a shot at the boss. "It's a football term."

Parris didn't miss a beat. "Stay out of this, Knox."

"Yessir." The insolent man smirked openly.

Parris focused his attention on the chubby cop. "Officer Slocum, I am extremely grateful that you did not kill any innocent little children today."

Piggy responded with an enthusiastic nod. "Oh, me too, sir."

"Tell me about your unit."

The cop pointed in an easterly direction. "It's out yonder in a field. I guess it's pretty well bunged up." It was Piggy Slocum's nature to look on the bright side. "But it had about ninety-six thousand on it." He fixed the little porcine eyes on his boss. "I'd sure like to have me a four-wheel-drive vehicle for off-road patrolling. You think maybe the town council would buy me one a them Hummers?"

To Officer Knox's delight, the chief of police was grinding his teeth. "Slocum, you have just had a traumatic experience. It might have affected your brain in some way that medical science could not even imagine. So I don't believe you're quite ready for a Hummer. Before we put you in any kind of unit again, I think maybe you should have a nice, long rest. Six weeks, at least."

The chubby man grinned. "Like a vacation?"

Parris nodded. "Without pay."

Disappointment fairly dripped off Piggy's face. "No pay—but where could I go without any money for airplane tickets and hotels and whatnot?"

The chief of police was sorely tempted to tell him precisely where he could go.

Eddie Knox was painfully aware that while they were standing there, jawing with the chief, the criminals had not yet been apprehended. He cleared his throat. "Them old women was headed east toward the mountains, and couldn't have got very far. If we get a move on, we oughta be able to nab 'em."

"We will not nab 'em now or at any time in the foreseeable future." Parris smiled coldly at the amputee.

Knox started to ask why, realized that was just what the boss wanted.

Undeterred, Parris responded to the unasked question. "Because I don't want to find them. Because if I did find them, I'd probably discover that you'd scared hell out of a couple of elderly nuns who had stopped in our fair city for a brief moment of prayer. And that they were on their way back to oversee a leper colony somewhere south of the border, where they are venerated as living saints. And because, in the interest of protecting other innocent citizens from experiencing your peculiar brand of law enforcement, they might be willing to testify at your respective trials. Not that I would mind, except for the embarrassment that kind of publicity would bring to the department."

"Them wasn't no nuns," Knox mumbled. "One was an old Indian woman, the other was Anglo. And they was haulin' around the ugliest hound dog I have ever seen."

"They had an ugly dog in the car?" Parris threw his hands in the air. "Well that puts an altogether different light on the matter. You should've shot the unsightly animal right on the spot, cuffed the old ladies and slapped them around some till they come to their senses and agreed to purchase a toy poodle. Or a Yorkie or a Pek'."

Unmoved by this verbal assault, Eddie Knox played his hole card. "The Anglo woman, she was a dope fiend."

Parris's head started to swim. "A dope fiend? And how did you ascertain that, Officer Knox?"

Knox started to tell the boss about the needle the doper had pushed into her arm. *But he won't believe me.* "Ah, forget it."

The boss looked up at an empty sky. "I'd sure like to forget it. I'd like to go back to the office and pretend none of this ever happened. In fact, I'd like to go home and go to bed and pretend this whole *day* never happened. But I've got a job to do. And along the line of which, hear this—as of right now, you two are on suspension until a department inquiry determines whether or not to impose disciplinary action!" He turned on his heel and left.

They watched him go.

Piggy muttered under his breath: "Eddie, I think he's really, *really* mad at us this time. I bet he's gonna fire our butts."

Eddie Knox put his arm around his partner's shoulders. "Ah, don't worry, Pig. Sure, the fat's in the fire right now, but once all the facts come out, we'll be heroes. Mark my words—in a couple a weeks, I'll be promoted to sergeant. And you—why, you'll be toolin' around town in a black-and-white Hummer big as a Abrams Main Battle Tank."

Slocum's pudgy face grinned all over. "You really think so?"

Knox sighed. *This man is dumber than a germ.*

Halfway back to the station, the Granite Creek chief of police stopped at a red light. Unknown to the conscious portion of his mind, the Sub-basement Subliminal Department had been putting the bits and pieces together. Organizing. Calculating. Correlating. Now, the finished product was forwarded upstairs.

Old white woman.

Old black Oldsmobile.

License plate that's not in the data bank.

Old Indian woman who claims she doesn't need a driver's license.

Old Indian woman who runs over a cop's foot.

Ugliest hound Knox has ever seen.

The light turned green.

Oblivious to the Go signal, he stared straight ahead. *Surely* not.

There were four sedans, two pickups, and a UPS van lined up behind the chief's unit. Suspecting that this was some kind of sly police trickery, not one driver blew a horn at the stationary black-and-white.

GCPD's top cop shook his head. *It just couldn't be.*

But of course, it could.

Parris made a tight U-turn.

31

DAISY AND LOUISE-MARIE'S EXCELLENT ADVENTURE

The old Olds rolled on down the road.

What a morning. Daisy Perika had learned to drive a car—and she had dodged that pushy town cop. The tribal elder was highly pleased with herself.

Sidewinder, always game for a ride, had his paws draped over the front seat. Tongue lolling out of his toothy mouth, he drooled happily, stared this way and that, all the while making the occasional canine whine, constantly emitting a distinctly doggish odor. In his field of endeavor, he was a high achiever.

Soaked to the bone in anxiety, Louise-Marie LaForte kept peppering her chauffeur with questions, to which the Ute woman provided only such responses as she thought necessary to keep the owner of the vehicle off balance.

"Back there in town," Louise Marie chirped, "what did that policeman want?"

"He wanted to know who owned this car."

Louise-Marie's pink skin blanched to a chalky gray. "But whatever for?"

Daisy squinted at the horizon, wondered how far it was to Garcia's Crossing. "That blue-suit said he wanted to put a big fine on the owner—for having a Mexican license on her bumper."

"Well, how ridiculous—that is a perfectly lovely plate!" Louise-Marie aimed the unpatched eye at the driver. "What did you tell him?"

"I told him this old rust bucket wasn't mine." The speedometer needle jittered at thirty-five. She let up on the gas. "And when he said he wasn't buying none of that, I told him to check with the rightful owner. He asked me who that unfortunate soul might be, so I gave him your name. He wanted to know where you live, and I told him that too."

"Daisy! How could you *do* such a thing—" She noticed the Ute woman's mischievous smile. "Oh, you're teasing me." A hopeful look. "Aren't you?"

"I expect Officer Fuzz'll be waiting for you when you get home. If you don't have the greenback dollars to pay the bribe, they'll probably chunk you into the jailhouse with the other outlaws." She shot the one-eyed woman a stern look. "But don't expect me to come and bail you out. Only income I have is my tribal allotment and Social Security." She returned her gaze to the highway in front of the hood, cringed as a big bread truck zoomed by. "That and a few dollars I make from doing a cure now and then. And selling my home-made medicines."

"Well, I don't believe you told that policeman my name. In fact, I don't believe a single word you're saying." Louise-Marie was of the firm opinion that if you *didn't believe* a thing hard enough, why, the thing *just wasn't so*.

Daisy chuckled. "I bet you'll believe it when they haul this old rattletrap away to the graveyard for dead cars. And you end up in the jug with a bunch of wild-eyed criminals."

I just won't pay her the least bit of attention. Louise-Marie turned her bleary eye toward the vistas ahead. To the east, through a faintly bluish mist, mountains rose up to touch the clouds. There were rolling, rocky hills off to the right, a small stream paralleling the road on the left. "Where are we going?"

I guess I can tell her that much. "Garcia's Crossing."

"I never heard of such a place." Feeling a sudden surge of "nerves," the French-Canadian woman began to pat a vein-lined hand on her knee. "Why are we going there?"

"To find somebody." *Here comes another big truck. I wonder why they have to drive so fast?* Daisy pulled to the right, edging onto the bumpy shoulder.

"Oh!" Louise-Marie grabbed at the dashboard. "I don't know if I should've let you drive." She breathed a sigh of relief when all four wheels were back on the blacktop. "Who is this somebody we're hoping to find?"

"A young white woman."

"Why do we want to find her?"

"Because," Daisy said with logic that did not invite dispute, "she is missing." *And because I'd like to teach that big jug-head nephew of mine a thing or two. Like how I can find somebody that he can't. Which proves that I'm a whole lot smarter than he thinks I am. Even smarter than he thinks he is, which is quite a lot and then some.*

During this interval, Louise-Marie had been thinking. "Missing from where?"

The driver was about to respond with a tart retort, when she saw it. Daisy pointed with a lift of her chin. "Look—up the road."

Her passenger looked. "I don't see nothing."

"That's because you're blind in one eye and can't see a mountain out of the other." She took one hand off the wheel long enough to point straight ahead. "On the right. That's St. Cuthbert's."

Louise-Marie leaned forward. "A church?"

"No, a combination pool hall and bowling alley."

They were now within a hundred yards of the structure. Louise-Marie was beginning to make out the architectural features. "Why would a pool hall and bowling alley have a steeple with a cross on top?"

Daisy sighed. "Because it's a church, potato head!"

Louise-Marie was becoming dreadfully confused. "But you said—"

"Don't pay no attention to what I said."

The ancient sign they passed—peppered with rusty bullet holes—informed them that they were entering Garcia's Crossing, population 99.

Daisy grinned. *Ninety of 'em must be away on business.* She could see only one residence close to St. Cuthbert's—a brown stucco house behind the church. *That should be the rectory.* But would Pansy Blinkoe be staying there? The more she thought about it, the more sense it made. Especially if Alonzo and Prudence were illegals. It was not uncommon for kindly priests to give shelter to people who had no other place to go.

The Ute woman saw another sign. This one was considerably larger, and on the left side, directly across the road from St. Cuthbert's. It read: POKEY JOE'S GENERAL STORE.

The two-story building behind the sign was unpainted clapboard, leaning tentatively as if on the verge of slipping away to a better site. Three old-fashioned Texaco pumps were lined up out front. Daisy slowed until she spotted the entrance to the establishment. What the driver did *not* spot was the motorcycle in the oncoming lane, roaring down the road at seventy-six miles per hour. She was also blissfully unaware of the big Dodge pickup coming up fast from behind. It was for this reason that she made the left turn with considerable confidence.

To avoid the Olds, the guy on the Harley swerved into the oncoming lane, missed the pickup by a whisker, bounced along the shoulder, barely avoided being pitched into the ditch. The motorcyclist cursed the black Oldsmobile, the white Dodge truck, his dark karma, the universe, and every malignant atom in it.

The pickup driver cursed the black Oldsmobile, the speeding motorcyclist, plus all Democrats and Republicans. The registered Independent did not care whether or not the other drivers were attached to the major political parties; bad-mouthing the Jackasses and Elephants was merely force of habit, and highly satisfying.

Louise-Marie had seen something whoosh by. Something black and blurry. Then a white something, var-oooming in the other direction. "What was that?"

Having knocked a galvanized water can aside, Daisy was braking to a sliding stop on the graveled surface. "What was what?"

"I think somebody almost hit us."

"I'm not surprised. Most of these dumbos go way too fast and don't pay no attention to us careful drivers. I don't think half of 'em know *how* to drive a car." Daisy eyed the gearshift. "Tell me again, what do I do with this gizmo when I want to stop?"

"Put it in P."

"Oh. Right." She did this. "How do I shut the motor down?"

Louise-Marie pointed to a chrome-plated slot under the gear shift. "You just turn that doodad to Off. Then give me the key."

Daisy fumbled with the ignition switch until the engine stuttered to a stop, passed the key to Louise-Marie. It was a great relief to be motionless again. She sat there for a de-lightful moment, enjoying the immobility. The stillness. The quiet. It was not to last.

"My head is starting to pound, and I can see little wavy lines in front of my eye." Louise-Marie took a deep breath, moaned. "I think my sugar's getting too *low*. I need to get me something to eat."

"They should have some food in this big store." Daisy managed to get her stiff legs out of the car. After retrieving her walking stick from the rear, she heard a rumbling sound, a crunch of tires on the gravel. She turned to see a young man on a motorcycle. He was filthy with road dust, had hair like a tangled mop, wore black leather and a malicious scowl.

Stringy-Hair was glaring at her. "You the old biddy who run me off the road?"

All these young people nowadays look so angry all the time. Like they never learned no manners. "Don't you talk to me like that," she snapped. "And why don't you take a bath and get a job!"

He said something that sounded like *rich* or *itch* but was neither. Something else sounded like *arrrgh* and was.

"Mess with me," Daisy raised her sturdy oak staff like the club it was, "I'll whack you upside of your ugly gourd head. And while you're laid out flat, I'll sic Sidewinder on you—he'll chew all the meat off your bones!"

Hearing his name mentioned, the hound felt summoned. He lurched out of the car to confront the stranger. Instantly, the back of his neck bristled. *"Arrrgh,"* Sidewinder said to Stringy-Hair.

Having recently uttered the same expletive, the motorcyclist understood. He growled, raised a filthy finger at the dog. Having had the final eloquent word, he revved the Harley engine to a roar that rattled the old women's bones, sped away victorious—kicking gravel in a magnificent arc.

Louise-Marie was perplexed by life in general and by this encounter in particular. "Who was that?"

"Bugs-on-His-Teeth," the Ute woman replied. She shook her stick at the departing villain.

It is just amazing how Daisy seems to know everybody and everything. But what a strange name. "What did Mr. Bugs-Teeth want?"

"To strangle us and steal our purses, I expect." Daisy sighed at the injustice of it all. "That's why I don't like to travel these days. A civilized person is likely meet up with really nasty people. Tramps and savages and the like."

With the hound at their heels, the women went into the store. The inside was filled with dust and twilight. And every sort of merchandise imaginable. But not a human being in sight.

Until a tall, stout woman descended the stairs. The proprietor was outfitted in faded overalls and heavy men's boots.

Girlish black bangs made a perfectly straight line above the double arches of painted-on eyebrows. She paused to unfasten a chain that stretched across the bottom step. The brass links supported a hand-painted sign which warned customers that the space upstairs was private living quarters—keep out. She gave the trio a stern, uncompromising look. "I'm sorry, but we have strict rules 'bout what kinda creatures can come into the store."

"Oh, it's all right," Daisy said with a quick glance at Sidewinder, another at her patch-eyed companion. "He's her Seeing Eye hound."

Pokey Joe glowered at Daisy. "I was speaking to the *dog*."

32

POKEY JOE

At the proprietor's invitation, Daisy Perika and Louise-Marie had taken seats by the potbellied iron stove.

The Ute woman was having a go at a ham-and-cheese sandwich.

Sidewinder was watching every bite.

Daisy gave the hound a flinty-eyed look. *Don't you even think about it.*

The French-Canadian customer took a ladylike sip of her Seven Up, a nibble of Twinkie. "I was talking to the dog. Hah—that's a good one," Louise-Marie cackled. "I'll have to remember that, and pull it on somebody who brings a dog into my house." She began to consider the list of potential candidates.

POLICE WORK

Cruising along the county road, Scott Parris was beginning to entertain doubts about this course of action. *I don't know what caused me to think Charlie's aunt Daisy could be out tooling around in Louise-Marie's beat-up old car. I bet that elderly lady has never driven a car in her whole life. No, it'll turn out to be some other old Indian woman that ran over Eddie Knox's wooden foot.* The recollection of Knox's outraged correction made him smile. *Make that high-tech carbon-fiber-whatever foot.* But any way you looked at it, this search was a long shot. *The Olds was heading east, and the driver knows we know that, so unless she's balmy, she headed in another direction to throw us off. Or maybe she's parked somewhere in the national forest till things cool down. There's not one chance in a hundred that I'll be lucky enough to spot—*
And then he spotted it.

Bold as brass, parked right in front of Pokey Joe's.

The chief of police slowed. *If that ain't Louise-Marie's old car, I'll eat my hat. And boots to boot. So Daisy must be with her.* He considered going inside straightway and confronting them. *But that way I'd never find out what they're up to. And this pair is always up to something. Something that'll give me a serious case of heartburn.* Parris drove a few yards farther, just past Hank's Auto Repairs, which had been shut down long enough for a sizable elm branch to grow through a front window. He pulled his unit behind the abandoned building, into a brushy patch of willows. *I'll just sit here awhile and watch the Olds. Play it by ear.*

MEANWHILE, BACK AT THE GENERAL STORE

Pokey Joe hitched her thumbs behind the overall straps, eyed the white woman. "You feel better after the soda-pop, darlin'?"

"Sure do," the one-eyed diabetic said. "I think my sugar is about normal now. Or maybe a little more."

P.J. turned her attention to the silent Indian. "Anything I can do for you?"

"Make me another sandwich," Daisy said. "Just like the first one."

"Comin' right up."

Daisy and her pal watched the big woman disappear behind the counter.

Sidewinder licked his lips. Cast a hopeful glance at Louise-Marie's Twinkie.

When Pokey Joe returned with the second ham-and-cheese on white bread, Daisy accepted it without a word, passed it to her friend. "After you get all the sugar you want, you'd better chomp down on some food that'll do you some good."

Louise-Marie sniffed at it. "What thank you kindly, Daisy dear." She took a bite of the sandwich, another from the Twinkie, then repeated the rotation. *These go good together.*

The overalled woman departed, returned with a meaty ham bone wrapped in brown butcher paper. She leaned to pat the dog's head. "You look hungry too, bub." She placed the aromatic gift on the floor, immediately under his muzzle.

Offended by this charity, Sidewinder turned up his nose.

Pokey Joe raised a penciled-on eyebrow. "I never heard of a dog that didn't like ham bones."

Rather than explain, Daisy preferred to let Nature take its course.

A few heartbeats later, Nature did.

In a blurred move, Sidewinder snatched the sandwich from Louise-Marie's hand.

The startled woman shrieked, tossed her Twinkie across the store.

The Ute woman cackled a raspy laugh.

The lady who had offered the ham bone howled. "Hooo-eeee—I reckon that hound likes people food better than pig bones!"

Louise-Marie shook her finger at the animal. "Bad, bad dog. You scared me out of a year's growth!"

Having swallowed the sandwich, Sidewinder trotted away to recover the cast-off pastry.

Pokey Joe patted Louise-Marie on the back. "Don't you fret, sweetie—I'll bring you another Twinkie." And she did.

Having had about all the fun she could stand in one day, Daisy decided it was time to get down to serious business. She smiled at the owner of the store. "That's a nice-looking old church across the road. I believe I seen it once or twice when I was a little girl."

That must've been a hundred years ago. Pokey Joe looked through the front window. "St. Cuthbert's hasn't been a real church for twenty years or more. I guess most of the Cath'lics either croaked or moved away from here. Come to think of it, almost everybody has croaked or moved away." *I oughta pack up and go too. Before I croak or go broke.*

The Ute woman executed an expert follow-through. "I noticed a brown house out behind the church—is that the rectory?"

Pokey Joe shrugged. "Might've been a long time ago, but not anymore. That's Mr. DeSoto's place."

Having acquired a name, Daisy pressed for more. "It must be a blessing to have a close neighbor."

"I don't think of DeSoto as a neighbor—or even a cus-tomer." Pokey Joe's expression morphed from blandly neu-tral to mildly annoyed. "Except for topping off his gas tank once in a while, he hardly ever stops here to buy anything. I don't even know how he makes a living."

Daisy saw the opportunity, grabbed it by the throat. "Maybe he takes in boarders. I know this young lady who moved out to Garcia's Crossing a little while back. From what I hear, she rented a room right next to the church."

"I don't know who DeSoto shares his house with." Pokey Joe took a swipe at a horsefly with her hand, missed it by a millimeter. "But he has visitors from time to time." She watched the insolent insect circle her head. "They generally come and go in the middle of the night."

I knew it! Daisy clasped her hands together to keep them from trembling.

Pokey Joe made a second try, snagged the fly, squashed it flat, wiped her palm on the overall bib. "For all I know, ol'

DeSoto could be operating a bed-and-breakfast over there, but I doubt he'd pull in any classy tourists. For one thing, he's a reg'lar slob. For another, he packs a little pistol in his hip pocket. Not that I got anything against slobs and guns, mind you—but I got a feelin' this DeSoto is a bad egg." The proprietor was distracted by the toot-toot of a horn. "'Scuse me, ladies. Looks like I got a live customer out front." She departed in long, purposeful strides that shook the floor.

Louise-Marie cleared her throat. "I think that's really nice."

Daisy had almost forgotten her companion. "What?"

"This isn't one of those self-service places, it's the old-timey kind." Louise-Marie pointed. "Look, she's filling that man's gas tank."

"I don't care if she gives him a shave and a haircut," Daisy grumped. "I've got to go find someone."

Louise-Marie raised an eyebrow. "That white woman who's missing?"

Daisy nodded. "Her name is Pansy Blinkoe—after her husband was murdered, she took off."

Murdered? And then Louise-Marie remembered. "I read about that Blinkoe fella in the newspaper—somebody blew him up in his boat. But I didn't hear anything about his wife running away. Why d'you suppose she'd do such a thing?"

Daisy had thought long and hard about this. "Because Mrs. Blinkoe knows who killed her husband. And the killer knows she knows. She's hiding, so he don't murder her too." She shot her friend a grim look. "And I'll bet you a silver dollar to a copper dime that Mrs. Blinkoe's holed up in that house behind the church."

"But why do you think—"

"Don't ask," the shaman snapped.

Not the least offended by this rebuke, Louise-Marie finished off the second Twinkie, wiped at her mouth with a dainty little embroidered hankie.

Daisy reached for her walking stick, pushed herself up from the bench.

Louise-Marie's pulse picked up a few beats. "What do you intend to do?"

"What *we* are going to do is walk right over there to that house behind the church, and knock on the door."

Her timid companion blinked the eye that could. "Oh dear. Isn't that . . . well, rather *brash*?"

Daisy regarded her companion with frank contempt. "If you're scared of this DeSoto fella, you don't have to come— I'll take care of things by myself." With Sidewinder tagging along at her heels, she hobbled away toward the door, knowing full well what would happen.

It did.

Like a jack-in-the-box, Louise-Marie popped up. "Wait— wait for me!"

From his concealment in the willow brush, Scott Parris waited. Watched. Those pesky little demons commonly known as "second thoughts" had come to torment him. *Those two may be in Pokey Joe's till the cows come home.* There were also third thoughts. *I'm wasting time.* And fourth. *I oughta just go in there and find out what— Wait a minute. Here they come outta the front door.* He started the engine. *I'll let them get in the Olds, follow 'em a mile or so down the road, then switch on the emergency lights and siren.* He smiled at the image of how his unexpected appearance would rattle the pair of elderly women. *It'll make a great tale to tell ol' Charlie Moon. After I pull 'em over, I'll give 'em a good talking-to, then I'll— What's this? They're not getting in the car.* Fascinated, the lawman watched events unfold. *What is going on here?*

This raised a second question. *Why does an old Ute woman cross a road?*

A third: *Why does an old Anglo woman follow her?*

Finally: *Why the heck do I care?*

But care he did.

While checking her customer's oil, Pokey Joe noticed the women and the dog crossing the highway. *Guess they're going to have a look at the old church.* It was not like there was anything else to see in Garcia's Crossing.

33

A MEANINGFUL CONVERSATION WITH MR. DESOTO

Daisy paused to gaze at what remained of St. Cuthbert's. It seemed smaller and more modest than when she was a child. Most of the stained-glass windows had been broken, the milky-white statue of the Virgin was spotted with lichens and moss. Scattered around the image were a few scruffy little rosebushes that seemed determined to survive. For a bright moment, the harsh work of Time faded. She was nine again, and Momma and Daddy were here, and little brother Tom-Tom. The tot was running after something that only the very young treasure. A dusty moth, perhaps, or a grasshopper. Salty tears filled her eyes, her heart ached as if it might fracture and break. She was startled when someone touched her.

"What is it, dear?" Louise-Marie patted her arm.

"Oh, nothing." Daisy brushed a sleeve across her face. "Just got some grit in my eye." She nodded to indicate the dirt driveway beside the abandoned church building. "We can follow that back to Mr. DeSoto's house."

Sidewinder watched until he understood the plan, then doggedly led the way.

A picket fence that had once enclosed the church property was mostly rotted away; a riotous party of tumbleweeds, kinnikinnick, and chokecherry had come to stay. As they passed the ancient cemetery, it became apparent that there were not many relatives left in Garcia's Crossing to tend the graves. Only the larger headstones were visible above the undergrowth. A few marble vaults—mute testimony of more prosperous times—were covered by a dismal species of waxy-gray vines.

To catch up with her companion, Louise-Marie took a few quick steps. "I never did like walking past graveyards. Even in the broad daylight."

The Ute woman held her silence until they were past the burial ground. When their destination was in sight, Daisy paused, leaned on her oak staff.

A rusted-out Chevrolet van was parked near a tumbledown shed, a low-slung, expensive-looking sedan was sheltered in the sparse shade of a Russian olive. The DeSoto house was a long, narrow, peak-roofed structure. Having cracked in the heat of many summers, the stucco walls resembled the bottom of a sun-baked stream. The front entrance faced the back of the church. There was no porch. A pine board on a pair of cinder blocks served as a step. On each side of the door, small windows with almost-closed yellow shades suggested suspicious little half-lidded eyes set on a broad, stupid face. A robin strutted about in the dusty yard, evidently hoping to discover an earthworm that had little enough sense to be in this place.

Now past the cemetery, Louise-Marie had eased her pace and fallen a few paces behind the bold Ute woman. "Before we just walk up and knock on the door, I think we ought to have us a *plan*."

Daisy was about to respond when something warm and

furry rustled in the brush beside the lane, then bounded off toward a cluster of sage.

In hopes of a cottontail lunch, Sidewinder tore off after the insolent white flag.

Louise-Marie watched the chase, shuddered. "Oh, I hope he doesn't catch the poor little bunny rabbit."

"That poor little bunny rabbit is probably covered with bloodsucking ticks big as your thumb, and fleas that carry the plague." Daisy chuckled. "And that old dog has the misery in his joints, just like me. He couldn't catch a cold if he slept in the rain for a month."

Her Disney image shattered, the tiny woman turned her gaze toward the dreary home. "I don't like the looks of this place. And I don't think we should be here—just the two of us alone."

Daisy tried to think of something tart to say. But there *was* something bad here. She could feel it down into her marrow. "Go back to the car, if you want to. If something happens, and I don't come back in ten minutes—you tell that big woman in the store to telephone the police."

Unnerved by this sober statement from her friend, Louise-Marie shifted gears and found some traction. "No—I won't leave you alone." She bent with a grunt, picked up a stick. "If you're staying, so am I."

Daisy shook her head at the sight. *Here I am, a hundred miles from a home that's burnt to the ground, walking into who-knows-what, and what've I got to protect me? A silly old woman with a little switch in her hand, a dimwit dog that goes off chasing rabbits.* Almost unconsciously, she asked God for help.

Her perfunctory prayer had been anticipated long before Daisy had been conceived in her mother's womb—yea, even before the first star had warmed to a dull, reddish glow.

Having left his unit parked by Louise-Marie's Oldsmobile, Scott Parris took up a position in the weed-choked space beside St. Cuthbert's. He watched the elderly women exchange words, then march up to the door of the stucco house. Daisy Perika had a habit of getting herself into trouble, and taking the French-Canadian woman along for the ride. He scratched at an itch on his ear. *What is she up to this time?*

Daisy started to put her foot onto the small plank that served as a step, hesitated. The board looked like it might fall off the cinder blocks. She reached out with the oak staff, gave the door a light tap. She heard no steps in the house, but had the uneasy sensation that someone was watching her. Someone was.

Someone stared through a narrow slit set high on the cellar wall.

Daisy tapped on the door again, harder this time. Out of the corner of her eye, she saw a flash of movement by a tattered curtain.

The women waited.

Finally, Louise-Marie made this observation in a hopeful tone: "Maybe there's nobody home."

"Oh, they're here all right."

Somewhere, far off in the brush near the church, there was an urgent whine from Sidewinder.

The Ute woman supposed that he had run the cottontail into a hole.

Louise-Marie entertained a hideous vision of the hound ripping a poor little flea-and-tick-infested bunny rabbit into bloody shreds. The world was a hard place.

Daisy Perika was about to knock again when—

The doorknob turned.

The Ute elder tightened the grip on her sturdy walking staff.

Louise-Marie readied her puny stick.

The man who appeared in the doorway had utterly failed in his lifelong aspiration. A red-hot dandy was what he wanted to be. This vain ambition was the reason for the seven-hundred-dollar ostrich-skin boots, skin-tight black jeans, turquoise-studded snakeskin belt, and canary-yellow silk shirt decorated with a scattering of embroidered butterflies. Spiffy duds, all in all—and he might just have pulled it off. Except for a few minor deficits—such as a shirttail hanging out over a bulging gut; greasy, slicked-back hair; and a mustache too thin to be manly. The stern judges in the Dandy of the Year contest would have winced and subtracted extra points on account of being appalled. There were other deficiencies that the pitiful soul could not be held responsible for—a deeply pockmarked face, a knobby nose, a chin decorated with a slug-shaped mole. This latter feature wriggled as his lips worked with a plastic toothpick. He stared at the visitors with flat, unblinking eyes.

Never one to hesitate in passing harsh judgments, Daisy sized him up in a glance. *This pineapple head's the kind of back-alley pimp that gives flesh peddlers a bad name.*

The man pulled a pack of cigarettes from his shirt pocket. Spitting out the toothpick, he stuck a filter tip between his lips. "What?"

With a sickening epiphany, Daisy realized that Louise-Marie had been right. *I should've worked out a plan before I knocked on his door.* To gain a patch of time, she cleared her throat. Cleared it again. Then: "Are you Mr. DeSoto?"

He produced a plastic lighter, flicked it three times, touched a flame to the tip of the cigarette. "Who wants to know?"

"I'm Daisy." She gestured with an elbow to indicate the woman behind her. "That's Louise-Marie."

He blew a smoke ring over the Ute woman's head. "So whatta you want?"

Daisy had barely opened her mouth when she heard the words behind her.

"We're with the Salvation Army—we visit sick folks and shut-ins."

The Ute woman turned to stare at her one-eyed friend.

Louise-Marie LaForte was blushing crimson. She gave Daisy a pleading look. *I just felt like I should say something.*

Daisy grinned at her companion. *Well, the old mare has taken the bit in her mouth, I'll just let her run with it for a while.*

DeSoto's lips twisted into a quasi smile. "Salvation Army—you two old biddies?"

The Ute elder shot him a sizzling look. "Who're you calling *biddies,* you two-bit piece of horse—"

Alarmed that the Indian stick of dynamite was about to explode in their midst, Louise-Marie intervened. "Mr. DeSoto, we are here to . . . uh . . . to bring you some nice books to read." *That was good.*

"Books?" The cigarette hung precariously on his lower lip. "I thought the Salvation Army dished out bread and soup."

Though not having told a lie since she was six years old, L.M. fell headlong into the job. "That's right, sir. But we also distribute all sorts of wholesome literature." In an attempt to conjure up examples, she fell back on her own collection. "For instance, we provide *Aunt Celia's Country Cookbook, The American Heritage Dictionary, Birds of the Rocky Mountain West, Guys and Dolls, See Here, Private Hargrove,* and . . . and the Holy Bible."

The man snorted. "Bible?"

Sensing that her friend's line was going a bit limp, Daisy took up the slack. "You know, that black book with gold on the edges of the pages." She took a step closer to the man. "If you was to read one, you'd find out what God expects from you. For one thing, hospitality to strangers."

"Izzat right?" He blew smoke in her face.

Daisy coughed. "I wish you wouldn't do that."

He chuckled. Blew another puff at the funny old woman.

The Ute elder held her breath until the smoke had passed her by. Then: "Now listen to me, you pineapple-headed potgut—don't you do that again."

The blackguard sucked in another lungful of smoke.

She added in a menacing tone: "I'll hit you *hard.*" Where it'll hurt.

Noting that the little woman wielding the big stick was looking at his crotch, he sensibly allowed the fumes to escape through a pair of hairy nostrils.

Sensing that she was getting the upper hand, Daisy pointed at his house. "You go inside, and tell Prudence and Alonzo that there's some ladies at the door that wants to have a word with them."

The cigarette wobbled between his lips. "You get offa my property or I'll—".

"Keep your yap shut till I've had my say!" Like a cougar about to pounce, Daisy hunched her shoulders. "And while you're at it, tell that pretty white girl you're hiding that I want to see her too."

DeSoto retreated into the doorway. "Go away, you crazy old woman!"

"Don't you talk to me like that, Pineapple Head!" She shook the walking stick at the hideously pockmarked man, raised her voice loud enough for Pansy Blinkoe to hear—*and Pansy heard every word.* "Now you tell that silly yellow-haired girl to come out here—and tell me why she left her home to stay with a blivit like you!"

Though not a person who would ever be mistaken for a scholar, it must be said that DeSoto had an Inquiring Mind. He also harbored an aching suspicion that he had been insulted. "What's a blivit?"

Daisy explained to him that a blivit was two hundred pounds of manure in a sixty-pound bag. Though it must be admitted that she used a vulgar synonym for "manure."

Being not entirely without feelings, DeSoto was hurt. He muttered a vile remark, making reference to the mean old woman's ancestry, then slammed the door in her face.

Daisy banged the knobby end of her stick on the wall, dislodging a sizable chunk of stucco.

Louise-Marie tugged at her friend's arm. "I don't think he is going to cooperate—we might as well go back to the car."

"Not till I talk to Pansy!" The Ute woman took a hearty lick at the door. *Bam!*

The hound loped up, woofed happily at the excited woman.

Daisy turned an accusing eye on the dog. "Where was you when I needed you, you old sack of bones—off chasing a varmint? You could've made yourself useful, bit a big hunk outta that slick-haired pimp!"

DeSoto appeared at the window, waving a pistol. "Go away!"

Daisy yelled back: "You let me talk to that young woman, or I'll call the cops on you!"

Right on cue, Scott Parris came trotting across the yard. "What's going on here?"

Daisy and her pal were struck dumb by this unexpected appearance. Startled by the sight of the silver shield pinned on the lawman's shirt, DeSoto backed away from the window.

34

POLICE BRUTALITY

Scott Parris pulled himself up to his full height, which—with the gradual compression of his spinal column over the years—was down to an even six feet. He folded muscular arms across a broad chest, glared at the pair of elderly women.

This blatant attempt at intimidation had the expected effect on Louise-Marie LaForte, who cowered behind the Ute woman.

Daisy was another matter. She stared straight back at the tough-looking lawman, went on the offensive. "What're you doing here?"

The Granite Creek chief of police knitted his brow into a halfhearted scowl. "Seems to me that's what I should be asking you."

Hah—got him on the run. "I asked you first."

He tried not to grin. "As it happens, I'm out looking for a desperate criminal. And I'm talking about someone who's a real and present danger to society."

"Then you've come to the right place." Daisy pointed at the DeSoto residence. "He's hiding in there."

Parris glanced at the door. "Who?"

"Pineapple Head DeSoto."

"Pineapple Head?"

"Soon as you see his ugly, pockmarked face you'll know why I call him that." Daisy lowered her voice. "And that primped-up pimp's up to no good, you can count on that. If you don't believe me, just ask him to let you talk to Prudence. Or Alonzo. Or that yella-headed white woman. See where *that* gets you!"

The lawman looked at Daisy's French-Canadian companion. "Do you have any idea what she's talking about?"

Having already represented herself and the wicked Ute woman as pious soldiers enrolled in the Salvation Army, Louise-Marie was not about to tell another lie. She shook her head.

Parris produced a ferocious scowl, pointed toward the lane. "You two start walking."

Louise-Marie sprinted off like a famished hen at feeding time.

The Indian woman glared poisoned arrows at the lawman, staunchly stood her ground.

Parris pointed harder. "Go."

Daisy grumbled something in her native tongue that was extremely rude. Having had this final say, she grudgingly followed her faint-hearted friend.

DeSoto peeked through a crack in the curtains, mumbled a curse of his own.

Ignoring the blare of the TV set, Pokey Joe stood at the store window. *Here comes that good-looking cop, and he's herding them two old women like they was sheep. I bet they've done something real bad.* This was lots better than *As the World Turns.*

• • •

As they approached the Oldsmobile, Sidewinder loped up to the rear door and whined. Parris patted the old dog on the head. "You won't be riding home in that." He allowed some time for this to sink in.

It did.

"Oh," Louise-Marie said, "I guess you're going to drive Daisy and the doggy back to her nephew's ranch." She smiled sweetly, began to rummage around in her purse for the car key. "I suppose that's just as well. It's getting late and I should drive directly home."

"I don't think you'll be needing this." The chief of police deftly removed the key from her hand. "Not till I see a valid driver's license."

"Driver's license?" The French-Canadian woman did not hide the hurt. "I don't think I have one of those things with me."

"Hah!" Daisy said.

It was not clear to whom this comment was directed.

"No driver's license, eh?" Parris pointed at the rear bumper. "You want to tell me where you got that Mexican plate?"

Louise-Marie beamed with pride. "It's from my late husband's collection. He was a big traveler, you see—and whenever he went somewhere, he always brought back a license plate. It was like a keepsake. Why, I suppose I must have hundreds of 'em in the garage."

The lawman almost wished he had not asked, but this had to be pursued. "When was the last time you had a current Colorado plate on this vehicle?"

Louise-Marie counted fingers, muttered something about Adlai Stevenson, tried to remember the other guy. Finally, she smiled. "It was when General Dwight Eisenhower was elected president. For his second term."

Parris stared in disbelief. "Really?"

"Sure. That was when we bought the car. It was brand-new then."

Well, that tears it. "Get all of the stuff out of your car that you want to take with you." He opened the trunk on his unit. "You can put it in here."

Louise-Marie's visible eye doubled in size. "Do you mean to say—"

"Even without a legal plate, I could write you a ticket and issue you a temporary permit to drive it home. But seeing as how you don't have a driver's license, that's not an option." With a shrewd glint in his eye, he turned to Daisy. "Of course, if Mrs. Perika has a ticket to get behind the wheel, maybe she'd like to drive this fine Oldsmobile."

The Ute woman shook her head. "Not me."

Never one to argue with an authority figure, Louise-Marie began to cart little bits of this and that from the Olds to the policeman's car.

Parris took his best friend's aunt aside. "A couple of hours ago, a person driving a car of this description passed through my fair city. When this particular person was pulled over by one of my officers, she made a getaway to evade arrest. And in the process, ran over my officer's foot."

Daisy absorbed this with a poker face that Parris could not help but admire.

He continued. "All told, the driver of the Oldsmobile is probably guilty of about six misdemeanors and a couple of felonies." After a dramatic pause, he said: "Would you care to speculate about who that driver was?"

The Ute woman gave Louise-Marie a worried look. "Not with all those charges hanging over her." Her voice dropped to a whisper. "Why, if she got throwed in jail, she'd never live through the first night in a cell. I expect her poor old heart would give out. Or she'd hang herself with her stocking."

"Then you're hinting that Louise-Marie was driving the car? That she ran over Officer Knox's foot?"

Daisy shook her head. "I didn't hint no such thing." She assumed a primly virtuous look. "I'd never rat on a friend."

"You won't have to," Parris said. "Officer Knox will be able to identify the driver." He pulled down the brim of his felt hat. The shadow across his brow gave him a sinister look. "But you don't need to worry. You and Louise-Marie don't look at all alike. I'm sure he'll point to the right suspect."

"Suspect?"

Parris nodded. "When we put both of you in the lineup." He cleared his throat. "With a half-dozen other ladies who're more or less the same age as you two."

She reached out to straighten his bolo tie. "That's a nice piece of turquoise."

He lowered his chin to inspect the ornament. "Yes it is."

"Someone give you that for a present?"

He felt his face burn. "If memory serves, I believe it was a Christmas gift. From somebody by the name of Daisy."

"Oh my, is that a fact—somebody with the same name as me?" She clasped a hand to her mouth. "Oh, now I remember—*I* gave you that expensive handmade Zuni tie."

Manipulative old woman. "Yes, you did."

"Well think of that. I must have saved up for a long time. From my pitiful little Social Security checks."

He took this hit below the belt and came back with a sharp jab. "That was the same Christmas I gave you that three-hundred-dollar AM-FM radio."

"Oh, I remember that. It burnt up with my trailer." She sniffed. "I guess it wasn't fireproof."

"This bolo tie never does quite hang straight." He gave it a good yank. "I guess it's off balance or something."

Daisy fell into a thoughtful silence before she spoke. "I'd sure hate to see that nervous old white woman have to get in a lineup."

"You're a good friend to Louise-Marie," Parris said. "But I don't think there's anything you can do to save her now. If she did the hit-and-run, she'll have to wear the ball and chain on her ankle. And break rocks with a five-pound sledge."

The Ute elder edged closer to the lawman. "Maybe we could cut a deal."

Parris looked down his nose at the woman. "I hope that don't mean what it sounds like."

"Oh, I wouldn't try to bribe you with cash money or anything like that."

Having expected something at least that naughty, he was disappointed. "What, then?"

"If you'll let Louise-Marie off, and not get me involved—

not that I've done anything to break the law—I'll help you solve a *real* crime."

He let the doubt show all over his face. "I don't know—we'd have to be talking about a particularly serious offense. Something even worse than running down one of my officers. And I can't imagine what that'd be."

Daisy could. "How about cold-blooded murder."

"So who got murdered?"

"Well, I hope you haven't already forgot about that rich man with the funny two-pointed beard. But in case you did, he got ripped limb from limb in a big explosion."

"Manfred Blinkoe?"

"Unless you know of another dead man whose boat was blown sky-high in Moccasin Lake."

"How would you come to know anything about the Blinkoe business?" The question was no sooner past his lips than he realized he did not want to hear the answer.

Daisy did not want to tell him. Generally speaking, Scott Parris was a lot more understanding about her "methods" than Charlie Moon was. But it was a good practice never to tell a cop more than you absolutely had to. "I have my ways. That's all I can say."

He nodded. "Okay. I guess you've got sources to protect." *Like that little dwarf who lives in Spirit Canyon.* "So tell me—who dynamited Dr. Blinkoe's houseboat?"

She cast a wary glance toward the DeSoto residence. "I have some suspicions, but I'm not quite ready to say."

Parris's face broke into a broad grin. "Great. Now we're getting somewhere."

Daisy gave him a nasty look. "If you want to know where Pansy Blinkoe's hiding out, you'd best mind your manners."

"From this moment, I'm on my best behavior." He was beginning to enjoy her little game. "But please don't tell me you think she's somewhere between Mexico City and Anchorage. Try to be a little more specific."

"I can tell you *exactly* where she is."

"Okay. Exactly would be close enough."

Daisy pointed toward a spot across the road. "She's right over there."

The lawman turned to look. "In the church building?"

The elderly woman strained, but could not remember. So she had to ask. "Who was that doofus deputy who worked for Andy Griffith?"

"You mean in that old Mayberry TV show?"

"That's the one."

"That was Barney Fife." Parris smiled fondly at the childhood memory. "Andy, he'd only let ol' Barney carry one bullet for his gun. And Barney had to keep that cartridge in his pocket."

"I know all about the bullet and Aunt Bea and cute little Oafie. Now ask me—"

"Opie."

"Forget about Mayberry. Now ask me again."

This caused him to pause and reflect. "Ask you what?"

"About Pansy being over there across the road, in the church."

"Okay. Is Mrs. Pansy Blinkoe hiding out in the church?"

"No, Barney Fife, she's holed in with that pimp DeSoto." Having said this, Daisy felt considerably better.

S. Parris, aka B. Fife, groaned. *I should have known.* "So that's why you were over there harassing an innocent citizen, trying to break his door down with your walking stick?"

"If Pineapple Head DeSoto is innocent, I'm Saint What's-her-name." Not being able to remember things like names was a constant annoyance. "And he's probably not even an American citizen. I bet he's from Panama or Massachusetts or someplace like that!"

Gently, Parris put a hand on her shoulder and did his best imitation of an amiable Carolina drawl. "Aunt Bea, if you would tell me just one thing—"

"My name ain't Aunt Bea."

"And you're not a thing like that sweet little lady. But what I'd like to know is—what makes you think Mrs. Blinkoe is hiding in the DeSoto residence?"

Daisy got that stubborn look.

"Oh, right." He flashed a disarming grin. "You have your *ways*."

"Hmmpf," she said. And meant it.

He tried a shot in the dark. "I'd bet a dollar to a Dr Pepper it was a dream."

"Then you'd lose your dollar, Mr. Smart Mouth, 'cause it wasn't no dream. It was a vision that—" *Oh, I shouldn't have said that. I let him trick me.*

"A vision." Parris slammed fist against palm. "Well, that throws a whole new light on things." He took some time, as if thinking the thing up one way and down the other. "Okay. Here's the deal. Three A.M. tomorrow, me and a dozen hand-picked officers will throw a cordon around the place. We'll give DeSoto one minute flat to produce Mrs. Blinkoe. He doesn't, we go in guns blazing. We'll shoot every living soul full of holes, then burn his house to the ground."

Daisy glared at the insolent man. "You used to be a fairly nice person, for a *matukach*."

"Excuse me, madam—I do not mean to seem overly sensitive. But to my ears, this does not sound like the preamble to a heartfelt compliment."

"But now you've got a mean streak a yard wide. I guess it comes from hanging around with my smart-aleck nephew."

"I'll go along with that. For years now, my motto has been: 'Don't blame me—it's all Charlie Moon's fault.'"

"Ahem." This was Louise-Marie's way of making her presence known. "I've got all my stuff in the trunk of your police car."

"I thank you," Parris said. *Now I have to decide where to stash the Olds so it doesn't get spotted by one of my officers.*

Unable to stand the suspense any longer, Pokey Joe emerged from the her place of business to confront the lawman. With a closer look, his face seemed familiar. "Hey—ain't you that cop from town who came out here last year and arrested the jerk who kept breakin' into my store at night and stealin' all my sugar-cured hams and free-range eggs?"

Scott Parris tipped his felt hat. "Yes ma'am. It was me that put the pinch on the breakfast burglar."

She flashed him a toothy smile. "Well, I'm glad to see you again. If there's ever anything I can do for you, I hope you won't mind asking."

"As a matter of fact, there is and I don't." He gave her the ignition key. "These ladies, who are friends of mine, have had a bit of trouble with their automobile. It appears that someone has substituted a Mexican plate for the legal one that was issued by the great state of Colorado. Until we can get this straightened out, I would appreciate it if you would keep an eye on Mrs. LaForte's vintage Oldsmobile. I would appreciate it even more if you would park it in an out-of-the-way spot, so some ardent collector of classic automobiles doesn't steal it."

Pokey Joe eyed the key, the car, the fine-looking man. "Why, I wouldn't mind a-tall." She hopped into the Olds, drove it behind her store.

Parris gave Daisy a hearty one-armed hug. "Please get inside my fine black-and-white automobile and make yourself extremely comfortable."

Daisy gave the cop car a thoughtful look. *I don't want Louise-Marie where she can talk to him.* "I'll sit up front."

"Sorry," the lawman said. "The front passenger seat is reserved for petty criminals like jaywalkers, shoplifters, and little boys who pull the rabbi's beard. But the man behind the wheel—which happens to be me—needs protection from truly dangerous felons, like tribal elders who corrupt sweet little French-Canadian ladies, hit-and-run drivers, and meddlers who make a general nuisance of themselves. By departmental rules, such hardcases are required to ride in the backseat, behind the bulletproof partition." He looked down at the Columbine hound. "Along with any nonhumans that happen to require transportation."

Sidewinder emitted an eager whine, wagged his whiplike tail.

Daisy was miffed. "If you don't like that bolo tie that I scrimped and saved for, you can give it back."

"I will," Scott Parris said. "Soon as you return the expensive radio I gave you." He opened the rear door.

"I already told you," Daisy muttered, "that contraption was burned up in the fire. If you know how I can give you back something that's nothing but ashes scattered to the four winds, please explain it so I can understand!"

"Get in the car," he explained.

35

MEAN OLD WOMAN

Scott Parris thought long and hard about how best to deal with this sticky issue. They had left Pokey Joe's General Store miles behind them before the Granite Creek chief of police came to a decision. He addressed himself to the tiny woman in the passenger seat. "I'll work out a way to get your car back to Ignacio. But from now on, you'll have to keep the plate up-to-date." He could see only the patched eye, thought she might be asleep.

Louise-Marie LaForte was wide awake. "Whatever you think is best."

"Do you think you could find a qualified driver to take you places—like to the grocery store or the doctor's office?"

Louise-Marie nodded. "There's Henry, who lives next door." *He's only eleven, but he drives almost as good as me.*

"Well, I hope you'll talk to him."

Daisy Perika was seated directly behind the driver. The

hound was curled up on the seat beside her, his head resting in her lap. The angry woman was barely aware of the dog. Her entire attention was on a spot between the lawman's collar and hairline. The shaman was doing her best to raise a blister.

Her victim felt an itch on the back of his neck. He tried to scratch it away.

The Ute woman grinned. *I ain't quite lost my touch.*

Parris scratched again. *I must've got a mosquito bite.*

RESIDUE OF A LIFE

Charlie Moon was wandering around the grounds of his aunt's former home, picking up bits of this and pieces of that. A ballpoint pen here, a plastic hair clasp there, a little blue bottle filled with ground-up leaves, a scorched coffee can wedged into the crotch of a piñon branch. There was no way of knowing what might constitute a treasure for the tribal elder. He had just squatted to retrieve a blackened dime when the telephone in his jacket pocket warbled. The tribal investigator checked the caller ID, smiled. His best friend's voice would be just the tonic.

SMOOTHING THINGS OVER

Daisy knew perfectly well whom Scott Parris was calling. "You're not supposed to use one of those phones while you're driving," she said. "There's a rule against that!"

"There are exemptions for us sworn officers of the law," he said over his shoulder, and heard Charlie Moon's hello in his ear. Parris responded in his usual hearty tone. "Hey, pardner—how're you doing?"

Straining to eavesdrop on both sides of the conversation, Daisy leaned forward, turned her ear toward a patch of tiny perforations in the plastic partition. She was able to hear the white policeman's words, but her nephew might as well have been on Mars.

"I'm glad to hear it," Parris said. "Oh, I'm fine as frog's hair." He listened to a query about what he was up to. "Oh, nothin' much. Had to make a little run out east of town—to assist a pair of elderly motorists." Two heartbeats. "They were experiencing problems with an old, black Oldsmobile." A longer silence. "No, nothing like that. Turns out they had a faulty license plate." He smiled at the response. "I'll give you one guess, 'cause that's all you'll need." Parris snickered. "Well, that's one of 'em." He nodded at the invisible communicant. "Right again, your aunt was with her Canadian sidekick. But you don't need to worry, they're both all right. I'll deliver Daisy to the Columbine in about an hour, then I'll run Louise-Marie down to Ignacio." He listened to a welcome offer. *That'd save me a long and tiresome round trip.* "I'll ask her." Parris spoke to the passenger beside him. "Charlie would like for you to stay the night at his ranch. He says you'd be welcome as a warm breeze in December."

Louise-Marie shook her little gray head back and forth.

"She appreciates the offer, but I think she'd like to sleep in her own bed tonight." *Which means I'll be on the road till way after dark.* "Okay, pardner. See you later."

Daisy thought her thoughts. *Scott never intended to put me and Louise-Marie in no lineup. And I don't think he means to tell Charlie about the run-in I had with that pockmarked pimp or how I run over that white cop's foot. Scott's doing everything he can to keep me and Louise-Marie out of trouble. So I guess I'll stop trying to burn a blister on his neck.* She waited until they had passed through Granite Creek, then tapped on the Plexiglas shield.

Parris glanced at the rearview mirror. "Yeah?"

Daisy spoke through the patch of tiny holes. "I had some time to think about it." She took a deep breath. "I guess you can keep that expensive bolo tie I gave you."

"I am much obliged." He grinned at the reflection. "And

you can keep the cinders and ashes from that expensive radio that got toasted."

The sly old woman smiled. *Scott's all right. For a blue-eyed* matukach *devil.* Despite some setbacks, this had turned out to be a pretty good day. A hundred times better than sitting alone at home, wishing something interesting would happen. She leaned her head back on the seat, stared at a dim image of herself that looked back from the Plexiglas shield.

Sidewinder mumbled something in his sleep.

Daisy's hand was resting on the hound's head.

For a hundred ticks and tocks of the cosmic clock, nothing unusual happened.

Then—

Daisy was mildly intrigued when her reflection faded away from the polished plastic. She was absolutely electrified by the image that replaced it.

Why, it's me and Louise-Marie. And we're walking down that little road toward Pineapple Head's house. But we look really tall, like someone was looking up at us—someone whose face is close to the ground. Could it be the pitukupf? She did not think so. The little man rarely strayed more than a few miles from his badger hole in *Cañón del Espíritu.* And then she knew—

In an instant, and with a flash of opalescent light, she was jerked away from ordinary consciousness into that timeless, twilight place.

The Shaman's strange world was without color. But it did not matter that Daisy's vision was limited to shades of gray—she could smell dozens of wonderful scents that she had never known before. Underneath her, four soft feet padded along—her black nose sniffed and snuffed at this and that. She was searching for something. Something warm, something fleshy. Now she was moving more quickly along a dirt lane, beside an old fence row. Then the rabbit jumped up from a clump of sage, bounded off. Her heart raced with the most elemental joy she had ever known—she chased after the cottontail with a wild abandon! Her world was a forest of leafy bushes, her

own hoarse barking—and the overpowering odor of the flee-
ing rabbit's fear. The chase seemed as if it would never end,
then she was digging in the earth with her front paws. The
terrified rodent was not there. She heard herself whining.

Quite unexpectedly, there was someone standing beside
her. She looked up at the young woman, who smiled and said
something. The human's words were unintelligible, but
friendly, even empathetic—as if she was also familiar with
struggle, anguish, loss.

Daisy jerked with an unpleasant twitch, as if a spike of electrical current had passed along her spine. She looked at the
sleeping dog's head in her lap, and understood. *You seen her,*
didn't you? Pansy Blinkoe was in that house with Pineapple
Head, all right—but when she saw me and Louise-Marie
coming, she must've slipped away, run off to hide in the
bushes. For a moment, she considered telling the white policeman what she now knew for a fact. *But he'd want to know*
how I could be so sure, and I could never tell him how I'd
seen what was in this dog's mind. So I'll keep this to myself
until I can figure out what to do about it.

Scott Parris was pleased with how he had managed a po-
tentially sticky situation. *Eddie Knox won't try to find out*
who ran over his foot; he'll just be relieved when I change my
mind about putting him and Slocum on suspension. Louise-
Marie will get a legal plate put on her Olds, and that man
who lives next door will do the driving for her. And I put
enough of a scare into Daisy that she's finally learned her
lesson. He exhaled a gratifying sigh. *By tomorrow, this busi-*
ness will have all blown over.

They moved on down the road, along the arrow of time—
into an unknown, unknowable future.

36

GRUMPY OLD WOMAN

After Scott Parris had deposited Daisy at the Columbine and departed with Louise-Marie LaForte, the Ute woman went directly to her downstairs bedroom and shut the door. An hour later, hearing Charlie Moon drive up, she slipped into bed with all her clothes on and switched off the light. When he tapped lightly on her door, asked if she was all right, she pretended to be sound asleep, even to the deceit of faking a snore. She listened tensely while he had his evening meal, then made his way upstairs to his bed.

Even after the entire house was dark, Daisy could find no rest. Well past midnight, she lay wide-awake in the comfortable four-poster, staring up at a dark void where the ceiling ought to be. The events of this singular day kept racing through her mind. Louise-Marie LaForte, with a patch over her eye, almost running the car off the Too Late bridge. That mean white policeman, telling her to get out of the car, then dancing around after she ran over his foot. The police car chasing after her, then running off the road. Pokey Joe in her tentlike overalls, dispensing sandwiches and Twinkies. Pockmarked Pineapple Head DeSoto, his bulging belly hanging out from under his sissy yellow shirt.

Finally, at a small hour, Daisy drifted off into a troubled sleep. Almost immediately, she was plagued with the most bizarre dream. She was running and tumbling through the brush and the brambles. At one moment she was the terrified rabbit, then she would assume the role of the pursuing hound. But always—in the background—was the slim form of the yellow-haired white woman. Pansy Blinkoe watched the chasing game, clapped her hands to see such sport.

The first hint of daylight came absurdly early.

When she heard her nephew moving around in the kitchen, Daisy put her feet on the cold hardwood floor. *Oh, God. I am too old to keep on living—I should've been in the ground a dozen years ago.* She took a deep breath and tried to think a positive thought. *Once I get myself up, I'll start to feel better.* One creaking joint at a time, she got herself up. She did not feel the least bit better. On the contrary, what she saw in the full-length mirror made her shudder. *What a pitiful old woman—I look like death warmed over.*

Charlie Moon tapped on the door. "You ready for some coffee?"

"I'm ready for a coffin."

"What?"

"Never mind. Once I manage to pull myself together, I'll be out." *If I stay alive that long.* But the wonderful scent of fresh coffee seeped through the cracks around the door, and this did the trick. As she began to pull on her day clothes, the old woman started thinking about yesterday, and the week before—all the things she was angry about. And what she could do to get even. By the time she stomped into the big ranch-house kitchen, Daisy was glaring at her nephew, ready to tear into him tooth and claw. She was momentarily deterred by something that struck her as quite odd. "Why're you dolled up in your best suit of clothes?"

Moon hitched his thumbs in his vest pockets. "I aim to go see a lady."

"A *white* woman, I'll bet."

"You would win the wager." He gave her a sly look. "You and Louise-Marie have a good time yesterday?"

"Good enough." *Just you say one smart-aleck thing about what me and her was up to, and I'll pick up this chair and break it over your head.*

Moon pulled the intended weapon away from the table, helped her settle into it. "I'm glad you got to spend some time with your friend. Going for a nice ride must've been just the thing to cheer you up." He patted her shoulder. "I'm sorry there was trouble with the car. Lucky thing Scott happened by, and brought you back home."

"Hmmph," she said. *He's just softening me up.*

He seated himself across the table. "Did you get a good night's sleep?"

Hah—now the questions start. Well, I'll just ignore him. She sipped at the coffee, made a face. "This is weak as Sister Sarah's mint tea."

Moon stared at the tar-black brew. "I'll make another pot, just for you." He was getting up from his chair when she waved him back.

"Never mind. I'll eat and drink whatever's put in front of me." She tried a forkful of scrambled eggs, was highly annoyed that she could find nothing to complain about. "After all, it's not like I'm family or nothing—I'm just a guest in your fine big ranch house. Who'm I, to expect things should be made to suit me?"

He grinned over a plate of eggs and chili. "I guess you didn't sleep all that well."

"I slept just fine." *I'll ask him before he asks me.* "So what did you do yesterday?"

He shrugged the broad shoulders. "Had a confab with my foreman about the fence repairs along the north pasture. Stopped over at the Big Hat to check on my new hands. Then I spent the rest of the day down at your place, cleaning things up some."

She shot him a look. "I didn't know there was anything left to clean up."

"There's still quite a bit of odds and ends scattered around. I thought I'd gather some of it up for you."

This aroused the old woman's curiosity. "Well where is it?"

"There's a couple of cardboard boxes out in the pickup."

"You could've brought 'em inside."

"I'll do that later. But I did bring you in a sample." He got up, went to an oak cabinet, found what he was looking for. He placed the blackened coffee can on the table by her coffee cup. "I put some of the smaller things in this."

She glared at the thing. "Where did you get that?"

She must not be quite awake yet. "These are some things that I picked up around your yard—"

"No. I mean *that.*" She pointed at the container.

"The coffee can?" He seated himself. "The blast had blown it into a tree, so I picked it off a branch, and—"

"Then you can put it back."

Moon arched an eyebrow. "Beg your pardon?"

"That ain't mine."

"What ain't yours?"

She turned the can so he could see a small patch of paint that remained. "What color is that?"

I bet this is a trick question. "Well, I'd say . . . green."

"What color can does Folgers regular coffee come in?"

"Oh, right. Red. I guess you don't buy much decaf—"

"During my whole life, I never bought nothing but good old red-can regular coffee. I wouldn't have no other kind in my kitchen." She gave her cup a suspicious look. "You surely wouldn't—"

"No," Moon said quickly. "That's not decaf."

She sniffed. "What's wrong with your well-water? This smells like kerosene."

"I'll be glad to make another pot—"

"Ah, don't bother. I've drunk worse stuff than this and liked it." She peered into the can. "Looks like a pile of burnt-up junk to me."

"That's not far from the truth. But before we toss it, you

might want to scratch around some. There might be a pretty pinto pony in there somewhere."

"A pony?" *That is just about the dumbest thing I ever heard.* She turned the can upside down to dump the junk on the table, proceeded to sort through the odds and ends. "Except for this old silver dime, I don't see anything here that's worth a thimble of monkey spit." It hit her hard. Tears began to well in her eyes. "After all these years, I don't have nothing left. *Nothing.*"

He watched her across the table, not knowing what to say. "You still have that nice telephone I bought you."

She lifted the bulky pendant in her hand, blinked at it. "This ain't worth the kindling wood it'd take to burn it up."

Moon buttered a biscuit. "What's wrong with it?"

I've been really hateful this morning. I shouldn't complain about this silly little telephone. But remembering a particular grudge against her nephew, she could not help herself. "I'll tell you what's wrong with it—when you call a person on it and leave 'em a message, they don't ever call you back."

The grin found his face again. "That might not be the phone's fault."

Her scowl trumped his grin. "And what do you mean by that?"

Moon realized he'd gone a wisecrack too far. "Well . . . uh . . . I . . ."

Daisy knew she had him by the neck. "Ask me *who it was* I called that didn't call me back."

"Okay. Who it was?"

"I'll tell you who—it was a big smart aleck that goes by the name of Charlie Moon."

I might've known. "When did you call me?"

She had to stop and think back. "The day before that night my trailer burnt down."

"Was the message about something important?"

"It might've been."

"Want to tell me what?"

"No I don't. I left you a phone message. If you wasn't interested enough to call me back then, you wouldn't care to hear about it again."

"Try me."

She shook her head.

He got up from his chair, came to her side. "Let me have a look at your pendant phone."

"You can keep it for all I care." She took the loop from around her neck, returned the birthday present to her nephew. "A broken telephone is worse than not having one at all."

"I'm going into town today, I'll drop it off where I bought it, see that they get it fixed." He inspected the small instrument. There was no obvious sign of damage. "Now show me exactly what you did."

He thinks I'm too dumb to call him on the phone. "I don't care to be cross-examined this early in the morning. Not before I've finished this fine cup of kerosene."

"If you don't show me what you did, I won't know what to tell the technician."

"Oh, all right." She snatched the miniature marvel of modern technology away from him. "First, I pushed this button to dial your cell phone, but all I got was a recording. So I pushed the other button, for the phone here at the ranch house. Dolly Bushman answered and told me you'd gone to see that lawyer fella. The one with the beady eyes that're too close together."

"I'm guessing you mean Trottman."

"That's the one. Dolly gave me his number, and after I punched it in with a toothpick, all I got was another stupid recording. So then I pushed that other button to get your cell phone again."

"Which other button?"

"This button right here," she snapped. "Can't you remember nothing?"

There was a merry sparkle in his eye. "What happened then?"

"Just like the time before, you didn't pick up—all I got was that dumb recording. But this time, I left you a message."

He nodded. "Oh, sure, *that* message—the one about how you wanted a new TV set and—"

"It wasn't about no TV! I told you I knew exactly where that Pansy Blinkoe woman was hiding and—" She caught herself. "That wasn't fair—you know I didn't mean to tell you that. You *tricked* me."

"Did I?"

Her high-temperature glare fairly sizzled his skin.

Moon thought he'd try again. "So where is Mrs. Blinkoe hiding?"

"After you get this dumb thing fixed, I'll tell you." She slapped the pendant telephone into his hand. "I'll call you, and leave you another message."

He got the message.

Charlie Moon strode across the yard with a brown paper bag in his hand, got into the Columbine Expedition, sniffed at the paper bag, put it on the passenger seat. He rummaged around in the glove compartment for his cell phone, turned it on, dialed a very smart lady he had not seen for years. Her answering machine responded with a recording of the familiar voice.

> *If you're wanting to sell me something, forget it. I don't want it, and even if I did, I couldn't afford it. The ringer on my telephone is turned off. If you're someone I know, and you want to talk to me in person, come to my house and knock on the door. Anytime between ten A.M. and six P.M.*

Guess I'll just have to go knock on her door. He called the FBI office in Durango, listened to an automated response which informed him that no one was in, but to leave a message and ". . . if your business is urgent, please dial the Denver Field Office." Moon shook his head. *Don't anybody answer their phone anymore?* The tribal investigator left Special Agent McTeague a message to the effect that at three P.M. today, he would be at Big Tony's, desperately lonely, and hoped she could find time to join him. "And if you do, I'll have something for you—not to mention a free lunch." With this double-barreled incentive, he disconnected.

The tribal investigator started the engine, was about to

pull away when he remembered the "important message" Aunt Daisy claimed to have left him. He dialed his cell phone answering service. There were no messages. *Maybe the phone company has messed up.* He removed his aunt's pendant telephone from his shirt pocket, pressed the button Daisy said she had used to call and leave him a message. His cell phone did not ring. *Maybe it's on the blink. When was the last time I got a call on it?* Unable to remember, he pressed Daisy's pendant telephone to his ear, listened to a few final rings, then the computer-generated voice.

> *The number you have dialed is not responding. If you wish to leave a message, please press one and wait for the tone.*

After inspecting each tiny label on each tiny button, squinting at the telephone number on LCD screen, Moon concluded that his aunt's miniature telephone was working just fine. The problem was on the other end.

He dialed the foreman's residence, heard Bushman's gruff hello.

"G'morning, Pete. Listen close, because I'm a little pressed for time. First, I'm on my way to town and I'm going to lock the Columbine's front gate. I want it *kept* locked till I say otherwise, so make sure all the cowboys know that. Second, I want you to post three men in eight-hour shifts to ride herd on my aunt. I don't want her leaving the ranch without my say-so, and if she goes for a walk, the man on duty will have to keep a close eye on her." A pause. "Yeah, I know how we're already shorthanded, but that's how it's gonna be. And one more thing—issue the man on guard a rifle and a sidearm." Another pause. "Because if a cowboy is assigned to guard duty, he expects to be armed. Now see to it, Pete. I'll listen to all eleven dozen of your complaints when I get back." And *they'll go in one ear and right out the other.*

37

PAYING A CALL ON MISS ATHERTON

Charlie Moon pulled the Expedition up to a crumbling curb, parked under the shade of a mulberry tree. The property was concealed by a hedge of rosebushes that had not been trimmed since Mr. Reagan was president. Three particularly fine butter-colored blossoms were hanging over the sidewalk, well within the public domain. The lawman recognized the clear hazard to public health—some innocent child might come zipping by on a skateboard and get a thorn in the eye. Seeing his duty, Moon did not hesitate. He unfolded his pocketknife, removed the prickly stems.

He pushed a rusty wrought-iron gate open, followed the remnants of a bricked walk through a weedy lawn. Smothered with purple lilacs, choked with Virginia creepers, the little brick house seemed to be gasping for a final breath. The painted-concrete front porch was bordered by clusters of forlorn four-o'clocks and pots of sickly geraniums. He stepped on a horsehair welcome mat, wiped each boot toe on the back of his trousers, tapped lightly on the door. He pretended not to notice the small, roundish face that appeared in a window, behind a filmy net of lace curtain.

The eighty-year-old woman blinked at the seven-foot-tall man. *My goodness, what is Charlie Moon doing here—and all dressed up like he was going to the senior prom?* The lady paused momentarily by a mirror, blinked through trifocals at a mop of white hair, patted a bit of silver fluff into place.

As the door opened, the Ute removed his dove-gray John B. Stetson hat.

The five-foot-two woman looked up at him. "Well knock me over with a canary feather, if it isn't Beanstalk Charlie."

That had been his high school nickname from the time he'd gotten his fourteen-year-old growth spurt. "It's me all right." He had been afraid of her way back then, and Miss Atherton looked just as tough as she'd ever been. "Uh—I'm sorry to just drop in, but when I called you on the phone this morning—"

She laughed, shushed him with a flutter of a blue-veined hand. "Oh, I've got where I detest these modern so-called conveniences. If a person won't come here and see me, why, I'd rather they just leave me be." She noticed what he had in his hand. Arched an eyebrow.

"This is for you." He presented the offering.

She accepted the freshly harvested blossoms. "Oh—I absolutely *love* any kind of flower. And yellow roses are my very favorite." The teacher smiled at her former high-school pupil. "How did you know, Charlie?"

"Trade secret," the lawman said.

"No, really."

"I asked around in the local bars and pool halls. Talked to a couple of your scruffy boyfriends. Both of 'em said yellow roses was just the thing."

"Oh, foo—I haven't had a boyfriend since the big war. And come to think of it, I guess I don't have any manners." She stepped aside, made an inviting gesture with the bouquet. "Please come inside."

The immaculate inner sanctum was the antithesis of the
seedy lawn. There were lace doilies on every chair arm, a
faint scent of peach blossoms in the air, not a molecule of
dust from one flower-papered wall to another. He hoped he
wasn't tracking dirt on the spotless blue carpet.

Miss Atherton ushered her unexpected guest to an over-
stuffed couch, put the roses in a crystal vase, vanished into
the kitchen to make some green tea, reappeared shortly with
this healthy beverage. She also brought an offering of salted
cashews, tiny cookies, and candied fruit—all arranged in perfect symmetry on a lacquered Japanese tray.

Moon enjoyed the cookies and nuts, tried a sugared plum,
pretended to like the tea—which was about as good as any
sample of hot water a man might happen to find in a translu-
cent china cup. But after taking a taste or two, he concluded
that heated H_2O had a distinct edge on this grass-tinted brew.
Having been a well-brought-up boy, he drank it just the same.

They talked for an hour or more. About old times, old
friends, how it was way back then when everything was better.

Finally, she said: "I know very well you haven't come here
for idle conversation." She eyed the crisply pressed suit. "In
fact, it appears that you have merely stopped by on your way."

"On my way where?"

"To see some nice young lady." Her eyes sparkled. "Am I
right?"

A grin split Moon's dark face. "You're a long way from
being wrong."

"Who is she?"

"Lila Mae McTeague's her name."

"I knew a McTeague once, in Indianapolis. I believe he
sold men's shoes." *Or was it ladies' hats?*

"Sounds like a boyfriend."

"Almost." Her eyes began to glaze over at the memory. "I
think he had a crush on me." *Perhaps I should have stayed in
Indiana. . . .*

He held his silence while the old woman dreamed her
dreams.

Presently, she returned to the present. "We've just about

used up the small talk, Charles. Is there anything in particular you have on your mind?"

"Oh, this and that. Denver politics. Major League baseball. The price of beef." He gave her a peculiar look. "Or we could talk about your particular specialty."

"Whatever do you mean?"

"I mean the stuff you tried to teach me when I was a junior at Ignacio High."

"English or biology?" *He could certainly do with a refresher in the former.*

"Oh, I don't have a problem with English. It's the science of living things that's lately raised some questions in my mind." He turned a frosted cookie in his hands. "When I was a young fellow, there was lots of things I didn't pay nearly enough attention to. But lately, some of these issues have begun to pique my interest. Even keep me awake at night."

Charlie had always been an unusual, unpredictable boy. "Biology is a rather broad field, especially nowadays, but I do try to keep up. What are you interested in?"

"When it comes to breeding cattle," the rancher said, "I guess I know my business about as well as the next stockman—I mean about reproduction and such." He frowned with intense concentration. "If I was to cross a Hereford with a Brahma, or an Angus with a buffalo, I'd know what kind of calf to expect. But there's some other things I'm not so sure about."

Barely able to bear the suspense, the bright-eyed little schoolteacher put her teacup on the tray, leaned forward. She asked what, exactly, it was that he wanted to know.

Moon told her. Exactly.

The schoolmarm shook her head in a manner that suggested a mild disappointment in this former pupil. "Charles, I am surprised that you should have the least doubt on such an elementary issue. Such an outcome as you report is, well . . . so unlikely as to be immediately dismissed."

"But not impossible?"

"There are rare exceptions." She blinked at him. "But we're talking *very* long odds."

"A lot depends on this." The tribal investigator stared at the cookie. "I need to be dead sure." Her scholarly assurance had given him some hope, but he was only halfway there. He needed technical assistance from someone who could be trusted to keep her mouth shut. "Miss Atherton, do you have a computer?"

"Well of course I do." Pride of ownership sparkled in her eyes. "A 3.6-gigahertz laptop with over 200 megabytes of RAM and a 600-gigabyte hard drive."

"And I bet you know how to find things on the Internet."

"In my sleep. What shall I Google for you?"

"Google?"

"Charles, Charles—you are *so* behind the times." Miss Atherton sighed. "What sort of information do you require?"

He told her.

"If it's there, I'll find it." She brought the laptop to the parlor, got right to work.

Thirty minutes later, Charlie Moon was feeling good. No, three notches better than good. Blissful, even. Happy enough to drink a half-pint of hot, greenish water and enjoy every drop. He lifted the cup to salute the elderly scholar. "Miss Atherton, if you've got any left in the pot, can I have another dose of this fine beverage?"

"*May* I," she shot back.

"What?"

"*May* I have another cup of green tea."

"Sure," he said. "While you're pouring some for me, help yourself to a shot."

38

AT BIG TONY'S

Giving lie to the vile rumor that he operated on "Indian time," the tribal investigator arrived at the restaurant four minutes early. McTeague's government-issue Ford sedan was not yet in the parking lot, the lunch crowd was long gone, the proprietor was behind the counter, munching on a king-size carrot.

Big Tony saw the customer, waved the vegetable like a flag. "How ya doin', Chollie?"

"Fine, Tony. How're you?"

"I'm on a horrible diet and I don't want to talk about it." The chef scowled at his customer, snapped off another bite of the orange root. "What's that paper bag—you bring your own lunch?"

"Just a precaution—I'm sure there's something on the menu that'll strike my fancy." Moon homed in on his favorite spot by the window, jerked out a chair.

Tony brought a menu and a mug of coffee, gave the table a hearty swipe. "You eatin' alone today?"

"Sure hope not." Moon spooned six helpings of sugar into the beverage. "I'm expecting an exceptional lady."

"Whatta you mean by 'ceptional?"

"I mean she's a knockout on wheels and brainy to boot. And not only that, she is gainfully employed and well-heeled. Did I mention that she will be paying the bill?"

This produced a derisive snort. "That'll be the day—when some good-looking doll with the do-re-mi buys *you* lunch."

"Would you care to place a modest wager on that?" Moon laid a twenty-dollar bill on the table. "Mr. Jackson says she picks up the check."

For Tony, a bet involving hard cash in plain sight was harder to resist than a jelly doughnut soaked in honey. "Even Steven?"

"Unless you want to give me ten-to-one."

"Hah! That'll be the day." The proprietor removed a crisp pair of tens from his wallet, covered the twenty. "You want I should put this dough in the usual spot?"

"Certainly." Moon consulted the menu. "How's the lasagna?"

Tony removed a cranberry-glass bud vase from a tiny bric-a-brac shelf, stuffed the rolled-up bills into it. "Please, don't talk to me about that." He gazed wistfully at the menu, imagined a big slab of *that,* licked his lips. "In fact, don't even say the name of it out loud."

"L-word makes your mouth water, huh?"

The famished fellow nodded. "Like Niagara Falls after a forty days and forty nights of rain upstream."

Moon made a face. "Try to go a little lighter on the vivid descriptions of your drooling, Tony. You're not exactly helping my appetite."

"Listen to me, Chollie—you skinny guys don't have no idea what a serious appetite is. If I should fall offa this diet, I'll start off with a whole tray of baked . . . of baked *you know what.* And that'd be just for starters." He turned his broad backside toward the customer. "If this knockout-on-wheels lady happens to show up, and you two get around to deciding what you want to eat, don't tell me nothing out loud—just put a finger on the menu."

39

A GIFT FOR THE LADY

At three minutes and fourteen seconds past the hour, FBI special agent Lila Mae McTeague burst through the door.

Moon got up to pull a chair out for the lady. He also scowled at his watch. "Among us Native Americans, promptness is considered a cardinal virtue."

"Can it," she said, and seated herself. "I've had a hectic day."

Big Tony plopped a glass of water in front of the new arrival. He smiled down at the elegant woman. *Chollie wasn't kidding. She's right up there with Audrey Hepburn. In fact, she's a good head taller than Audrey was.*

Moon explained the rule that was in effect during Big Tony's current diet.

McTeague dutifully tapped the menu at her entrée selection, verbally requested iced tea. After Moon had put his finger on the lasagna and the restaurateur had departed, she gave her date the eye. "Well?"

He gave it right back to her. "Well what?"

"Well what's on your mind?"

Moon reached across the table, took her hand in his. "I'll tell you what's on my mind. You and me. Cozy little cabin on a lake." He gazed at the ceiling. "Big sky full of twinkling stars and—"

"None of your blarney." The pretty woman blushed, pulled her hand away. "I'm on duty."

"Hmm," he said.

She straightened the collar of her blouse. "What does that mean?"

"It means that I'm cogitating. And what I come up with is this—if you are on duty, then maybe I shouldn't give you the present I brought."

She flashed him a little-girl smile. "What did you bring me?"

"Guess."

"Apricot bonbons?"

He shook his head. "I wouldn't want to add an ounce to your trim figure."

Another blush. "Flowers, then."

"Nope. I had some yellow roses this morning, but I gave 'em to another lady friend."

She lost the smile, arched a perfect brow. "What, then?"

He reached under the table, placed his offering between the candle holders. "This."

McTeague made a face. "You brought me a present in a brown paper bag?"

"I was in a hurry."

She looked inside. "Charlie—it's nothing but a filthy old tin can."

"They hardly ever make 'em out of tin anymore, McTeague. That is genuine American steel."

The FBI agent sniffed. "And it stinks!"

"Now don't go out of your way to hurt my feelings—I'm not made of stone."

She sniffed again. "But it *does* stink."

"It does not *stink*," he said. "It has a particular kind of pungent scent."

"Like what?"

"You're one of Uncle Sam's finest. You tell me."

A third sniff. This one more technical. "Kerosene?"

"That's what my aunt Daisy's nose thought." *Only she thought she was smelling her cup of coffee.*

She gave the can a long, hard look. "Is this some sort of evidence from your aunt's trailer fire?"

"There is no fooling Special Agent McTeague." He took a deep breath. "I've said it before, I'll say it again. There is no fooling Special Agent McTeague."

"Okay, okay. I'll send it off to Forensics in D.C." A thoughtful pause. "What should our white-smocked beaker geeks expect to find?"

"If we was lucky enough to win the lottery, there'd be some prints on the can that wasn't mine."

"And discounting such an unlikely piece of good fortune?"

He shrugged. "It's a shot in the dark."

McTeague studied the Ute's face. "Thank you for the stinky can."

He raised his coffee mug. "You are entirely welcome."

"Now, in exchange for the piece of trash, I've got something for you."

"Okay." He grinned. "But don't go overboard. This is a public place."

"Don't get your hopes up, cowboy." The FBI agent leaned forward, lowered her voice. "My gift comes in two parts. First, there's the information, then the advice. Both have something to do with your professional relationship to the late Dr. Manfred Wilhelm Blinkoe."

Moon did not look pleased. "This sounds like something that will ruin my lunch."

She continued, without a trace of sympathy. "Since his houseboat was destroyed, we've been collecting fragments that wash up here and there. Divers have recovered some of the heavier remnants. Forensics have detected traces of high explosives on a portion of the engine's output manifold. We're talking TNT—a type that is commonly used in mining and road construction. Your client was obviously murdered."

HUDSON BOOKSELLERS
Store #474
DFW TERMINAL C GATE 4-28

Bulb Reg CID 106 1:01 pm 08/20/06

S SHADOW MAN	1 @	6.99	6.99
S 0312936648			
SUBTOTAL			6.99
SALES TAX - 7.5%			.51
TOTAL			7.50
MASTER CARD PAYMENT			7.50

HAVE A SAFE AND WONDERFUL FLIGHT
BOOK OF THE MONTH
LIPSTICK JUNGLE
By Candace Bushnell

```
              424241522889
           HUDSON NEWS - DALLAS
          DFW TERMINAL B GATE 21
           GRAPEVINE, TX  75261
               972-456-5204


       MERCHANT 8100 300003432977 012
         DATE : 08/20/06  01:03 PM


   ACCOUNT #:  XXXXXXXXXXXX1805
   TYPE:       MASTERCARD


   REF #   31
   BATCH #:   232001
   AUTH #:    780361


   SALE             $       7.50


   I AGREE TO PAY THE ABOVE TOTAL AMOUNT
   ACCORDING TO THE CARD ISSUER AGREEMENT
   (MERCHANT AGREEMENT IF CREDIT VOUCHER)

   X_____
                 SIGNATURE


   TOP COPY-MERCHANT  BOTTOM-COPY CUSTOMER
```

The lawman toyed with his coffee mug. "I appreciate the information. I bet I can guess the advice."

"I'm sure you can." She reached across the table to touch his hand. "I know it's tough to lose a client. You'll want to find out what happened to Dr. Blinkoe. But leave it alone. This particular homicide is Bureau business. I have permission to keep you informed about our progress, but the bottom line is this: You stay clear of the case."

"Okay."

She shot him a suspicious look. "I warn you to keep clear of the Blinkoe homicide, and that's all you've got to say— 'okay'?"

He seemed to be thinking hard. "Okay, *ma'am*?"

She was about to reply when the waiter arrived with her iced tea.

The angry man in the pickup watched Big Tony's Restaurant from across the street. He took a sip of whiskey from a pewter flask; his hungry stomach rumbled. *So what're the skinny Indian and the FBI gal gabbing about?* The silenced rifle was behind the seat. *I could shoot 'em both from right here.* He grinned. *Sure, knock 'em off in broad daylight, then just drive away. Boy, howdy—wouldn't that be something to write home about? If I had a real home* . . . The grin gradually slipped away. *I've got to be patient. Wait till I can get the job done right.*

40

THE LUNA COUNTY INCIDENT REVISITED

Having finished a meal that had been dominated by the woman's wary stare, Moon wiped his mouth with a linen napkin, leaned back in his chair. "How did you like your grub?"

A little shrug. "It was okay."

He grinned. "That's all you can say—just 'okay'?"

"You are beginning to annoy me." Special Agent McTeague tossed an olive at him.

Moon executed a deft one-hand catch. "Well, that's a beginning."

"Let me be more succinct." Her tone was acidic. "You are giving me heartburn."

"I never wanted to do that—what can I do to make up for it?"

"Behave like every other local cop who believes he's been

stepped on by the Bureau. Put up a big fuss, bang your fist on the table, yell about how the FBI has no right to order you off the Blinkoe homicide case."

"I would if I could—but my heart wouldn't be in it."

"Even so. Humor me."

"Okay, I'll try to give you some trouble." He helped himself to an after-dinner mint. "I suppose I could ask you why the FBI has latched on to this particular killing. But that's no good. You wouldn't tell me."

"Perhaps." She flashed the sunshine smile. "But you won't know unless you ask straight-out."

"I'm way too shy for the direct approach. Would you mind if I worked my way up to a guess?"

"I could say yes." She avoided his level gaze. "But that wouldn't stop you."

"Thank you for the encouragement. Here goes: First time I met Dr. Blinkoe was when he came to my aunt Daisy's place with his lawyer. While my relative entertained Mr. Trotter, me and this potential client had a private talk. Blinkoe claimed he was sure someone had already tried to shoot him that night on the restaurant patio. He wanted me to help him stay alive. When I asked why he didn't go to the cops on the public payroll, he told me he'd already talked to our local chief of police, who didn't believe the shooter had intended to put a hole through him. And as far as the feds were concerned, they weren't. Concerned, I mean. Blinkoe claimed the FBI didn't care a nickel's worth whether he got shot or not." The gambler was holding sorry cards. He hoped McTeague would show her hand.

"Did Dr. Blinkoe tell you *why* he was not the Bureau's favorite orthodontist?"

Moon played the bluff. "Every cop shop in a dozen states has heard one version or another of the story. But the fact is, when some cold-blooded killer was stalking Blinkoe, he knew the FBI wouldn't turn a finger to help him. The way he saw it, the feds wanted him behind bars for the rest of his natural life." He paused. "But seeing as how the U.S. govern-

ment hadn't managed to get that done . . . maybe the Bureau
would be satisfied just to see him dead. That way, they could
close the case—without making the least effort to find out
what'd *really* happened."

She clenched her hands into fists. "So that's what he told
you. And you believed him?"

Moon shrugged. "I don't necessarily believe everything a
client tells me." He put on a sad expression. "Even when it
looks like he was an innocent victim of circumstantial evidence."

"Him—innocent?" Agent McTeague rolled her pretty
eyes. "That's a laugh."

"Sounds like you've read his file."

"Cover to cover." She tapped a finger on the table. "And
we're talking upwards of two hundred pages."

"I don't doubt he's misbehaved from time to time—most
of us have something to be ashamed of." Moon looked
ashamed of some unconfessed sin. "But there's no hard proof
he was mixed up in that *particular* business. From time to
time, even the FBI makes mistakes."

"There was no mistake," she snapped. "Blinkoe was there,
manning the machine gun, when the cartel soldiers were
killed in the shootout. The wounded pilot and his partners—
by which I mean Blinkoe and the Colombian national—got
away in the Humvee and the laundry truck with at least
twenty bags of cash."

*Machine gun. Cartel. Pilot. Humvee. Laundry truck. Bags
of cash.* This was a fit for only one of the felonies he'd heard
of during the past decade. Now Charlie Moon knew what
Blinkoe had been suspected of—and in all likelihood was
guilty of. Suppressing the satisfied expression required all of
his willpower. "Well, whoever the pilot's partners were, that
was quite some operation. The DC-3 they swiped from the
aircraft museum near Santa Fe was supposed to land just
south of the border in old Mexico. But the pilot puts the crate
down a few miles *north* of the border, in New Mexico, where
some of his buddies are waiting."

"You are rather well informed." She arched an eyebrow at

the tribal investigator. "Did Manfred Blinkoe tell you about this?"

"Nope." *You did.* "It was a pretty big deal at the time. There were stories in the newspapers, and on the TV. And from what I recall, the DC-3 jockey and his buddies were never found."

"Your information from the popular media is incomplete."

He grinned. "Then fill me in."

She hesitated, then: "The pilot—a Mr. Hitchcock—was mortally wounded in the firefight. Manfred Blinkoe and his Colombian pal—a Mr. Pablo Feliciano—loaded the pilot into the laundry truck with the stolen money, but he died before they arrived at their destination. They disposed of the corpse in an arroyo somewhere in the Gila Wilderness. Hours later, they concealed their ill-gotten gains at a prearranged location."

Moon performed a rapid calculation: Three minus one minus one more equals one. "Of the three fellas who allegedly set up the hijacking, the pilot died that same night. On the reasonable assumption that Dr. Blinkoe did not inform on *himself,* Señor Feliciano must have been the guy who talked."

She smiled at this faultless piece of deduction. "Only a few weeks after the incident, Pablo Feliciano was arrested in Sonora on a murder charge. He made a deal with the *federales.* In hopes of having the charges reduced to manslaughter, he agreed to rat out his U.S. partners in the hijacking. A team of DEA and FBI agents interviewed him in the Hermosillo *calabozo.*"

"And he implicated Dr. Blinkoe?"

"Of course." She gave him an expectant look. "This is where you ask me why Manfred Blinkoe was never formally charged by the Department of Justice."

"Okay. Why was Dr. Blinkoe never formally charged by the Department of Justice?"

"Before the DEA could obtain a legally deposed statement, someone detonated a charge of high explosive against the cell-block wall. Three prisoners died as a result, but about two dozen others escaped during the confusion—including Mr. Feliciano. There were several rumors floating around about who had set up the jailbreak. Would you like to hear the one I like best?"

Eager to please the lady, Moon nodded.

"Okay, here's my favorite: According to this theory, the Colombian drug cartel was behind it—they blew up half the jail just to get access to Feliciano. This score-settling scenario is supported by reports of his subsequent death, but his body hasn't turned up."

"So Hitchcock is dead, Feliciano is either dead or in hiding, and all you've got on Dr. Blinkoe is hearsay evidence from a known felon."

"Sadly, that is about the size of it. It would have helped to have Feliciano's sworn testimony in a court of law that Manfred Blinkoe participated in the theft of the cartel's money-filled laundry bags."

He thought it would be fun to twist this she-cat's tail a couple of more turns. And just maybe, crank out some additional information. "That's not the way I heard it," Moon said. "The word going around was that Dr. Blinkoe was clean as a brand-new butterfly wing. In fact, he was in North Carolina at the time, attending a medical conference. The shootout was actually between two gangs of Colombian drug dealers who—"

"What you heard from your doughnut-munching police-station buddies were baseless rumors. According to Mr. Feliciano's informal testimony, Blinkoe and Hitchcock were his partners in the hijacking. On top of that, Blinkoe was the machine gunner. Without provocation, he shot down several Colombian citizens. The fact that they were drug runners is quite beside the point—Blinkoe was a cold-blooded murderer."

The Ute looked troubled. "It is bad form to speak ill of the lately deceased."

"Spare me the pithy proverbs. Alive, Blinkoe was a rotten apple. Now he is a dead rotten apple." *If he's actually dead . . .*

"You are a tough lady, McTeague."

"That may be. Do you want to hear—as the famous news broadcaster Mr. Paul Harvey might say—the 'rest of the story'?"

"You bet. I have my ear to the radio."

"The Colombian who ratted out Blinkoe also told us where the bags of cash were cached."

"You have a way with words, Agent McTeague. But from the sad look on your pan, I'm gonna guess that when the feds got to the spot, those bags of greenbacks were gone."

"Of course they were gone. Manfred Blinkoe had undoubtedly heard through the grapevine about the leak south of the border. But this wasn't some story Feliciano made up—forensics evidence of the presence of the loot was found."

"Forensics evidence—what are we taking about?"

"A single twenty-dollar bill. Beside President Jackson, it featured a dime-sized smirking smiley face, sketched in red ink." The FBI agent looked as if she would like to bite a railroad spike. "It is obvious that Dr. Blinkoe left this item behind to taunt the federal authorities."

"Not a smart thing to do."

"I hope you will remember that. But the main point is that your recently deceased client had removed the laundry bags filled with twenty-dollar bills. Dr. Blinkoe probably deposited this very considerable fortune in several foreign bank accounts."

"Well, that's an interesting story. If those bags of money aren't fiction, somebody must've made off with 'em. But except for some tale told by a felon locked up in a Mexican jail, there's no proof my client had anything to do with—"

"Your *former* client, Charlie. And I'm not interested in hearing an account of his protestations about being an innocent bystander or whatever." She had twisted her linen napkin into a knot. "I *hate* it when bad guys get away."

"I hate to mention money. But what was the take?"

"An estimated eighty million dollars."

Moon made a low whistle. "That much?"

She nodded. "I am authorized to tell you that the Department of the Treasury is offering a substantial reward for information leading to the recovery of the cash."

"How substantial?"

"Ten percent of the amount recovered. So if you should happen to come across any information that might assist the government—such as numbers to foreign bank accounts—it would be well worth your while to pass such information on."

"Seems unlikely to come up, but for the sake of discussion, let's say it did. I'd have to think about what I should do." He leaned back in his chair. Thought about it. "I don't know, somehow it just wouldn't seem right to turn that drug money over to the Treasury."

"I beg your pardon?"

"Well, that cash came from private U.S. citizens who were buying crack and heroin and Mary Jane and the like. Seems to me like the money ought to be returned to those poor, addicted souls."

She stared. "Tell me you are kidding."

"Okay, I'm kidding." He grinned at her big eyes. "But there is another problem."

"I don't want to hear about it."

"Suit yourself."

"Oh, go ahead. Tell me before you burst."

"We rural westerners don't burst. We bust."

"Okay, cowboy. Tell me before you bust."

"If I knew where eighty million in unmarked cash was stashed, why should I settle for a measly ten percent?" He leaned forward, elbows on the table. "Why not take it all?"

She flashed a charming smile. "Because I would have a low opinion of a man who did such a thing?"

"But how would you know?"

"If you should buy up eighty million dollars in prime ranch land and purebred cattle and shiny red pickup trucks, I would become mildly suspicious."

"Yeah." He sighed. "There is that."

She suddenly looked very tired. "I will not rest until this mess is sorted out."

"Look, McTeague—don't take your work so personal, or it'll get you down. That drug-money heist happened quite a while back. Whoever was responsible, odds are ninety-nine to one against the stash ever turning up—or anybody going to jail." He took a sip of tepid coffee. "But let's get back to more recent times, and the issue of who took a shot at Dr. Blinkoe—and when that didn't take him out, blew Blinkoe's houseboat sky-high with a charge of dynamite. Does the Bureau figure it had something to do with that DC-3 hijacking?"

Her lips went thin. "That possibility has occurred to us. It is possible that the drug cartel has decided to get even with the only survivor of the team that hijacked their stolen aircraft, mowed down their soldiers like grass, and hauled away several bags of their ill-gotten gains."

"Well, I'm more than happy to let the FBI and DEA deal with the drug cartel."

She pitched him a hardball. "So who is your lady friend?"

Moon caught it, felt the sting. "Which lady friend?"

"The one you gave my roses to."

"Oh. That was Miss Atherton."

"Is she good-looking?"

Moon thought about it. "She's what I'd call *cute.*"

The FBI agent closed her eyes, frowned, scanned the pages. "Are we talking about *Phyllis* Atherton? Your eighty-year-old schoolteacher?"

He stared. "How did you know about her?"

"I have what is commonly known as a photographic memory." She laughed at him. "You have a pretty thick file too."

This is an amazing woman. "And you've read it all?"

"Every page, including footnotes." She winked at her date. "I know every bad thing you've ever done. All of your former girlfriends' names."

Charlie Moon was trying to think of a suitable response when the waiter arrived with the check, smiled benignly at the diners, departed like a wisp of fluff in a summer breeze. Moon noticed Big Tony heading into the kitchen, probably to nag the hired help. He produced his wallet, cracked the pocket where he kept his greenbacks. "Dang!"

Lila Mae McTeague looked up. "What?"

"I *know* I had a brand-new twenty-dollar bill. Now all I see is a scruffy five and a couple of beat-up ones." He pocketed the billfold. "Well, it's not an earthshaking problem. After yelling and cussing some, the Big T always takes my IOUs."

"You don't have a credit card?"

He tried to look embarrassed. "I'd rather not talk about that."

She reached for her purse. "Never mind. I'll take care of the bill."

He shook his head. "No. I'd never stick a lady with the check. I'll have a man-to-man talk with Tony and—"

"No," she said firmly. "I said I'd take care of it and I will. So let's not have another word about it."

With a doubtful look, he shrugged.

McTeague shifted gears. "Charlie—there's something I should tell you about. But you must treat it as strictly confidential."

"I'm listening."

"It's about that body part that turned up in Moccasin Lake."

The tribal investigator nodded. "The infamous dismembered arm."

"Right. Which Mrs. Blinkoe identified as having once been a functional portion of her husband's body."

"So what about it, McTeague?"

"Bureau Forensics has completed a series of tests on the specimen—including a detailed DNA analysis." She watched his face very closely. "A comparison was made to tissues obtained from a prostate biopsy Dr. Blinkoe underwent eighteen months ago. Bottom line is this: That particular arm was never attached to Manfred Blinkoe's body."

Moon returned a blank stare.

"Excuse me, Charlie—but you don't seem particularly surprised."

"It's probably because in my duties as a law-enforcement professional, I've seen and heard just about everything. I am a hard man to surprise."

"I don't buy that."

"Then put it down to my legendary gambling skills."

"Your *what*?"

"I was referring to my exceptional poker face."

"Then you *are* surprised?"

He picked up a highly polished silver cream dispenser, carefully examined the reflection of his exceptional poker face. "I don't know, Lila Mae—I'm *so* good at this, it's really hard to tell."

"Charlie, don't fool around—this is serious. Some John Doe's arm has been found with Dr. Blinkoe's watch and ring on it. Which forces one to consider some rather disturbing possibilities."

"Such as?"

"Well, it's rather obvious—Blinkoe could still be alive. He might have staged the boat explosion to fake his disappearance. And to make it look convincing, he might have left a corpse behind—or at least a portion of a corpse—with his ring and watch attached to it."

"Yeah. I guess it could've happened like that." Moon turned the creamer in his hands. "But Dr. Blinkoe would be bound to know that a DNA test would ruin his evidence— even suggest he was still among the living. Seems a lot more likely some bad guy took Dr. Blinkoe's watch and ring by force."

"Oh, sure." She flung her hands in the air. "And then blew himself up in the houseboat!"

"That sounds just a tad unlikely, McTeague." He set the silver creamer aside. "But I won't say you couldn't be right. After all the strange things I've seen in this world, nothing amazes me."

"Listen, Charlie—if you know something you aren't telling me—"

The waiter appeared. "Was everything quite satisfactory?" Assured by both diners that it was, he continued. "I am directed to tell you that if you should wish to order dessert, it will be on the house."

Big Tony was wedged behind the counter, beaming at

Moon and the good-looking tootsie. *There ain't no way that long-legged cutie pie is goin' to pay for Chollie's lunch.*

"Thank you," McTeague said, "but I will not want any dessert."

This has to look good. Moon sighed, as if he had lost his appetite for sweet things. "Me neither." He gave the waiter a sad look. Sad enough to make an IRS auditor weep. Then he added a dash of humiliation. "Uh—tell Tony I need to have a word with him. In private."

"No!" McTeague snatched the check. "Lunch is on me."

Big Tony's double chin fell twenty dollars' worth.

41

FAMILY BUSINESS

At shortly after ten that night, special agent McTeague's telephone rang. She smiled at the readout on the caller ID screen. "Hello, Charlie."

"Hello yourself, McTeague."

She put her book aside, leaned back on a flowered sofa. "It's only been a few hours since we had lunch. You missing me already?"

"You bet."

"How much do you miss me?"

"Three or four bushels. Matter of fact, aside from an ailing heifer down in the riverside corral, you're all I can think about."

"I come in second to a sick cow. You are very sweet."

"Either that, or I suffer from limited mental capacity."

"I'll buy that. What's up?"

"At Big Tony's, while you were ruining my appetite with

all that talk about rotten human flesh, there was something I wanted to ask you about—it completely slipped my mind."

"Define 'it.' "

"Uh—I forget. Just a second. Oh, now I remember. It was about Mrs. Pansy Blinkoe."

"Before you ask—no, the Bureau has not located her. And her brother, Clayton Crowe, also continues to elude us."

"Then maybe you'll be interested in what's on my mind."

McTeague closed her eyes. "Don't tell me—another hunch."

"All right, I won't."

"It was merely a figure of speech, cowboy. It's okay for you to tell me."

"I'm glad you explained that."

"So what's on your mind?"

"I think you oughta check out Mrs. Blinkoe's family."

"That's routine procedure, Charlie. I already have a preliminary report on my desk from the field office in Nashville. Pansy Crowe grew up in western Tennessee with her parents and her older brother. She was a C student, a cheerleader, had a few minor run-ins with the law. Nothing too serious. Usual teenage stuff."

"What about her brother?"

"Clayton was a better student. He trained as a diesel mechanic." She curled up on the couch. "You have a particular interest in Pansy's brother?"

"I'd like to know what happened to him."

"So would I. But I'd much rather know where Pansy is hiding. Perhaps she's with her brother."

"Could be. But I think you should take a *close* look at her family."

"What, exactly, am I looking closely for?"

"First time I met Mrs. Blinkoe, I was struck by her pretty blue eyes."

McTeague smiled. "I'm sure you were."

"I think she got 'em from her parents."

"From what I've been told, that is nature's usual course."

"Well, I'd like to talk to you all night, Lila Mae."

"Would you?"

"But I got me a sick heifer to doctor."

"Good-bye, Dr. Moon."

"Good night, Special Agent McTeague."

42

ANOTHER MAN DONE GONE

Phillipe's Streamside Restaurant was immersed in that hushed transition between lunch and dinner, when tables were being draped with clean linen cloths and decorated with cunningly folded napkins and spotless silver flatware. It was also the time when the heavily tattooed dishwasher stepped outside to smoke a skinny little Jamaican cigar, whilst speculating about the ultimate meaning of Life and the Universe and what the Red Sox might accomplish late in the season.

With the entire customer parking lot at his disposal, Scott Parris edged his black-and-white into the shade of a perfectly conical blue spruce. He nodded at the meditating dishwasher, entered through the kitchen, exchanged a few words with the pasty-faced pastry chef, passed down a narrow hallway, knocked on a door marked MANAGER.

Phillipe jerked the door open, looked down the hall. "Did anyone see you come in?"

Parris responded in a serious tone. "Nope. I slid down the chimney."

As he closed the door behind the burly cop, the proprietor showed not the least sign of amusement.

The Granite Creek chief of police removed his hat, grinned at the nervous fellow. "So what'd you want to see me about?"

"It's my groundskeeper."

"Old Willie—the senior citizen who works for table scraps and a bed in the shed?"

Phillipe chose to ignore this display of impertinence. "Ever since the unfortunate incident—"

"You refer to the brutal murder of one of your customers?"

The thin man paled. "If you must be so blunt, yes. Ever since that unfortunate incident, my groundskeeper has been—how shall I say it?" He tried to think of just the right expression.

Parris waited.

It finally came to him. "Ill at ease."

The town's top cop leaned forward, his palms making spots on Phillipe's previously spotless glass-topped desk. "Is he worried we'll ID him as a witness to the killing?"

The businessman winced at the word. "I suppose that's a possibility."

"You want me to have a talk with Willie, reassure him the department won't mention his name to the media—that it?"

Phillipe's dark eyes did not blink. "That is not it."

Parris's patience was running close to the empty mark. "Then what *do* you want me to do?"

"I don't know." Phillipe nibbled at a fingernail. "It's just that he's gone."

"Gone where?"

"I haven't the least idea. My headwaiter informed me this morning that the old man was nowhere to be found. I took the liberty to inspect his lodgings—"

"You mean the equipment shed."

Phillipe glared across his desk at the coarse policeman. "All of his belongings appear to be in his quarters. It's as if . . . as if he simply walked away."

"This Old Willie—he have a last name?"

"Everyone has a last name." The restaurateur shrugged. "But he was not an official employee, so I didn't keep any records. He merely slept in the—" Phillipe was about to say *shed,* "in his assigned lodgings. If he volunteered to do some work, that was fine with me. But it was not required."

"You didn't pay him?"

Another shrug. "Oh, from time to time I gave him a few dollars." He frowned at a Tiffany lamp. "A man that old, he must have had a pension of some sort—or perhaps he was drawing Social Security."

"This prosperous old guy have a set of wheels?"

"I do not know. Employees are encouraged to park their vehicles across the highway, in the mall lot."

Parris looked out the window. "Let's go have a look at Willie's assigned lodgings."

The shed was crammed almost to overflowing with fifty-pound bags of fertilizer, gallon jugs of weed killer, an assortment of paint cans and brushes, and virtually every hand tool known to man. Plus a rusty gasoline-powered lawn mower, a garden tractor that looked almost new, a dirt-encrusted wheelbarrow, about a ton of fresh sod.

In a dark corner, the groundskeeper had cleared out a space for himself. There was a folding card table that—judging from the single plate, knife, and fork, and the stack of paperback books—evidently did double duty for Old Willie's dining and reading needs. On the wall above a makeshift cot topped with a plastic-covered mattress, there was a rough pine shelf that supported a cheap-looking radio and a Kerr jar with a green toothbrush and tube of toothpaste stuffed inside. A Cattleman's Bank calendar was suspended from a nail. Parris turned backward through the pages. The aged man, who'd had so few days left, had been marking them off one by one. The marks stopped at the day before yesterday.

"You see," Phillipe said with an expansive gesture, "all of his meager belongings are still here. Why would he just walk away?"

Parris felt a sour coldness settling into his stomach. He was absolutely certain that the old man had not simply "walked away." On that night when the woman on the restaurant patio was shot in the head, maybe Old Willie had seen more than he'd admitted to. And even if he hadn't, maybe the shooter had decided to eliminate a potential witness.

43

THE WALK-IN

At least three days every week, Special Agent McTeague worked out of her Granite Creek office. The rented space was a small corner room above the Cattleman's Bank. It had an old-fashioned door with a transom, a ceiling fan that creak-creaked, cracked plaster walls, and a pair of tall windows that looked out over Third and Main. It was late in the afternoon, time to clean off her desk. The FBI employee was spinning the file cabinet's combination lock when she heard footsteps slowly ascending the uncarpeted stairs. Boots, she decided. Men's boots. He walked like an old man—a tired old man. The heels clicked slowly down the hallway, stopped outside the door marked PRIVATE.

Her presence in Granite Creek was supposed to go unnoticed, but word had gotten around and the locals were curious about the Bureau's new office in town. From time to time, someone stopped by "just to say hello"—obviously hoping to find out why the "G-men" were setting up shop here. Prevailing opinion was that it must have something to do with Rocky Mountain Polytechnic University. Some of those college students were probably involved in a project that had upset the feds, like making a radiation bomb or hacking into an air-force computer—you could never tell what. Crazy kids.

There was a tentative tapping. McTeague pressed the intercom button. "Who's there?"

A muffled voice answered. "You the FBI lady?"

She smiled at the door. "Who wants to know?"

"Uh—I'd rather not say."

The agent switched on a black-and-white video monitor. It was hard-wired to a miniature TV camera mounted in the hallway, just above her office door. The LCD screen slipped a few frames, then stabilized the image of a man in a raincoat. Two-thirds of his face was concealed under the brim of a tattered cowboy hat. Under the cuffs of the faded jeans were the expected cowboy boots. The federal cop automatically made mental notes. Height was hard to determine with the steep camera angle, but this was a Caucasian, medium build, a few days' growth of beard. *Looks like a derelict.* Just yesterday, a wild-eyed Korean who called himself Emperor Chan-Spong of the Thirteenth Planet had arrived to report a landing of space aliens just north of town. *This could be one of the emperor's drinking buddies. Probably wants to confess to kidnapping the Lindbergh baby.* "Okay. Give me a moment to open the door." There was a standard dead bolt, another that was electrically operated from a switch under her desk.

"No!" The scruffy-looking man took a step backward. "I'm not comin' in." He scratched at the stubble on his chin. "You that new FBI lady that's come to town, or her secretary?"

"This is a small office, we don't have a secretary. I'm Special Agent McTeague."

The visitor leaned closer to the door, as if he were trying to see though the thick oak panel.

"Look up at the camera over the door," she said. "And show me some ID."

He shook his head. "Oh, I can't do that, miss—because I don't carry none."

She glanced at her wristwatch. "It's almost quitting time and I'm looking at a long drive home. So either state your business or hit the bricks."

"What I have to say won't take but a minute." He pushed his hands deep into the raincoat pockets. "I have some information you'll be interested in."

Sure you do. "About what?"

He squared his shoulders. "I know something about that guy whose boat blew sky-high up yonder on the lake. That Mr. Blinky."

"I assume you mean Dr. Blinkoe."

He nodded the cowboy hat. "Yeah. That's the guy."

"I suppose you saw the story on the TV news." *He'll have some half-baked theory about what really happened, expect a ten-thousand-dollar reward.*

"No, I read about what happened in the newspaper. And I'm ninety-nine percent sure I can help you." A hesitant pause. "But times is tough, so I don't beat my gums for nothin'." He pulled his right hand from the coat pocket, rubbed finger and thumb together in the universal gesture. "If you can spare me a buck or two, I'll give you a little tip."

If I give him something, maybe he'll go away. McTeague reached into her purse, squatted to slip two dollars under the door.

"Thank you, miss." He picked up the payment, pocketed it.

She gave the pitiful figure on the monitor a stiff smile. "It's getting late. Why don't you gather your thoughts for a few days, come back next Tuesday at ten A.M. and we'll talk for a few minutes."

"Next Tuesday, I may be dead."

Great, a paranoid. "Who would want to kill you?"

"The bad guy, if he finds out I'm ready to spill my guts to a fed." He glanced toward the dimly lighted stairwell, as if an assassin might be lurking there.

She frowned at the image on the monitor. "So who's this bad guy?"

The odd person pulled his hat brim down a notch. "I don't dare say." He hesitated. "But he's a sure-enough hardcase, I can tell you that." He dragged the coat sleeve across his nose. "You know, it's kinda funny—ever since I was just a pup, I've wanted to be an undercover agent for the FBI." A raspy cough. "I'm ready to go to work startin' right now—but only if you pay me a reg'lar salary. Let's say twenty dollars a week. My code name'll be 'Scarf.'" He glanced over his shoulder again. "I made it up while I was climbin' the stairs."

She gave his video image a smile, this time the genuine article. "Mr. Scarf, do you have—"

"Not *Mr.* Scarf." His tone suggested a painful exasperation at having to deal with someone who did not understand how these things worked. "Just plain *Scarf.*"

"Very well, uh—Scarf. Do you have the telephone number for this office?"

"Uh, no." Just Plain Scarf fumbled in the raincoat pockets. "Wait just a minute till I find my pencil."

"That won't be necessary." She slid her card under the door, stood up to watch him snatch it off the floor.

"Okay, I got it." He put his hand under the raincoat, slipped the card into a shirt pocket. "I'll be ringin' you up soon as I have somethin' to tell you." He rubbed his hands together. "Now there's the matter of money to talk about. Startin' a week from now, you can leave my twenty bucks under that flower pot in front of the bank downstairs. The one with them red-and-yella tulips."

Special Agent McTeague watched his black-and-white image turn way, heard the boot heels click-click down the hallway. She sighed. *With any luck at all, this will be the last I see of this pathetic old geezer.*

corral.

44

THE OUTLAW HORSE

Even for an energetic young man in his prime, Charlie Moon
had entirely too much work to do. Yesterday, he had spent the
full day carrying heavy rocks and two-by-eights. Day before
that, he'd hauled a truckload of feed and grain from Mc-
Cabe's Mercantile, stacked it in the Sour Creek shed. Today,
urgent business had brought him to the Big Hat. County
Agent Forrest Wakefield was running tests on 120 head of
Herefords and Moon was determined to keep a close eye on
things. They were working at the north corral, which was attached to a low, long horse barn. Wakefield was supervising
one of his summer employees. While a crew of Columbine
cowboys worked the beeves through a squeeze chute, the veterinary student was drawing blood samples. The trick was to
get the animals clamped in without a mishap. If a steer fell in
the chute, getting it back on its feet again was tedious work.
When a Mexican cowboy slapped a wild-eyed Hereford on

the rump, Moon watched that last animal lope across the corral, through an open gate into a fenced pasture. "Well, that about does it."

Wakefield nodded, wiped a shirtsleeve across his forehead. "Yeah. And I'm danged glad to see the last of 'em." He instructed his assistant to take the blood samples to the truck.

Moon watched the sturdy young woman carry the stainless steel case away. "When'll you have the results?"

"Couple of weeks." Wakefield eyed the tall Ute. "Guess I'd better hit the road." He added wistfully: "I imagine you're about to have some lunch."

"Yeah, it's got to be a habit." Moon squinted at the midday sun. "We do that every day, along about noon."

The hungry man looked toward the ranch house. "That new fella still doing the cooking?"

Moon nodded. "Cap's the only hand we got who can boil coffee and burn meat."

Concerned that he was not getting through to the Ute, Wakefield dropped a five-pound hint. "I bet he's fixing up something that'll stick to a man's ribs."

"Oh, nothing special." Moon wore an innocent expression. "Today's menu is fried chicken, smashed potatoes and brown gravy, green peas cooked in butter. Biscuits made from scratch." He paused to let that sink in, added: "And rhubarb cobbler."

The hopeful diner raised his nose to sniff the air. "When I was a little boy, we had fried chicken almost every Sunday."

"Well, ol' Cap makes it just like Momma did."

"And rhubarb is my favorite kinda pie."

Moon grinned down at the six-footer. "Then you and your assistant better have lunch with us."

The county agent felt his stomach growl. "Oh, we wouldn't want to impose. And I really oughta get on down the road."

"Another time, then."

"Well, if you twist my arm—"

Someone cleared his throat.

Moon turned to see his youthful straw boss. "What is it, Kyd?"

Jerome Kydmann, aka the Wyoming Kyd, removed his white Stetson in a respectful gesture. "Sir, it's about that horse."

The Ute's face darkened. "Sweet Alice?"

"Yes sir." *The boss don't like to hear this kind of news but it's my job to tell him.* "You remember how last week, she threw Little Joe Piper into the side of the barn, broke his right arm and his collarbone?"

The rancher nodded.

"And the week before that, how she pitched Portuguese Tom over the corral fence? And how ever since, his eyes are crossed and he ain't been able to walk a straight line?"

Another nod.

"And how on Independence Day, that ornery horse—"

"I know Sweet Alice's history, Kyd. Get to the point."

Jerome Kydmann lowered his gaze to his hat, rotated it in his hands. "Well, Pete Bushman, he thinks—"

"I know what my foreman thinks. Pete told me yesterday we ought to sell Sweet Alice. To one of them packers that grinds horses up for dog food." The Ute shook his head. "Before I'd do that, I'd shoot her dead."

The Wyoming Kyd took a deep breath, shot the boss a man-to-man gaze. "I am speaking for the wrangler and all of the men. The way we see it, all she does is cripple up one good cowboy after another." He paused. "Sir, there is some horses that can't be rode, much less gentled for regular work." He glared at the animal, who was standing in the corral—listening to every word. "And that is sure-enough one of 'em."

Moon looked down his nose at the earnest young man. "There is no such thing as a horse that can't be rode."

The Kyd straightened his back to the last notch. "In all due respect, sir—that is a lot of hooey."

"Hooey?" Moon swallowed a smile. "That's pretty strong language."

Kydmann stood his ground. "That's what I said." He spat at a fence post, said it again. Louder this time. "Hooey!"

Moon turned to the county agent. "Forrest, you're a recognized expert on beeves and horses and other hoofed animals. What do you think?"

Wakefield gave the horse a thoughtful look.

Sweet Alice eyed him right back.

After being stared down, the county agent had his say. "The Wyoming Kyd could be right, Charlie. There are some animals that can't be domesticated."

Emboldened by this support, Kydmann pointed his chin toward the placid-looking beast. "That's the truth. And a blind man with both eyes closed can see—that is one of 'em."

Looking past the men, down the lane, Charlie Moon saw something else. Topping a ridge, a puff of dust following a motor vehicle. He recognized the automobile. "Among my people," the Ute said in a disdainful tone, "we take a different view. Our belief is that there are no bad horses. Just bad riders."

"Hah!" Kydmann said.

Moon gave his employee a gentle, fatherly look. "Say whatever's on your mind."

The Wyoming Kyd clamped the white Stetson onto his head, pulled it down so it folded his ears. "You mean that?"

"I do. You got something rattling around in your craw, spit it out."

"Okay, then." Kydmann took his time to think up the words, say them just right. "In all due respect, sir—it is us cowboys that end up with the bruises and broken legs and cracked skulls. It is your employees who are expected to take the risks." He took a deep breath. "*You* have never tried to ride that bronc."

Moon took the gut punch without flinching. "There is a reason for that." The boss of the outfit considered the callow youth with a sad, worldly-wise expression such as managers commonly use to intimidate the help. "It has to do with keeping up morale amongst the men."

Kydmann's blank look made it clear that he did not follow this line of reasoning.

"I did not want to show off," Moon explained. Considering who was coming up the lane, he was working up an irresistible urge to show off. "Seeing me break that old nag in a minute flat would've made you less-able riders look downright pitiful. Why, esprit de corps would've gone right down the drain."

The Wyoming Kyd allowed an expression of mild amusement to visit his pale face. "Well, that is mighty thoughtful of you."

Moon looked hurt. "I don't mean to call your word into question, but that remark sounds just the least bit insincere." He nodded to indicate the equine audience, who had moved closer. Sweet Alice had her neck over the fence rail. "Do you really think I can't stay on that mild-mannered horse?"

The Kyd nodded. "Not for long enough to say your prayers."

Moon laughed. "You want to lay some cash on the barrelhead?"

The younger man hesitated. Cowboys were always spitting Trouble right in the eye, but the First Rule around the Columbine was: Never Throw a Punch at the Boss. Not if you wanted to wake up tomorrow morning with your head still on your shoulders. Rule Number Two was: Don't Never Bet Against the Indian. Luck was always riding along in Charlie Moon's saddlebags. But this was just too good to pass up. The Wyoming Kyd cocked his head. "Even money?"

"If that's the best you can do."

Kydmann grinned to display a perfect set of teeth. "I will lay you a month's pay you can't stay in the saddle for . . . for fourteen seconds."

"Ten."

"Twelve."

The stockman reached for his wallet. "You're on, Kyd."

Fifty yards away, in the shade of a shaggy, centenarian cottonwood, the gray Ford sedan was pulling to a stop. The puff of dust that had tagged along behind now waltzed past the automobile, and kept dancing right along till it was gone with the wind.

g who was coming up the lane, he was working up an ire

45

THE LONGEST RIDE

As Special Agent Lila Mae McTeague cut the ignition, a grizzled old cowboy approached the FBI sedan, walking with a limp. He leaned to look in the window at the handsome woman, presented a friendly grin through a prickly undergrowth of salt-and-pepper whiskers. "Howdy."

"Good morning," she said.

He gave her a grandfatherly look. "You lost?"

"No, I've been to the Big Hat before. But I don't remember meeting you."

He tipped his broad-brimmed straw hat. "That's because I only signed on a few days ago. They call me Dollar Bill, or just Dollar for short." He waited in vain for her to show some curiosity about how he had acquired this handle. "They call me Dollar Bill, 'cause I keep the first dollar I ever earned in my hat." D.B. removed his lid to expose a tangle of gray hair. He removed a seventy-year-old greenback from behind the sweatband, which was in almost as sorry a shape as its owner.

"I am pleased to meet you." She smiled at the wrinkled face. "They call me McTeague, because that is my name."

He beamed at her. "You are pretty as a spotted puppy under a little red wagon."

She beamed back. "Thank you. A lady always appreciates a well-meant compliment."

He donned the straw hat. "Well, I guess I'd better get on down to the corral, so's I don't miss the big hullabaloo. You want to come with me?"

She eyed the crowd. "What's all the excitement about?"

He did a shrug-and-grin. "From what they tell me, same thing as happens here ever' week or two—a cowboy with more guts than brains has taken it in his head to ride Sweet Alice."

"I assume we are talking about a horse."

"Some of the boys would say so," Dollar said darkly. He spat three times on the cottonwood bark, used the toe of his boot to make an *X* in the sand, added in a husky whisper: "Others hold to the 'pinon that Sweet Alice is a she-devil that slipped into a horsehide."

She smiled at the superstitious man. "Then she's a hard one to ride?"

"Ride? Hah! That ol' cayuse has never been broke—and no man-child on the Big Hat or the Columbine has been able to straddle her saddle for long as it takes to sneeze. And those dumb enough to try have ended up with broken bones and busted heads . . . and worse." Seeing as how a lady was present, he did not elaborate on what was *worse*.

"But someone is about to try it again?"

"Oh, sure." Dollar Bill heard the "why" in her voice. "All because of some damn-fool bet."

Bet? Her heart skipped a beat. "Where is Charlie Moon?"

"Oh, the boss's down there with the rest of the boys." He chuckled, shook his head. "He's the damn fool that's goin' to get his brains kicked out, and all for a month's pay. It'll be quite somethin' to see."

She felt her skin go cold. "He won't actually get hurt, will he?"

"Oh, he'll get *hurt* all right. Question is—how bad. When I left, the odds was even money he'd get at least one bone busted, one-to-three he'd get himself kilt." He gave her a hopeful look. "You like to put some money in the pot?"

"Certainly not!" McTeague clinched her fists. "Someone has to put a stop to this!"

Dollar Bill was pleased at the prospect of this new wrinkle. "You want to come an' try?"

Before he had gotten all the words past his lips, the woman was marching off toward the corral. "Stomping postholes," as cowboys like to say.

She would, of course, be too late.

Charlie Moon had seen her coming. Before she had a chance to say, "Are you out of your mind or what?" the tall man was in the saddle. "Okay," he muttered to the sullen beast, "do your best stuff."

It seemed that Sweet Alice was all out of *stuff*. The ugly mare simply stood there on spraddled legs, looking bored with mindless cowboys, weary of the burdens life had put on her swayed back.

Seeing McTeague arrive at the corral fence with a look of wide-eyed alarm, the Ute felt the shame burning on his neck. This predicament was the rodeo cowboy's worst nightmare. *I'm goin' to look like a regular idiot sittin' here on a stuffed animal that don't have the common decency to at least put on a little show—*

A keg of equine dynamite exploded underneath him.

It was like getting hit in the butt with a sledgehammer. The occasional bronc rider felt his spine jam up against the base of his skull, his eyes pop halfway out of their sockets, his teeth snap down on the tip of his tongue. And that was the good part. For the next few heartbeats Charlie Moon did not think about the pretty woman who was watching, or even the horse who was determined to do him in.

There was no time for *thinking*.

All of his instincts were focused on staying in the saddle.
And staying alive.

Blood in her eye, the wily old horse went up with her head
pointed north, twisted like a pretzel come to life, hit the earth
looking in the general direction of New Mexico.

Cowboys were whooping it up, yelling encouragement
that was—depending on how they had placed their bets—directed to either horse or rider.

The animal flipped her muscular rump almost vertical,
seesawed this way and that, reared up like a black bear bat-
ting at peaches, did a double-crawfish, landed on her stubby
forelegs, completely left the earth, launched into a half-
sunfish, hit the ground with a thunderous thump that shook
every post in the corral fence.

What a fine show! The cowboys waved their hats in the air.

His Stetson gone, his molars jarred loose, Charlie Moon
hung on. Every second in the saddle was like an hour inside
an Oklahoma tornado.

It was about to get worse.

On the far side of the corral from the spectators, Sweet Alice seemed to lose her footing. (Later on, some of the cowboys would claim that the she-devil had done this on purpose,
and with evil intent.) Whether with malice aforethought or
not, the mare fell hard against the fence. There was a sickening crunch of *something* breaking. Creosote-soaked railings,
for sure—the spectators could see the splinters fly. But some
of that cracking sounded awfully like bones fracturing.

The horse laid on the rider for a horrific moment, then
struggled to her feet.

Sensing the cold hand of Death, the cowboys stood as
silent as tombstones.

Calm as you please, Sweet Alice lowered her head, sniffed
at the still form on the ground.

McTeague wanted to move but her limbs would not respond. "Oh, God," she said, "Oh God."

By this prayer, the spell of paralysis was broken.

The Wyoming Kyd was the first to vault the fence. The

young cowboy sprinted across the corral, brushed past the outlaw horse. The county agent—closest thing to a doctor for thirty miles—was not far behind.

The Kyd dropped to his knees. The boss's eyes were shut, his body limp.

The veterinarian was there a heartbeat later. Forrest Wakefield poked and prodded, carefully examined Charlie Moon's prone form. His initial impression was that this did not look good. If the man survived, he would probably have a broken back.

One by one, the other cowboys gathered around. With the head of the outfit down, they waited for the Kyd to take command.

Wakefield felt for a pulse under the thrown cowboy's jaw. He put his ear to the Ute's mouth, hoping for a whisper of breath.

They spectators stared.

The veterinarian looked at Kydmann, shook his head.

Kydmann could not believe it. He put his ear to the Ute's mouth. Confirmed the horse doctor's diagnosis.

This was going to be a hard thing to do; both men set their jaws.

The Kyd called on the Mexican cowboy, muttered a few hushed words in Spanish.

Señor Cruz nodded, went back to the crowd. The word was passed to the employees.

One of the cowboys picked up the Ute's black Stetson, knocked off the dust, pushed out the dimples, placed it on the fallen hero's chest.

Jerome Kydmann got to his feet. The young dandy removed his spotless white hat, pressed it against his heart.

The other men followed suit, pulling off their soiled, sweaty hats, hanging their heads in mournful fashion.

The veterinarian nodded to his assistant. "There's nothing for us to do here," he murmured. "Let's go." The stunned young woman followed her supervisor back to the county agent's truck.

The bow was bent double, the sinew pulled tight. It was as if time had stopped.

Sensing that something had to be done that was appropriate for the moment, Portuguese Tom thought he might sing "Rock of Ages." Problem was, he could not remember the lines. Falling back on something more familiar, he cleared his throat. In a voice that crackled with age and the ravages of raw whiskey, he began to whine a few lines from an old campfire song:

> *There, down in the corral, jus' standin' alone,*
> *Was that old cavayo, old strawberry roan.*
> *His knees was knobby, he had big pigeon toes,*
> *Little piggy eyes and a big Roman nose.*

A pair of the older hands joined in for the chorus:

> *Well, it's oh, that strawberry roan,*
> *Oh, that strawberry roan!*
> *He's ewe-necked and old, with a long lower jaw,*
> *You can see with one eye he's a reg'lar outlaw.*
> *Oh, that strawberry roan!*

Transfixed in numb horror, McTeague beheld the eerie performance. *Charlie must be dead.*

The dirge continued:

> *Well I puts on my spurs and I coils up my twine,*
> *I piled my loop on him, I'm sure feeling fine.*
> *I piled my loop on him, and well I knew then,*
> *If I rode this old pony, I'd sure earn my ten.*

The woman forced herself to move.

> *Well it's oh, that strawberry roan,*
> *Oh, that strawberry roan!*
> *He lowered his old neck and I think he unwound,*

He seemed to quit living down there on the ground.
Oh, that strawberry roan!

Lila Mae McTeague climbed the corral fence, pushed through the cluster of cowboys, knelt by the man who'd had little enough sense to ride Sweet Alice. The FBI agent pressed her thumb under Moon's jaw, felt an instant surge of hope. "He's still got a pulse." She counted seven pulses in ten seconds, multiplied by six. "About seventy."

Taking but slight notice of her arrival, more sad-eyed cowboys had joined in the song:

He went up towards the east and came down towards
the west,
To stay in his middle I'm doin' my best,
He's about the worst bucker I've seen on the range,
He can turn on a nickel and give you some change.

The FBI agent had lowered her cheek to his parted lips. She waited for some evidence of air moving, felt nothing. *Oh, my God. He's not breathing.* All business now, she tilted Moon's head back, put her mouth against his, exhaled the breath of life into his lungs.

The singers were improving with practice. Harmony was now close and sweet, like a well-honed barbershop quartet.

Well, it's oh, that strawberry roan,
Oh, that strawberry roan!
He goes up on all fours and comes down on his side,
I don't know what keeps him from losin' his hide.
Oh, that strawberry roan!

Oblivious to the singing, McTeague continued her work. *Out with the bad air. In with the good. Out with the bad . . . If he doesn't start breathing on his own pretty soon . . .* But she brushed aside that grim possibility.

◆ ◆ ◆

As if sensing that her valiant efforts were pointless, the cowboys' tones had become softer, almost funereal. Tears rolled down one old cowhand's leathery cheeks.

> *I loses my stirrup and also my hat,*
> *I starts pulling leather, I'm blind as a bat;*
> *With a big forward jump he goes up on high,*
> *Leaves me sittin' on nothin' way up in the sky.*

Lila Mae McTeague paused from her strenuous mouth-to-mouth efforts to check the man's pulse. It was still there, which meant his heart was getting oxygen. Oddly, it was also strong—thumping like a drum under her thumb. And much, much faster. At least 130.

> *Well, it's oh, that strawberry roan,*
> *Oh, that strawberry roan!*
> *I'll bet all my money the man ain't alive*
> *That can stay with old Straw-berry when he makes his*
> *high dive.*
> *Oh, that strawberry roan!*

The FBI agent was a qualified EMT. First in her class at Quantico. She also had a remarkable memory. Running through the written and oral instructions from her training, she tried to recall what a racing pulse could mean in a case like this. McTeague eliminated a half-dozen unlikely possibilities. Arrived at the truth of the matter.

"Charlie," she said.

No response from the patient.

She slapped him on the cheek. "Charlie Moon!"

He was still as death.

The woman glared at the sculptured face. Waited for the inevitable.

The laws of human physiology are writ in stone. After twenty-one painful seconds, the prone man sucked in a deep breath.

I knew it. He was faking all along!

The patient emitted a pitiful groan, a melancholy sigh.

"Save it!"

Moon opened one eye, peered up at a pitiless face. "What . . . who are you?" After a thoughtful pause, he made a guess. "An angel come to take me to heaven?"

The lady tried to look stern. "You should be ashamed of yourself!" She turned to the choir. "And you morons were in on this."

There were a few sheepish grins.

McTeague pointed to no place in particular. "Get out of here, all of you!"

The crew wandered off this way and that, mumbling. The general consensus was that this town woman had no sense of humor.

After a tense silence, Moon asked the Big Question: "What was my time?"

"Your what?"

"My time in the saddle. If I didn't stay on for twelve seconds, I owe the Kyd a month's pay."

McTeague shook her head, sighed.

The bronc rider closed his eyes. *These women just don't understand.*

He's such a little boy. She touched his face. "Is anything broken?"

Moon wiggled his fingers. Then his toes. "I don't think so."

"Do you hurt anywhere?"

"Everywhere." He groaned again. "Even my hair."

She raised his head, put it in her lap. Stroked his forehead with her hand.

"Ah," he said, closing his eyes against the noonday sun. "That's much better."

46

PICNIC

The man who called himself "Cap" approached the corral with some trepidation. Having been one of the few souls on the Big Hat to miss the excitement, the cook had heard from the cowboys how that outlaw horse had attempted to murder the boss, and come within a gnat's eyebrow of getting the job done—but Charlie Moon wasn't quite dead, and he'd whispered to the vet and the Wyoming Kyd that he wanted to play a little prank on the FBI lady and the word got passed around and all the boys fell right in with it. The cook had also heard about how the hot-tempered woman had ordered everyone away from the scene of the mischief. On top of all that, Cap—like a sizable portion of Charlie Moon's other employees—had his reasons to stay clear of the FBI agent and other sworn officers of the law. But the outfit's hash slinger had a job to do, and he took his responsibilities seriously. The seriously nearsighted man entered the corral through the gate, bumped into a hefty post, meandered over toward the pair. He was within a couple of yards before he could make out exactly who was there. A man, whom he took to be Charlie Moon, was stretched out on his back. The Ute's head was resting in a woman's lap. They were talking in low, intimate tones, and seemed unaware of his presence.

Cap rattled the covered lunch bucket.

The woman gave him a look.

"Uh—I thought the boss might like some lunch."

McTeague focused her big eyes on the stainless steel bucket. "I don't think he feels like eating just yet."

Moon sniffed. "What'd you bring, Cap?"

"Oh, nothing much. Few pieces of fried chicken. Buttered corn on the cob. Mashed potatoes. And some rhubarb cobbler." He rattled the bucket again. "It's good and hot."

"Well," the stricken man said with a moaning groan, "just set it down. Maybe the lady would like to have a bite."

Cap left the pail on the ground, departed. On the way out of the corral, he bumped into the same post again. And called it an unseemly name.

McTeague watched him head more or less toward the Big Hat headquarters. "The man needs to see an ophthalmologist."

"If he could *see* an ophthalmologist, there wouldn't be no need for him to—"

"You know what I mean."

"Cap already has himself a serviceable pair of spectacles."

"Why doesn't he wear them?"

"He does, sometimes." Moon managed a wan smile. "But whenever you're around, he takes 'em off."

"Why on earth would he do that?"

"If you don't know, I ain't gonna tell you."

She blushed. "Don't be silly, Charlie."

"False modesty doesn't become a pretty gal like you, Lila Mae." *Fried chicken sounds like just the ticket.* "Did you notice Cap has grown himself a fuzzy little beard?"

"Of course I did. It looks nice on him. He has a smallish chin."

"I'll tell him you said that."

"Not the part about his chin."

"That'll take half the fun out of it." He grinned at a drumstick-shaped cloud. "I feel a bit of an appetite comin' on."

She opened the lunch bucket, was overwhelmed by a mix of delicious aromas wafting up from therein. "What would you like?"

"I was hoping for some dessert," he gasped. "How about another helping of that artificial resuscitation?"

Smiling, the lady unwrapped the foil from an ear of corn. "Stick this in your mouth."

He gave the food a cross-eyed look. "I don't think I can eat while I'm flat on my back."

"Do you feel like sitting up?"

Moon raised himself on an elbow. Groaned with a painful intensity that made the woman wince.

"Easy, now." She reached out to steady him. "You might have a broken rib. And your blood pressure may be unstable. Get up very slowly or you might faint."

"Cowboys don't *faint,*" he grumbled. "And if there's any bones busted, I'd just as soon find out right now."

She helped Moon get onto one knee, gradually onto his feet.

He leaned on a corner post, gave the woman a peculiar, unfocused look. "Oh . . . you were right . . . I feel like I'm gonna topple over—"

Lila Mae McTeague reached out to catch him.

Moon picked her up, danced around the corral.

"What are you doing!"

"I think they call it a hornpipe," he shouted. "But I never did one with a partner before."

A half-dozen cowboys showed up from nowhere to gawk at the spectacle. There were several "wa-hoos," "yi-pees," and one "way to go, boss!"

"Charlie Moon—put me down!"

He looked like he might not. "Or what?"

She showed him a fist.

Disappointed in her lack of enthusiasm, he eased her down.

Disappointed that he had given up so easily, she attempted

an expression of outrage. "You are the most annoying man I have ever met."

"Thank you." He found his hat, clamped it on his head. "You are the nicest lady I ever did a hornpipe with." He held his arms out. "How about it—want to go for another round?"

"I am not accustomed to dancing in manure-caked corrals." McTeague looked toward a clump of willows, pointed. "Let's go over there by the pond."

"Western ranches don't have ponds. That is a stock tank."

"Then let's go over by the stock tank."

"Behind those bushes, where nobody can see us?"

"Precisely."

"And what'll we do over there?"

She picked up the lunch bucket. "We'll have our lunch."

Pulled by equine curiosity, Sweet Alice followed them through the break in the fence. While the human beings enjoyed their meal, the horse took turns munching at grass, slurping water from the stock tank.

After the fried chicken and corn on the cob and potatoes and pie had been dealt with, Charlie Moon picked his teeth with a willow twig. "So, how're things with you, McTeague?"

"Tolerable," she said.

"In these parts, the word is *tol'able.*"

"I am not from 'these parts,' thank you." She wiped her mouth with a snow-white linen napkin. "I wouldn't have been surprised to get a tin plate of greasy fatback, burned pinto beans, and month-old biscuits that would break a bulldog's teeth. But the food was simply scrumptious."

"The grub on the Big Hat is always first-rate." Moon winked at her. "And Cap brought them fancy napkins just for you."

She remembered the cook's missing spectacles and smiled. "Do you really think he has a crush on me?"

"Hey, anything is possible."

"And what does that mean?"

"Do I have to explain it?"

"You certainly do."

"Well, ol' Cap, he's a regular hairy-chested man just like the rest of us. When a fine-looking woman comes around, he's bound by the laws of nature to stop and take notice. Even show off a little bit. But that's as far as it'll go. You shouldn't expect any candy or flowers from my five-star hash slinger."

"He is bashful, then?"

"It's not so much that. I expect the fact that you're a FBI pistol-packing momma puts him a little on edge."

"I see your point. It bears remembering that your ranch is a haven for all sorts of petty felons."

"There's nothing petty about *these* felons. But it is a fact that when you come around, quite a few of my employees get nervous."

"As no doubt they should. But you may tell Cap that I have not the least intention of searching out evidence of any frightful deeds he has done."

"I am sure he will appreciate it."

She shifted gears. "You knew all along, didn't you?"

"Knew what?"

"That Bureau Forensics would determine that the arm found in Moccasin Lake was not Dr. Blinkoe's limb."

"I am still digesting my lunch." He grimaced. "Couldn't we talk about something else?"

"Charlie, don't try to kid me. You knew all along that wasn't Blinkoe's arm. The question is: *How* did you know?"

"Just for the sake of civil conversation, I guess I could humor you—pretend I'm every bit as clever as you think I am."

"Yes you could. So go right ahead."

He thought about it. "It might have been because what the lady fisherman snagged on her hook was a *left* arm. And I'd seen Blinkoe wearing that ring on his right hand."

She shook her head. "He always wore the ring on his left hand."

"Ah—then maybe I remembered seeing the ring on a different *finger*." He nodded to agree with himself. "Yeah. That must've been it."

"Afraid not," she said. "The ring was on the same pinkie

where Dr. Blinkoe always wore it. The Bureau has several photographs to prove this point."

"Then it must've just been a gut feeling. I never did trust that slicker." The Ute's face reflected the pain of a hurtful memory. "First time we met, Blinkoe tried to cheat me at cards."

McTeague rolled her eyes. "Thank you *so* much for sharing this meaningful anecdote with me."

She's got the dangdest prettiest eyes I ever saw. "You're entirely welcome, ma'am."

"But you still have not provided a satisfactory explanation."

Moon shrugged. "I've never admitted I knew it wasn't Dr. Blinkoe's arm. Being a fella with a well-developed sense of humor, I've merely been humoring you."

"Charlie, did I ever tell you that you are the most annoying man I have ever met?"

"Just a few minutes ago."

"I meant every single word of it. And I think you're being evasive."

"It's not likely—I don't even know the meaning of the word."

"It is a variation on 'evasion.'"

"Oh, right. Like the Evasion of the Giant Space-Crickets."

"Don't be silly, Charlie. 'Evasive' means 'intentionally ambiguous or vague.'"

"I bet you had to look that up in a dictionary."

She made another shot at it, aiming for his ego. "I bet you had some devilishly clever reason to believe that dismembered arm belonged to a John Doe. You probably spotted some obscure little clue that I missed entirely."

"You might be right."

"But you're not going to tell me."

"If I did, it'd only upset you."

"Okay. Have it your way." *Sooner or later, I'll find out.* "The primary issue is that the severed limb was never attached to Dr. Blinkoe's torso. Which raises two rather interesting questions."

He nodded. "Number one—whose severed limb is it? Number two—how did Blinkoe's ring and watch get on the John Doe's finger and wrist?"

"So what do you think?"

He winked at her. "I think you liked doing the hornpipe with me."

She ignored this latest evasion. "I suppose you also know what I found out about Pansy Blinkoe's family."

He nodded. "But I don't want to annoy you, so I'll pretend like I don't."

McTeague smirked. "I don't believe you."

"What don't you believe—that I know or that I don't?"

"That you don't. You're bluffing."

"Okay, I'm bluffing. So go ahead and tell me what you found out about Mrs. Blinkoe's parents." He paused. "And her *so-called* brother."

The FBI agent threw her napkin at him. "You *did* know!"

He presented the wide eyes. "Know what?"

"Don't give me that innocent-as-a-newborn-babe expression. *How* did you know?"

"That the fellow who calls himself Clayton Crowe is not, never was, and never will be Pansy Crowe-Blinkoe's brother?"

She waited.

"Maybe it was like knowing that severed arm hadn't been ripped from Blinkoe's shoulder—just a highly experienced lawman's razor-edged intuition."

McTeague threw her head back. "Bilge water!"

The Ute looked tossed aside his willow toothpick. "Nautical phraseology is wasted on an Indian raised in the arid West."

"I bet you understand hogwash, tommyrot, applesauce, and . . . and claptrap!"

Moon did not hide his disappointment. "Those expressions are a bit overused."

Lila Mae gave him a venomous look. "How about *rattlesnake spit!*"

What a woman. "Okay, I'll admit it—I wasn't completely clueless."

"Don't tempt me, Charlie."

"Right. Well, what it all boiled down to was Clayton's big brown eyes. Blue-eyed parents like Mr. and Mrs. Crowe are both endowed with a pair of genes for blue irises. They can produce all the blue-eyed babies they are of a mind to. But it is almost impossible for them to have brown-eyed offspring—which suggests a number of more likely possibilities. Like the mother had an unseemly relationship with a man who carried at least one brown gene. Which could mean he was, like the song says—a Brown-eyed Handsome Man."

"Not all brown-eyed men are handsome."

"I hope that remark was not intended to hurt my feelings."

"I wish I could reassure you."

"You're a hard-hearted woman, McTeague. But to get back to what we were talking about, I didn't believe for a moment that Mrs. Crowe had given birth to this brown-eyed Clayton."

"I'll say this, Charlie—you are far more perceptive than I would have thought."

"Thank you. But most of the credit should go to my extremely capable high-school teacher, Miss Atherton. I thought I recalled something about eye colors and inheritance from her biology class, but I had to go see the lady and check it out."

"I am very impressed." A hesitation. "I don't suppose you know who the so-called Clayton Crowe actually is."

Moon was genuinely sorry and it showed on his face.

"Tell me you're kidding."

"I would if I could. But once again, I owe it all to Miss Atherton. That clever lady got on the Internet, found facsimiles of all four of Pansy Crowe's high-school yearbooks. The Clayton Crowe in the apartment over the Blinkoe garage was actually Roger Culpepper. Pansy and Culpepper were Queen and King of the Fall Festival. There were three or four pictures of them together. It didn't take a quantum mechanic to figure out he was her old boyfriend. Mr. Culpepper must've hit hard times, looked up his former sweetheart. I guess Pansy couldn't turn him away from her door, so they cooked up that story that he was her brother. Dr. Blinkoe bought it,

and agreed to let him stay in the apartment over the garage."
Moon thought about it. "I think Pansy was just softhearted. I
doubt her and the so-called Clayton ever did anything they
shouldn't have."

Special Agent McTeague stared at this remarkable man.
"Do you actually believe that?"

He nodded. "I'm not saying there wasn't still some romantic attraction between them."

"But you really believe it was a . . . a chaste relationship?"

"That's the way I see it."

"Charlie, you are a hopeless romantic."

"I certainly hope so."

"There is one thing you don't know."

"If I don't, it's because Miss Atherton didn't tell me."

"Six days ago, Roger Culpepper, aka Clayton Crowe, was
stopped near Garden City, Kansas."

Moon raised an eyebrow. "Stopped from doing what?"

"Not from. Stopped *for* doing what. By a Garden City police officer."

"Okay. What was what?"

"Driving Pansy Blinkoe's pickup truck. Through a red
light."

"Where was Pansy at the time?"

"Not with her high-school sweetheart."

"And how did Culpepper aka Crowe explain having possession of Mrs. Blinkoe's fine motor vehicle?"

"He lied, of course. Said she had loaned it to him. Along
with her credit card, which he'd used an hour earlier to purchase fuel at a truck stop in Dodge City."

" 'Loaned it to him,' eh? Culpepper must've been rattled.
A six-year-old with his hand in the cookie jar would've
thought up a better story."

"After he had a few hours to think it over, he came up with
another one."

"I bet it was a dandy."

"Culpepper claims he returned to his garage apartment
late one night, realized his 'sister' was gone. This disturbed

him, because 'sis' generally wasn't away so late at night. He rode his motorcycle into Granite Creek, intending to cruise around. He claims he spotted her pickup parked at the Lullaby Motel. Key was in the ignition, her spare credit card stashed in the ash tray. Culpepper says he figures Pansy is shacked up with some guy in the motel, so he decides to teach her a lesson. He muscles his motorcycle into the pickup bed, drives away. He intended to leave the truck a few miles out of town, but before he knew it, the sun was up and he was across the border in Kansas."

"And he never admitted to being anything but Pansy's brother?"

"He was only interrogated twice."

"Please don't tell me they turned him loose."

"I won't, because that would be a lie. During the second day of his incarceration in the Finney County lockup, he faked a heart attack and was rushed to the hospital. While in the emergency room, Culpepper apparently experienced a remarkable recovery. Feeling no urgent need for medical care, he apparently left the premises while no one was looking. And has not been seen since."

"A slippery fellow."

"Indeed."

"Tell me, McTeague—did you say that Mr. Culpepper used Pansy Blinkoe's credit card to purchase gasoline in Dodge *before* he was picked up near Garden City?"

"That's right."

"Then he was heading west on Route 50. Toward the Colorado border."

She shrugged. "Perhaps he was coming back to visit his 'little sister.'"

"One cannot entirely rule it out." Moon edged closer to the pretty lady. "How about we stop talking shop?"

She was agreeable to this proposal, and said so.

After the intense work of the morning, the afternoon was spent in a most pleasant fashion.

But like a breath of honeysuckle perfume or the trill of a mockingbird, such sweetness passes all too quickly.

While the sun was still over the Buckhorns, Lila Mae McTeague said her good-bye, drove away in the government-issue Ford Motor Company product.

47

GIVING IT ANOTHER SHOT

After a light supper of broiled beefsteaks, baked potatoes, and great-northern beans—during which Sweet Alice and the hot-tempered FBI agent were the chief topics of conversation—Cap closed the Big Hat kitchen for the day. There were disputes among the cowboy gamblers about whether or not those few seconds when the horse didn't move counted as honest time in the saddle, but the point was moot because it turned out that during all the excitement, no one had kept the boss's time. Staying aloofly above the fray, Charlie Moon wrote Jerome Kydmann a check for an extra month's pay. All in all, it had been an outstanding day. In twos and threes, the cowboys drifted away. Most to the drafty bunkhouse, a few to night duties.

It was generally assumed that the boss would head back to the other side of the Buckhorns. But before he returned to the Columbine, Moon had some unfinished business to attend to.

And so he hung around, finding this and that to do, until a silver-dollar moon was rolling high over the prairie—and he was alone. He headed for the corral, which had been repaired during the afternoon. Under his breath, he hummed a few bars of "Strawberry Roan."

She was waiting for him.

He climbed the mended fence, seated himself on the top rail.

Sweet Alice whinnied, brushed off a horsefly with her tail.

Moon pushed back his Stetson, looked the horse right in the eye. He delivered a stern monologue, explaining the hard facts of life on this planet. What the owner of the outfit had to say can be summed up pretty much as follows:

1. Broncs who cannot be gentled are of no use on a working ranch.
2. Horses who try to murder their riders can't be sold even for rodeo stock.
3. There is a steady demand for horseflesh over at the Pueblo packing plant, where Perky Puppy Pet Food is ground up and put into fifteen-ounce cans.

He paused to let this sink in.

Alice approached, put her nose against his leg.

"All right," he said. "I'll give you one more chance."

In a moment, the cowboy was back in the saddle again. Almost every muscle in Moon's body was sore from his earlier experience. He waited for the inevitable explosion. Very few things are inevitable. There was no explosion. He gently flicked the reins, nudged S. Alice with his knee. The mare trotted gaily around the corral, yielding to the horseman's every whim. After a few minutes of this exercise, he opened the gate.

Off they went at a canter.

The Ute was overflowing with joy. *Wait till the boys see this!*

He rode the horse along the spine of Dinosaur Ridge,

south along the skyline fence, back along the lane from the highway. Moon fairly beamed with pride. *This horse is gentle enough for a little girl to ride.* He realized that she might still get snuffy from time to time, and maybe Sweet Alice liked to show off when she had an audience. But all she had ever needed was a good talking-to. "You've been a good ol' nag tonight," he said. "You've earned your sweet self a long drink of water." He patted her on the shoulder, rode her up to the stock tank.

Concealed by the night and a grotesque grove of dwarfish oak, the bushwhacker lay on his belly. He squinted through the 9X scope mounted on the silenced Savage 110FP Tactical Rifle. As the horse loped along in an easy gait, the target in the saddle was bouncing up and down four or five inches. *But that don't matter—not at this range.* And there was not a hint of a breeze. This time, it would be a dead-easy shot. He centered the crosshairs on the rider's spine. *Now won't you be surprised when I knock a big hole in your back. . . .*

As they approached the stock tank, Sweet Alice trotted along like there was nothing in front of her but dry land. She did not respond to the reins, and when the anxious rider yelled "whoa!" she did not slow. Perhaps the command sounded too much like "go!" But near the edge of the water, the horse seemed to experience a sudden change of mind. She lowered her head, planted stubby forelegs firmly in the mud, stopped like she'd hit a brick wall.

Aside from going along for the ride, there was not much Charlie Moon could do—it was a matter of forward momentum. In barely one momentum, he had slid down Sweet Alice's neck, sailed past her pointy ears.

Because his entire concentration was focused on the upcoming landing, Moon heard neither the small "pop" of the silenced rifle shot—nor the 190 grains of lead that hummed past his head.

In a cartoon, the caption would have been "Ker-splash."

The actual sound was more like *splat* as he landed on his butt in about two feet of muddy water. As he sat there, the chocolate-tinted liquid lapped around his chest.

Because he had his back to the beast, she walked a full half-circle to reach the other side of the tank. It was evident that Sweet Alice went to this place because she hankered to see the rider's face.

It was a waste of equine effort.

Moon's expression was a black hole under the black Stetson. Which is to say that no light whatever came from within. Not a solitary photon. Moreover, no words proceeded from his mouth. Considering what he was thinking, this was just as well.

The outlaw mare pawed at the bank, whinnied a brash horse-laugh.

Having slipped away into the night, the rifleman did not witness this low comedy.

48

YOU-KNOW-WHO

Special Agent McTeague was working late when the telephone rang. She glanced at the caller ID, noted that the call was from a public telephone somewhere in Granite Creek. Brushing aside a wisp of coal-black hair, she pressed the instrument against her ear. "FBI." She counted three raspy breaths before the caller spoke.

"This the FBI lady?"

I didn't think I'd ever hear from you again. She switched on the digital recorder. "This is Special Agent McTeague at the Bureau's Granite Creek office. Who's calling, please?"

"This is you-know-who."

"Thanks for not making me guess."

"It's me." His voice dropped to a throaty whisper. "Scarf."

"Oh, *that* you-know-who." *This should be good for a giggle.* "What's on your mind, Mr. S?"

"It's not *Mister*—just plain *Scarf.*"

"So what's up, Just Plain Scarf?"

His tone suggested that he did not appreciate the flippancy. "You got the twenty bucks for me?"

"Depends on what you've got for me. Don't be wasting my time."

"I figured you might like to know where that Mr. Blinky is holed up."

The telephone felt like ice in her hand. The Bureau had not released the results of the dismembered-arm DNA tests to the media. As far as the general public was concerned, Manfred Blinkoe had died when his boat exploded in Moccasin Lake. "What do you mean?"

"I mean he's alive and spry as a spring chicken—and I can tell you where he is!"

"Before you say another word, I must inform you that any attempt to mislead an official FBI investigation is a very serious offense and—"

"Don't be wasting *my* time, FBI lady. Put twenty bucks under that flower pot I told you about, and I'll be in touch with you."

McTeague heard a click on the line. *Troublesome old crank. He doesn't know a thing about the Blinkoe homicide— he's simply attempting to extort a few bucks from the Bureau.* She placed the headset back in the cradle. *Still, twenty dollars isn't all that much money.*

49

A BRAND-NEW DAY

When Daisy Perika opened her eyes, the promise of another dawn was merely a grayish glow over the Buckhorn range. The sleepy woman rolled over under the quilt, wondered whether her nephew was already up, attending to his beefy business. For a full minute, she lay very still, listening. Aside from the occasional creak or groan in the timbers, there were no sounds in the big log house. As elderly folk are apt to, she got up slowly, making certain that knee and elbow and shoulder joints were equal to the task. With a few grunts and groans, Daisy pulled on a cotton dress, slipped her cold feet into a pair of fleece-lined moccasins, padded down the hall and into the parlor. Charlie Moon's wide-brimmed black hat was not hanging on the peg by the door. She pulled a heavy drape aside, peeked out the window. His automobile and the stake-bed GMC were gone, so she knew he was off somewhere with a truckload of cowboys. The Columbine was a

huge ranch, and now Charlie owned another big piece of
property on the east side of the Buckhorns. What with hundreds of cattle to deal with, fences that always needed mending, hay crops that needed tending, her nephew had too much
work to do. *Charlie's way too ambitious, even for a young
man.* That was what came from living among the hard-driven
matukach. The Ute elder's mouth wrinkled into a wry smile.
*But I'm old and wise, so I'll spend my last days having a
good time.* She marched into the huge kitchen, put the perco-
lator on the stove.

Minutes later the tribal elder stepped out onto the east
wing of the wraparound porch, prepared to enjoy the day's
first cup of strong coffee. She leaned her walking stick
against the wall, plumped her bottom down into a cane-back
chair, rested her gaze on a long, rocky ridge that someOne
had lovingly decorated with aspen and spruce. She watched
dawn's liquid gold spilling extravagantly over the jagged
edge of the Buckhorns. *God is no miser.*

Daisy sipped at the steaming black liquid. Weary of trials
and troubles and regrets, she tried to think of nothing. This is
almost impossible to do—especially when something is nagging at you. And something was. She tried very had to dis-
miss whatever it was. Which was about as effective as trying
very hard to go to sleep.

Shortly after the sun topped the snowy peaks, it came to
her. *Today, something's different here.* The shaman knew this
was true—she could feel it in her marrow, smell it in the crisp
morning air. For some time, she puzzled about it, wondering
what had made everything seem so fresh and new. Daisy was
about to go inside for a second cup of coffee, when she felt
the warm breath on her ankle. She gave the hound a long,
thoughtful look. "Good morning, Mr. Dog." She refused to
address Sidewinder by his given name.

The animal fixed her with a piercing canine stare, whim-
pered. Looked away in a particular direction. Looked back
at her.

Daisy wondered what was on his mind. *He's acting kind*

of fidgety. She considered various possibilities. *Maybe he didn't sleep good last night. Or it could be he's worried about something.* But what did dogs worry about? *I expect what he needs is some conversation.* Completely relaxed, and happier than she had been in months, the Ute elder talked to the dog. She offered the beast a juicy selection of tales, parables and fables about her long life and hard times. Though most of her tellings were about the usual day-to-day things (the best way to bake a pan of biscuits, how to take skunk smell off your clothes), there were accounts of quite remarkable events (like that Sunday morning when the *pitukupf* came to church). She even confessed two or three dark secrets—like about that time she had stolen a Navajo charm pendant from a superstitious *matukach*, and how her third husband had *really* died, and one other misdeed that cannot be mentioned.

As the narrative flowed along, the dog listened with rapt attention. At the proper moments, Sidewinder would respond with a wag of the tail, a knowing jerk of the head. He also made small noises. An urgent growl, a canine whine, an occasional ruffing bark.

None of these attempts to communicate made the least sense to the human being.

Finally, something of quite a different nature did arouse the shaman's curiosity. This occurred when she happened to close her eyes, and in little patches here and there—saw snatches of black-and-white pictures in the creature's memory. There were woolly-gob weeds and tall saw grass. The corral down by the river. More weeds and grass. A startled deer leaping over a rotten log. But what was this? Cone-shaped trees. A little log cabin. Parked by the hitching post, an old automobile that hadn't been there for months! So *that* was what was so special about this day.

Immediately, Daisy got up, took hold of her oak walking stick.

Knowing where she was going, the hound did his following up front.

A stiff breeze whipped at her skirt.

◆ ◆ ◆

Little Butch took his duty seriously. Every day when he showed up for his eight-hour shift, he would check the Marlin rifle and the heavy pistol holstered on his side. Happy to have something more to do. than stand around, the armed Columbine cowboy trailed forty paces behind Daisy Perika, ready and willing to gun down any man or beast who posed the slightest threat to the boss's aunt. The hound was aware of the guard's presence, but Butch managed to stay out of Daisy's sight.

It took the frail woman almost twenty minutes to top the ridge. She paused at the edge of the glade, where quivering aspens and blackish blue spruce provided a welcome shade. Having gotten her wind back and having gotten the wind to her back, she found a deer path and trudged through the small forest. The boisterous dog bounded through an undergrowth of ferns, sniffing at the delectable scents of rodents and toadstools. Occasionally, when the woman paused and closed her eyes for a moment, she caught flashes of what the animal saw. The twisted root of a dwarf oak. A perfectly formed brown pine cone. A fat chipmunk, scampering into a hole under a mossy bank.

Daisy emerged from the sunny side of the woods to see a rolling prairie reaching out to embrace the alpine lake. Over to her left, isolated on the open land like a tiny island in a sea of grass, was that smaller cluster of trees. And nestled among them, the log cabin that was several years older than the aged woman. She was not surprised to see the priest's venerable black Buick parked at the hitching post. Having been sniffing the scent of a dead something or other, Sidewinder decided on a detour, trotted off across the prairie.

Father Raes Delfino was in a deep, restful sleep. The sound came from very far away. Louder now. Insistent. Painful. It was, he thought, as if someone were banging his head with a knobby shillelagh—and this was not an Irish priest. The bone-weary man kept his eyes tightly shut. *It must've been my imagination. Perhaps if I keep quite still, I will be able to go back to sleep and—*

Bam-bam-bam!

He turned on his side, scowled at the clock on the bedside table.

Bam-bam-bam!

It was like a nightmare. When the priest had retired from his parish on the Southern Ute reservation, Charlie Moon had offered him the use of this rustic cabin so he would have a quiet retreat from the noise and tumult of the world. *Who on earth would be banging on my door at this hour? Certainly not Charlie. And the cowboys mostly leave me alone. It could be that cranky old foreman, come to annoy me about something. Perhaps if I don't respond, whoever it is will go away.*

Bam! "Hey—I know you're in there. Open the door." *Bam!*

God help me. It is Daisy Perika. But what on earth is she doing here? He got up, stepped into his black gabardine trousers. *Charlie must've invited her to the Columbine for a few days.*

Bam-bam-bam!

He pulled on a shirt, padded through the small parlor to the door.

"You might as well open up—I ain't goin' away." *Bam-bam-bam!*

Father Raes opened the door. Blinked at his visitor.

"Hah," she said. "I knew you was in there!" Daisy Perika stared at the unbuttoned shirt, the bare feet. "What—you was still in bed?" She pointed her walking stick at the sun, used a distinctly accusative tone. "It's almost an hour into daylight."

The kindly man yawned.

She regarded him with a beady-eyed frown. "Why didn't you let me know you was back?"

"For one thing," he mumbled, "I didn't know you were here at the Columbine. For another," he grumbled, "I got in well past midnight." Another yawn. "It was about three A.M. when I finally got into bed."

She shook her head in mock dismay. "You shouldn't be staying out so late at night." Daisy bumped her way past him, gave the parlor a close inspection. As she had expected, it was neat and clean.

"Come right in." He closed the door. "Make yourself completely at home."

"Thank you," she said brightly. "I don't mind if I do."

He sighed. "Would you like some breakfast?"

Daisy raised her brows in mock surprise. "Breakfast—this late in the day? Why, it'll soon be time for lunch." She clucked her tongue. "Not having a regular job has caused you to slack off some."

He mumbled something she could not hear.

Daisy followed him into the kitchen, watched the sleep-deprived man muddle through his preparations. The fruits of his labors were a saucepan of pasty oatmeal, a pot of black tea.

She seated herself across the table, watched him eat and drink.

After he had washed his bowl and cup, the priest suggested they go to the parlor.

Before he could get there, Daisy had plopped into his rocking chair. "So tell me about your travels."

Father Raes sat on a lumpy couch. Somewhat refreshed by breaking his fast, the priest proceeded to tell the Ute woman about strange cities, grand palaces, a visit to the Vatican, even an audience with the Pope.

She listened to the entire account without interrupting.

Finally, he said: "What's been happening in your life?"

"Oh, not much." She watched an agitated little beetle scuttle across the hardwood floor. "Nothing I'd want to talk about."

He knew she was aching to tell him about her latest misadventures. "Very well. I would not wish to intrude upon your privacy."

Annoyed that he would not press her, Daisy was obliged to tell him why she was staying at the Columbine.

The kindly man was horrified to hear about the destruction

of her home. But so thankful she had escaped alive. He paused to thank God for her deliverance from the fire.

The tribal elder assured him that she would buy another trailer, and be back at the mouth of *Cañón del Espíritu* before the first snow fell. Moving on to more interesting things, she told him about meeting Manfred Blinkoe and his lawyer, Spencer Trottman, and how Blinkoe had hired Charlie Moon to find out who'd taken a shot at him and accidentally killed that poor woman at the restaurant. Sensing that she had his full attention, Daisy gave a brief account of the terrible explosion that had destroyed Blinkoe's houseboat, and how a mangled arm had been dragged in by a fisherman.

The priest winced at this.

The storyteller told him how Mrs. Blinkoe had disappeared. The wily old shaman would not reveal *exactly* how she knew where Pansy Blinkoe was hiding. Though she would not dare mention the *pitukupf*, Daisy thought it would be all right to describe her vision of Pansy Blinkoe. Even in the Bible, prophets and the like had dreams and visions. But as she told him about "seeing" Pansy in that little room, chatting with Prudence and Alonzo, Daisy thought the priest's expression suggested some suspicion that the "little man" might have been involved. She hurried on, describing how she had talked Louise-Marie LaForte into driving her to Garcia's Crossing. She left out certain irrelevant events, like the wild encounter with the policemen in Granite Creek. But when she got to the part about that lying pot-gut, pineapple-head pimp who was hiding Pansy Blinkoe in his house, Daisy gave the priest an accurate, word-for-word account of the encounter with DeSoto.

Father Raes Delfino shook his head. "Daisy, Daisy," he said. "What am I going to do with you?"

She was wide-eyed with surprise. "What do you mean by that?"

"Those terrible things you said to that man—a practicing Christian would never do such a thing!"

Daisy snorted. "Well, I guess I'm a little out of practice."

Already wound up, he threw her a low curve. "When was the last time you were inside a church?"

The old slugger knocked his best pitch right back at him. "When was the last time you said Mass at St. Ignatius?"

His mouth gaped. "Daisy—that was more than a year ago!"

She could have told him that Charlie Moon took her to church practically every Sunday morning, even admitted that the visiting priest was a pretty decent fellow. But pulling Father Raes's chain was lots more fun. "My, my—you haven't said Mass for that long?" She gave him a sorrowful look. "Well—I guess you must be out of practice too."

The priest thought he saw the glint of mischief in her eye. "As you well know, I am retired."

"Me too." The tribal elder rocked in the chair. Began to hum "Rock of Ages."

He cleared his throat. "There has been a visiting priest at St. Ignacio's."

"Oh, sure, I heard about Father What's-his-name." She dismissed What's-his-name with a flick of her wrist. "He's from back East, I don't remember exactly where. Boston or Providence or Long Island—one of them uppity places." Daisy frowned. "What do them Johnny Rebs call 'em?" She closed her eyes. "Oh, now I remember—damn Yankees."

Father Raes paled. "Daisy—shame on you!"

"Oh *I* wouldn't say that—to me he's a *danged* Yankee." While the priest fumed, Daisy hummed another bar or two of the hymn. "They tell me all his sermons are about fundraising and a new rectory and theology and useless stuff like that." It occurred to her that Father Raes's single vanity was pride in his several university degrees. She stopped the rocker, leaned closer to her victim. "And you know what else? They say he's got himself a Ph.D. I bet that's why he thinks he's such a big hotshot."

The scholar felt his temperature rising. "I happen to hold a doctorate myself."

"Oh," she said. Shook her head. "I might've known."

The kindhearted cleric choked back a surge of righteous anger. "Daisy, I regret the necessity to say this—but I must."

He fixed her with a steely glare. "I am greatly disappointed in you."

"Now you've hurt my feelings." She started rocking again, humming "Bringing in the Sheaves." "But I won't hold it against you. Tell you what—if you ever say the Mass at St. Ignatius again, I'll drop by. Just to see if you still remember how."

Father Raes set his jaw. "Daisy, there is no excuse for your absence from church during the past year."

Daisy jutted out her chin. *I've been there fifty more times than you have.* But she couldn't admit to that.

He clasped his hands. "But there is another matter that causes me even more concern for the state of your soul."

She snorted. "My soul is as good as it ever was."

"Sad to say, that is probably so. But those insults you hurled at Mr. DeSoto—such behavior amounts to a grievous sin."

Daisy slowed her rocking. "Is 'grievous' as bad as 'mortal'?"

"Don't try to change the subject."

She raised an eyebrow. "What's the subject?"

Unmoved by this devious subterfuge, Father Raes cocked his gun, unloaded both barrels. "Repentance. And penance."

Either of these harsh projectiles would have pierced the old sinner's skin. The combination quite did her in.

50

HER WORRIED MIND

Daisy Perika had left her interview with Father Raes convinced that she had done nothing wrong in recognizing De-Soto for what he certainly was. A blivit is a blivit! And telling Pineapple Head exactly what she thought about him was certainly the right thing to do. Honesty Is the Best Policy, and Tell It Like It Is—those were in the Bible, weren't they? But even with Truth and Justice and a mistaken understanding of Holy Scripture solidly in her corner, Daisy realized that the Catholic priest had taken a quite different view of the matter, and she had no doubt that God would side with Father Raes—who probably had talked to Him as soon as she'd left the log cabin. The tribal elder tried not to think about it, and was reasonably successful during the daytime. But after night would cover the Columbine, and she was in her bed, it did not matter what she tried to think about. The priest's words would come back to haunt her.

Shame on you . . . I am greatly disappointed in you . . . concern for the state of your soul . . . those insults you hurled at this Mr. DeSoto . . . a grievous sin . . . Repentance . . . Penance.

Even after she had drifted away into something resembling sleep, the backslider's troubled conscience would not let her rest. The dream varied, but went more or less like this: Father Raes would appear at the foot of her bed, weeping and sighing as if his heart would break. Whenever he had a minute to spare from his various criminal activities, DeSoto would join the priest, a halo glowing around his ugly face! Pineapple Head would bare his chest, as if prepared to absorb the arrows of her insults with the patience of a holy martyr. Lastly, Father What's-his-name would join the trio, and say a prayer for the troublesome old woman. The pockmarked hypocrite, pretending to be a saint—flanked by two sad-faced priests. It was just about more than a person could bear.

After three nights of this terrible torment, Daisy made up her mind.

At breakfast, she glared across the table at Charlie Moon. "This is the first meal we've had together in a week."

Her nephew deftly inserted a tablespoon of blackberry jam into a hot biscuit.

"Did you hear what I said?"

He nodded at the biscuit. "Seven days a week, sunup to sundown—a rancher's life is nothing but work, work, work."

"I've been talking to some of your hired hands." She stirred her coffee, smirked at the hardworking man. "They say a horse pitched you onto a fence."

He shrugged. "Don't ever believe anything these cowboys tell you."

"My father broke wild horses for sixty years and *he* was never bucked off."

"Well, ol' Granddad was quite a man." A man who claimed to have found a ninety-pound gold nugget on Shellhammer Ridge and ate a bushel of raw turnips at one sitting and fought off an enraged grizzly with his Russell Barlow pocketknife. Not necessarily on the same day, of course.

She pushed the cup aside. "Charlie, I am sick and tired of sitting here by myself. Never going nowhere."

"I'll tell Butch to take you into Granite Creek."

Daisy shook her head. "I don't want none of your smelly cowboys taking me nowhere. But before winter comes, you can drive me down to Ignacio. We can have some lunch at Angel's." She hesitated. "And then I want to go have a look at my place."

A shadow passed over the Ute's face. "There's nothing left of your trailer. After the fire inspector got finished with his work, I had all the debris hauled off."

"I don't care, I'll still want to see the land." Daisy gazed at the tranquil picture in her mind. "I'll go for a long walk in Spirit Canyon." *And talk to some of my old friends.* There were dozens of ghosts in *Cañon del Espíritu.* And there was the *pitukupf,* of course. She did not particularly like the little man, but when you had been away from home for a long time, any neighbor was a welcome sight. There were good spirits there too, even some that came to call from Upper World—like Nahum Yaciiti. The old shepherd, who was one of God's Holy People, had come to comfort her on the night of the fire. *Maybe, if I was back where I belong, Nahum would come to see me. If he did, we could talk about this and that.* It did not occur to the shaman that his spirit would ever visit the Columbine. Nahum, she assumed, would be as uncomfortable in the high country as she was. Even in the middle of the summer, the nights here were ice-cold.

"Okay." There was a twinkle in Moon's eye. "Before the first big snow, I'll take you back to the old home place."

Daisy gave no evidence of having heard him. "I've been thinking."

Uh-oh. Charlie Moon tried not to look alarmed.

"I don't have hardly any stuff left, so I don't need that much room. Just a two-burner stove and a small table, and a toilet, and a little cot to sleep on. I have enough money saved up to buy me one of them little camping trailers—if it was used. You could tow it out to my place, and hook it up to the electric and water."

He turned this over in his mind. "Well, that's something worth thinking about."

"Don't think about it, do it!"

He got up from the table.

"Where do you think you're going?"

He grinned. "Well, I *think* I'm going over to the Big Hat, then—"

"You better think again!"

"What?"

She pointed at his empty chair. "Sit down."

He sat.

She leaned over the table, fixing him with a stare. "Today, you are taking me over to Garcia's Crossing."

What's at Garcia's Crossing? He did not bat an eye. "Okay, let's go."

Daisy regarded him with considerable suspicion. "What—no argument from Mr. I'm-So-Busy-I-Don't-Have-Time-to-Spit?"

He bathed her in a warm smile. "I wouldn't want you to call up one of your friends."

Her voice lost its edge. "What do you mean by that?"

There was a merry twinkle in his eye. "I mean it's better to have *me* for your driver than, oh, let's say—someone who tools around in a rickety old Oldsmobile, terrorizing law-abiding motorists."

"Louise-Marie is a perfectly good driver."

"I'm sure she is. Now are we gonna sit here all morning and talk about it, or do you want to hop in the car and start rolling on down the road?"

"I'm too old to hop. And you haven't asked me *why* I want to go."

I'll give her a little more rope. "You really think I don't know?"

I should've known. "Scott Parris told you all about it, didn't he?"

Aha! "If he did, it would be in the strictest confidence. I'd be honor-bound not to admit it."

Daisy scratched at a spot on the tablecloth. "I knew I shouldn't have trusted that white policeman. You and him are thick as thieves."

"It's true," Moon said. "There's hardly anything he don't tell me."

"Scott's a bigmouth. And so are you." She got up with a groan. "I'll fix us some sandwiches and a thermos of coffee. You be ready to leave in twenty minutes." As an afterthought, she added: "And bring that ugly dog of yours along."

He raised an eyebrow. "You enjoy Sidewinder's company?"

She brushed this off with a gesture. "At least when I talk to a dog, I can be fairly sure he won't repeat what I say to every nitwit in the county."

Charlie Moon dialed the familiar number, waited to hear the familiar voice. After four rings, it boomed in his ear.

"Police department, Chief Parris here."

"Hello, Chief. This is your faithful Indian friend."

"Charlie, how are you?"

"Troubled. I have been waiting for some time . . ." he looked at his watch, figured it amounted to about four minutes, "for you to give me a call. And tell me what I needed to know."

"Is this some kind of riddle?"

"Are you some kind of friend who keeps secrets from his best buddy?"

"Secrets?" A nervous cough. "What about?"

"About what my aunt Daisy did. That business at Garcia's Crossing."

"Oh . . . that."

The Ute filled the space with silence.

"Charlie—you there?"

Moon grunted. He could see the white man blushing, pulling at his shirt collar.

"So you found out about it."

"It was bound to happen, pardner." Moon did his best imitation of a man who'd been let down by his best friend. "Just wish I'd heard it from you."

There was an uneasy silence before Parris mumbled into the mouthpiece. "Look, there was no real harm done. I just thought it'd be best if we let it rest."

"Just the same . . ." Moon let his words trail off.

"What'd you hear?"

Enough to want to hear more. "Enough to make me worry."

"Well, it wasn't no big deal. You must've heard an exaggerated account."

"Maybe so. You want to tell me your version of what happened?"

Parris didn't. But he did.

51

MAKING AMENDS

The drive was spent in silence. After the requisite number of miles had accumulated on the odometer, they approached the outskirts of Granite Creek, passed the Mountain Man Bar and Grille, the Ford dealership, the new Wal-Mart superstore, the BelMar Trailer Court, the rodeo grounds.

None of this was of the least interest to Sidewinder, who was stretched out on the backseat, enjoying a blissful sleep. In his dream, the aged hound was a puppy again. He was yipping and running and rollicking through the grass, chasing a black mouse.

As Charlie Moon watched the blacktop slip under the Expedition, he wondered what his aunt was thinking about.

Daisy Perika's imagination was operating in overdrive. Recalling her previous passage along this route, she was haunted by the possibility that she might encounter that nasty white cop again. Despite this worry, she could not help but smile at the remembrance of his comical image in the Oldsmobile's rearview mirror—hopping around on one leg like a crippled ape. She assured herself that a second confrontation was unlikely. First of all, how would that mean policeman know she was coming through his town again? And even if he did know—he would not want to have a face-to-face with her nephew. *Nobody* messed with Charlie Moon. With this comforting thought, she settled down, closed her eyes against the bright sunlight.

Moon reached over to the passenger side, lowered the sunshade.

By then, they had left the town behind. It seemed as if they might drive on forever without exchanging a word.

It was Sidewinder who broke the spell. Having watched the mouse escape into a cluster of prickly-pear cactus, the dog abruptly awakened to a world of reality that included hunger pains, aching joints, dozens of fascinating scents. The animal put his front feet on the front seat, plopped his head onto Daisy's shoulder.

"Oh," she said, pretending to be annoyed. "Go bother somebody else!"

Aside from Charlie Moon, there was no one else to bother and the hound had made his choice. In a gesture of endearment, he licked her on the ear.

"Aaaagh!" Daisy took a swat, missed his nose by an inch. Having failed in this violent act, she found a handkerchief in her pocket. "Now I've got dog spit in my ear."

Moon kept his eye on the clump of cottonwoods down the road. "They say dog spit is loaded with antibiotics."

She wiped at the offended ear. "Who'd say a fool thing like that?"

He admitted that he did not recall, then slipped in a casual remark. "After what happened, I'm surprised you wanted to go back to Garcia's Crossing."

Daisy almost made a tart retort, then clamped her mouth shut.

He cast her a crosswise glance. "Maybe you still think Mr. DeSoto is hiding Pansy Blinkoe in his house." There being no response, Moon continued the conversation with himself. "Nah, that's not likely." He considered other possibilities. "I bet you think he's got her stashed in his *garage*."

Daisy took a deep breath, exhaled her version of a pithy proverb she'd heard long ago at the reservation boarding school. "It is better for a big jug head to keep his mouth shut and have people think he's most likely a fool, than to start talking nonsense and remove all doubt."

He nodded at this sage observation.

She waited in vain for her nephew to make another crack. Evidently, he had taken her advice to heart. Pleased, she decided to satisfy his unseemly curiosity. "When I was here last time, and talking to Mr. DeSoto, I kind of . . . lost my temper a little bit."

Moon looked doubtful because he was. "I find that hard to believe. The part about 'a little bit'."

She ignored this. "After I had a talk with Father Raes, I made up my mind to come back. And apologize to Pineapple Head for what I'd said."

Her nephew found this *impossible* to believe.

Daisy continued in a pious tone. "A Christian lady should not say unkind things to bad people." She sniffed. "Even if every word of what she says is true."

Moon smiled at the Garcia's Crossing sign on the shoulder. "I'm proud to be your relative—you are a good example to us all."

She nodded her agreement to this sensible remark. "It's up to us elders to set the standard, so you young people will learn how to behave."

He slowed to the forty-mph speed limit. "Where is Mr. DeSoto's house?"

Pleased that Mr. Smarty Hat didn't know *everything,* she pointed. "You can turn right there, just on the other side of St. Cuthbert's."

Across the highway from St. Cuthbert's Catholic Church, inside the musty, dusty darkness of Pokey Joe's General Store, the large woman in the oversized overalls watched through a fly-spotted window. The owner of the business establishment did not recognize the automobile turning into the dirt lane by the church, or the man behind the wheel—but that little woman in the passenger seat looked awfully familiar. Pokey Joe wondered why that old Indian woman had returned to Garcia's Crossing.

Daisy Perika jerked at Moon's sleeve. "Don't drive up in his yard—park behind the church."

"Is there any reason why—"

"I intend to do this by myself," she snapped. "You can wait in the car."

As he braked to a stop, Moon did not conceal his disappointment. "I've never seen you apologize to a living soul. I thought it'd be something I should witness, so I can tell my great-grandchildren about it."

She snorted. "Before you can have great-grandchildren, you gotta have children. And before you can have children, you gotta find yourself a wife."

"That'll be no problem." He came around to open her door, winked at his aunt. "I've got several hot prospects."

She threw her head back. "Ha-ha."

He had no ready response for this unkind remark. "You sure you don't want me to come along for protection?" He took her arm as she got out.

She was grateful when her feet touched the ground. "I don't need no protection."

"I was thinking of Mr. DeSoto."

Daisy chuckled. "Don't worry. If he behaves himself, I won't hurt him."

"Yeah, but what if he gives you a crosswise look?"

"Then you can call his next of kin, ask 'em where they want the body sent."

Charlie Moon watched his aunt stomp off with her walking stick, the hound at her heels. He wondered what life would be like without the mischievous old woman.

◆ ◆ ◆

The almost-repentant sinner stood at the entrance to the loathsome man's residence and prayed. *God, you and me both know what kind of yahoo this DeSoto is. But it's my duty to do what Father Raes tells me, even if it don't make no sense at all, so here I am.* She summoned up all of her resolve, which would barely have filled a ladybug's thimble. *Well, here goes.* She tapped the door with her stick.

A raven winged its dark way over the roof, came to rest on the top of a telephone pole.

She tapped again. Harder.

The homely face appeared at the window, scowled. "It's you."

Daisy called upon the blessed virtue of Patience. When dealing with outright fools, one could not have too much of this commodity. "I know it's me." She said this sweetly.

DeSoto, whose midday meal had been interrupted, was no little bit annoyed, as well as bewildered. "What're you doin' here?"

She responded slowly, as if addressing a backward child. "If you'll open the door, I'll tell you."

The pistol appeared in his hand. "You can tell me now."

When dealing with a man who exhibited bad manners, Daisy had no need to call upon the virtue of Stubbornness—she had tons of the stuff close at hand. She stood her ground, shook her head. "Come to the door, we'll talk," she said. Then added: "Unless you're scared of a little woman who's old enough to be your great-grandmother." She snickered. "But I guess that's why you're packing a gun. You're afraid I might hurt you."

That did it.

The face disappeared from the window, the door opened wide. The small revolver concealed in a hip pocket, DeSoto strutted out onto the board supported by cinder blocks. The ever-present cigarette dangled from his lips.

Charlie Moon had been watching his aunt from the cemetery. From what he could see, it appeared that her conversation with Mr. DeSoto was going along okay. The Ute heard footsteps, turned to see a smallish Hispanic man in coveralls and a battered cowboy hat. The fellow had a claw hammer in his hand, a Leatherman tool on his belt, a proprietary look on his face.

"Excuse me," the hammer wielder said in a polite but firm manner, "but who are you?"

Moon introduced himself.

The old-fashioned gentleman tipped the brim of his hat. "I'm Henry Martinez."

Moon noted that Henry's surname was engraved on most of the mausoleums in the cemetery, probably eight out of ten tombstones. He smiled at the pleasant man. "They should call this place Martinez town."

"I suppose they should." Henry M. smiled back. "Nobody even remembers old Garcia's first name. Or what it was he crossed." His eyes narrowed. "If you don't mind my asking—what are you doing here?"

Moon glanced toward the house behind the cemetery. "I brought my aunt."

The member of the Martinez clan glanced at the Expedition, didn't see anyone sitting up. It happened two or three times a year, people making unauthorized use of church property. *This Indian's probably got her in the back of the car, rolled up in a blanket.* "Uh . . . if you plan to bury her here, you'll need to get permission first."

The Ute put on his best poker face. "You're right about that." He sighed. "If I buried Aunt Daisy without her say-so, she'd get mad as a scalded cat."

It was clear that Mr. Martinez did not appreciate this sort of graveside humor.

"She's come to visit Mr. DeSoto," Moon explained. He nodded to indicate the residence across the cemetery fence.

"Oh, him." Martinez frowned, started to say something, resisted the temptation to gossip.

Moon wondered what the man didn't want to tell him about, decided to walk around it. "Looks like you're a carpenter."

"Jack-of-all-trades, master of none—that's me." Martinez gestured with the hammer. "With the church closed down, we have problems with vandals. Windows get broken, graffiti painted on the walls, that sort of thing." He turned to gaze at the building. "I came by last week, found the lock on the back door broken. That's what I'm here to fix."

Daisy had to look at the repulsive man, but she tried not to dwell on his pockmarked face, the big hairy stomach bulging out from under the dirty orange T-shirt, the obscene remark printed on said garment. She could not help but notice that his belly button was half filled with something that looked like cotton fuzz, and wondered whether this odious person ever took a bath. *I might as well get this over with.* She cleared her throat, began the memorized speech. "Last time I was here, I said some things I shouldn't." This was extremely difficult. "I came back to . . ." It was, in fact, nearly impossible. *Help me, God.*

DeSoto was openly suspicious. "You came back to *what?*"

If I don't say it now, I never will. "I came back to . . . to apologize."

He stared dumbly at the wrinkled face.

Having gotten past the A-word, Daisy was relieved. She hurried on, eager to complete the ordeal. "I'm sorry about saying those unkind things."

The object of her apology was not blessed with a fine memory for details. All he could recall about the encounter with the old woman was that it had been unpleasant. He craved to have his recollection refreshed. "What things?"

She shrugged. "Oh, about how you're a pineapple head."

He nodded. "Oh, yeah. I remember that."

To be helpful, she added: "And potbellied."

He belched a garlicky odor, scratched indolently at that prominent portion of his anatomy. Which reminded Daisy of another observation she had made.

"And I called you a blivit."

He chuckled. "Oh, yeah. I remember that, too." He gave

her an admiring look. "You sure are a dirty-mouthed old woman. You remind me of my aunt Hilda."

Daisy had to bite her tongue. *I have to remember, I am dealing with the head philistine.*

"So," he said. "Is that it?"

The visitor nodded. "That's it."

Feeling quite at ease now, DeSoto took a draw on the cigarette, looked around for some sign of an automobile. "You come out here by yourself?"

"Sure. I hitchhiked all the way from Ignacio."

He blew smoke in the old woman's face. "Must be hard for a crazy person to thumb a ride."

Daisy closed her eyes, tried to imagine what Father Raes would do in a situation like this.

"When they find out you're gone, I bet they won't even come looking for you." He snickered. "I mean the people who run the asylum for feebleminded old Indian broads."

The church handyman had gone off to hammer at something, and Charlie Moon was about to resume the surveillance of his aunt. The tribal investigator would have witnessed something quite memorable—the sort of once-in-a-lifetime event that is not to be missed. But, alas—it was not to be; Sidewinder had sidled up by his knee. The hound was whining. Moon squatted to scratch the dog behind the ear. "What's the matter, old fella—you ready to go home?" No, that wasn't it. This was the old dog's "come with me" whine. Ignoring the drama across the cemetery fence, Moon followed along behind. *I bet he's got something treed.* But after a few steps, he smelled something unpleasant, and recalled the animal's scholarly interest in the subject of week-old roadkill and other unsavory left-behinds. *Sidewinder's found himself something ripe. I sure hope it ain't a skunk.* Moon slowed his pace. *I'd better go back and see how Aunt Daisy is getting along. . . .*

Daisy Perika tried to count to ten, made it all the way to two before she spoke to the obnoxious man. "I came back here to apologize, and that's what I did. You've got no reason to say nasty things to me."

Removing the cigarette from his mouth, DeSoto reached out, tapped ash on the woman's head.

She clenched her fists, grimaced. *I've had just about enough.*

He laughed in her face.

This was enough.

Daisy snatched the cigarette from his fingers. Well aware of the hazards of such objects—which range from cancer and cardiovascular disease to starting wildfires—she thought it best to put the thing out. Immediately. This, she would later claim, was why she stuffed the burning end of the cylinder into DeSoto's disgusting belly button.

Where the fuzz was.

This tinder in the tender orifice burst into a torchlike flame.

Having had his attention diverted by the smelly thing the Columbine hound had found, Moon was startled to hear the shrill scream. *What now—*

The scene across the fence was one that boggled the mind.

Mr. DeSoto was leaping around, patting his belly *hard*— like it was a drum. The *slap-slap* provided a comical rhythm to accompany his energetic dance.

Aunt Daisy was laughing so hard it looked like she might fall on her face.

Though perplexed by this bizarre piece of theater, he came to an instant decision. *I'd better get her outta here.*

During the long drive back to the Columbine, a westerly breeze rippled the grass, a dusky twilight swept across the prairie. It was that unsettling few minutes of half-blindness that heralds night—not dark enough for headlights, not quite enough light to see what might be scurrying across the blacktop.

Having waited in vain for Charlie Moon to show some curiosity about her small adventure, Daisy volunteered a brief account of her meeting with DeSoto.

As he strained to see the road ahead, Moon would merely nod or grunt.

Her nephew's apparent lack of interest annoyed Daisy Perika no end.

Despite appearances, the driver had heard every word.

Daisy leaned her head back on the seat, closed her eyes. As the miles slipped away with the minutes, she spent them reliving the day's delightful experience.

On the far horizon, Charlie Moon watched the arrival of a furry herd of buffalo clouds. He was a man who knew too much—and yet not quite enough.

52

THE BAG MAN

When the Mercedes sedan pulled into his yard, Mr. DeSoto was in his cellar, tending to business. He did not hear the marvelously engineered German engine purr—only the soft crunch of tires on the gravel. Pausing in his work, he took a look through the narrow ground-level window, grunted with displeasure at the sight of an unfamiliar automobile.

DeSoto stuffed his pistol into a hip pocket that was concealed under the tail of his purple shirt. He grunted his way up the cellar stairs, arrived in time to hear the rhythmic knock. Shave-and-a-Haircut . . . Six-Bits.

Easing the door open, DeSoto frowned at the man in the gray hat, gray suit, gray gloves, gray boots. He shot a wary glance at the expensive gray sedan, where a driver sat behind the wheel. Unable to make out the features of the man concealed by the smoke-tinted windshield, he took another suspicious look at his visitor. "Who're you?"

The gray man's thin mouth smiled. Hard eyes glittered behind the pink-lensed spectacles. "A potential benefactor." He pitched the repulsive man a leather pouch.

DeSoto caught it, was surprised at the weight of the thing.

The potential benefactor spoke in a disinterested monotone: "Inside, you will find a dozen Krugerrands. According to the most recent quote on the Jo-burg exchange, that amounts to just over five thousand dollars." He waited for a moment, watched the stupid man's stupid face. "If you sincerely believe you can help me, you may keep them as a down payment for future services rendered. If you are not able to provide the necessary assistance, it will be in your best interests to return the Krugerrands to me immediately."

The greedy man weighed the gold in his hand. "Whatta you want me to do?" DeSoto managed a nervous grin. "Punch somebody's ticket?"

The visitor lost the humorless smile. "Don't ask questions. I'll tell you whatever you need to know."

"Uh—awright." He jingled the bag, heard the reassuring clink of precious metals.

"As we attempt to communicate, there's no need for you to strain your minuscule mental powers." The gray man's lips curled in a sneer. "Just nod for 'yes,' shake your head for 'no.'" A pause. "Think you can manage that?"

DeSoto almost spoke, then remembered to nod. He wanted ever so much to open the pouch, examine the contents, but something about the arrogant visitor prevented him.

The gray man looked past DeSoto, addressed his remarks to the ugly stucco house. "On top of the advance, I am authorized by my employer to offer one hundred Krugerrands for certain information. I don't care where you get this information, or how. Do you understand what I'm saying?"

A nod from the pockmarked man.

"The information I require is in the possession of a Mrs. Pansy Blinkoe." He shifted his gaze, watched DeSoto's face intently. "If you know nothing about this woman or where she might be contacted, now is the time to return the dozen Krugerrands. But if you believe you can help me, nod."

A hesitation, then a nod.

"Good. Now listen carefully, because I'm going to tell you exactly where she keeps this information. And I'll only tell you once." His rapt audience listened. He told him.

DeSoto gulped, started to speak—thought better of it.

The gray man glanced at the cellar window. "Do you wish to tell me something now?"

DeSoto licked his lips, squeezed the leather pouch. Shook his head.

"That is acceptable. I suppose you'll need some time to do whatever you need to do. But as soon as you have something useful to tell me about Mrs. Blinkoe—or the information I'm after—hang that hideous shirt you're wearing on the clothesline." He pointed a gloved finger at the cotton rope strung between two rusty poles. "And hang it *upside down*. Can you remember that?"

The man with the bag of gold coins nodded.

Amused, the visitor smiled. "One last thing. *Do not mess with me*. If you do . . ." He told him exactly what he would do. And how long he'd take doing it.

The lurid description had the intended impact on DeSoto, who broke into a cold sweat. But he did not give up the pouch of Krugerrands.

As they motored away from Garcia's Crossing, the gray man spoke to his chauffeur. "Mr. DeSoto is a putrid pimple on the face of our fair civilization. Way I see it, he'll hold on to the gold and give us nothing in return—aside from measured doses of misinformation." He removed the rose-tinted glasses, waved at a pretty girl on a blue bicycle. "If there's anything I cannot stand, it is a dishonest man."

The man at the wheel nodded his agreement.

The gray man leaned toward the front seat. "If this punk tries to jerk us around, I say we teach him a lesson."

53

THE EXCELLENT BENEFITS OF TRUE CONTRITION

Late in the afternoon, Father Raes dropped by the Columbine headquarters. He was disappointed to learn from Daisy Perika that her nephew was not at home. She had seen Charlie Moon leave with the county agent again, probably to go check on some sick cows.

"All day and half the night—it's nothing but work-work-work for Charlie." She glowered out a kitchen window. "He don't own this ranch—it owns *him*!" While spewing off for another minute or two, she made a pot of extraordinarily strong coffee, and invited the priest to join her in the parlor.

Seated before the massive fireplace, they watched magical flames transform ordinary pine into glowing embers and crumbling cinders.

Unable to take more than a sip or two of the brackish brew, the priest cupped the cup in his hands. "So. How have you been getting along?"

Daisy shrugged. "Okay."

The kind man smiled, firelight danced in his dark eyes. "Did you consider my advice?"

She gave him a wary look. "You mean about making nicey-nice to Pineapple—to Mr. DeSoto?"

"In a manner of speaking, yes." *Just as I expected, she has not done it.* "And did you attempt to make amends?"

Daisy nodded the old gray head. "Charlie took me out there. And I apologized up one side and down the other."

The coffee cup almost slipped from the priest's grip. *This is truly astounding.* He tried not to sound surprised. "And having done so, I'm sure you felt better."

"Yes I did." She allowed herself the merest hint of a smile. "*Lots* better."

Being a teacher at heart, the Jesuit was determined to make certain the tribal elder understood the significance of what she had done. "Though the gentleman was undoubtedly blessed by your act of humility and contrition, I have no doubt that you received the greater blessing."

The shameless woman put on a saintly expression. "I expect you're right about that."

GARCIA'S CROSSING

One Minute before Midnight

In certain inner circles, where old men converse with those in other worlds and sacred pipe-smoke twists and twirls, the one who came calling is called by a *secret name.*

Makes No Tracks also makes no sound. Except when he intends to.

Having counted the gold Krugerrands at least twenty times, DeSoto had the pouch suspended from his pock-marked neck, concealed under his hideous shirt. Ever since the big Mercedes had pulled away, he had tried to decide how he should respond to the gray man's proposition. Having worn himself out in this futile effort, he had finally fallen into a restless sleep. DeSoto was dozing in front of the television when he was awakened by the heavy *thunk* of a stone hitting the metal roof. He groaned. *It's those damn stupid kids, chunking rocks at my house again.* The disgruntled tenant got up from his reclining chair. With the pistol in his hand, he stomped to the door, opened it a crack.

A sinister broom swept away the sounds of night.

Cricket forewings ceased to stridulate.

A bloated owl paused in mid-regurgitation.

DeSoto's heart began to palpitate. He opened the door—just far enough to poke the revolver out. Then his head—just far enough to catch the big fist on his jaw.

He would remember nothing after the smashing right hook—until almost an hour later. As he began to drift up toward something resembling consciousness, the dazed man thought he heard the toilet flush. And flush again. And again. The sounds reminded him of his worst hangovers. *Or that bad case of the flu, when I threw up my socks. Maybe somebody's sick—* He suddenly had a terrible sense that *something was missing.* His hand leaped to his neck, trembling fingers scurried around in a frantic search. The heavy pouch was gone. Now, somebody was definitely sick. When he eventually discovered what else was missing, sickness would be replaced by utter terror.

In DeSoto's chosen line of work, failure was punishable by death.

54

A COMPELLING PROPOSITION

When the office door opened, Spencer Trottman was searching his desk for a client's business card. A tall, slender man entered—carrying a small black suitcase. He was decked out in an expensive ash-gray suit, suede gloves and Tony Lama boots of the same sooty shade, topped off with a matching Golden Gate cowboy hat. He observed the attorney through the proverbial rose-colored glasses. Literally. "You're Mr. Trottman, am I right?"

"You are and I am." The attorney got to his feet. "And you?"

The newcomer mirrored the professional smile, shook the lawyer's hand. "Me, I'm new in town." He glanced at the window. A smoke-gray Mercedes was parked at the curb. "Matter of fact, I just blew in with the wind."

"I don't believe you've mentioned your name."

The stranger gave the attorney a slow, appraising look. "My friends call me Smitty. I suppose you can too."

"Okay, Smitty. Have a seat." Trottman indicated a comfortable armchair by a potted palm.

"Thanks, but what I need is some standing-up time."

Trottman seated himself behind the desk. He prided himself on being able to size up his man. *This one is interested in real-estate investments.* "How may I help you?"

"Now that's the spirit! I like a man who gets right down to the meat on the bone." Smitty produced a gray suede pouch from an inside jacket pocket.

The attorney watched the mysterious stranger remove twelve South African Krugerrands, line them up on his desk. "This should cover a few minutes of your time."

Trottman nodded, stared dumbly at the golden disks, nodded.

The visitor produced a gray cell phone that matched his suit and hat and boots and Mercedes. "'Scuse me for a sec. Gotta make a call."

The attorney watched with keen anticipation. *He's representing a well-heeled investor who prefers to remain anonymous.*

Having pressed a programmed button, Smitty spoke into the small instrument. "Yes sir, I'm here. Is he ready?" A pause. "Okay, put him on." He smiled. "Hello there, hotshot—I'm with your lawyer. You want to have a word or two with him? Good, I thought you would." He offered the cell phone to Spencer Trottman.

Puzzled, the attorney pressed the phone against his ear. "Who is this?"

Though strained, the voice was crisp and clear. "It's me."

Trottman felt the blood drain from his face. "Manfred? You're *alive?*"

"For the time being. Look, Spence, I'm in a bad spot and I don't know how long they'll let me talk. So don't ask any questions, just listen and do *exactly* what I say. You understand?"

"Of course." *This cannot be happening.* "Please continue."

"I need something. And it's really, really important that you get it for me."

"What?"

"A series of numbers."

Manfred Blinkoe's attorney had heard the rumors about the millions hijacked from the Colombian drug cartel, and the alleged foreign bank accounts. *It must all be true.* He heard himself say: "Account numbers?"

"No questions, Spence—please!"

"Uh—I'm sorry."

"I kept one set on the boat—we can forget about that. Pansy has the other copy."

"Manfred, I haven't seen Mrs. Blinkoe for quite some time—"

"Keep your mouth shut and listen, dammit! You've got to talk to her, get those numbers. Do you understand what I'm saying?"

"Yes. Certainly." Spencer Trottman looked up at Smitty, whose long face was grinning wolfishly.

Blinkoe's voice continued. "Thing is—Pansy don't even know she's got the numbers."

"But, Manfred, if your wife doesn't—"

"Just shut up and listen!" There was a brief silence. "I'm sorry, Spence. It's just that I'm in *serious* trouble." An intake of breath. "Now pay attention—Pansy has the information *right on the tip of her tongue.*"

As a remarkable notion occurred to him, Trottman frowned. "Did she learn the numbers under hypnosis? Is there some trigger phrase one must utter to release her from—"

"If you'll keep quiet for ten seconds, I'll explain."

The attorney listened. Could barely believe his ears. "Manfred, are you serious?"

"Serious don't half cover it, Spence. If you don't get Pansy to provide that information within twenty-four hours, these—uh—gentlemen are going to make things very tough for me. This situation I'm looking at is what you could call *terminal.*"

"But I have no idea where Mrs. Blinkoe is—"

"Then you better get busy and find her. I am in serious trouble and—"

Trottman heard a distinct *click*. Almost before he realized what had happened, Smitty had removed the cell phone from his grasp.

The visitor placed the leather suitcase on the lawyer's desk. "The Krugerrands were chicken feed. Now I'll show you something that'd make a duck's mouth water." He opened the case. "Take a gander at that."

Trottman stared in disbelief at the wrapped stacks of twenty-dollar bills. *I wonder how much . . .*

Smitty read his mind, and smiled. "A hundred grand. I'll leave it here, let you count it."

"But I don't understand."

"It's yours, Mr. Trottman. A good-faith down payment for services we expect you to render."

"But as I have already told Dr. Blinkoe, I have no idea whether Mrs. Blinkoe will contact me—"

Smitty leaned on the lawyer's desk with gloved hands, stared through the pink spectacles. "The outfit I work for has more cash flow than General Motors and Ford combined. It's not like my bosses worry about a thousand bucks falling through a crack now and then. But a few million here, a few million there, it cannot be ignored. If such misbehavior is not properly dealt with, it could set a bad example. So a meeting is called, a decision is made. What it comes down to is this: If Mrs. Blinkoe would like to get her hands on five million bucks, all she has to do is come up with the numbers to those foreign bank accounts where her old man stashed our liquid assets. She comes across, I will deliver the five mil' tomorrow afternoon, her husband will be cut loose in good health. The Blinkoes will have a potful of cash to purchase expensive trinkets and fancy duds and this and that. And you will have your fee on the five mil', which I imagine will be at least twenty percent. But my bosses are not patient men, Mr. Trottman. You will get a call," he checked his wristwatch, "at precisely ten forty-two A.M. tomorrow. You have the list of numbers for us, everything is jake. You don't, your client is history." He gave the attorney a lopsided grin. "And I would not want to make odds on your probable life span, or Mrs. Blinkoe's. And don't even think about calling the cops. My outfit has top-notch technicians placed in every phone company in the USA. Every time you call for a pizza, we know whether you asked for Italian sausage or anchovies." A grimace. "Or pineapple. Did you know that some weirdoes are asking for *fruit* on their pizza?" He shook his head. "I mean, what next—prunes?"

Trottman's mouth gaped. "But . . . but . . ."

Smitty shook a finger in his face. "Don't give me no *buts*." He paused to straighten a cuff. "To tell you the honest truth, hardly anybody expects you to hear from Mrs. Blinkoe. Among the higher-ups in my organization, the general consensus is that she has already left the country." He glanced at the case stuffed with greenbacks. "If I were you, I'd try to spend that little bit of cash fast as I can. If Mrs. Blinkoe don't happen to contact you pretty quick, you'll be goin' to that bad place where a hundred thousand bucks won't buy you a shot glass of cold water." With this observation, Sooty-Suit turned on his Tony Lama heel and departed.

Half an hour after the door had closed on his earlier life, the attorney was still pacing back and forth, occasionally pausing to stare at the paneled wall where his law diploma hung. The sheepskin was slightly skewed. He reached out to straighten the frame. *What on earth should I do? Call the authorities, no doubt, and report this astonishing incident.* But there were other things to consider. Two other things. Mentally, he enumerated them.

1. If Pansy does not yield up the account numbers, Manfred will no doubt be murdered.
2. If she does, quite a substantial amount of cash will be forthcoming.

Spencer Trottman's Juris Doctor diploma was surrounded by scores of photographs of himself with important people. He squinted to examine a recent photographic image. The picture had been snapped the last time he had dined at Phillipe's. He was standing between Manfred and Pansy

Blinkoe. *Manfred looks oddly pensive, like he was worried about something or other.*

Mrs. Blinkoe, on the other hand, appeared absolutely ecstatic. Indeed, behind Pretty Pansy's beautiful toothpaste-advertisement smile, there was a sly look. As if she knew a delightful secret.

55

A LONG NIGHT'S WORK

The best friends sat side by side in the darkness.

The GCPD chief of police zipped a wool-lined leather jacket to his chin. "You'd never believe it was summertime—it's cold up here."

The tribal investigator did not respond.

Scott Parris blinked at a waning moon. "What time is it?"

Charlie Moon pressed the button on his wristwatch, eyed the luminescent green disk. "Eleven minutes past one."

"When I was a rookie cop, I always looked forward to stuff like this. Stuff that detectives do. But after a dozen times sitting in a car all night, drinking gallons of bad coffee, always waiting for somebody who never showed, always needing to pee—that was enough for me. And this ain't that much different. There's nothing to see. Nothing to hear."

The Ute saw a coyote trot through the cemetery. Listened to a ghostly breeze rattle dead elm leaves.

"I hate stakeouts, Charlie."

"I hate stakeout partners who talk all night."

"You have hurt my feelings. I'm not gonna say another word."

There was a *whuf-whuf* of wings as a famished mouse hunter passed by.

Parris grimaced at the unseen fowl. "I never liked owls."

Moon hung a Cheshire grin. "Why's that?"

"Ah, when I was a ten-year-old kid in Indiana I paid nineteen dollars and ninety-nine cents for one of those 'you can learn to be a taxidermist at home' courses. You know—the kinda thing that was advertised on the backs of comic books."

"And you didn't get your money's worth?"

"All I can tell you is *never ever* kill an owl." The failed taxidermist cringed at the memory. "And if you do, don't skin it. And if you skin it, don't try to stuff it with sawdust."

"Unpleasant experience, huh?"

"Write this down in your book, Charlie—owls *stink*. And we're not talking ordinary stink, like skunk spray or rotten eggs. And taking a bath don't help; owl stink seeps down deep into your pores, and stays there till you shed your old skin and grow a new covering."

"I'll try to remember that." The Ute hoped for a few minutes of silence.

"And another thing. I feel stupid, perched up here on top of Mr. DeSoto's roof. Not to mention how it makes my butt ache."

Several semiclever responses came to mind, but Moon let the opportunity pass.

Grunting, Parris got to his feet. He hung the heels of his cowboy boots over the pinnacle of the peaked structure. "You know who I feel like?"

"Nope."

"Here's a hint—I'm a fictional character."

The Ute chuckled. "Inspector Clouseau."

"Charlie, that was a cheap shot."

"Okay. You're the Fiddler on the Roof."

Parris's response was somewhat tart. "Do you see anything tucked under my chin that resembles a violin?"

"Good point. But I'm fresh out of guesses."

"I'm an animal."

"Sure. I can see it now. You're a long-legged stork, about to take wing and fly away to wherever those big white birds go when they get bored with work."

"You're not very good at this, Charlie."

"You have hurt my feelings. I'm not going to guess anymore."

"I'll make it dead-easy for you. I feel like that beagle."

"The one who lays on his back, on top of the doghouse?"

"Right." Having helped his circulation, Parris seated himself again. "But it wasn't no ordinary doghouse."

Moon nodded. "Mr. Snoopy had a pool table downstairs."

Parris sighed. "My favorite character was Heathcliff."

"Who?"

"The little bird that flew upside down."

"That was Woodstock."

There was a tense silence, during which Parris cogitated so hard it made his head hurt. "You sure about that?"

"Sure enough to give you two-to-one."

"Forget it."

"I *can't* forget it. Matter of fact, I remember every single one of Woodstock's little feathered friends."

Parris snorted. "Poppycock."

"Nope, Poppycock wasn't one of 'em. There was Bill—"

"There wasn't no bird in the strip by the name of Bill."

"—And Conrad, and Harriet. And Oliver."

"I know a bluff when I see one, Charlie. You're making those names up."

"Lay your money down, Chief. I'll give you three-to-one."

"I don't intend to lay no money down on a tilted roof that's slippery as snail spit." He could almost hear Moon's smirk. "Remind me again why two grown men are sitting on top of Mr. DeSoto's house at one o'clock in the morning."

"Because you accepted my gracious invitation. And it's closer to one-fifteen."

"Why did I accept your gracious invitation?"

"Because it is in your interest to determine the whereabouts of Mrs. Pansy Crowe Blinkoe."

"Is Mrs. Blinkoe staying in Mr. DeSoto's house?"

"I'd rather not say."

"Okay, have it your way. But tell me this—what do we do if DeSoto comes home?"

"I don't know about you, but I intend to be very quiet."

The chief of police was not reassured. "But what if he looks up here and spots us and—"

"Scott, you don't need to worry too much about DeSoto coming home."

"Why?"

"You don't want to know. Trust me."

"Trust you? Charlie, you know saying something like that just gets me worried sick. I've got to know—so start talking."

"Okay, pardner. It's like this—a certain Someone found out DeSoto was using his cellar to stash about forty kilos of cocaine, all in pint-size plastic sandwich bags."

"Charlie, please don't tell me *how* you know this."

"That suits me just fine, pardner. Now, the way Someone figured it, DeSoto was providing a temporary storage location for big-time operators, who were likely moving the stuff up from Juarez." Moon paused. "You got the picture so far?"

Parris nodded. "I can guess what happens next."

"No need to guess—I'll tell you straight out. Mr. Someone found the stash, flushed it down the toilet. Soon as DeSoto figured out what'd happened—and realized the bad guys would skin him alive when they found out their property had gone down the drain—he hit the road. The man was doing ninety miles an hour before he got out of Garcia's Crossing, which is only about a half mile wide. This is why I have a feeling he ain't comin' back anytime soon."

"Charlie, you should have tipped the DEA, let them handle this DeSoto punk—"

The tribal investigator raised his hand for silence.

There was a pair of headlights off to the west. But the

pickup did not slow. The lawmen watched the taillights vanish over a distant rise.

Parris broke the silence. "Let's just pretend you never said a word to me about Mr. DeSoto."

"Mr. Who?"

The chief of police sighed. "I've got a couple of sandwiches in my coat pocket."

"What kind?"

"Ham-and-Swiss-cheese kind. Grilled."

"Grilled sounds good."

"They should still be warm. I wrapped 'em in paper towels."

The Ute considered his choices. "Okay, I'll have a grilled ham and Swiss. You can have the other one."

Parris gave his friend the preferred sandwich.

"What else've you got in your pockets?"

"Cookies."

"What kind?"

"Pecan Sandies."

"That'll be just dandy." Moon was about to take a bite of the lukewarm sandwich when his friend intervened.

"Hold it!"

"What?"

"You can't eat that ham-and-Swiss, or have any dessert—not till you tell me what you know that I don't know."

"Pardner, that would take a long, long time. I could starve to death."

"I mean about the Blinkoe business."

Moon felt a severe case of Stubborn coming on. But the sandwich smelled good, and a Pecan Sandie would sure hit the well-known spot. "It is common knowledge that Pansy Blinkoe has an older brother by the name of Clayton Crowe."

Parris made a big show of enjoying a cookie, and said with a mouthful: "I am well aware of this."

"Did you know that the man who calls himself Clayton Crowe is not her brother?"

"Well of course I do." The chief of police swallowed.

"The fake Clayton Crowe was Pansy's high school sweetheart—a guy by the name of Roger Culpepper."

The tribal investigator stared at his friend. "Where'd you hear that?"

"Oh, through the grapevine." Parris smiled in the darkness. "From what I hear, some clever FBI agent figured it all out. Something about genes and eye color. But you're tight with Agent McTeague, so I suppose you already know about that." He took a bite from his sandwich. After swallowing, he continued. "While guys like you and me do all right with ordinary police work, it takes those college-trained feds to do the really clever stuff."

The college-trained Ute made a guttural sound.

"What'd you say?"

"Uh—nothing."

"Oh, go ahead and eat your sandwich." Parris's smile was making his face hurt. *Sooner or later, I'll tell Charlie that I know he was the one who figured it out. And how McTeague has been bragging about him.* But there was no hurry.

While his *matukach* friend was uncharacteristically silent, Moon finished his ham-and-Swiss. He cleared his throat. "Could I have a cookie?"

Feeling guilty, Parris gave him two.

"Thank you."

"Charlie, did you know the feds tracked down the real Clayton Crowe?"

"No." *Nobody ever tells me nothing.*

"Way I heard it, the FBI had some trouble running him to ground, but they eventually found out he'd volunteered to serve in the Peace Corps. Got sent to Haiti to help some little village clean up their drinking water. Died last month during a cholera epidemic."

The Ute blinked at a star that winked back at him. "I'm sorry to hear it."

"Me too."

The winds sighed. The galaxy whirled.

Parris shook his head. "I keep thinking about Mrs.

Blinkoe—with her boyfriend living right there under her roof. Well—*garage* roof. That is really sick. And dangerous." He rolled the possibilities over in his mind. "If Dr. Blinkoe found out what was going on, he might've murdered the both of 'em. And there's the other possibility. If Mrs. Blinkoe and her so-called brother thought the husband had caught on to what they were up to, they might've knocked him off."

Moon nodded. "The possibilities for mayhem are almost endless."

"Way I see it, Mrs. Blinkoe is hiding out somewhere with her boyfriend." Parris frowned at the starry sky. "But here at Garcia's Crossing? I don't think so. It just don't make sense that the lady and her main squeeze would pick a spot so close to home."

Another pair of headlights was coming from the west. The lawmen watched the vehicle slow to a crawl. And turn. But not into DeSoto's driveway.

Parris whispered: "Charlie, it's coming around the other side of the church. And he's turned off his lights!"

They could hear tires crunching in the gravel. Then silence. The automobile had stopped in the weed-choked church parking lot, at the edge of the cemetery.

The chief of police nudged the tribal investigator, whispered. "Whatta we do now?"

Moon returned the whisper. "Now we make our move—but slow and easy."

56

AN ODIOUS TASK

The blackness was identical to what he had encountered once upon another time. That experience had been in the depths of a limestone cavern in southern Yucatán, where the long-dead Maya had worshipped Kukulcán, their plumed serpent god. It had been sufficiently unsettling, being a hundred yards underground where the indigenous people sacrificed their children to the pagan image. He had been utterly terrified when the gasoline generator that energized the string of electrical lights coughed several times—then stuttered to a stop. The darkness that enveloped him had been complete, as in that awful place where lost souls shall wail and gnash their teeth. But on this occasion, he was not a frightened tourist. This night-within-night was his protective cloak. Still, one must see well enough to get the job done. *Just a quick glance, that's all I need.* It was, in fact, all he *wanted.*

The intruder held a handkerchief over his nose, scratched

a match along the gritty sandstone floor. Illuminated by the yellowish flicker of light, what he saw was even more over-powering than the horrible stench. A panic seized him, he shook the match as if his fingers were on fire. It refused to be extinguished. He put it to his lips, blew it out.

Even without the feeble light, the horrific vision would not go away. He closed his eyes. Willed the total blackness to return. *Begged* for it. As if in response to a blasphemous prayer, it did. Soundlessly, he mouthed his thoughts. *I must not lose control. This will be a difficult task, but it simply must be done.*

Somewhat restored by this reminder, he reached out. Touched a silken garment. *That wasn't so bad.* The man put on a masklike smile. *It's not like I can be harmed by a corpse.* He willed his hand to move along the torso. Toward the head. Touching rotting flesh, his fingertips instinctively recoiled.

The would-be thief could feel a heavy drumming under his ribs. *That must have been the neck.* Perspiration dripped off his face. *Why didn't I think about rubber gloves?* He for-got about the stink, took a deep breath, gagged. *It's only dead tissue. I've got to get hold of myself. I'm almost there. Okay . . . steady now. This won't take a minute. If it's too tight, I'll use the pliers. . . .*

All jutting chin and clenched teeth, Parris felt for the reassur-ing coldness of the .38-caliber Smith & Wesson holstered un-der his armpit. It was there. He was ready for business.

Moon whispered, "Let's work our way around to the rear of the church."

Trailing the Ute—who made about as much noise as a cat's shadow—Parris worried that he would step on that proverbial twig, which would go off like a two-dollar fire-cracker. "Charlie, if these turn out to be drug dealers, I say we cancel their tickets."

Moon ducked an elm branch. "Whatever works for you is fine with me."

"Just wanted to make sure we're of the same mind—"

There was a eerie, soul-chilling wail that froze both lawmen stiff as posts. But only for an instant.

In a sprint that left his partner behind, Charlie Moon crossed DeSoto's yard, vaulted the cemetery fence.

Scott Parris ran up the lane toward St. Cuthbert's Catholic Church, found the creaking gate. Stubby revolver in hand, the chief of police went stumbling among the tombstones. After tripping over a root and almost falling, he called out in a hoarse stage whisper: "Charlie—where *are* you?"

Moon switched on a small flashlight. "Over here."

Aided by the splash of anti-night, Parris hurried toward his friend.

The Ute was standing at the cemetery's largest mausoleum, where a rusty steel-plate doorway stood wide-open.

The older man was breathing hard. "What's happened?"

It did not bear thinking about. Much less looking at. "You'd better brace yourself." Moon aimed the beam through the entrance.

The hardened cop looked inside the structure. "Oh my God."

There was a pair of pink marble vaults, one on each side of the room. There would presumably be coffins inside that held the remains of those long dead to this world. These mortuary details were of small interest to the stunned chief of police.

Spencer Trottman was sitting with his back against the limestone wall, his wide eyes staring straight into hell.

Pansy Blinkoe's rotting corpse was on the dusty floor beside the newly dead man—her teeth clenched firmly on his fingers.

Moon responded to Parris's unasked question. "Had to be a heart attack." Having seen enough and too much, he moved the beam of light onto a red purse that had been tossed under one of the vaults.

Feeling a sour surge of nausea, Parris turned, leaned against the mausoleum's outer wall. *I will not throw up. I will not throw up.* Presently, the queasiness subsided. The chief of police switched on his flashlight, forced himself to turn, look upon the obscenity. "Charlie—I'm guessing you knew Mrs. Blinkoe was here."

The tribal investigator nodded.

"So how'd you know?"

Feeling as cold as the woman's corpse, Moon resisted the urge to shiver. "Few days ago, I brought Aunt Daisy out here. While she was talking to Mr. DeSoto, I was watching from the cemetery. Sidewinder led me over to this place, and I smelled something. At the time, I figured it was a dead . . ." He choked on *dead animal*. It was a long moment before the tribal investigator regained his powers of speech. "The door wasn't locked, so I had a look inside."

Parris shook his head. "But how'd you know Dr. Blinkoe's family lawyer would show up tonight?"

"I didn't for sure," Moon said. "It was kind of a shot in the dark."

"You can explain that later," Parris mumbled. He found his cell phone. "I'm gonna call out my entire police force. And some state cops. Till some uniforms show up, we'll stand guard, make sure the evidence isn't disturbed."

Moon nodded. *Especially Mrs. Blinkoe's purse.*

57

EARLY IN THE MORNING

Two GCPD officers on the graveyard shift were first to respond to the call. They stood guard at the tomb.

Informed that there would soon be a sizable influx of police, Pokey Joe realized the cops would be followed by a flock of journalists and dozens of curious locals. Already counting the potential profits, the canny businesswoman was making the necessary preparations to cash in. Two huge urns of coffee were perking while she was working. The industrious cook was laying up a supply of fried-egg sandwiches, pork link sausages, and honey-dipped waffles. *Make it and they will come.*

Parris and Moon were out by the gas pumps, watching for the first shimmering hint of dawn. Feeling much better after an egg sandwich and a pint cup of 90-proof java, the chief of police cleared his throat. "Charlie, I'm going to ask you some simple questions. I'm hoping for some simple answers."

Moon watched the steam rise off his Styrofoam cup of coffee. "I'll do the best I can, pardner."

"Okay, here goes—why did the Blinkoe family attorney show up tonight?"

Moon closed his eyes, looked backward. Yesterday seemed so far away. "About fifteen hours ago, Mr. Trottman had a visitor."

"Who?"

The Ute thought he might as well tell him. *By noon, Forrest Wakefield will be bragging to anyone who'll listen.* "It was a friend of mine. But I want you to know right up front that Wakefield didn't break any law or—"

"Charlie, just tell me what'n hell your county agent was doing in Trottman's office."

"First, I'll have to give you some background. Even though Dr. Wakefield is a highly skilled practitioner of veterinary medicine, and has a steady job with excellent benefits—the man has never been completely happy in his work. He's always felt called to another, higher vocation."

Parris recalled his own youthful aspirations. "Like what—taxidermy?"

"Even better than that. Wakefield has a yen to be a professional actor."

The chief of police was beginning to get a glimmer of the plot. "You sent this county agent–wannabe actor to a clever attorney's office to commit a sordid act of make-believe?" Parris shook his head. "You must've been desperate to try something like that."

"Wakefield might've fallen on his face, but he didn't." Moon took considerable pride in what the amateur thespian had accomplished. "But before he performed for Trottman, we paid a visit to Mr. DeSoto—"

"Wait a minute—what's this 'we' business?" Parris pitched his empty cup into a trash can. "Am I to understand that you was in on the act?"

Moon nodded. "To make things look really high-class, Wakefield figured he needed a chauffeur. I drove him out to Garcia's Crossing in a rented Mercedes. Wakefield tried to bribe DeSoto into telling us what he knew about Pansy Blinkoe. But after a couple of days, we concluded he either didn't know a thing or wasn't going to tell us. So late one night, Someone went back to his place and convinced him to return our down payment. That same Someone searched his house and found the white powder in his cellar."

Parris groaned. "Charlie, please don't tell me nothing your favorite chief of police shouldn't know."

"Suits me, pardner. I also drove Wakefield to see Dr. Blinkoe's family attorney. Our fine actor—who is on a roll by now—convinced Trottman he was employed by an international drug cartel."

"Well, what can I say—the vet obviously has a gift."

"He certainly does. But he also had some help."

"For example?"

"A bag of Krugerrands and a suitcase full of greenbacks. Enough to buy a brand-new Porsche and then some."

"Pardon me for sounding doubtful, but where would a moderately compensated government employee get that kind of dough?"

"From a citizen who has lots of the stuff." *Several laundry bags full.*

Parris aimed a suspicious look at his sly friend. "Charlie, are you in touch with Manfred Blinkoe?"

"I can't say one way or the other. The man either is or was my client."

"You're starting to talk like a lawyer."

"I hope you meant that as a compliment."

"Hope whatever you want. But let's get back to this second farce you staged. Your county agent—with a suitcase full of money to help him make his case—convinces Spencer Trottman that he is representing an international criminal organization."

Moon nodded. "He also convinced Trottman that Dr.

Blinkoe had provided his wife with some information that was worth bushels and bushels of cash—which the big-time bad guys were determined to get their hands on."

"Okay, Chucky. You've got my attention. What was that *something*?"

"Several strings of numbers."

"I am cranky and short of sleep. Please keep this simple."

"These sets of numbers were for various foreign bank accounts where Manfred Blinkoe had *allegedly* hidden the cartel's cash. I'm talking about the stuff that was taken from the hijacked DC-3."

The chief of police stared at his Indian friend. "And how did our county agent *allegedly* come to know about these accounts?"

The tribal investigator tried not to look smug. "I told him."

"And how did *you* come to know about these foreign bank accounts?"

"Oh, I didn't need to know about 'em—I made the whole thing up."

"It was a fabrication—a pack of lies?"

"I prefer to think of my fable as a useful piece of fiction—a necessary element of Wakefield's script." Moon was thoroughly enjoying himself. "See, it was a kind of carrot-and-stick deal. If the family attorney could get the information from Mrs. Blinkoe within twenty-four hours, things would turn out very nice for him. If he couldn't come up with the numbers, Trottman's chances for a long and happy life wouldn't be worth a politician's promise."

"And Blinkoe's attorney believed this wild tale?"

"He must have. He showed up where he'd left the woman's body."

Parris turned his glare on a defenseless gas pump. "I still don't get it. If the lawyer was searching for a list of numbers, why didn't he look in her purse?"

"Trottman already knew Blinkoe had made his bride a dental plate. And he was led to believe that Blinkoe had etched the numbers on the denture."

Parris looked down the road, saw a pair headlights coming

up fast. Right above them, emergency lights were blinking. *That'll be the state cops.* "So Trottman comes back to the place where he's stashed the corpse, tries to remove Mrs. Blinkoe's artificial teeth, gets his hand caught in her mouth . . . or something." *Something I'd rather not think about.* He rubbed at bloodshot eyes, remembered Daisy Perika's "vision." "Charlie, what exactly did your aunt know that brought her out here—to this *particular* piece of nowhere—to look for Mrs. Blinkoe?"

Moon shrugged. "Only God knows."

For the moment, there was no more to be said.

But across the highway, at the cemetery, there was something to be read.

GCPD Officer Alicia Martin aimed her five-cell flashlight at a mossy spot above the mausoleum entrance. On a surface just below a slitlike vent, the beam illuminated a simple memorial, which, once upon a faraway time, had been chiseled into the limestone.

ALONZO MARTINEZ 1851–1912
PRUDENCE MARTINEZ 1864–1939

58

WHATEVER LILA WANTS

By the time the sun had topped the eastern range, five Granite Creek PD black-and-white units were on site, along with two low-slung Chevrolets from the state-police detachment and a pair of ambulances that would serve as body wagons—all with emergency lights flashing. The cemetery crime scene had been taped off, thoroughly photographed with film and digital cameras. Physical evidence had been bagged and tagged. Until further notice, three two-officer teams constituted of a Granite Creek PD uniform and a state Smokey would guard St. Cuthbert's cemetery in eight-hour shifts.

Jurisdictional issues had been settled. Almost.

There was the matter of the FBI's intense interest in what the chief of police referred to as "this weird Blinkoe business." The way Scott Parris and Charlie Moon had it figured was this: Within minutes of arriving at her Granite Creek office, Special Agent Lila Mae McTeague would hear about the big commotion at Garcia's Crossing. Moon expected her to show up before 10:00 A.M. Parris thought it would take the fed a tad longer than that. The inevitable wager was made.

The lawmen were standing in front of Pokey Joe's General Store when she drove up at six minutes past ten, skidded to a stop on the loose gravel.

Moon gave his buddy a dollar.

The good friends waited for the storm to begin.

McTeague got out of her car, looked from one man to the other, chose the ranking officer. She marched up to Parris like she was ready to punch him out. "What's going on here?"

The chief of police gave her an account of recent events, including almost everything Charlie Moon had told him. He provided a brief summary of the "drug cartel" sting Moon's county agent had pulled off in Trottman's office, but thought it best not to mention the DeSoto business. *If he wants to, Charlie can tell her about that.*

The FBI agent did not give the Ute a second glance. "When you discovered the bodies in the mortuary, why wasn't I informed immediately?"

Parris reminded her, somewhat curtly, that Garcia's Crossing was in his jurisdiction. He was not obligated to inform the FBI. Before she exploded, he told the lady that he would be grateful for all the help he could get from the Federal Bureau of Investigation.

It was like being slapped in the face, then kissed to make it better. Staggered, all McTeague could think of to say was: "Has any of the evidence been examined?"

Parris glanced toward the cemetery. "Doc Simpson will deal with the human remains. But I'd be pleased if the Bureau would submit the late Mrs. Blinkoe's purse and its contents to its forensic experts. And you're welcome to whatever you find in Trottman's pockets."

McTeague stared at the shrewd lawman, wondering what his game was. "I'd like to have a look at the crime scene."

Parris gave her a little salute. "Follow the blinking lights."

McTeague shot a quick look at Charlie Moon, stalked off across the highway.

Parris checked his watch. "Two bits says she'll be back in less than twenty minutes."

"You're on."

She was back just short of sixteen, with Pansy's red purse and some other odds and ends.

Moon flipped a shiny Tennessee quarter to Parris.

Without a word to the gamblers, she placed the plastic evidence bag in the trunk of her government-issue Ford sedan.

The tribal investigator leaned on the sleek automobile, smiled upon his favorite fed. "Good morning."

She returned the look, but not the smile.

"Uh—when you check out the lady's purse, you might find an expensive compact. I hope you'll have a close look at it."

"Why do you hope?"

"The compact was a present from Dr. Blinkoe to his wife."

"That hardly responds to my question."

"I've had a long, sleepless night." Moon covered a yawn. "It's the best I can do."

"Your best, is it?" She turned away to greet an exuberant Dr. Simpson, who was crossing the highway, chattering cheerfully with an assistant about the "imminent onset of rigor mortis."

The tribal investigator gamely accepted this abrupt dismissal.

"What a woman," Parris muttered.

Charlie Moon nodded. *Yes indeed.*

59

REVELATION AT THE COPPER STREET DELICATESSEN

Lunch was her quiet time. Special Agent McTeague was about to take a bite from a toasted tuna-salad sandwich, when she heard the hissing sound.

"Hssst."

It came from the booth behind her. She closed her eyes. *Please, God, don't let it be who I think it is.*

It was too late for this particular prayer. The thing had already been decided.

Louder this time, and longer. *"Hsssssssst!"*

McTeague put a hand to her ear. "Hark! What is this I hear—a punctured tire going flat?"

"No." But he did sound somewhat deflated. "It's only me."

"Right. Mr. S."

"It's not mister, just plain—"

"I know. How've you been, Just Plain Scarf?"

"Not so loud with my code name—somebody might hear you."

"Sorry. I suppose my tradecraft could use some sprucing up."

"You can say that again."

"Very well. I suppose my—"

"I wish you wouldn't treat me like some kinda loony."

"I'm sorry." She smiled at her sandwich. "Truly I am."

"You should be. A man has his pride, you know."

The lady was well aware of this serious shortcoming among the hairy-legged gender. "Pride goeth before the fall," she said. "And hear this—if you intend to make a habit of stalking a federal agent, you are heading for a *hard* fall. You sneak up behind me just one more time, I'll fling you on the ground, cuff you, read you your wrongs, then beat you black and blue. And that's just the *good* part."

"You don't need to get testy." A sullen pause. "You didn't leave the twenty bucks under the flower pot."

"I considered it, but came to the conclusion that such generosity on my part would only encourage you. I do hope you are not slightly offended."

"No, I guess not." A sniff. "That food sure smells good."

She sighed. *Even dimwits need sustenance.* "Are you hungry?"

"Let's just say I could use a few dollars for groceries."

"How many dollars—twenty?"

"That'd do nicely. And I'm ready to earn it."

"I'm listening." She helped herself to a cheese-flavored potato chip.

"You want to hear somethin' about that Mr. Blinky?"

"Like where he is?"

"That's what I mean, all right."

"Sure." She sipped a tall glass of iced tea.

"Then listen up, 'cause here's the honest truth—Blinky's holed up out west of town. At a cattle ranch."

She choked on the tea, coughed.

There was a "heh-heh," then: "I thought that'd get your attention."

McTeague coughed again. "Which ranch west of town?"

"The spread that Ute Indian pays taxes on. Well, Mr. Moon actually owns two ranches. But the Big Hat's where Blinky's at."

She fumbled in her purse, found the microcassette recorder. "Do you know this for a fact?"

"Dang tootin' I do!"

McTeague pressed the Record button. "Describe Dr. Blinkoe."

He recited a description that matched what had been in the newspapers.

"Have you actually seen him?"

"I dang sure have."

"When?" .

"Plenty of times, including just this morning—why, I was closer to that forked-beard tooth yanker than I am to you."

It's a stupid question, but I have to ask. "As far as you know, is Mr. Moon aware that Dr. Blinkoe is on his property?"

"Know it? Why of course he knows it—that sneaky Indian's been hiding Blinky on the Big Hat." A few heartbeats. "Now where's my twenty dollars?"

McTeague folded a bill, held it over her shoulder—where it was instantly snatched away. The FBI agent hated to pursue this, but she could not look the other way. Not even for Charlie Moon. "Scarf, would you like to have twenty more?"

"Maybe. But before I say yes, I'll have to know exactly what for."

"Have I ever seen you before? At the ranch, I mean."

"Uh . . . maybe. I mean yeah. You've seen me all right."

"Tell me your name."

A quick intake of breath. "Look, miss—if that Indian finds out I've been carrying tales about him, he'd skin me alive, grind me up like so much man-burger, feed me to the cattle."

She smiled. "Bovines do not eat human flesh."

A rude snort. "That's what *you* think—they'll eat anything that's got calories—even other cows, if the meat's mixed in with their regular feed. Those beeves are nothin' but big-eyed, lip-smacking cannibals."

"You needn't worry about being fed to the Herefords. The Bureau will protect your identity." While Scarf tried to make up his mind, she heard the thumpity-thump of his fingers on the table.

"I don't know," he mumbled. "If I told you who I was, there's always the chance Moon might find out. I'd have to leave the state. On toppa the extra twenty, I'd need some serious travel money."

"That can be taken care of. It's your call."

A ten-second eternity.

"Uh—first, let me see that extra twenty bucks."

A second bill was passed from booth to booth.

"Okay, FBI lady. A dollar's a dollar and a deal's a deal."

The federal agent held her breath.

"Out at the Big Hat, they call me Cap."

"Yes, of course, I remember you very—" McTeague heard the heavy sound of boot heels as the Big Hat cook headed for the delicatessen's rear exit.

TILDA THE HUN

Charlie Moon had dropped by Scott Parris's office to read a faxed report. According to the document, Nebraska state-police detectives had discovered an illegal beef-butchering operation on a bankrupt chicken farm just outside of Omaha. The Ute rancher pored over page after page, but it turned out the hides and heads had been disposed of. This being so, there were no brands or nose prints to be had. Disappointed, Moon was about to head back to the ranch and a colicky horse and a grouchy aunt. Parris reminded the busy man that he'd been in town for only fifteen minutes, assured him that a coffee break would be just the thing. And while we're sipping java and chomping down on delectable sugar-encrusted pastries, why not enjoy a hand of straight poker? He didn't have to twist Moon's arm all that hard.

Parris checked his hand, asked for three cards. Moon dealt them, gave himself two. They were concentrating on coffee and doughnuts and probabilities when the handsome woman opened the door, marched across the hardwood floor, arched an eyebrow at the older man. "So—this is how you spend your time at the taxpayers' expense."

"Who asked you?" Parris gave the FBI agent a stony-faced look. "And besides, I'm on my lunch hour."

She rolled her eyes. "At three in the afternoon?"

"He's telling the honest truth," Moon said. "If I was forced to, I'd be happy to testify under oath in a court of law that Scott hasn't done a lick of work since he started his lunch hour at ten-twenty this morning."

Parris shot a flake of the flinty gaze at the Indian. "I know you don't mean well, partner—but please don't try to help me."

"Whatever you say." Moon grinned at the pretty lady. "You want some coffee, or a doughnut?"

"Thank you, no."

The Ute gentleman got up, pulled out a chair. "You want us to deal you in?"

"Unlike a certain chief of police I could mention, I am on duty." She settled herself in the seat. "Besides, I'd hate to take all your hard cash, not to mention IOUs."

Both men stared at the woman. Parris asked the question. "You play poker?"

McTeague laughed. "Does Barry Bonds play baseball? Does Bill Gates make money? Does—"

"Does she know when to put a sock in it?" Parris checked his cards. *Nuts.* "Aside from a persistent desire to persecute and pester me, what brings you here?"

"The invitation, of course."

"I never invited you," Parris grumped. "You just barged in like Aunt Audrey at suppertime, or Tilda the Hun crashing through the gates of—"

"That's Atilla."

"Tilda was his older sister," Parris snapped. "Tilda the Hun also had a habit of showing up where she wasn't invited."

"Very well—enjoy your silly historical fantasies. But I was referring to *Charlie's* gracious invitation." She cranked the big eyes up to full size, turned them on the Ute.

Moon's heart skipped a few beats. "Uh—you figure *I* invited you here?"

"I was on the way back to my office, saw your car parked out front, cleverly deduced that you were visiting Chief What's-his-name, thought I'd drop in and say: 'Yes, I don't mind if I do.'"

Lost in her eyes, Moon heard himself say: "Don't mind if you do *what*?"

"Last time I had a meal at the Big Hat, you told me I could come back whenever I 'had a hankering to.'" She almost smiled. "I have a hankering."

"I'd like to oblige you." Moon's expression had switched from balmy to scattered clouds. "But there's a small problem."

She presented a passable poker face. "Problem?"

"My cook hasn't been doing any cooking for the past week or so."

"I am sorry to hear that."

"You and all the hungry cowboys on the Big Hat—and don't forget those Columbine chow hounds that'll fight a starving pit bull for a meaty soup bone." The manager of the two-ranch spread shook his head. "My employees will use any excuse to come sniffing around this gifted pot-and-pan-banger's kitchen. But lately, Cap's been feeling somewhat poorly."

Her poker face had hardened into a brittle mask. "I hope he recovers soon from whatever's ailing him."

"Oh, I'm sure Cap'll be feeling better by and by. In the meantime, I'll treat you to a Wonder Woman–size dinner at the Mountain Man Bar and Grille—"

"No."

"What?"

"You made me a promise, and I'm calling it in." She tapped a crimson fingernail on his chest. "I will take my breakfast at the Big Hat. Tomorrow morning."

He frowned at the determined woman. "But with my hundred-horsepower hash slinger only hittin' on about two cylinders, there's no way I can lay out a meal that'd suit a lady of your refined tastes and delicate sensibilities and huge appetite, so why don't we just ooze on over to the Mountain Man this evening and—"

"Just this once, we shall limp along without your chef's expert services." She picked a piece of lint off Moon's sleeve. "From what I've heard, you're a pretty fair hand with a skillet."

He lowered his gaze, put on a bashful "aw shucks, ma'am" expression. If he had been outside and near a source of small stones, Moon would have kicked at a pebble. "My cooking ain't nothing to brag about."

"Charlie, your boyish modesty is one of your most endearing qualities. But my mind is made up. I will see you at the Big Hat tomorrow, nine A.M. sharp." She flashed a dazzling smile. "I like my bacon extra-crispy, my eggs scrambled, my biscuits red-hot." She got up, glanced over Parris's shoulder at his cards. "Pair of deuces and some trash. Oh well, make the best of it." Little heels went *clickety-click*. Big door went *bang*.

Besides having his hand exposed and his professional character demeaned, Scott Parris hated being left out of things. Had since he was three hours old. He laid his cards aside. "Charlie, I don't want to commit some kind of fawx pass, but—"

"Fox *what*?"

"Say it however you want, the point is—" The middle-aged man paused, stared blankly at a paneled wall.

Moon set his cards aside. "So what's the point?"

Parris scratched at his thinning hair. "I disremember." Mentally backing up one step at a time, he retraced his verbal tracks. "Oh yeah. I don't want to make no social blunder, so tell me straight out—am I or am I not invited to this greasy, gut-busting breakfast at the Big Hat?"

"You're always more than welcome at my table, pardner." Moon clapped him on the back. "And I expect this'll be a meal you don't want to miss."

Parris blinked at the door the fed had slammed behind her. "You think Special Agent McTeague is gonna grill you in your own kitchen?"

"Till I sizzle." The Ute grinned at his best friend. "Remember how she likes her bacon?"

60

PERCHED IN THE CATBIRD SEAT

Special Agent Lila Mae McTeague polished off her scrambled eggs, biscuits, and extra-crispy bacon with an enthusiasm that would have raised awe among an assembly of famished lumberjacks. The avid diner noticed that the men around the table were staring at her. "I was hungry," she said, and buttered another hot biscuit.

"It's all right," Moon replied with frank admiration. "A man who's stood over a hot woodstove all morning appreciates a lady with a healthy appetite."

Scott Parris nodded. "I like a woman who don't pick at her food like a bird." He punctuated this assertion with a healthy belch.

Forrest Wakefield wiped his mouth with a cotton napkin that matched the red-and-white-checkered oilcloth on the table. "That was an excellent breakfast." He shot a look at his host. "And I appreciate the invitation to the feast."

"You're welcome," Moon said. "I'm glad you're here to finish up your work."

McTeague smiled at Moon's fellow plotter. As if she didn't know, she asked: "What sort of work do you do, Mr. Wakefield?"

Pleased at the woman's interest in his career, he blushed. "I'm with the United States Department of Agriculture."

"Ah," she said, "a brother fed."

Feeling self-conscious in the company of a strikingly pretty FBI agent, a tough-as-nails chief of police, and a legendary tribal investigator, Wakefield took a halfhearted stab at a fragment of fried potato. "I'm just a county agent."

"*Just?* Don't be so doggone modest," Moon boomed. "Why, without our county extension agents serving agriculture in all the fifty states, where would we be?" When no one responded to his rhetorical question, the beef rancher provided the answer himself. "Why, we'd be knee-deep in alfalfa rot, cotton-chewing boll weevils, and sickly sheep and cattle—that's where we'd be."

Parris regarded his improvised biscuit-bacon-potato sandwich. "And eating bread full of rat droppings and pork crawling with worms."

"Hear, hear," McTeague said. "Hooray for the USDA." It was clear to one and all that she was in a fine mood.

Warmed by this unanimous praise, Wakefield blushed to the roots of his hair.

McTeague got up from her chair. "Charlie, since you cooked the meal, I'll wash the dishes."

The Ute was immediately on his feet. "Oh no you won't."

"I won't?"

"Of course not. At the Big Hat, ladies don't wet their delicate hands in dishwater—that's a man's work."

She seated herself. "Well, if you insist."

"I certainly do." Having made his point, Moon also sat down. He pointed to his friend. "Scott'll do the dishes."

Parris glared at his host. "Why me?"

Moon ignored the pointless question, smiled at the attractive lady. "And while Scott washes and Forrest wipes, you and me can go for a nice walk, down by the creek."

Special Agent McTeague shook her head.

"No?"

She looked from one man to the other. The dejected tribal investigator. The chief of police, who was munching another biscuit, this one filled to overflowing with blackberry jam. The county agent, who was showing distinct signs of unease. "Before we go for a stroll, I have few things that I wish to say."

"Go right ahead." Moon scooted away from the table, hitched his thumbs in his belt. "I believe I speak for all of us when I say you have a captive audience."

"Thank you." She turned to the county agent. "Even Mr. Wakefield may find my account of some interest."

The USDA employee was staring vacantly at the remnants of food on his plate.

McTeague continued. "From what I have heard, Mr. Wakefield played an important role in the plot to persuade Mr. Trottman to return to where he had left Pansy Blinkoe's corpse—and remove the denture from her mouth."

"Forrest was doing a job for me," Moon said. "And I was acting in my professional capacity as a licensed investigator working on behalf of Dr. and Mrs. Blinkoe."

"I am aware," McTeague said, "that Mr. Wakefield was acting on your instructions. And as far as I know, what he did probably falls barely within the bounds of legal behavior."

To Wakefield's sensitive ear, this sounded very much like criticism.

She added: "Though there is an ethical question when someone—particularly a U.S. government employee—misrepresents himself to a member of the legal profession."

"He was not misrepresenting," Moon reminded the lady. "He was *acting*."

"That's right," Wakefield said. "I have always wanted to strut and fret my hour on the stage." Caught up in his part, he thumped the table, raised his voice. "Since when is it unethical for an American citizen to practice his chosen avocation? Whatever happened to liberty and freedom and justice for all?"

"I am deeply sorry," McTeague said. "If I had brought a star-spangled banner to breakfast, I would wave it and sing the national anthem—while tap-dancing on the table."

All three men would have liked to witness the long-legged lady kicking up a storm, and Scott Parris barely stopped short of saying so when she gave him The Look.

"I know exactly what you're thinking, Scott—keep it to yourself." McTeague turned her gaze on Charlie Moon. "I also know what's been going on."

Moon smiled at his fanciful image of the dancing FBI agent. "Then you're two or three steps ahead of me."

She shook her head at the childish man. "Charlie, Charlie—did you actually think you could mess around with the FBI and not be found out?"

Moon's expression suggested that he had certainly hoped so.

McTeague continued. "I am aware that even before that dismembered arm with Manfred Blinkoe's watch and ring was found by the fisherman—"

"Fisherwoman."

"Charlie, please do not interrupt me."

"Sorry."

She looked at the beamed ceiling. "Where was I?"

Being well fed and full of caffeine, Parris was in a helpful mood. "You were aware that even before that dismembered arm—"

"Right. Thank you, Scott." McTeague paused to take a breath, fixed the Ute with a paralyzing stare. "I am aware that even before that dismembered human arm was found by the fisher*woman*—and not very long after the Blinkoe houseboat exploded on Moccasin Lake—you knew that Dr. Blinkoe was alive and well."

Moon gave her an innocent look. "So?"

"So?" McTeague banged her fist on the table hard enough to rattle dishes. "So you should have informed the FBI!"

He thought about it. "That's a debatable point—I didn't even inform the chief of police, and he's my best buddy."

"That's right," Parris said. "And you don't hear me whining and griping about—"

"Shut up, Scott." She said this without taking her eyes off Moon. "That's how you knew the dismembered arm wasn't Dr. Blinkoe's. And all along, Blinkoe has been feeding you information. That's how you knew the compact he gave his wife was bugged. That's how—"

"Whoa, Nelly."

"What did you say?"

"Excuse me." Moon's tone was meant to be calming. "It's just an old expression. What I really meant was: 'Excuse me for a dang moment, Special Agent McTeague.' But seeing as how you're all in favor of sharing information, why don't you tell us what you found on the tape in Mrs. Blinkoe's compact?"

"There was no tape in the compact, Charlie." She gave him a pitying look. "You really should make an effort to get up-to-date on the latest technology."

"Okay, educate me."

"The compact was voice activated, and had over eighty gigabytes of RAM—"

"Ram means one of two things to me," Moon said. "Either a he-goat or a Dodge truck."

McTeague responded with admirable patience. "It is also an acronym for random access memory."

"Sure. Random access memory." He didn't bat an eyelash. "That's the third thing."

He is so cute. "Because of the modest bandwidth necessary for recording the human voice, that much digital memory can hold hours and hours of recorded conversation."

Moon propped his elbows on the table. "So what was recorded during all those hours and hours?"

McTeague shrugged. "Oh, some of this, some of that."

"Skip the this and that—let's get down to the nitty-gritty. The brass tacks. The bottom line. What I mean to say is—tell us the good part."

Scott Parris nodded his agreement with this sentiment.

"Very well," McTeague said. "In a nutshell, we were able to determine that Mrs. Blinkoe's so-called brother—who was actually her high-school sweetheart—played no significant role in the recent spate of criminal activities."

Moon knew as much, and was still aiming for the nitty-gritty, et cetera. "Was the tape turning that night when she thought she'd seen her dead husband at the window, and drove her pickup into town to see the family attorney?"

Ignoring his stubborn insistence on 1940s technology, McTeague nodded. "Mrs. Blinkoe drove her pickup to Spencer Trottman's home. He tried to calm her, convince her that whatever or whoever she had seen at her bedroom window, it could not have been her husband. Manfred was most certainly dead. This being so, she was a widow and free to take another husband—someone who would appreciate her, treat her with the kindness and respect she deserved."

The Ute had guessed the rest. "Trottman asked Pansy Blinkoe to marry him. And she turned him down flat." Only a couple of years ago, Charlie Moon's proposal had been rejected even before he had a chance to utter it.

"Not only did she refuse," McTeague said, "she evidently thought it was terribly funny. When Spencer proposed, she *laughed* at him."

Parris shook his head. "Always a serious mistake."

"It was her final mistake." McTeague recalled listening to the horrible curses and shrieks on the compact's concealed digital recorder. "Trottman slapped her, she fought back, he strangled her on the spot. From a detailed analysis of the sounds for the next eighty-nine minutes, it is apparent that Trottman put Mrs. Blinkoe's body and purse in her pickup, drove the vehicle to Garcia's Crossing. He stopped at the abandoned church, placed her body in the Martinez crypt. Because he left the purse with the compact in the crypt with the corpse, we have no recordings after his departure. But it is reasonable to assume that he drove her pickup back to Granite Creek, left it in the motel parking lot—along with her keys. Trottman must have walked back to his home, believed he was safe. But after thinking the thing through, he realized that once the woman was reported missing, the Blinkoe telephone records would be checked—and her late-night telephone call to the family attorney's residence would be discovered. So he not only reported Mrs. Blinkoe's absence from her home, he also reported their telephone conversation accurately—and preserved the recording for the authorities. It supported his story about being worried when she didn't show up, not getting any answers to his repeated calls to the Blinkoe residence—which he made after he returned from Garcia's Crossing. To make the thing look even better, he drove out to the Blinkoe estate—presumably to determine whether anything was amiss. There's little doubt that Mr. Trottman broke the window in the back door to make it look as if someone had entered the house before he arrived. Once the setup was ready, he called the police."

Parris grimaced at the thought of how he'd been taken in.

McTeague paused long enough to examine her elegant hands. *I really need a manicure.* "And it seems quite likely that the man posing as Pansy Blinkoe's brother was telling the truth. Sometime that night, he returned to his apartment above the Blinkoe garage, noticed that Pansy's vehicle was not in its usual spot. He rode his motorcycle into town, drove around until he spotted her pickup parked at the motel—with the key in the ignition. Assuming she was in the motel with another man, Mr. Culpepper got hot under the collar. He hoisted his cycle into the back of the truck, drove it away. And so on." She turned to Moon. "What made you suspicious of Trottman?"

Moon stared into his coffee cup. "One day last month, my aunt got a peculiar notion that she knew where Pansy Blinkoe was." He hesitated. "For one reason or another, she thought the woman was hiding out at Garcia's Crossing—someplace close to St. Cuthbert's Catholic Church."

Parris, Wakefield, McTeague—all felt a chill.

It was the woman who asked the question. "But how could she have possibly known . . . ?"

Moon raised his palms. "Don't ask me." He waited for a few heartbeats. "Anyway, my aunt was anxious to tell me about it, so she used this little satellite telephone I gave her for a birthday present. She pushed the button programmed to dial my cell phone, but I had it turned off. She didn't want to leave a message, so she called the Columbine land line. My foreman's wife answered, told Aunt Daisy I was on my way to Spencer Trottman's office, and gave her Trottman's number. But when my aunt called, Trottman didn't answer. So she decided to ring my cell phone again and leave me a message. Problem is, she pressed the wrong button, ended up leaving the message for Trottman."

McTeague asked for clarification. "How did you determine this?"

Moon appreciated the question. "When I pressed the Redial button on her phone, Trottman's number came up on the readout—which proves that was the last number she'd called." He shook his head at the irony of it all. "Imagine the lawyer's surprise when he checks his messages, and hears Aunt Daisy telling me where to find Pansy Blinkoe—and she's got it right! He must've thought she'd seen him stash the body in the church cemetery. He can't just sit around and wait until she tells me about it. So he goes out to the res that night with a green coffee can and some smelly kerosene, and sets fire to her home."

The FBI agent glared at her image of the dead man's ghost. "In an attempt to cover up the murder of Pansy Blinkoe, Trottman attempted to murder your aunt."

Parris frowned. "But what about the murder of the Chicago woman on the restaurant patio? D'you suppose the shooter was Trottman—aiming at Blinkoe?"

"The Bureau has ruled that out," McTeague said. "We have witnesses who place Trottman at a location six hundred miles away when the shot was fired. We haven't eliminated Trottman as a suspect in the dynamiting of Dr. Blinkoe's boat, but it seems far more likely that the event was engineered by the Colombian drug cartel." She aimed her big eyes at the Ute. "Would you like to comment on that possibility?"

She's hoping I'll implicate Blinkoe in that DC-3 hijacking. "I don't know who set the charge on the houseboat," Moon executed an elegant side step. "But what the guy with the dynamite didn't know was that my client had taken my advice, and hired on a couple of tough guys to guard his body. Blinkoe arranged to meet his hired guns a few miles down the lake from his home. These knuckle-draggers brought a vehicle to a designated point on the shore. The idea was to remove their client from his fancy boat, take him to a safe house. It didn't occur to these guys that somebody might have already tampered with the boat. While Guard A took Dr. Blinkoe ashore, Guard B was still on the craft, waiting with a submachine gun in case somebody attempted to board. Most likely, when the dynamite was touched off, he was expecting a quiet, peaceful night."

"So," Parris said, "it was Guard B's dismembered arm that was fished out of the lake."

Moon nodded, waited for the inevitable question from McTeague.

"But why was Guard B wearing Blinkoe's watch and ring?"

Moon told her. "Soon as they showed up, Blinkoe suggested a friendly game of poker. Guard A was not interested, but Blinkoe and Guard B got right down to business. They only played one hand."

"He lost his jewelry and timepiece in a one deal of the cards?" The chief of police chuckled. "Well, I don't believe it!"

"Believe it," Moon said. "Way it happened, Guard B was holding a pair of sevens, and Blinkoe had three queens and a couple of aces."

Parris could not follow this. "Excuse me, but in any kind of poker I've ever heard of, whether played on earth or any distant planet you may wish to name—a full house will beat a pair of sevens every time. This universal rule is, as they say—according to Mr. Hoyle. Look it up in his little book."

Moon admitted that this was the way poker was played.

"Then how," McTeague asked, "did Dr. Blinkoe lose his property?"

The tribal investigator came clean about his disreputable

client. "Guard B caught Dr. B. dealing from the bottom of the deck."

Parris grimaced. "Ouch!"

"You may well say so. Being more than a little irked, Guard B jerked the expensive Swiss chronometer off the boat captain's wrist. And when Dr. Blinkoe hesitated to remove the other ornament from his digit, Guard B produced a wicked-looking blade and threatened to take it finger and all. And no doubt meant it."

"I don't blame him one iota." Parris offered this statement with a flinty expression. "There ain't nothing worse than an orthodontist who cheats at cards."

Having once made a similar observation to Dr. Blinkoe, Moon was not inclined to argue the point. Though he considered cattle rustlers and horse thieves pretty much in the same category.

McTeague posed a question. "This face that Pansy Blinkoe saw in her mirror—was that her husband staring in her bedroom window?"

Moon shook his head. "According to what I've heard, it was not."

The FBI agent tried to slip one in on her favorite Indian. "And who is the source of your information?"

The tribal investigator pretended to be astonished at such an unseemly question. "I will pretend I did not hear that."

She started to grind her perfect teeth, barely caught herself before serious damage was done to enamel. "Then I will ask you again, louder this time: How do you come to know all these details—like about Dr. Blinkoe cheating his bodyguard in a poker game?"

"I am a professional investigator, who has a solemn ethical duty to protect the interests of his client." He leaned across the table, met her hard gaze. "Drive red-hot splinters under my toenails, McTeague. Gouge out my eyes with a sharp spoon. Make me listen to all the acid rock and hip-hop that's been recorded for the past umpteen years." He shook his head. "Still, I will not tell you."

"If you don't, I shall be chagrined. And very disappointed in you."

"Well, that's another matter entirely. My source is my client, of course. Dr. Manfred Wilhelm Blinkoe."

"I had assumed as much."

"Then there was no need to threaten me with red-hot splinters, eye gouging, and so on."

"I did not threaten you—"

"Now that you've put the scare into me, would you like to know where Dr. Blinkoe is hiding out?"

"Yes. I most certainly would."

"Then you'll have to use threats of *serious* violence."

"Charlie, this has gone about far enough. If you don't start talking instantly—"

"Does the FBI intend to charge my client with anything?"

There was a tense moment while they eyed each other.

"Barring the discovery of new evidence, not in connection with recent events."

"Good. What about that business about the so-called DC-3 hijacking?"

"That was not 'so-called,' as you call it. The aircraft was most definitely hijacked. And several bags of cash were stolen."

"Stolen from who—the government?"

She wondered where he was going with this. "You are well aware that the money was forcibly taken from employees of a major drug cartel."

"Let me get this straight—the FBI has been working overtime just to get some stolen money returned to a bunch of dope pushers?"

"Well, of course not! Once the funds are recovered and appropriate legal procedures are completed, the cash will be confiscated by the U.S. Treasury."

"Oh, then the drug cartel stole the money from the Treasury?"

"Don't be silly. You know very well where the money came from."

Moon nodded. "I sure do. From U.S. citizens who happen to be addicts." He grinned at the pretty woman. "So does the U.S. government want to return the cash to the addicts—or spend the money on treatment programs?" He glanced at his county agent. "Or even give it to the Department of Agriculture? No." He thumped the table to drive is point home. "They want to put it in Fort Knox. Then spend it on no telling what. Foreign aid to the North Koreans, or the Iranians." He shook his head. "As an official U.S. taxpayer, this does not sound right to me."

She fixed him with a triple-strength glare. "Shut up."

He did.

"And listen."

He did this too.

"Charlie—I want you to tell me where Dr. Blinkoe is hiding."

The chief of police banged a spoon on his plate. "Excuse me for interrupting."

McTeague turned a scowl on Parris. "What?"

"You just told Charlie to shut up. Now you're asking him questions. Out in the Wild and Woolly West, this is what we call a conversational contradiction."

Sighing, McTeague addressed herself to the Ute. "Charlie, you may feel free to speak."

"Okay."

"Tell me where I can find Dr. Blinkoe."

"Oh, *that's* all you wanted to know?"

"It is not a matter of what I want to *know*." She smiled like a happy crocodile. "It's about what I want you to *tell* me."

Moon blinked. Not once but twice. "Excuse me?"

Her smile got bigger. Toothier. "I already know where Blinkoe's holed up. I just want you to tell me. So that we may remain on friendly terms." She added quickly: "Professionally."

"You're bluffing."

"I never bluff."

"Then you're not a poker player." He watched for a tell,

saw nothing. "How would you know where Dr. Blinkoe is hanging his beret?"

Her expression could only be described as smug. "The FBI has its methods."

"I don't like the sound of this, Agent McTeague. If you've tapped my phone or planted bugs on my private property, you'd better have a warrant signed by a judge."

"If you find evidence of an unwarranted intrusion, Mr. Moon, I suggest you file a formal complaint."

"If it's not bugs, then you've got yourself an informer." He looked very sad. "What'd you do, dig up an old charge on one of my cowboys—tell him to either play ball with the FBI or look at umpteen years in a federal jug?"

"I refuse to continue this pointless conversation." McTeague pitched her napkin aside, got up from her chair. "I wish to talk to your chef."

"Cap?"

"Do you have another one?"

Moon admitted that he did not. And inquired why she wished to exchange words with his kitchen employee. Was Cap the informer?

McTeague tried to look appalled by this suggestion. "You mentioned that he was not feeling well. This is not meant to be a reflection on the breakfast you prepared—I'm sure you did your best. But I wish to determine for myself the state of his health—and inquire about when he might be attending to his kitchen duties again."

The rancher got up, stomped across the kitchen, rapped on a knotty-pine door. "Cap, d'you feel up to having some company?"

The ranch cook, who had been listening at a knot-hole, backed several paces away, called out in a feeble voice: "Who is it?"

Moon told him.

"Sure, boss. I guess that'll be all right."

The Ute opened the door, stood aside.

Special Agent McTeague entered the room.

Moon looked over her shoulder at the pitiful-looking man. "You want me to come in and be a witness?"

The hireling, who was sitting on his bed, shook his head. "Oh, no sir. That won't be necessary."

"Okay. But just holler if you need me." Moon shut the door, went to the cookstove to get the pot. "You fellas need some fresh coffee?"

Scott Parris did not, Forrest Wakefield asked for half a cup.

When his duty was done, Moon seated himself across from his guests.

Parris regarded his friend with a suspicious look. "Why's McTeague so interested in your cook?"

Moon shrugged. "I guess we'll have to wait and see."

61

THE INFORMER

McTeague found a straight-back chair, pulled it up to face the sickly-looking man.

Cap, aka Scarf, had grown a bushy little beard. He was also wearing a glum expression and a black armband.

She whispered: "How are you?"

The Big Hat cook looked back through bleary eyes. "I've been better."

McTeague pointed at the black strip of silk encircling his biceps. "What's that for?"

He exhaled a long, melancholy sigh. "There's been a death in the family."

"I'm very sorry. Someone close to you?"

He nodded. "But I don't feel like talking about it right now."

She leaned closer. "I regret the necessity to approach you so directly, but I was concerned that Charlie Moon had learned that you were informing on him. I'm going to take you into protective custody."

"You won't be taking me anywhere—not unless you've got a warrant with my John Henry on it." There was a momentary glint of amusement in the sad eyes. "Anything else on your mind?"

She got right to the point. "Cap, I appreciate your tipping me off that Dr. Blinkoe is in hiding on Moon's property. But now I need to talk to him."

"You intend to put the cuffs on ol' Blinky?"

"Not unless he confesses to a felony. He's more like—a material witness. Do you know precisely where he's hiding?"

"Well, he moves around a lot." The ranch cook rubbed his eyes. "But I think I can put the finger on the slippery bugger for you."

She glanced at the closed door. "Will Charlie Moon try to stop you?"

"Oh, I doubt it. I think the boss knows the jig is about up."

"Then let's get it done." She had a damn-the-torpedoes full-speed-ahead look. "I am ready to confront Dr. Blinkoe!"

"Okay, I'll see what I can do." Cap scratched at the scruffy hair sprouting from his chin, blinked the nearsighted eyes. "But I'll need a couple a minutes to wash up, and put my glasses on so I'm not bumping into things." He got off the bed with an old-man groan, toddled off into a small bathroom.

McTeague got up from the uncomfortable chair, paced back and forth.

Right on the mark at two minutes, the Big Hat cook appeared in the bathroom doorway. In the manner of one making a dramatic presentation, he spread his arms wide. "Ta-da!" Cap was wearing a pair of thick spectacles, had a small pillow stuffed under his shirt to simulate a belly. Moreover, he had trimmed a cleft into his beard—which gave it a distinctly forked appearance.

Staggered at the sight, McTeague took two steps backward, bumped into the straight-back chair, sat down hard.

She aimed a shaky finger at her informer. "You're . . . you're . . ." She could not make herself say it.

With a slight bow, a foppish flourish of his hand, he said it for her. "Dr. Manfred Wilhelm Blinkoe at your service, m'lady."

M'lady felt a swirling surge of nausea and dizziness, was terrified that she might vomit or faint. Or both.

Thumbs hooked under suspenders, Blinkoe smirked. "Yes 'tis true. Your trusted informer is actually the sly fellow you've been searching high and low for. Seeing me for who I truly am must come as a bit of a shock, eh?"

He might as well have referred to the 1811 New Madrid earthquake as a minor tremor.

She fought to regain a modicum of self-control. "But why . . ."

"Why?" Dr. Blinkoe considered the question with a thoughtful cock of his head. "Why does the red-breasted robin sing on a warm June morn? Why does the speckled trout leap heavenward from the glistening waters—why, for the *fun* of it!"

With a mind of its own and a single thought, McTeague's hand was moving closer to her automatic weapon.

Blinkoe paled. *Women have such a poorly developed sense of humor.* "You surely aren't thinking of shooting me?"

She glanced at the closed door, on the other side of which the Ute was hanging out with his pals. "Charlie Moon—he put you up to this . . . this Scarf business!"

The impostor shook his head. "Certainly not. He was unaware that I have been occasionally posing as an informer to the FBI." Blinkoe smiled. "Well, until late last night, when I told the big galoot about my devilish escapade. He showed a particularly keen interest in what transpired at our meeting at the Copper Street Deli. And even when he learned that you had paid a bribe of filthy lucre to his trusted cook to inform on him, Moon's extreme chagrin was entirely reserved for me. In this gallant's view, I have treated you quite unfairly—practically entrapped you, as it were. In short, Mr.

Charles Moon is entirely innocent of the Scarf affair. I proudly claim the entire responsibility for my slyly conniving self."

"Is that so?" *While he's in the mood, I'd better keep him talking.* "And did your sly, conniving self arrange the sinking of your houseboat—with the hope of being presumed dead?"

"Sadly, no." He sighed. "I am embarrassed to admit that such a clever ploy never occurred to me. For that singularly dramatic act, person or persons unknown must assume the entire credit."

"Not that I'll believe a single word of it, but I would like to hear your version of recent events."

"And so you shall." Blinkoe seated himself on the edge of the bed, dangling his feet inches above the floor. "Ever since the shooting of that poor woman on the restaurant patio, I have been convinced that someone is out to murder me. On Mr. Moon's recommendation, I decided to hire a pair of professional bodyguards, and lie low for a while. I believe you already know about our clandestine meeting on the lake, the hand of poker which led to a minor misunderstanding and the loss of my watch and ring, so I'll skip over that. While the humorless cardplayer stayed behind on the *Sweet Solitude*—standing in for my honorable self—the other thug and yours truly paddled away in the little rubber boat. We'd barely gotten ashore when my lovely houseboat was utterly destroyed by the most dramatic explosion you can imagine. The surviving bodyguard was fairly rattled, and of course so was I. But we stayed with the original plan—which was to go into hiding." He paused to gaze at the ceiling, where a tiny green wasp was buzzing around the light fixture.

McTeague could not bear the silence. "But after a few days, you became terribly lonely, and went home one night to get a glimpse of your lovely young wife—"

"I will not deny that I thought about it." He watched the winged insect with a painfully intense concentration. "But the fact of the matter is that I did not. I was nowhere near my residence when Pansy was frightened by that face she saw in the mirror."

"Do you actually expect me to believe that?"

"What you choose to believe, Special Agent McTeague, is of little concern to me." He smiled at the uptight fed. "Shall I continue with my gripping narrative?"

"Please do. I am hanging on every word."

"Thank you kindly." He effected another slight bow. "Let us slip back to a few days after my boat was destroyed. I had tired of my makeshift hideout and the mind-numbing company of the surviving bodyguard—I refer to my chum Curly, of course—whose entire vocabulary is barely twenty words. I decided to impose myself upon the hospitality of Charlie Moon, who was—in a manner of speaking—in my employ. And so I did. On the night when my wife saw the fearsome face, I was in this very house."

"And I bet you have witnesses to prove it."

"Yes, seven in all."

"Quite a crowd."

"It was the night of the monthly poker game."

"I hope you lost your shirt."

"As it happened, I was not to be counted among the happy participants." Blinkoe's expression reflected his pique at the hurtful memory. "On Mr. Moon's real estate, I am barred from all games of chance. It is a most appalling form of discrimination. No doubt, several of my civil rights have been severely violated."

"Just for the sake of civil conversation, let's say I believe you were here when some Peeping Tom frightened your wife. Do you have a theory about his identity?"

"No theory is required, G-woman." He removed a miniature Swiss Army folding knife from his vest pocket, opened the stainless-steel scissors, clipped away at a stray thread dangling from a shift button. "I know precisely who it was."

"A neighborhood pervert?"

"Certainly not."

"The man who posed as your wife's brother?"

This produced a pained expression. "Please, let us not mention that scoundrel who so flagrantly abused my hospitality. Just imagine—posing to be someone who he was not!"

McTeague almost smiled. "Then who was the face in the mirror?"

He returned the knife to his pocket. "It was the Shadow Man."

"The *what*?"

"My doppelgänger. Or if you prefer—my ghostly twin."

McTeague took a deep breath. "Excuse me for saying so. But if that is not the most absurd thing I have heard in my entire life, it's got to be in the top two percent."

"Indeed?" Eyes bulging behind the thick spectacles, Blinkoe fixed her with a disdainful stare. "You are a strict materialist, then?"

"If you're asking whether I believe in phantoms and goblins, the answer is . . . is . . ." For a fleeting moment, it was as if the man had split into almost identical duplicates. Worse still, one of the faces winked at her. McTeague closed her eyes. *This is not happening.* Thankfully, when she opened them, it was not. Manfred Wilhelm Blinkoe was singular again. *I don't know how he did it, but he must have hypnotized me!* It occurred to her that a few dentists use hypnotism in the practice of their craft.

Blinkoe appeared to be genuinely puzzled by her startled expression. "Agent McTeague, are you all right?"

"Of course I am." Taking care not to look him directly in the eyes, she continued the interrogation. "When you showed up at the Big Hat, I expect Charlie Moon rolled out the red carpet for you."

"Being the charming person that I am, you would naturally think so. I thought the kindly Indian fellow would be only too happy to give me shelter from the storms and tumults of this wicked world. But believe it or not, while Mr. Moon was extremely pleased to learn that I was still alive, it was not his intention to conceal me on his property."

DUBIOUS was written all over her face. "It wasn't?"

"Sadly, no. Even though I had committed no crime, he suggested that I turn myself in to a legally constituted authority." He gave her a tender look. "More particularly, to yourself."

What a fat pack of lies. "Why me?"

"In my opinion, because he is inordinately fond of you. He evidently hoped your career would benefit by my unselfish act."

She blushed a pretty pink. "Then why didn't you—turn yourself in to me, I mean?"

"Well, seemingly having no viable long-term alternative, throwing myself on the mercy of the FBI was my earnest intention. Though Mr. Moon put no undue pressure on me to leave his protection—that would have violated his sentimental notions of cowboy hospitality—I decided to pay you a call. And I meant to do the right thing. Really I did. But wouldn't you know it—just as I approached your threshold, I thought about how I had shaved off my beard and dropped sixteen pounds, and wondered whether you would believe that this sad little package could possibly be Dr. Manfred Wilhelm Blinkoe, well-known orthodontist, celebrated bon vivant and debonair man-about-town—and I was blessed with this absolutely *wonderful* inspiration. I transformed myself into an eccentric transient who—for a few paltry pieces of silver—was willing to provide the FBI with some sort of valuable information. I knew you'd think I was some kind of nut." He paused to enjoy her anger.

"So this Scarf business was just a stupid joke?"

"Tut-tut, G-woman," He shook a stubby finger at her. "You should never speak disparagingly about the sacred subject of jokes. What is this universe but a divinely stupendous jest? Besides," he added, "it occurred to me that my cunning little prank might serve a useful purpose. You see, if I were to gradually work my way up to telling you that Dr. Manfred W. Blinkoe was enjoying room and board on the Big Hat, I would be informing on *myself*. This would effectively protect Mr. Moon—my most gracious host—from future charges of having given shelter to—"

"To a felon!"

"No-no-no." He shook the finger again. "To a person *suspected* of having allegedly committed a few paltry felonies in connection with that unfortunate DC-3 hijacking incident. But more to the point, had the Federal Department of Injustice become aware of Mr. Moon's having secretly given shelter to a *person of interest* to the FBI, why, that rabid pack of lawyers might have harassed my kindly Indian benefactor. But by my making an open admission to an FBI special agent that Dr. Manfred Blinkoe—which happened to be *myself*—was staying at the Big Hat, the FBI would be highly unlikely to lend its support to a legal complaint against either Mr. Moon or myself. Don't you see?"

McTeague did see. And she did not like what she saw.

Blinkoe clasped his hands. "It is all just *so* delicious."

The FBI agent had a bad taste in her mouth. "One way or another, Blinkoe, I'll get you for this."

"Your professional animosity is understandable, and all things are possible—given sufficient time. But as the years pass—and you grow old and embittered in your impotence to wreak revenge—I shall remember this particular adventure with special relish. No doubt, Special Agent McTeague, comic songs will be written and a television movie made about how I came to be an 'informer' to the FBI on *myself*." He leaped to his feet, struck a ludicrous flamenco pose. "No doubt, I will be asked to play the lead." Full of himself, Blinkoe did a little heel-tapping jig on the oak floor. "There is nothing you can charge me with, FBI lady—I am a free spirit, immune to prosecution and persecution." A disdainful snap of the fingers.

Desperate for something to hang him with, McTeague raised clenched fists. "You—you have deliberately misled an official FBI investigation."

Blinkoe raised his nose for an arrogant sniff. "On the contrary, I have been entirely straight with you—everything I told you was absolutely true. I *did* know that Mr. Moon was hiding Dr. Manfred Blinkoe on his property, and I made it perfectly clear at our initial meeting that Scarf was not my real name. And just minutes ago, while I was still posing as Cap, I agreed to reveal Dr. Blinkoe's precise whereabouts—which I have most certainly done." He resumed the heel-tapping, wailed a few strained phrases from *Solo por verte bailar.*

The man is certifiably insane. And I'm a bloody fool. Lila Mae McTeague knew she should not ask. It was *so* unprofessional. "What makes you believe that Charlie—that Mr. Moon is . . . ah . . . fond of me?" *Inordinately fond*.

Mildly winded by his exertions, the dancer plopped onto the bed. "My dear lady, I may be nearsighted without my prescription spectacles, but I am not stone blind." He added delicately: "And I'm certain that he must be very concerned—knowing the difficult position you find yourself in."

"What do you mean by that?"

"Well, it is obvious enough. How would your future with the FBI be affected if it became known that you were paying Manfred Blinkoe to inform on *himself*. The effect would certainly not be a positive one. I am sure that our mutual Indian friend would stop at nothing to protect you."

She felt her face getting warm, but refused to blush. "But you're just champing at the bit to blackmail me—"

"Oh, no. Kick the horsy metaphor out of the saddle. The stuff about songs and TV movies and such was mere whimsy. I do not intend to utter a word about my delightful little charade as Scarf." Blinkoe blinked behind the thick spectacles. "Unless I should be forced, under oath, to tell the truth, the whole truth, et cetera, and so on and so forth."

McTeague got to her feet. "Tell me one thing."

He popped off the bed. "Anything, m'lady."

"Where did you hide the bags of money you took from the DC-3?"

"Oh no." He shook his head. "Anything but that. Ask me something else."

Having run short of relevant questions, she pointed her nose at the black armband. "Is that for your wife?"

"Of course." Manfred Blinkoe's eyes moistened. "Poor little Pansy. Though somewhat of a shrew, she was such a pretty thing. I shall miss her all of my remaining days." He smirked at the FBI agent. "Is that all?"

"No, it's not all." McTeague fixed him with a look that would have shaken a lesser man. "You can tell your story about making a fool of me wherever you want. Buy a megaphone and shout it from the rooftops. Get an interview on *60 Minutes*. It doesn't matter to me, not one whit. I'm going to spend the rest of my career, however short or long it may be—nailing you."

His bow was low, this time, and earnestly solemn. "Dear lady, I would have been disappointed if you had chosen any other course. And even if you hound me to the ends of the earth, I will never mention my harmless little prank. Indeed, I have decided that even if I am cross-examined under oath, I shall not admit to having hoodwinked you so thoroughly."

"Really?"

"Of course. It shall be no strain upon me to deny the facts." He gave her a prideful look. "I am a congenital liar of the first order."

Having heard the hinges squeak, Charlie Moon met McTeague at the door, closed it behind her. *She looks rattled. Cap must've dropped the bomb.* "You all right?"

She nodded, took note of the empty room. "Where has Scott gone—and your remarkable county agent?"

"I sent 'em out." He turned to look out a window. "They're down by the horse barn, looking at a frisky mare."

She smiled, though wanly. "Sweet Alice?"

The Ute shook his head. "After giving the matter some thought, I turned her loose." He nodded to indicate the west. "She stays over there amongst the canyons and mesas, with the wild ones. From what I hear, she's found herself a feller."

Me too. She reached out to take his hand. "Charlie, are you inordinately fond of me?"

It took him a moment to swallow the rock in his throat. "Yes ma'am, I am."

"If I was to go far, far away—would you miss me?"

"Nope—wouldn't be any time for that. By the time you'd crossed the county line, I'd be right on your trail. And I'd hunt you down."

"You aren't angry with me for . . . for paying one of your employees to inform on you?"

"Oh, sure I am. I'm mad as a dog with porcupine quills in his nose." He pulled her into a gentle embrace. "But by and by, I'll get over it."

She hugged him back. "I have some quills in my nose too. About your cook."

"Yeah. I know. He's given me some heartburn too."

"I'd better go now." She glanced at the closed door. "Take good care of . . . Cap."

"Ah, don't worry yourself about that rascal." Moon laughed. "He can take care of himself."

"Yes. I daresay he can."

He felt her slip away. Watched her go.

62

YOU CAN GO HOME AGAIN

Charlie Moon was up at the cold crack of dawn, working hard to make an honest dollar. The rancher was in the Columbine headquarters kitchen, where all important business was conducted. A cup of sugary black coffee in one hand, he thumbed through the expenses ledger with the other, trying to make sense of Pete Bushman's scribbled entries. He turned a page, read a long column of costly necessities. Fifty bushels of feed corn for the horses, sixteen bushels of oats, a twelve-hundred-watt portable electric generator, two sacks of alfalfa seed, a rebuilt transmission for the John Deere tractor. On the following page there was a list of two-by-fours, two-by-sixes, dressed pine logs, five pounds of ProPanel screws, the same weight of tenpenny nails, ten bags of cement, and on and on and on. In that grim race between income and expenses, the dark horse was leading by a nose. In the stillness of the big log house, Moon heard footsteps in the hallway. He glanced at his watch. *What is she doing up so early?* He got up, pulled a chair out for his elderly relative. "Good morning."

Daisy Perika padded into the kitchen, passed by her nephew without so much as a grunt. She went directly to the cabinet over the sink, found a mug, poured herself a cup of strong coffee.

Having noticed that she had *that look,* he waited.

Ignoring the offered chair at his elbow, Daisy seated herself across from Charlie Moon, banged the coffee mug on the table.

He eased himself into his chair, waited.

Daisy took a sip of the scalding liquid. "We have to talk."

Moon closed the ledger. "What about?"

"I've been hearing some tales." She stirred a spoonful of sugar into her coffee. "Word is, the tribe has put a gate on the road to Spirit Canyon."

"Where'd you hear that?"

"Not from you." Her dark eyes flashed with anger. "Louise-Marie called me last night while you were out punching cows or whatever it is you do."

Moon put on his best there's-nothing-to-worry-about expression. "The tribal chairman put the gate up to keep people from wandering around where your home used to be—"

"Oscar Sweetwater never did me a favor in my life." She scowled at him. "You know what else Louise-Marie told me?"

He pretended to think about it. "Hard as I try, I can't imagine."

"She heard from Alice Pink, who was told by Judson Cedar Bear, that the tribal council has already set up a house trailer on my property!"

"Well, I can explain that," Moon said. "Oscar had a little camping trailer put there temporarily. It's for tribal members who volunteered to guard the site against sightseers and looters and—"

"Guard my hind leg—they're nothing but squatters that hope I'm not coming back! First thing you know, Oscar'll have half of his good-for-nothing relatives living out there in canvas tipis and tar-paper shacks and I won't be able to elbow my way in unless I shoot every last one of 'em between the eyes!"

"Look, nothing like that's going to happen. I'll see to it that—"

"Shut your mouth and listen to what I'm telling you." She banged her fist on the table five times, once for each word: "I—am—going—home—today."

Moon frowned across the table at the wrinkled face. "You don't like it here?"

Daisy lowered her gaze to the red-and-white-checkered oilcloth. "This place is all right. But it ain't the same as being in my own place."

Moon reached across the table to cover her gnarled little hand with his big paw. "Why not wait for two or three more weeks until—"

Daisy jerked her hand away. "I'm going home." She aimed a trembling finger at her nephew's nose. "If you don't drive me there, I'll call Louise-Marie to come get me."

He gave her a long, thoughtful look. "Since you two had that bad run-in with the police in Granite Creek, Louise-Marie's been having some difficulties. In the transportation department."

"What do you mean by that?"

Moon tried not to grin. "SUPD and the Ignacio town police are keeping a close eye on her. If she's spotted on a public highway in that old Oldsmobile, she'll be fined for driving without an operator's license. And for not having current plates."

Daisy snorted. "None of that's ever stopped her before."

"Well, there's something that will. Louise-Marie's motor vehicle won't start."

The tribal elder thought this sounded suspicious. "What's wrong with it?"

"From what I hear, there's some kind of problem with the ignition system." The chief of the Ignacio town police had the

Oldsmobile's distributor rotor locked in his desk, and such antique parts were hard to come by.

The determined old woman dismissed the Louise-Marie plan with a flippant wave of her hand. "Then I'll call somebody else to come get me. And if that don't work, I'll stick out my thumb and hitchhike. And if nobody'll pick me up, I'll walk." She fixed the beady black eyes on her young relative. "But one way or another, I am going home today. If you don't believe it, you just stand out on the porch and watch me get smaller."

Moon knew she meant it. "After we have a good breakfast, and I get a few things done, I'll drive you down there."

Daisy drained her cup, slammed it down. Flushed by victory and caffeine, she grinned wickedly at her nephew. "I knew you'd see it my way." It was great fun, pushing him around.

Moon watched his aged aunt hobble down the hallway toward her bedroom, where she'd be getting her "stuff" together.

It was close to sundown as Moon maneuvered the Expedition along the dirt road that would eventually be swallowed by the mouth of *Cañón del Espíritu*.

Daisy knew every arroyo, hill, and ridge—practically every tree. As they approached the spot she had called home for most of her life, her heart began to race. "I wish we could've come when there was still good light."

"Sorry," Moon said. "I had some business to attend to before I could leave the ranch. You'd be surprised how much work there is running an outfit the size of the Col—"

"I probably would, but I don't want to hear about it right this minute."

The amiable man held his silence.

With an unnerving suddenness, Daisy demonstrated her capability to astonish him. "Charlie, do you think God really loves people like Mr. DeSoto?"

Moon smiled. "Yes. I do."

Having no doubt that her kindhearted nephew was right,

the old woman sighed. The way the universe worked was an inexplicable mystery.

A few minutes passed. They were much closer now.

Eager to see even the faintest remnants of her former home, Daisy began to fidget. Unaware that she was patting her hands on her thighs, she leaned forward to look through the broad windshield. *It's just around this bend. . . .*

Charlie Moon slowed as he made the turn, braked to a stop at the new steel gate. The obstruction featured a large NO TRESPASSING sign. A massive brass padlock secured the gate to a sturdy post.

Daisy shook her head. "My family has lived on this land for five generations. The tribe's got no right to lock me out of here."

He showed her a key, got out to remove the padlock.

When they were a few yards farther down the road, a tribal member emerged from a pale green camping trailer that was almost hidden in a cluster of junipers. He was a short, stocky man in faded jeans and a red felt shirt. "That's Eddie Tipton," Daisy muttered under her breath. "I *knew* it'd be some of the tribal chairman's no-account kin." She shot a dark look at her nephew, whom she suspected of not keeping up on the all-important issue of who was related to who. Or whom. "In case you don't remember, Eddie Tipton is Oscar Sweetwater's second cousin."

Moon could not resist the temptation. "In case you don't remember, you're Oscar's *first* cousin."

She groaned. "Don't remind me."

Eddie glared at the Expedition until he recognized it. The guard's face broke into a big smile, he waved at the tribal investigator.

Moon stopped by the small trailer, cut the ignition.

Eddie nodded politely at Daisy before coming around the car to say a big hello to Charlie Moon.

They exchanged the obligatory greetings, moved on to a discussion of crops and cattle and the urgent need for moisture. Though there was not a cloud in the sky, Eddie claimed he could smell a good rain off to the northwest. He predicted it would show up over the res well before midnight.

Daisy would glare first at the guard, then at the ugly little camp trailer the tribal chairman had put on her allotment without even asking her permission, then at Eddie Tipton again, then back at the trailer and so on. Eventually, she got a painful crick in her neck and settled on the compromise of scowling at a black moth that had settled on the windshield.

When Eddie had exhausted his supply of words, he advised Moon to "take it easy," tipped his hat at the curmudgeonly old woman, and withdrew inside the miniature trailer.

Moon turned to his aunt. "Now you can see why there's a gate on the road. And you don't have to worry about Eddie squatting on your land. He's got a brand-new three-bedroom, two-bath house a mile south of Ignacio. And Eddie's wife'd never want to live out here in the sticks."

Daisy grudgingly admitted that there was probably no danger from this quarter. *But who knows about Oscar Sweetwater's other relatives. Let one of 'em in to guard the place, next week there could be a dozen more camped out here.*

Charlie Moon was backing the Expedition into a space between a pair of century-old ponderosas, when his aunt punched him on the arm.

"What d'you think you're doing?"

"I think I'm turning the car around, so we can head back to the Columbine."

"Not till I have a look at my place, you're not." She opened the door.

"Look, it's getting late. Soon as there's something ready for you to move into, I'll bring you back and—"

She slammed the door in his face. Without a word, Daisy was off, thumping the dirt road with her oak walking stick.

He shook his head, shifted down to Low.

A few yards behind the hobbling pedestrian, he tooted the horn, called out, "If you're bound to go, get in."

She raised the stick in the air, yelled back over her shoulder. "I may be old as sin, but my legs work just fine."

Defeated, he parked the car, got out to walk beside her.

Daisy was only dimly aware of his presence. The sun had fallen behind Three Sisters Mesa; the land was immersed in a diffuse pinkish blue twilight. As the tribal elder trod along, she thought she could hear the mutter of ghostly voices on the sweet evening breeze. The shaman smiled. Though she had seen only three human ghosts on Charlie's ranch, there were dozens of ancient spirits inhabiting this sacred place. She heard the voices again. *Some of 'em must have come up from the canyon to welcome me home. Except there's no home here for me anymore. After I look at the cinders the fire left behind, I'll go back to the ranch with Charlie. But tomorrow, I'll start making some calls. Somebody must have a used trailer home I can afford to buy, and I'll badger Charlie till he hauls it out here and hooks it up to the electric and a new propane tank.*

Daisy came into the clearing.

The ghostly voices fell silent.

There was no sooty debris left from the fiery explosion. Not a cinder in sight.

But the clearing was no longer clear.

There was something directly in front of her. A redbrick walk. It led up to a new house, expertly constructed from a dozen varieties of local stone. It was capped with a peaked red metal roof that had a stone chimney on each end. A front porch ran the entire length of the dwelling; there were half a dozen flower pots on the redwood planking, and a fine rocking chair. It was her worst nightmare. *Oh no ... they've fooled Charlie Moon. One of Sweetwater's kin has already built a house here!* For a terrible moment, her heart almost failed her.

Then, the delusion vanished. She understood. Daisy could not speak.

Moon's tone was apologetic. "Sorry it's not quite finished. I've had men from the ranch working here every day I could spare 'em. The electricity is on and the new well pump is working, and the gas is hooked up. We're going to have a phone line run in, but that won't be done till sometime next week." He had hoped to delay her return until a surprise housewarming party could be organized. Her patted the mute woman on the back. "You want to go inside?"

She wiped away the tears, nodded.

In a trancelike state, Daisy followed her nephew through the glistening kitchen, which had a massive sandstone fireplace with a black iron pot hanging on an iron hook. Charlie Moon described the features of each new appliance. He took her through the empty dining room, into the large parlor—which had a couch long enough for her seven-foot nephew to nap on and a magnificent fireplace with a stack of split pine all ready for lighting. The tour ended in her bedroom, where a sturdy cedar bedstead had been placed by a window with a fine view of Three Sisters Mesa and the mouth of *Cañon del Espíritu*. Worried that she would awaken from this wonderful dream, Daisy peered into a large, empty closet, then inspected a gleaming blue-and-white bathroom that was several times as large as the cramped facility in her former home.

Finally, the old woman could take no more. She sat down on the couch and wept.

Embarrassed, Moon went outside to unload the car of her "stuff." Just in case he could not prevent his aunt from discovering her new home, he had brought along a supply of food and a few other necessities. He took his time putting these things away.

Not many words were needed to express her gratitude, so she used only a few. But she hugged the breath out of her nephew.

It was an hour after dark when Charlie Moon said good night. He expressed the opinion that she would be quite safe here with Eddie Tipton on guard.

Daisy reminded him that she had lived by the mouth of *Cañon del Espíritu* all of her life, and had managed to take care of herself. She didn't need any of Oscar Sweetwater's pushy, land-grabbing kinfolk looking after her.

She stood outside and watched him drive away. A delightful rain was beginning to patter in the dust. This was perfect. She yawned. *I'm tired and I'm going to bed.* The weary woman closed the heavy front door, turned the deadbolt latch, padded off to her bedroom, kicked off her shoes, didn't bother to remove her clothes.

The new bed was wonderfully comfortable.

She sighed.

The new house was remarkably quiet.

She turned over on her other side.

Too quiet.

She could see the rain pelting hard on the window. But she could not hear it. Not through the double-paned glazing. And not on the roof, which had a thick sheet of insulation underneath.

Daisy closed her eyes. She was so very tired.

She could not sleep.

Presently, the Ute elder knew what she must do. The insomniac got up, slipped on her shoes and a coat Moon had hung in the closet, picked up a flashlight, went outside into the rain, headed for the little trailer up the lane. Upon her arrival, she banged on the door.

After a delay, the door opened. Eddie Tipton's sleepy face presented itself in the blinding ray of her flashlight.

"What—whatsamatter?"

Daisy aimed the beam at his rusty pickup. "You have to go home right away."

He received this news with an expression of alarm. "Why?"

"Your wife needs you."

"Did she call you on the phone?"

Daisy shook her head. "Phone's not hooked up yet."

He stared at the peculiar old woman. *Daisy don't need a telephone—she's got other ways of knowing things.* He pulled a garish pink plastic jacket over his shirt. "Charlie said I should look after you. You sure you'll be all right?"

She smirked. "I'll manage."

After assuring her he'd be back the next day, the guard pulled away in the truck.

Daisy stood there for a while in the drizzle of rain. Finally, full of the scent of sage and juniper, she opened the camping trailer's squeaky door, closed it behind her, climbed onto the hard little bunk that smelled of Eddie Tipton's sweat and tobacco. The worn-out woman snuggled under her coat. Rain peppered on the thin metal roof, rattled on the plastic windows. A sudden gust of wind shook the little structure. The rain got harder.

She pulled the coat over her chin. *Ahh. That's better. I'll tell Oscar Sweetwater to leave this trailer here. Just in case I ever need another guard . . . or a spare room for a visitor . . . or a place to store some . . .* Before the thought was completed, she had drifted off into the deepest, sweetest of sleeps.

63

A DISAGREEABLE LATE-NIGHT ENCOUNTER

As the luxury automobile droned southward along the black-top, the driver could be described in a single word—*focused*. Indeed, Manfred Wilhelm Blinkoe had but one thought: *Free at last!* Only minutes earlier, he had crossed that invisible line that separates Colorado from New Mexico. In this in-stance, it also served as a boundary between his troubled past and a future as yet unseen.

The autopilot portion of his mind, which was keeping track of those essential things, alerted him to the fact that he had not eaten in almost ten hours. Moreover, his bladder was overfull. The conscious intellect decided that a clean rest-room would be quite welcome, followed by a grilled cheese sandwich and potato chips. He was wondering how far it was to the next settlement when a tiny point of light pricked the fabric of night. Arriving at a lonely crossroads, where there was only a single structure in sight, he pulled the SUV into a parking lot adjacent to a convenience store. With little concern for his convenience, the business establishment was closed up tight, and was dark except for a hundred-watt spotlight aimed at a rusty CONOCO sign. *I must remember to keep a candy bar in the glove compartment.* Abandoning the soft warmth of his Mercedes cocoon, the modest tourist retired to a shadowy spot and relieved himself.

Upon his return, he was astonished to encounter a gangly old man in ragged overalls and an equally shabby denim jacket. *Egad—where did this piece of flotsam float in from?* The derelict was picking a gray moth corpse off the grille of Blinkoe's expensive automobile. He addressed the offender in a not-unfriendly tone. "Ahoy there, my good fellow—take care not to smudge my recently waxed German motorcar."

Very deliberately, the cadaverous character turned a bearded face toward the younger, cleaner man. An absurdly long pipe dangled down over his fuzzy chin. Despite this impediment, the thin lips managed a hopeful grin. "Got any spare change, mister?"

Manfred Blinkoe knew the game. *The old dunder-kluck won't depart unless I bribe him. And if I drive away without crossing his grimy paw with silver, he'll probably hold a sharp object out and rake a streak of paint off my car.* He fumbled in his wallet, thumbing past twenties, tens, and fives—until he finally discovered a scruffy one-dollar bill. The reluctant philanthropist poked it at the pathetic character.

The elderly man accepted the greenback. "Thanks, Manny." He rolled the bill into a tight little cylinder.

He gaped at the stranger. "Uh . . . excuse me, old duffer—but what was that you said?"

Ignoring the inquiry, the gaunt man produced a plastic cigarette lighter, with which he proceeded to ignite the tip of the currency. He used the resultant torch to put fire to the tobacco in the bowl of his pipe.

Blinkoe gawked at the familiar gesture. *Who do I know who used to do that?*

The old-timer sucked in a helping of carcinogenic smoke, dropped the smoldering remains of the currency on the gravel, ground it under the heel of his boot. "Look's like me'n you are headed in the same direction." He exhaled an aromatic blue cloud.

Blinkoe stared at the bushy face, comparing it to a thousand others stored in his memory.

Dunder-kluck chuckled. "You still can't place me?"

"I cannot." The busy man was tiring of the game. "But I'm sure you must have a name."

"At that fancy-pants restaurant they called me Old Willie. Later on, when I got me a job on that rootin'-tootin' big cattle ranch, I told them dimwit cowboys my handle was Dollar Bill." The eyes glinted with a volatile mixture of hateful memories. "But you can call me Bad News."

"Very well, Bad News." The dapper little man tipped an imaginary hat. "You may call me Rude McDude, but as I have definite places to go and important things to do, let us terminate this conv—" He recognized the eyes. "Oh, my God."

As Old Willie, aka Dollar Bill, aka Bad News mouthed a response, his false teeth clicked on the pipe stem. "Way too late for prayers, Manny."

"Bill Hitchcock—is that actually *you*?"

"In the flesh, what little there is left on these old bones." William "Pappy" Hitchcock pointed the eight-inch pipe stem at something that was shrouded in the night. "That's my pickup—over there by the Dumpster." Amused at the astonishment on his former comrade's face, he added: "All the way from Charlie Moon's ranch, I've been right on your tail. You and me got a serious score to settle."

"But what—"

"What?" Hitchcock's wild eyes goggled. "You and Pablo Feliciano left me in that arroyo, oozin' out my life's blood like a stuck pig." Smoke spilled from his nostrils, waterfalled over the untrimmed mustache. "That's what."

Blinkoe blinked. "But we thought you were dead." Seeing the reflection of his lie in the angry man's eyes, he added quickly: "Or very near to it."

"You should've made damn sure." *Put a bullet in my head.*

"Honestly, Bill—who could have imagined that you

would have survived?" Blinkoe waved his arms like an exasperated penguin. "And we had just met that state-police vehicle, siren screaming, emergency lights flashing—it was apparent that the authorities had been alerted to the shootout. We could hardly afford to be stopped by the coppers with a bloody—a dying man in the truck amongst all those laundry bags stuffed with the drug cartel's cash!"

"But the cops didn't stop you." If looks could destroy, Blinkoe would have collapsed in a heap. "And I didn't die. All night, my wounds pained like ten kinds of hell. I tried hard as I could to shrug off the body, but flesh and soul were stuck tight to one another." The horrific memory provoked an involuntary shudder that rippled along his frame, threatening to loosen the old man's joints. Regaining his composure, Hitchcock continued. "I s'pose I must've finally passed out around first light." A glazed expression passed like a shadow over the DC-3 pilot's features. "I remember having this nightmare—you and me was walking along this lonely little road. You had a hold of my hand and was taking me somewhere I didn't want to go. I figured I was dead and you was too." He smiled at some private joke. "But round about noon, I woke up and saw this toothless Basque shepherd grinning at me. His ugly mutt was licking my face like it was a cherry lollipop." He jammed his right hand into a jacket pocket. "Took me quite a while to get healed up, but soon as I could travel I went to where the three of us had planned to hide all them bags of greenbacks so I could take my cut. But imagine my surprise—it wasn't there. Except for a twenty-dollar bill nailed to a juniper, which someone had drawn a silly grinny-face on."

The other thief made a little cough. "I suppose you want an explanation."

"It might help ease my troubled mind."

Manfred Blinkoe recalled that night as the best of his entire life. "After Pablo and I were—er—separated from you, we proceeded directly to the prearranged location and concealed the profits resulting from the night's business transaction—aside from two bags each, which we opted to retain for . . . miscellaneous expenses. But we agreed to leave the bulk of our assets concealed until such time as the hijacking incident was long forgotten. Then—"

"Let me guess. A few weeks later, you heard how Pablo had been picked up by the *federales* on a murder rap." William Hitchcock chewed on the pipe stem. "Knowing ol' Pablo, you figured he'd cut himself a deal—he'd rat you out on the hijacking, and maybe even tell John Law where to find the cartel's cash. So you hurried back and moved all those laundry bags to someplace where nobody but you could find 'em."

"You are approximately half right." Blinkoe cleared his throat. "But let us back up to the night of the hijacking. After we'd hidden the stuff, Pablo and I shook hands and parted company. But I parked the Humvee on Lobo Mesa and kept watch—just to make certain our wily Colombian friend wasn't planning to double back."

"And take everything for himself." The aged aviator nodded. "Smart move. You can never trust them foreigners."

"My sentiments exactly. And as soon as I was quite certain Pablo was not coming back, I returned to the site myself."

This candid revelation took a moment to sink in. "You mean to tell me you grabbed the stuff *before* Pablo got arrested?"

"Call it a premonition." Blinkoe pulled at the left fork of his beard. "I had this overwhelming compulsion to . . . to take sensible precautions."

"So what'd you do with all that money?"

"The task required four trips in the Humvee, but by late on the following day I had moved the considerable fortune to several other locations."

Hitchcock regarded his former partner with something approaching awe. "Manny, you are crooked as a barrel of snakes."

"Thank you." Blinkoe sniffed. "But *crooked* is saddled by a somewhat negative connotation. I much prefer the term *sly.* Or *devious,* if you like."

"Okay. You're sly and devious."

Sly and Devious took a deep breath. "But I am talking entirely too much about myself. What have you been doing during the interim?"

Hitchcock took a long, thoughtful pull on his pipe. "Oh, nothing much. Somma this. Somma that."

"Please, don't be so modest. I know you're always involved in some remarkably cheeky enterprise. So give me a for-example."

"Okay." He spat on a discarded oil can. "I crossed the border into Mexico and busted Pablo Feliciano outta that jail down in Hermosillo." He paused to admire the fiery trail of a pea-size meteorite. "After I got him outta town, we sat ourselves down by the riverside, tossed back a few cans of that fine Tecate brew, talked over them olden days till it was almost daylight. It was like whatta you call . . ." He swirled the pipe stem in the air, as if to stir up the word he was searching for. "Neuralgia."

The university graduate winced. "I'm sure you mean *nostalgia*."

Hitchcock glowered at his nitpicky audience. "I finally told Pablo how the money was missing from our hiding place, and he cussed a blue streak and swore he hadn't told a living soul about the hijacking, and it had to be your work and how me and him ought to hunt you down and rip your skin off in little strips till you 'fessed up."

"Pablo was always an inordinately passionate fellow."

"That's a fact. He couldn't stop saying how grateful he was to me for dynamiting the jailhouse—told me over and over how sorry he was he'd ever let you talk him into dumping me in that arroyo."

Blinkoe opened his mouth to protest.

"Shuddup, Manny. I told him not to worry about it. 'What's done is done,' sez I. Sooner or later, everybody gets what's coming to him. Then I cut the lying bastard's throat and rolled his body in the muddy waters of the Bavispe." Hitchcock grinned crookedly at the orthodontist. "You were number two on my short list, but I picked up a bad fever and dang near died. I think it must've been malaria, 'cause it kept coming back and knocking me off my pegs. It was nearly a year before I was able to travel again. I heard you was in Colorado, and finally run you down in Granite Creek. I spent a long time watching you, learning where you lived, all about your pretty wife, your fancy big houseboat, the names of all your big-shot friends, even where you liked to feed your face. Then I got me a piddlin' little job at your favorite restaurant and kinda hunkered down, waiting for my chance."

Blinkoe nodded. "Then it was you who shot that unfortunate lady at Phillipe's."

"Accidentally killing that poor woman is the thing that bothers me the most." Old Willie the groundskeeper felt a tear course down his leathery cheek, wiped it off with the back of his hand. "At that range, I don't know how I could've missed you—a blind man with a gimpy arm could of *thrown* the damned gun and hit you!" He heaved a dismal sigh. "And when I tried to take another pop at you, that two-bit little .22 jammed on me. So I pitched it into the stream and waited for the cops to show up so I could feed 'em a line about hearing the shot." He clenched the pipe between his teeth. "Later on, I followed you and your tin-hat lawyer out to that old Indian woman's trailer house, where you had a secret powwow with that tribal cop. And that time, let me tell you—Mrs. Hitchcock's number-one son wasn't packin' no nickel-and-dime *pistola*. I had me a fine high-power rifle and a jim-dandy scope. I was just about to pull the trigger when the wind started to blow, and messed up my shot."

The intended victim was having no trouble following the unfolding story line. "So you decided to plant the dynamite on my boat."

"Sure. And after it was blown to flinders, I finally crossed you off my list." The assassin grinned, shook his head. "But you are one slippery character, Manny. When I heard the rumor that it wasn't *your* arm that got fished out of the lake, I figured you'd pulled a fast one on me. Way I saw it, my best chance to find you again was to keep a close eye on that Ute lawman you was so chummy with. So Dollar Bill got himself a job on the big Indian's ranch. It seemed like a long shot, but guess what—I spotted you the very next day after I hired on. 'Manny is dead meat,' sez I. But that pug-faced bodyguard stuck to you like stink on a skunk. I got so danged frustrated at not being able to pop you, that one night I took a potshot at that Indian cop—just for meanness, I s'pose. Mr. Moon was on horseback. I had the crosshairs right on his spine, and when I pulled the trigger he went outta the saddle like a sledgehammer had smacked him square on the back. 'At least that tommyhawk tosser is outta the picture,' sez I—but come daylight, the Indian's walking around like nothing had happened." He paused long enough for a thoughtful puff. "I gotta admit it, Manny—that got me pretty spooked."

"Charlie Moon is a remarkably fortunate man." Blinkoe stared at the stone-cold killer. "And you, Bill—you are a very persistent fellow."

"That I am." Hitchcock took another drag on the pipe. "And you won't slip away this time."

"Pardon me for asking, but I am understandably curious—what, precisely, do you have in mind?"

"If the tables was turned, Manny—what'd you do?"

"Well, being a civilized man, I suppose I'd give you a good talking-to. 'Bill,' I'd say—'your behavior has not been strictly up to par.' I would demand a heartfelt apology. And, of course, my fair share of the loot."

"Nobody ever accused Bill Hitchcock of being *civilized*."

"A pity, but I cannot deny it."

"It had crossed my mind to slit your throat, just like I did for Pablo."

The intended victim took some time to mull this over, then—not wishing to offend—offered a carefully worded criticism. "Though I can appreciate the compelling symmetry of your plan, I do not find this finale entirely appealing. In fact, I feel obliged to suggest that you reconsider—"

"This ain't the Dixie Democrats Club, Manny. You don't get no vote."

"Fair enough. But I do have access to certain liquid assets. I refer to a fortune in excess of sixty-seven million, cached in the Gila Wilderness. Half of it is rightfully yours."

Hitchcock shook his head. "Money don't mean nothing to me."

Then you have certainly lost your mind.

Somewhere off on the western highlands, a coyote yip-yipped.

Unseen in a bushy mulberry tree, a hungry owl hooted.

Under a thirsty hollyhock, a fat black cricket chirruped.

Entranced by this offbeat musical ensemble, the adversaries assumed a temporary truce, and watched a crescent moon float up over the Sangre de Cristos.

Finally, Hitchcock grunted. This was a signal that he was ready to get down to serious business.

Blinkoe took a deep breath. "What now?"

"That's the question, ain't it?"

"It is indeed." M. W. Blinkoe turned to face his assailant. "As I await your decision with the keenest anticipation imaginable, I am all a-twitter."

"Twitter this." There was a quite audible *click*. Hitchcock pressed the business end of a switchblade knife against Blinkoe's belly. "Getting your throat cut's too quick and easy for the likes of you." With a mere flick of the wrist, he snipped an ivory button off the silk shirt. "I intend to poke about sixteen holes in your guts, leave you here to bleed until somebody finds you, which will likely be after the sun comes up." A dry chuckle. "Maybe the owl and the coyote'll fight over your sorry little carcass."

Showing only a marginal interest in this colorful threat, the odd little man turned his head to look over his left shoulder. He also arched an eyebrow. "Well, it's about time you showed up—where have you been keeping yourself?" Manfred Blinkoe paused, appeared to be listening to a reply—then: "Las Vegas is one of my favorite cities, second only to Reno—but then I'm *such* a degenerate." He glanced at the man with the knife in his hand. "I do not believe introductions are necessary—you are already acquainted with Mr. William Hitchcock, our plucky aviator friend." He lowered his voice to a conspiratorial whisper. "I hate to tell you this, but Bill has been up to some very naughty business. Murdering innocent women, blowing boats to smithereens, and smelling like something that crawled out of a highly polluted swamp."

The accused man furrowed thick eyebrows into a brutish scowl. "I know what you're up to, Manny—you figure you can freak me out. But that mule won't pull a plow—I never believed none of that silly crap about you having this invisible friend."

"Take care, old hardcase." The medical practitioner fixed the man with a hypnotic gaze. "It would not be wise to offend my companion. He can become quite feisty when riled."

As the orthodontist's words soaked into Hitchcock's brain, a shadow of something seemed to materialize beside Blinkoe. Hitchcock's jaw fell; the pipe drooped over his chin. "I don't care whether he's real or not. I'll just stick you and let him watch!"

"Oh piffle." Blinkoe pouted. "Shan't I have even a last word?"

I wish he didn't look so damn cocky. "Say it and die," Hitchcock growled.

The man at the tip of the blade opened his mouth, threw back his head in a haughty operatic gesture, sang it: *"Zyz-zy-vaaaaaaaaa!"*

As if a bee had stung him, Hitchcock's limbs jerked in an involuntary spasm.

"Sorry, William H. Didn't intend to startle you." Blinkoe smiled at the outraged expression on the other's face. "*Zyzzyva* was merely my notion of a whimsical witticism."

"Let me get this straight—I'm about to perforate your gut and you make some kinda dumb joke?"

The elfin jester was hurt. "*Dumb,* did you say?" *Also generous.* "But I forgive you." *And willing to assume responsibility.* "It is entirely my fault—I should not have expected *you* to appreciate the literal quality of my quip. Even a remarkably erudite person might not comprehend the off-side pun." Manfred Blinkoe now addressed the unseen presence. "You are quite right—I should not be discouraged by a single failure. I shall make one more attempt." He turned back to

Hitchcock. "Prepare yourself. Coming up—hopefully to meet with your hearty approval—is my absolutely final 'last word.'" Blinkoe cleared his throat, licked his lips. *"Velum."*

His fascinated persecutor glared. "What'n hell does *that* mean?"

"It is Latin, for 'soft palate'—but never touch it unless you are prepared for the well-known gag reflex." With that advice, the orthodontist's right hand shot upward, the heel of his palm connecting with the bowl of the long-stemmed pipe. The force of the unexpected blow drove the pipe stem through Hitchcock's *velum,* various nasal sinuses, a prominent artery, a thin sheath of bone, and six centimeters into the base of his brain. Death was virtually instantaneous.

As Manfred Blinkoe drove away, he waved a comradely salute at the corpse he had left in his wake. *"Adiós, amigo mío."* Down the road a piece, he broke into a song that suited the mood of the moment—a soul-wrenching dirge about the streets of Laredo. The singer could not recall the precise lyrics, but he (Manfred) saw himself as the young cowboy in the piece. The young cowboy who knew he'd done wrong.

SOUTHERN UTE RESERVATION

While Dr. Blinkoe was crooning his melancholy lament, Daisy Perika stirred on the small cot. She blinked into an inky darkness that spilled through the camping trailer's miniature window. Over the pattering of the rain, under the grumble of distant thunder, she could hear footsteps. And mutterings. *Somebody's out there.*

She pushed herself up on an elbow, peered through the plastic windowpane. Aside from the juniper and piñon branches shivering in the damp breeze, not a living thing stirred. But just as she was about to give it up, they materialized before her eyes. The shaman watched two *somethings* walk by—or, to put it another way, she observed some *things* that resembled human beings. They were holding hands.

The misty specter was leading the solid-looking one.

As she gawked at the remarkable spectacle, the one doing the leading was transformed from a shadowy assembly of torso and limbs into an entity with definite form and crisp features. He looked exactly like that oddball Blinkoe fellow—but Daisy knew he was not. The one being led was an older person, a skinny man she had never seen before. The odd couple was headed down the lane, toward the gaping mouth of *Cañón del Espíritu,* one of those appointed places for spirits to wait for the Last Day—and the earthshaking blast of that Final Trumpet. The apparitions vanished as suddenly as they had appeared.

Daisy lay back on the cot, pulled the coat over her face.

She considered herself a reasonable person. In the normal course of events, the tribal elder would have carefully considered all the evidence before reaching a preconceived conclusion. But lately, the course of events was anything but normal. She told herself that a person could stand only just so much, and enough was enough, and seeing wasn't always believing. And so, in contrast to her general practice, Daisy ignored the evidence presented by her senses and jumped *immediately* to a judgment that made her comfortable.

That wasn't real. The weary old woman closed her eyes. *And even if it was, there's nothing I can do about it.* She turned on her side, sighed. *It's none of my business.* But after a while, she was reminded Whose she was, and what His business was. Thus touched with grace, Daisy Perika offered up an earnest prayer for those lost, wandering souls. Having done this, she was prepared for rest, and so she made a personal request. For sleep.

And sleep she got. But not without dreams.

Dr. Manfred W. Blinkoe's shadow was perched on the foot of her cot, talking to Daisy as if they were old, dear friends. He had, he explained, just returned from a walk in Spirit Canyon, and it occurred to him that he should stop by and share an extraordinary story with the tribal elder. The tale's conception had occurred almost sixty-two years ago, in a pleasant little town in southern Illinois. As it happened, the fertilized egg fissioned into identical twins. But as time passed and the plot developed—one of the siblings did not. There was some physiological confusion, an unfortunate fusion—and one brother absorbed the other! At birth, the proud parents were presented with a single little fist-clenching son. Judging by external appearances, he was a normal seven-pound, four-ounce boy-child.

But deep inside himself, near his left kidney, little Manfred Wilhelm carried a tiny lump of angry, inflamed tissue. The mummified fetus contained microscopic bits of teeth and bone, patches of hair and skin, even components of a central nervous system. These contributions from father and mother had become the residue of his unchristened brother. Nevertheless, the internalized sibling did have a name. Teratoma.

Daisy Perika awoke with a convulsive start. She sat up, stared at the far end of the bed. There was, of course, no one there.

Why do I have these awful, crazy dreams? She collapsed back onto the thin foam mattress, snuggled under the overcoat. *I know what it is—it's all that scary medical stuff I see on* Oprah. Though she shuddered at the thought of such a sacrifice, virtue got the upper hand. *I'll have to stop watching so much of that educational television.*

Keep reading for an excerpt from
the next Charlie Moon mystery by JAMES D. DOSS

STONE BUTTERFLY

Coming soon in hardcover from St. Martin's Minotaur

COLORADO, SOUTHERN UTE RESERVATION
In the Shadow of Three Sisters Mesa

This being his weekly visit to his aged relative, Daisy Perika's long, lean nephew was seated at her kitchen table. It was evident that his entire attention was focused the tribe's weekly newspaper, more particularly a column by a Granite Creek astrologer-psychic, wherein the seer predicted that (following an earthquake of unprecedented magnitude) the Lost Civilization of Atlantis would surface in the South Pacific! Though it was absolutely certain that the calamity would occur on February tenth at 9:15 A.M. Mountain Standard Time, the stars and planets were somewhat foggy on the precise year of the event—which might be 2007, or perhaps 2077—depending upon whether or not Saturn decided to visit the House of Uranus whilst that latter planet was in diametric juxtaposition to the Twenty-Sixth Planet, which had not yet been discovered. The whole thing was a sham, of course.

(*Clarifying Note*: Reference is not made to the astrologer's immodest prophecy—but rather to the more unpretentious sham currently being committed by Charlie Moon, whose apparent interest in the newspaper was a pretense.)

As it happened, Moon had heard the tramp's shuffle-footed approach when the intruder was a good hundred yards away, and the full-time rancher, part-time tribal investigator thought it would be entertaining to see how his aunt would deal with this unwelcome guest. In happy anticipation of the fireworks to come, he turned another page of *Southern Ute Drum*, and waited for the fun to begin. In about six seconds, he estimated. And began to count them off. *One thousand and one. One thousand and two.*

If Daisy had not been concentrating all her attention on the preparation of a morning meal for herself and her nephew, she might have been aware of Yadkin Dixon's arrival. Or perhaps not—the hungry man was intentionally making a stealthy approach.

One thousand and three. One thousand and four.

The way Mr. Dixon saw it, a hard-hearted old woman who kicked at chipmunks and heaved stones at pretty, flitting bluebirds could not be expected to deal kindly with a self-educated economist who firmly believed in the concept of a free lunch. Or free breakfast, as the case might be.

One thousand and five. One thousand and six.

The first evidence of his unwanted presence was the tap-tap of a knuckle on the kitchen window—and his long, horsy face gawking at her through the glass. After a startled twitch, the Ute woman quickly turned away. In Daisy's Book of Bad Things, this particular pestilence fell into that same detestable category as the dull ache that visited her left hip on a rainy day. Her remedy was: Ignore the hateful thing, it would eventually go away.

Her attempt to pretend that Dixon did not exist was wasted on the thick-skinned beggar who camped out somewhere in the vicinity of her home. The persistent fellow was not about to leave without some nourishment to occupy that hollow space betwixt the Coors pewter belt buckle and his spine.

Shamming on unashamedly, Moon pretended to be engrossed in an article entitled "Treating Hemorrhoids With Acupuncture." *Ouch.*

After pretending for a full two seconds, Daisy gave up the game. Like Death and Taxes that were here to stay, Mr. Dixon was not going away. She wiped her hands on a polka dot apron, jerked the back door open.

Before she had a chance to say something uncivil, Dixon tipped a tattered slouch hat. "Good morning, ma'am—and God bless you." Though a greeting of this sort tended to disarm his ordinary marks, he might as well have expected a cheerful "Howdy-do" to charm a grinning-skull tattoo off the hairy hide of a whisky-soaked Hell's Angel.

Daisy marched outside, wagged a finger in his face. "Don't you start ma'am-ing me, you two-legged coyote." *Ugh—he smells like last week's fish.* She glared at the filthy white man. "What d'you want this time?" *As if I don't know.*

Charlie Moon also knew. And unseen by those outside, he had made his way to the cook stove, plopped several fat sausage links into a cast-iron skillet.

Mr. Dixon assumed a pitiful tone. "I wondered if you could spare a poor, homeless person a few leftovers from your table." His hopeful smile exposed yellowed teeth that resembled hard little kernels of unpopped corn. "Some cold, pasty oatmeal—or a few potato peels?"

"I gave you something to eat just last week." Daisy tried to recall the details and did. "It was a cheese sandwich, big enough to choke a bull moose." Though somewhat rusty from lack of use, Daisy's conscience gently reminded her that *the months-old cheese was fuzzy with blue mold and on top of that the bread was hard enough to break a brass monkey's teeth and*—Being one who did not accept criticism gracefully, she interrupted the inner voice: *I scraped the fur off that cheese. And even if the sliced bread was a little stale, you can't expect a dirt-poor widow woman to give her last slice of fresh bread to a man who hasn't used a toothbrush since that Goober-pea farmer from Georgia was president.*

Blissfully unaware of Daisy's internal dialogue, the hungry man rubbed his stomach. "Alas, I have long since digested that delectable delicacy." Dixon assumed a saintly expression he had recently seen on a stained glass window at St. Mark's Episcopal Church in Durango, where he had also tapped the Rector's Emergency Discretionary Fund for bus fare to Topeka so that he might attend his dear old mother's funeral (while Dear Old Mother was on a Caribbean cruise with her latest husband.) "I would be grateful for some broken soda crackers. Or a shriveled-up apple core."

Moon cracked three brown-shell eggs on the edge of the skillet, smiled appreciatively at the man's line of talk. It was always a pleasure to witness a highly skilled professional going about his work.

Daisy was not about to leave the subject of the white vagrant's last visit. "And after I fed you that sandwich, what did you do?" Like a well-rehearsed attorney, the prosecutor-persecutor answered her own question. "You thanked me by stealing a brand-new ax from my pile of piñon wood!"

The beggar—who was short of everything but pride—stiffened his back and lied: "I did no such thing."

Her nostrils flared dangerously. "Don't tell me that, you snake-eyed sneak-thief—I was watching you from that window." To identify the physical evidence which supported her accusation, the witness for the prosecution pointed to indicate the aforesaid window.

Little wheels turned in his head, tiny ratchets clicked and clacked, and so on and so forth. Figuratively, of course. "I might have absentmindedly picked up your ax." Dixon's highly plastic features effortlessly assumed the injured expression of one who—though painfully wounded by a malicious and false accusation—would not take offense. "But even if I did—all I ever intended was to borrow it for a few hours."

The hard-faced woman had a ready answer for that. "Then why didn't you bring it back?"

Having fended off many serious allegations over the years, Dixon did not miss a beat. "It is my faulty memory." He leaned forward, fixed his feisty accuser with an earnest gaze. "Ever since I was struck north of Clarksville, Tennessee, by that speeding L&N freight-train that was pulling eighteen box cars and a green caboose, I can hardly remember anything—even my name." He paused for a moment, evidently involved in an intense mental effort to recall what the initials Y. D. stood for, only to be defeated by the arduous task. "But be assured that as soon as I return to my modest encampment, I shall search for your—uh—dear me, you see—it has slipped away from me already." A cherubic smile. "Tell me again—what it was that is missing—a hammer from your tool shed?"

The old tea-kettle was approaching a boil; she hissed at him: "You took my new ax—and it was on my wood pile!"

Dixon stared at the neat stack of split piñon. "Hmmm." He nodded as if the light was beginning to dawn. "An *ax*, you say. Well, if I should find such an implement among my meager belongings, I shall bring it to you directly."

"Well, I won't hold my breath." Daisy exhaled. "And there's another thing." Inhaled. "You've got no right to be squatting on the Southern Ute reservation." She pointed at her house. "My nephew's inside, and he's a tribal policeman and—"

"Is that a fact?" Dixon's poor memory had made a remarkable recovery. "I was under the impression that Mr. Moon had retired from the Ute police department several years ago, to manage his cattle ranch."

"Charlie is a tribal investigator, and if I just snap my fingers"—She displayed a finger and thumb, all cocked to snap—"he'll trot out here and arrest you right on the spot and—"

"You called?"

Following Dixon's gaze, Daisy turned to see her nephew's lanky form in the doorway. Moon had brought with him a platter of scrambled eggs and pork sausage. These victuals were tastefully accompanied by a pair of oven-hot biscuits.

Yadkin Dixon fixed a hopeful gaze on the food. "It is good to see you, sir. I have continued to follow your career for some time now—and if I may say so, I am to be counted among your many admirers."

Moon chuckled at the blatant flattery, offered the plate to his ardent fan.

The gift was gratefully accepted by the famished man.

Daisy shook her head, turned to mutter misgivings to her overly generous relative: "Now that good-for-nothing bum'll be back every day, begging food, stealing anything that ain't nailed down." Knowing her words were wasted, she elbowed him aside, huffed and grumbled her way back into the kitchen.

Charlie Moon waited patiently while the enthusiastic diner devoured the hearty breakfast. After Dixon had wiped his mouth on his sleeve and burped, the tribal investigator gave him a look that would have shaken a more sensible man. This was accompanied by an order. "You bring that ax back *today*." As the sly fellow was opening his mouth to protest, the Ute cut him off: "And if you so much as steal a *look* at any of my aunt's property, I'll give Chief of Police White-horse a call. The very least he'll do is run you off the res. More likely, he'll put you up in the tribe's modern correctional facility for ninety days."

Normally such a threat would have caused Dixon to protest, or at least raise an eyebrow, but a full stomach has a calming effect on a man. He picked a pointy juniper needle off a convenient branch, thoughtfully picked his teeth, pondered the offer of a free room and three meals a day. Concluded that it would place too many restrictions on his cherished freedom of movement. "I will certainly return the lady's ax." He tossed the toothpick aside. "And henceforth, I promise not to—uh—borrow any property that belongs to your charming aunt." He raised his right hand to show Moon a soiled palm. "You have my word of honor, sir."

Great. With that and six bits I could buy me a seventy-five-cent cup of coffee. Moon looked up to watch a golden eagle float by. By the time he lowered his gaze, the scruffy-looking white man had ambled over to the Columbine Expedition.

The visitor caressed the Ford Motor Company product. "This is quite a spiffy motor car."

Moon winced at the greasy streaks Dixon's grubby fingers were tracing on the glistening fender. "I just waxed it."

"And you did a fairly decent job." Mr. Dixon got that faraway look in his eye, also cleared his throat. Which is a double warning that whether the unwary listener likes it or not, he is about to share a favorite memory. "Back in Michigan, when I was just a young lad, my daddy owned a cherry-red 1963 Jaguar XKE 3.8 Coupe. Pop kept it garaged, except on Sundays when he'd roll it out and take me for a ride into Lansing." His sigh was scented with nostalgia-blossom perfume. "Talk about your fine automobiles—there is absolutely *nothing* like a Jag."

AUNT DAISY'S VERY BAD DREAM

Daisy was busy at the propane range, putting the final touches on her nephew's breakfast. This amounted to one skillet filled with sizzling sausage and fried potatoes, another of fluffy scrambled eggs, plus a simmering pot of green chili stew. *Work, work, work—that's all I ever do.* As a gray mist slipped out of Spirit Canyon and settled over her mind, the cook sighed. *I bet that thieving white man'll be back here tomorrow, licking his lips and asking for any prime rib and baked potatoes that's left over from my lunch.* Recalling his whining request for an apple core, her wrinkled face crinkled into a crooked little smile. *I ought to give him a big, shiny red apple with enough pickleweed poison in it to kill a dozen smelly moochers—that'd teach him a lesson he wouldn't forget!* In Daisy's version of the heartwarming tale, this was how Snow White had dispensed with the witch, who should have known better than to trust a peculiar white girl who had run away from home to hang out with a truckload of dwarves. From the shaman's experience, one *pitukupf* in the neighborhood was sufficient.

Fortunately for Mr. Dixon, the cook had dismissed him from her malevolent thoughts. But Charlie Moon was not so lucky. As the broth began to froth and bubble, Daisy sensed the time was ripe to make some trouble—and commenced to stir the pot. "Charlie, there's something that's been bothering me."

Moon turned another page of the *Southern Ute Drum*. No sham this time.

"I've been having this same bad dream, over and over." No response. She turned up the volume. "Last night, I had it again. It was so scary I woke up with the sweats."

He frowned at a full-page listing of Upcoming Events, had a great notion. *I should take Lila Mae McTeague to the dance.* No two ways about it—the long-legged FBI agent would be the best-looking woman there.

The Ute elder turned to scowl at her nephew. "Did you hear what I said?"

"Sure." *I wonder if Lila Mae's ever been to a Bear Dance. Probably not.*

"Plop, plop, plop."

Moon shook a wrinkle out of the newspaper. "What?"

"That was the sound it made."

He stared at her hunched back. "The sound what made?"

"The blood."

"What blood?"

She brought him a man-size platter of eggs, sausage, and potatoes. "The blood dropping onto that dead man's face!"

"Oh. Right." He reached for a paper napkin, considered tucking it over his new white linen shirt with the mother-of-pearl buttons, decided to put it in his lap.

She hurried back to the stove. "You don't have the least idea what I've been talking about."

"Sure I do."

"Then tell me."

"The blood. It was going . . . uh . . . drip-drip."

"It was going plop-plop-*plop*." She turned down the ring of blue flame under the pot, tossed him another challenge. "And how was it that I happened to hear that blood going plop-plop-plop?"

With Aunt Daisy it was nine-to-one for a nightmare, so he played the odds. "You was having one of them weird dreams."

"I knew you wasn't paying no attention." She banged the

wooden spoon on the stove. "What I said was—I've been having the same *bad* dream, over and over."

Might as well get this over with. "Tell me all about it."

She sniffed. "Oh, you don't really want to know."

"Yes, I do. And if you keep me in suspense, I won't be able to eat a bite of breakfast."

That'll be a day to remember. Daisy brought the stewpot to the table. "I dreamed about a skinny little girl."

He watched her ladle a generous helping of green chili stew onto the mound of scrambled eggs. *That looks good enough to eat.* He took a taste. *It could use some salt.*

She reached out to tweak his ear. "You're supposed to ask me: 'Who is this skinny little girl?' "

"Consider yourself asked." He reached for the shaker.

She slapped his hand. "Don't do that—I've got it seasoned just right. I don't know who she is."

Momentarily deprived of salt, the Ute warrior raised his fork, expertly speared a sausage. "Then why should I have asked?"

"To show proper respect to a tribal elder."

"Right." He opened a steaming biscuit, inserted a generous helping of butter.

"I don't know who the girl is, because in these dreams, I don't ever see her face." She hobbled over to the stove. *Back and forth, back and forth—it's a wonder I don't wear a path ankle-deep into the floor.* "But I know she's in trouble. Serious trouble."

Behind her back, Moon snatched the shaker, added several dashes of sodium chloride, tasted the result. *That's some better.*

While preparing a plate for herself, Daisy paused to stare through the window at a diaphanous fluff of cloud floating over the big mesa. She watched it snag itself on the tallest of the Three Sisters. "In these dreams, the girl is standing over the dead man."

He took a sip of black coffee. *I forgot to put sugar in it.* He remedied this error with six heaping spoonfuls.

Daisy was silent for a long moment, watching the cloud that had become a misty wisp of gray hair on the petrified Pueblo woman's head. "And what makes it so awful, is that her little hands is soaked in blood."

As chance would have it, he had just poured tomato ketchup onto a heap of fried potatoes.

The shaman shuddered. "And that blood just keeps dripping off the tips of her fingers—onto the dead man's face."

Charlie Moon was not a squeamish diner, but food was meant to be savored. He eyed the bloody chunk of spud on his fork. *I wish she would wait till after I've had my breakfast to tell me about her nightmares.*

Daisy Perika brought her plate to the table, thoughtfully watched her nephew frown at a slice of ketchup-painted potato. "All night I could hear it, even when I was wide awake—all that blood dripping off her hands, onto that dead man's face." She saw the indecision on Charlie Moon's face. "There was so much that it puddled up in his eye-sockets."

Knowing she would finally tire of the subject, he decided the fried potatoes could wait. In the meantime, he would fortify himself with eggs and sausage and buttered biscuits.

The old woman settled herself into a chair. For a while, she absentmindedly picked at her scrambled eggs. After a few tentative bites, she lost interest in her meal. Fixed her gaze on a Wild Flower of the Month wall calendar. Began to hum her favorite Ute ballad, which she claimed had been stolen from her tribe by the British. Then, in a scratchy-creaky voice that would have seat a deaf man's teeth on edge, she sang thusly:

> *In Sweet Grass town, where I was born,*
> *There was a fair lass dwellin'. . . .*

And so on. Until she got to the good part:

> *O grandmo-ther, make my bed!*
> *O make it hard and narrow—*

> *My sweetheart died for me today,*
> *I'll be with him to-morrow.*

After the next and semi-final verse, and following his aunt's long, melancholy sigh, Charlie Moon concluded that he had won the waiting-game. He could almost taste his starchy, ketchup-tinctured victory.

From the corner of her eye, the tribal elder spotted the home-fry that was newly impaled on the tines of her nephew's fork. She mumbled a hastily devised and highly discordant epilogue:

> *And knowin' I'll be no man's wife,*
> *I'll slit my throat with a butcher knife . . .*

The crimson-dripping morsel was rising toward Moon's lips.

Her mumble rose to a mutter:

> *And my blood drips down,*
> *Down in the dust in Sweet Grass Town . . .*

She watched the fork slowing—possibly coming to a stop . . .

"Plop," Daisy said. "Plop-plop."